BLACK BLIZZARD

A Lyon County Adventure

GK JURRENS

UpLife
Press

BOOKS BY GK JURRENS

Contemporary Fiction (suspense)
Dangerous Dreams - Dream Runners Book 1
Fractured Dreams - Dream Runners Book 2

Futuristic Paranormal Fiction (mysteries)
Underground - Mayhem Book 1
Mean Streets - Mayhem Book 2
Post Earth - Mayhem Book 3
A Glimpse: Companion Guide to the Mayhem Trilogy

Historical Fiction (crime)
Black Blizzard - A Lyon County Adventure
Murder in Purgatory - A Lyon County Mystery

Non-fiction (nautical)
Moving a Boat and Her Crew
Restoring a Boat and Her Crew

Non-fiction (how-to)
Why Write? Why Publish? Passion? Profit? Both?

DEDICATION

My parents are long gone, but not forgotten. Born and raised of Dutch-German immigrant families in America circa the Great War with Germany that ended in 1918, I cut through the fog of my anemic memory to envision them as flawed saints. Better angels. Their five kids were always loved, an impossible task at times, and we never went hungry. Polio and poverty and countless crushed dreams during their earlier years and later merely presented uneven stepping stones for their proud legacy of faith and loyalty, whether or not we, as their children, returned those precious commodities in kind.

I imagine I may speak for the four of us "children" who still endure to honor their legacy in the year 2022. We still miss Mom's firm hand at the helm, handicaps and foibles notwithstanding, and "Daddy," the dreamer, the hugger, always the quickest draw on a corny joke under a goofy hat perched at a jaunty angle. Spread your wings and fly, our better angels. Your "crummy kids" will always remember.

On behalf of my siblings and myself, I dedicate this somewhat fanciful manuscript to our parents—our better angels:

- Edward Jurrens (1907 - 1980), Son of Gabbrrand Ubbe Jurrens and Henrietta Claussen
- Sophiena Bruns Jurrens (1911 - 1982), Daughter of Jacob Enno Bruns and Minnie Bruns

- GK Jurrens

DISCLAIMER & NOTICE

ACKNOWLEDGMENTS

The story you are about to read unfolds during the summer of 1933. The degree to which it feels authentic is in no small part due to the valuable insights, anecdotes, and materials generously shared with me by several contributors. Without them, this story would not have been possible. I am unabashed about revealing their names to you.

In their "order of appearance," during my research phase, I would first like to offer my undying gratitude to my niece, Ellie, for supplying my mother's diary, brief as it was, the first entry of which appears in her elegant hand on May 1, 1930.

And to my sister, Carol, my thanks for bequeathing to me not only rich anecdotal material, a generous box of old photographs dating back to the 1920s, but also for entrusting to my care another journal of daily life on the family farm in Iowa, also penned by our mother beginning October 1, 1947.

A pivotal four-hour interview with my brother Rod's mother-in-law, Dorothy, supplied me with myriad nitty-gritty details that added so much to this tale. At ninety years of age and sharper than me at almost twenty years younger, Dorothy was one of the few living souls from whom I could capture first-hand experience of life on a midwestern family farm during the 1930s and beyond. She shared in-depth anecdotes, photographs, and her own *extensive* documentation of farm life before, during and after the Great Depression, and what it took to keep their farm in the family for seven generations. Dorothy is a treasure.

I'd also like to thank my niece, Kristen, for reminding me to keep my characters "in voice" rather than to impose my own upon them.

And finally, I am honored to acknowledge all my beta readers, including one in-house, who offered constructive criticism so essential to this author's work. A special thanks to my aircraft and balloon advisors, Gus H and Tom L, respectively, for their help in contributing to the plausibility of Chief Dan's airship. To Judy H and Julia S for their brutal and essential word-craft expertise. And Bob J, I appreciate your review from someone else who may possess first-hand memories of the book's venue. To all who contributed to this manuscript, I thank you! - GK

INTRODUCTION

At the end of this book, you'll find references that you might find useful, even interesting:

- The **cast of major characters** and their respective roles are listed for you (see Appendix A),
- A **visual chart that lays out relationships** between all major characters within and across story lines (Appendix B),
- A **glossary of terms** commonly used in the early twentieth century (Appendix C).
- A **list of maps** that guide you around the book's significant locations (Appendix D).

Enjoy what I hope will be a thought-provoking and entertaining read.

EPIGRAPH

"We're all in the same boat on a stormy sea, and we owe each other a terrible loyalty."

- GK Chesterton

"Boileau said that kings, gods, and heroes only were fit subjects for literature. The writer can only write about what he admires. Present day kings aren't very inspiring, the gods are on vacation, and about the only heroes left are the scientists and the poor.... And since our race admires gallantry, the writer will deal with it where he finds it. He finds it in the struggling poor now."

- John Steinbeck in a 1939 radio interview

PREFACE

America trembled through an era of extremes. Millions perished. Not one, but two pandemics swept the globe following the *Great War* that ended in 1918. On October 29, 1929—Black Tuesday—the free-and-easy Roaring Twenties died a sudden and traumatic death. But the emotional reverberations and illicit vices it spawned did not. Hundreds hurled themselves through skyscraper windows, and tens of thousands across America surrendered their souls to Black Tuesday. Of those who survived its traumatic after-shocks, many drowned their sorrows, but even more were unwilling to do so. Some turned to their faith.

Then the world slipped from bleak to worse. The skies dried up and scorched the earth below. Shadows deepened over the creased land that once offered her keepers bounty for their labor. Farmers took reckless shortcuts hoping to save their acreages. Many could not. Instead of the new decade ushering in new hope, quite the opposite became the new reality.

The summer of 1931 on the Great Plains of Nebraska and Western Iowa felt like Armageddon. As time stalled, millions of Americans merely subsisted in the clutches of escalating squalor—starving and displaced from their homes. Hundreds of thousands more sought to re-discover Eden—elsewhere. Anywhere else. Those who stayed, struggled for a breath of air free of dust and despair under a drab sky that mocked their foolhardiness. And yes, most stayed put for fear of *the sickness*.

But even with faces swathed in handkerchiefs, and those lucky enough to own goggles for covering their eyes against the grit, they could not fill the hollow pit where a solid meal and contentment once settled. However, during zero-visibility dust storms they called *black blizzards,* the larger issue remained—the simple task of breathing more air than dirt.

Banks and private lenders alike gasped for their own survival. They called in notes on homes and farms and businesses that were no longer viable, hoping to turn an economic vacuum into an opportunity for their own survival. Somehow, a few ordinary folk still held money—in land, livestock, inventory, or precious metals. Many more leaned on the only two things of substance left—their faith and their community. Otherwise, the future might be too bleak to contemplate.

This is one such story.

❧

December 1932

MOST BIRDS OF PREY AREN'T LARGE, BUT THEIR QUARRY often disagrees. To a field mouse, anything larger than her poses a threat. Yesterday's brief thaw surrendered to an overnight freeze. The mouse's tiny nails clicked over the delicate ice crust. Her cheek bulged with a rare grain of winter wheat for her babies who awaited her return in their cozy underground burrow.

The forenoon sun promised a crisp but pleasant morning. A distant screech preceded a quicksilver shadow that cast doubt on the momma mouse's prospects. The red-tailed hawk swooped in for breakfast. Momma scurried. It was over.

The cycle of life was about to accelerate further, beginning with this otherwise sleepy morning in the rolling plains of northwest Iowa. The hawk, with breakfast in her talons for her own young, contemplated landing near the top of a power pole alongside Lyon County 14. But she thought better of it as she dodged a speeding motorcar slicing through the bitter wind. The auto swirled up a vortex of new snow in its wake, a feathery dusting that refused to stick after last night's freeze.

☙❧

THE DRIVER SWELLED WITH PRIDE AT THE CHROMIUM HOOD ornament of a leaping hound on the far end of his motorcar's sleek hood. It wasn't just that handsome marquis, but what it represented: prestige and respect. The brand-new auto had been a Christmas gift from Mr. Finn Malone of Chicago, Illinois. Her ultra-modern coachwork concealed her road-proven four-cylinder power plant. There were just too many stylish innovations to count over her predecessor, the Model A. Important folks drove cars like this.

The musky smell of tanned cowhide—and this kid's breath—filled the car's interior. No surprise, with those teeth. He did wonder what that was all about. Seemed out of place with those snappy duds. *Big city types. Immigrants, no less!* With a brilliant but hazy sun off to his left, the driver risked a glance at the big-city passenger to his right. The serene fellow with scary undercurrents gave him the creeps. Especially that lop-sided smirk, his brown teeth, and those eyes. He could still spot traces of blood around the edges of the kid's fingernails. And who in hell wore a black shirt with white buttons, anyway?

He'd met guys like this before in his line of work—thankfully, not often. More so these days. Short, but larger than life, he was Irish, not German like most folks around these parts. Sounded like a Mick too. Close-cropped ginger hair sprouted from beneath a flat-topped skimmer that shaded his youthful brow. Not very practical. Too damn cold for a straw hat. That overcoat he called his Crombie—whatever that meant—just had to cost a bundle. *Slickers!* Regardless, with the grim task at hand, the driver struggled to bury the charred-black corner of his conscience.

THE SCARY LITTLE GUNSEL THEY CALLED STICKS LEARY worked for Mr. Malone. That meant he was to be respected— on the surface, anyway—and not just because this kid was a shooter. Malone commanded, the world obeyed, and not just in the Windy City.

As Leary thumbed loose two huge buttons of his Crombie and flipped down its generous collar, the driver caught a metallic flash. A shiny pistol nestled under the kid's right armpit in a fancy shoulder holster. A show piece. So, he's a southpaw. Leary shrugged the coat forward with a jerk on both lapels. The cannon disappeared as the huge collar lay down, revealing the rangy kid's neck and a purplish circle beneath his jawbone. A puckered scar from a bullet wound to the left side of his scrawny throat. No, despite his youthful appearance, Leary was no kid.

He rolled his bug-eyes up to gaze at the driver in the rearview mirror. "Just watch the road, boy-o. Wouldn't do to put this pretty new sedan into the ditch, now would it?"

"Right. So, Mr. Leary, just curious. Who's under the blanket in the back?"

"It's just Sticks, 'kay?" Why did *Just Sticks'* smile not warm him up? "Don't ya be worryin' 'bout any a that just now."

The driver already knew who was under that blanket, but he didn't know why. Not that it mattered, other than worrying about the stink of the recently deceased. He'd been beckoned after the deed was done. Leary and another guy had loaded that cargo of dead weight before they allowed him back into his own brand new car. Leary had laughed, "Some jobs ya do yerself, yeh?" And there had been that spooky smirk with those jagged chompers and a cheerful glint in those crazy bug-eyes. *Well, in for a penny*....

The small Irishman, like a hellish leprechaun, continued with conversation meant to sound congenial, as if warming up to a recruit. He obviously enjoyed the sound of his own clipped voice dripping in that ridiculous brogue. Again, with the unconvincing smile. Or was he flirting with a leer?

The gunsel said, "I see why Finn likes the lay a the land out here. Borin' with a big "B" as far as the eye can see, yeh, boy-o?"

"If he's looking for rural isolation and no G-Men within a hundred miles, yep, this area should suit his needs."

They were only to drive a short distance south of George on Lyon County 14. Hopefully, this would be a brief conversation. The kid turned toward the driver, swiveling his left knee up onto the seat between them and slinging his left arm behind the driver's shoulder. The frontal assault from the kid's maw damn-near gagged him. "Tell me 'bout this dealership. Why should Finn get into this at all?"

He'd already explained this to Mr. Malone up in Worthington. With more obligatory deference than genuine sarcasm, he addressed the odious little creep. "Well, George, Iowa is a sleepy little town of about a thousand folks. Mostly farmers who've moved to town after making their bucks, or they just got too old to work the land. There's money there. But they're mostly poor folks getting by—especially these days. No local law enforcement. Only up in Rock Rapids, the county seat over ten miles northwest as the crow flies, and almost twice that by motorcar. Bairns Motors, the only dealership in George, buys respectability with a low profile. And they have a lot of square footage under roof. It's the perfect front. Plus, all the well-to-do farmers from the surrounding area buy their Chevies from Henry Bairns. It's a legitimate business, at least according to our expert consultant—our mutual friend."

Leary pasted a smug look on his face as he stretched thin leather gloves over his bony fingers. "Finn tells me yer a good soldier, and yer regular. That's worth somethin'."

An arrogant little prick, this Mick. The gunsel swiveled a practiced three-sixty with his dark bug-eyes showing lots of white. First ahead, then over his left shoulder, and the same over his right, shifting in his seat as he did so. There was that cannon again. Pausing, Leary didn't look the driver in the eye, only at his gloved hands on the wheel. "Pull over. Right here. Ya hang tight while I take out the trash." Dead serious.

The driver jerked the wheel. The car swerved to the edge of the road with two tires in stiff ditch weed. The tires crunched. He ground the gears before he settled the floor shifter into its sweet spot. He squeezed, then pulled the ratcheting brake handle with his left hand. The car skidded to a stop.

Leary slid out of the passenger's side, but stumbled in his city oxfords on the snowy weeds at the precipice of the shallow ditch. He'd have fallen without his chokehold on the handle inside of the still-open front door. Grabbed the rear door's exterior handle with his left hand, swung it open and back. The driver stole a glance at the passenger-side fender mirror. Partially blocked by the open door, he still saw Leary tugging his cargo from under the wool blanket and dragging it into the ditch. The blanket stayed on the floor behind the front seat.

With the task complete and his legs still dangling out of the door, Leary kicked his heels together. Jettisoned wet snow that clung to his warm shoes before swinging his legs back into the car. He tossed a small but heavy trophy from the kill into the driver's lap. "A keepsake fer yeh. Let's go."

Flat voice, no emotion. But when he caught the driver looking at him, he offered another one of those tiny foul-mouthed smirks—the left corner of his mouth higher and more puckered than the right. The driver stared down at the wet and cool Lyon County Deputy badge he now held in his right hand—scratched and dented. Retrieving a silk hanky, Leary polished his shoes. "What say you show me this town with the funny name, 'kay, Sheriff?"

Strictly speaking, dumping murdered deputies was not part of his job description as Sheriff.

What have I gotten myself into?

2

At twenty-five, Jacob Hardt predicted he would die young—lonely, bored and inconsequential on the dried-up patch of gray dirt he inherited from his parents two years ago, along with their debts.

Everyone called him Jake because he looked like a Jake. He was a simple farmer. But there was something darkly dangerous in his enormous, intelligent eyes that nestled a little too close together above a commanding aquiline nose.

With Jake, much was left unsaid and unsettled—like rocks rolling around in an empty milk can in the back of a truck on a rutted road. Old rumors hinted Jake almost killed a man who hurt someone he cared for. No names, but he carried a sharp edge on his shirtsleeve back then. Now, he buried all that beneath his likable demeanor. Everybody loved Jake. Well, almost everybody.

The hazy sun would rise again all too soon. Constant winds kept the finest Texas and Oklahoma grit airborne through their corner of Iowa and beyond. He had stuffed every window sill and door bottom with rags or pieces of clothing he could still wear—despite their aroma. He even crammed old newsprint into the key holes.

Guilt tinged his reluctance to get up for chores as he shrunk back under bulky covers in the pre-dawn darkness. *Jesse's udder must be close to bursting.* Ultimately, his own swollen bladder drove him out from under his lumpy goose-down comforter. He never bothered with sheets, not since Mom died. Resolute, he sprang from the old bed that belonged to his parents. His parents.... *Wasn't my fault, dammit. Or was it?*

In an instant, the chill leeched through his long-johns and especially the thin soles of his thick socks as he sat up and swung his legs to the planked floor. High time to throw on another log, even though wood was so damn scarce. But first, he grabbed a stick match from a shallow dish on the end table and lit the kerosene lamp to push back the inky darkness. Hadn't trimmed its finicky wick in a while. Not his sort of detail. If only he'd paid the electric bill.

A deep shiver grabbed hold and would not let go. Clutching the smoking lamp with its blackened glass by its wire bale, he held it out in front of him so he wouldn't stub another toe. The lamp stunk and swung as he pranced over the uneven planks that chilled his feet until they hurt. He reached his old slippers by the stove and slid into them. At least they weren't as cold as the floor. Old Blackie still gave off some warmth. He'd bring in a few more chunks of box elder from the pile in the mudroom today. Stock up the box in the kitchen.

Coffee in the pot on top of Blackie had grown cold, and that was okay, as long as it was thick and oily. His bladder and a trip to the two-holer out back could wait. He poured a cup and topped it off with a healthy dollop of Jesse's cream to ease the burning in his stomach. His prize milker wasn't giving as much these days, so not as much to skim. Nor were the other three, as if they were all cursed or something. *Stupid thinking. Snap out of it, plow hand.*

Compared to last summer's worst storm, the dust wasn't so bad these days, even though it still coated everything, even vertical surfaces, like it was magnetic or something. That monster blew sand and dust from Oklahoma all the way up to Chicago. Zero visibility made it harder to drive than in a white-out snow blizzard, and a lot darker. That storm had lasted more than a week. Most roads drifted over. Killed most crops, too. The few winter plows that would start and keep running shoveled powdery sand and dirt drifts around the clock for weeks. Nobody drove. Couldn't see. Couldn't breathe—even through a bandana. Anything that breathed sought shelter.

Jake shuddered as he remembered trying to find his way from the house to the barn to check on Queenie and the milkers. That day, it took him twenty minutes to crawl more than walk less than forty yards. Got turned around, and ended up at the hog pen, which offered no shelter, instead of the barn. So hard to breathe, he choked and coughed more than anything. Jake thought he might not make it. He remembered thinking, *How the heck are those hogs gettin' on? Probably got their noses together stuffed into a bale.* But Jake remembered focusing more on his own survival. Found the barn on his hands and knees with his face down low, gasping. Any longer and he might not be remembering at all right now. Months after that summer storm, he still shoveled piles of dirt from places it ought not to be.

Now warmed and dressed, he focused on the bright side as the sun threatened to peek over the eastern tree line across County 14. Today was Thursday—go-to-town day—assuming the wind wasn't too bad. Not that he liked town much, but that's where *she* was. Cold enough for another dusting of snow. That'd help. Every Thursday, he hoped to at least glimpse Sophie Bairns. He might even speak to her this week. *Aw, who am I kidding?* But a man needed his dreams, didn't he?

Thinking of dreams, maybe some day he'd even dig himself out from under this old patch of cracked dirt Daddy left him and get the hell out. Get some schooling like his friend Chief Dan. Invent something important and live a rich life, never dirty from digging again, and never again feel hollow from hunger and shame. Never smelling like hog shit, and being so small that some town and city folks look down at ya—*on* ya—if they'd notice ya at all. Like through one of them magnifying glasses. *But that's a far piece right now, and that's okay too.*

THIS THURSDAY HAD BEEN A BUST. JAKE HAD PURCHASED provisions, alright, but Sophie was nowhere in sight. Time to head home. Alone. Again. The bitter breeze shot tiny icicles that nibbled at his naked cheeks, rosy from the frigid air. They prickled. After he left town, he folded and tucked his good fedora into a hip pocket and jammed an old hat with ear flaps onto his head. Someone said his fedora, with a little wider brim than most, looked like it might've once belonged to Jimmy Cagney. Not that Jake knew who that was. The jaunty angle at which he wore it, though, telegraphed his mood. Jake's convivial demeanor infected those around him. Most of the time. Today, though, his fedora had looked ridiculous—misshapen, inappropriate. Made a lousy shield for frostbitten flesh. Besides, nothing, not even warmth, could sweeten his maudlin mood that worsened with every step. And not just because he hadn't seen Sophie.

Not so long ago, everything sparkled. The fields burst with yellow corn on green stalks with golden tassels that towered eight feet overhead by midsummer each year. And the cows' udders swelled twice a day from too much milk.

Then, the rain left, the black blizzards came, and everything spiraled. Especially after things went haywire out east. Men grew desperate.

With dead crops and no income, hope dwindled. Some took to stealing horses for food, or worse. A few took to cooking illegal hooch and selling it. Many lost everything as they clutched at straws in the dim light of day just to survive and to provide.

At least the youthful Jacob Hardt had no kids to feed. Yet. Hadn't found the right girl. Or had he, and she doesn't know it? Anyway, he found it hard enough to feed himself and his meager collection of inherited livestock.

Last summer had skulked away in shame. A dirty brown sky now surrendered to dingy white when the heavens teased mortals with a few snowflakes. Jake's joints creaked in protest of the cold, but his lungs now welcomed a little blowing snow. Breathing came easier.

He leaned into the cold and the howling prairie winds, praying the machinery would still work, come Spring. He prayed that all four cows would survive, and that his only ax handle wouldn't break chopping ice out of the water troughs. He prayed the fences would stay put. But the Good Lord cared less about his infrequent prayers of late. Regardless, a fickle Mother Nature made one vow in this season of change: it would get worse.

Still, he could not lose faith. Not completely, anyway. He still had the farm. And he inherited some decent livestock, even though he wondered daily how he would feed them. At least the well still pumped clear and strong. Yes, he'd be okay.

The few who knew Jake knew he was a dreamer. And like his daddy, Jake had always been a farmer, except for the year he slipped away to go to mechanical design school. The only time to imagine otherwise was when he slipped out of his bibs and stained brogans to venture into town on Thursdays, his favorite day of the week. He'd been careful with his only dress shirt that remained almost white, except inside its detachable collar and cuffs. His fancy black suspenders, wool vest, and high-waist trousers scratched at his pits and his privates. Plus, those fancy oxfords pinched his feet. But he hoped it would all be worth it. He was sure he looked more like a slicker than a sodbuster, except for his snow-white forehead that never saw the sun. Hats almost always concealed his prematurely balding head of dark brown hair. For now, his quilted cap with side flaps tied under his chin battled today's ear-numbing nor'wester.

There was something else about this simple farmer who knew no other profession. He seemed to outshine his hazy little life, even though there was an immense hole to fill. He had not even caught a glimpse of Sophie this week. That left him ill-prepared to face the coming week—alone. Again.

3

A nother week passed. Jake and Queenie headed home from town. This Thursday afternoon, Jake needed the old girl to stay focused. With reluctance, he slapped her rump. They both tolerated the biting chill in the air. Queenie shook her head to shake off the ice crystals from her flaring nostrils as they shot her steamy breath down and out. Looked like smoke. Jake imagined she was a dragon shooting flames. At least his quilted cap kept his ears from freezing. Even though he couldn't afford gloves, his oilskin coat sleeves were plenty long. Queenie didn't have any such protection.

"C'mon, don't let me down now, girl."

A twinge of guilt gnawed at his gut each time he smacked her butt. He convinced himself she didn't mind. His focus wandered—so often the case. He slapped her again, this time a little harder, maybe harder than necessary.

"Are you even paying attention?" Yet another slap.

She whipped her tired eyes around, as if questioning, but

she knew why. She wasn't getting any younger. And Jake was not growing more patient. She nickered in understanding as he snapped the reins against her flanks a fourth time. Queenie indulged him and picked up the pace ever so slightly, as if not to spoil the young man, or reward him too much for the abuse. Close now, he goaded her into a canter. He'd make it up to her later. When she slowed again, he smiled. *Good old Queenie, she's making a statement.*

From high atop the light buckboard's seat, he took a quick inventory of his costly larder bouncing in the back. Proud of his excellent memory—when he was motivated—he could recite the atrocious price of each victual, should anyone ask. *A pound of coffee for thirty cents seems high. Three plucked chickens cost a whole dollar? For pity's sake! A five-pound sack of sugar for thirty cents, a ten-pound bag of potatoes at eighteen cents, and a dozen eggs for the same, a pound of lard for fifteen cents... And them three loaves of bread for a dime didn't smell or feel too fresh, either.*

But no toilet paper was to be had in the store. Marvin, the owner, had said, "That might be true for all of Lyon County, Jake." The old gent had taken pity on him, a single farm kid living alone 'n all. Marvin had disappeared through his back room and returned half a minute later. "Son, here ya go." He stretched his arm out. He clutched a half-used-up copy of an old Sears-Roebuck from his one-holer behind the store. "Should be enough pages left there to hold ya over til next Thursday, *if* you're careful." He winked and grinned. "Maybe we'll have TP by then." Good ole Marvin and his heart of gold. Jake hadn't even asked.

Many of Marvin's shelves stood either sparse or downright bare. More than halfway home now, Jake fingered the few coins left in his pocket. Something to do. Guilt grabbed him as he had used a goodly amount of his remaining cash to *buy* them chickens and eggs. More 'n two dollars a week for store-bought provisions? *Downright ridiculous, but that ain't Marvin's fault, is it?* Once he'd settled in to the home place that was now his, he'd butcher and salt a hog, maybe buy a heifer. He'd borrow old Silas Hummel's bull stud to work on his own herd, and work his own chickens that were almost ready to lay, any day now. Then there'd be chicks, and.... But for now.... If only he weren't behind....

It seemed these days he just rotated through problems shy of any practical solutions. Jake resorted to worrying about the last and the next thirty-dollar farm payments to old Silas. Few private lenders were tolerant, especially these days, and especially Silas. He must be hurting too. It seemed Jake was always one telephone call or a neighborly visit from eviction. Winter was both the best time of year and the worst. Offered lots of time to tinker, the snow knocked down the dust, at least some of it, but no crops to harvest for cash, especially after last summer. *You just wait til I strike it big, Silas! You just wait!* He snickered, knowing full-well that would take time neither he nor his grumpy old neighbor could afford. But somehow he'd get by. He always did.

The farm was a far piece from town—six miles south of George on old County 14. The round trip to fetch supplies each week took most of a day. Jake engineered a way to see little Sophie Bairns from afar at least once each Thursday, except for last week. He'd sometimes spot her through the windows at her daddy's fancy dealership. Or he'd watch her limp a few blocks home from her friend's house, but she was never alone. He imagined talking to her—introducing himself —but that's usually when he decided Queenie had grown weary of waiting for him to make up his smitten mind. And he needed to get home before dark or they'd both likely freeze. That did not mean he wouldn't still *think* of Sophie. Like now.

Two hours later, Queenie pulled the old buckboard and

her abusive whip master into the yard. She knew to stop in front of the barn—home—such as it was, with its missing doors 'n all. Jake bemoaned the end of his weekly trip into town. Travel offered him time to think, when not maneuvering the ruts and bumps of old 14. But now he already missed Sophie, as if the encroaching darkness dragged him deeper into an empty hole. Alone. And she *still* didn't even know who he was, or how he felt about her.

He unhitched Queenie and rubbed her left rump, saw steam rising as she lost heat. She had the good sense to wander into the barn, out of the wind, and sidle up to a diminishing pile of hay that lay at the mouth of her open stall. *What would I do without you, Queenie?*

❧ 4 ☙

❦

Sophie Bairns determined she would not die a spinster. She could not allow her handicap—nor her over-protective parents—to define her.

Some folks thought this young girl outspoken, even though she spoke in a husky whisper, and rarely initiated a conversation. They came to her. At twenty-three, already of spinster age, she was both demure *and* demanding in any conversation on most any topic with anyone—women *or* men —much to her father's chagrin. She would avoid eye contact early in a discussion, but then the full force of her gaze rein-forced her strong opinions on most any topic once she joined in. However, if already inflamed, you were on your own.

Many suggested this comportment was unflattering for a genteel woman of the thirties who still lived with her parents, especially in her condition. But you dared not confront Sophie concerning her attitude for fear of an ample helping of most inappropriate comportment. All was delivered in her throaty whisper you'd hear very well from ten feet away. Her opinion would be reasonable once you got past the unexpected strength of this young woman who came across like a quiet force of nature—a straight-line wind with a Mona Lisa smile.

Sophie's cashmere eyes clashed with any of the crisp dresses she wore, as if she desired a notable contrast. She could thank her proper German mother for that—Hilda, her protector, her friend. The stiffness of heavy fabrics drew her. Perhaps a complex brocade that descended from a high collar to a mid-calf hem. That suited her. Soft eyes and medium-length auburn hair possessed of a natural curl and bounce adorned Sophie's interesting face. Like her soft locks were always just washed and dried without coifing—a bit fly-away, and that was okay, even if unconventional.

She smelled of lavender. Though her sculpted countenance appeared pleasant, a quiet desperation overshadowed her beauty, but did not complete her any more than her handicap. A stalwart spirit sprouted and flourished within Sophie, starting at an early age. Was she compensating for her helplessness early in life, a feeling that had constructed her moral and spiritual foundation brick by mortared brick? Yet those cashmere eyes often eclipsed her natural firmness, especially before she spoke. Advantage: little Sophie.

This girl inherited full cheeks from her Germanic mother's wider face, but she possessed a slender sharpness around her chin, borrowed from Father's chiseled jaw. The combination lent her a simple cherubic charm. Well, not quite simple. Nothing about Sophie was simple. A smile, though never quite realized, was never far away, as if she harbored some glorious secret. She had much to be thankful for, and she determined to let the world see it. In her own precise manner.

Sophie also determined her handicap only made her stalwart spirit even stronger *and* more resilient. You would notice almost nothing unusual about her physical stature as she stood before you. She'd clasp her hands in front. She looked like any other young woman, except for a slight curvature of her upper back, as if it had aged all on its own. This caused her to offer a cocked hip with the slightest hint of attitude. Slender, but well-nourished—her mother Hilda would claim —perhaps en route to becoming a full figured woman, her pronounced limp could not go unnoticed as she walked. But if you were around Sophie for a while, that limp *did* go unnoticed. Her right hand would lie across her lap as she sat, palm up, fingers curled with an unusual and unusable asymmetry. But she compensated with a dextrous left hand that disguised her right hand's partial paralysis and relentless cramping with clever clasped-hand gestures, the good hand supporting the nearly helpless one, but subtly so. That was just Sophie.

And if you were curious about what she was *thinking*, you just needed to *listen*. Soft-spoken did not mean unspoken. She could split wet oak with that husky whisper. This only child was a force of nature *and* a child of God.

Sophie was... reliable.

SITTING ON THE SOFA IN HER HER PARENTS' FRONT ROOM with her mother, Hilda, it was time to be very serious. "Mother, I'm leaving George City, and I need your blessing."

"*What*, dear? What are you saying?"

"Nursing school calls to me. I've applied to the Mounds Midway School of Nursing up in St. Paul, and I've been accepted."

"Sophie—"

She raised her outstretched palm to her mother, and rested it on her thigh. "Now I know what you're going to say, but I've decided. Will you support me in this decision?"

Sophie thought Mother would faint dead away upon

hearing this declaration. She knew her mother's head was spinning at the edge of precarious, like an off-balance top, as she tried to grapple with this news.

"We'll have to see what your father says about this, dear—"

"No, Mother. We will not. You will be my advocate with Father. I *need* this, Mother. Otherwise, I'll never know...."

"Alright, dear. I'll talk with your father. But I don't look forward to this. It will be a very difficult conversation."

"Oh, thank you!" With a couple of quick rocking motions to gather momentum, she rose from the small front room couch as she bubbled with excitement. She pleaded—with her outstretched arms and a huge smile that dimpled her cheeks—for her mother to rise.

HILDA BAIRNS' HEART ACHED SEEING HER LITTLE GIRL SO animated. Of course, she was no longer a little girl, but it still seemed so. She stood and Sophie threw her arms about her taller mother's neck, her confidence contra-punctuated with a small stumble as she tried to extend her reach with her orthopedic heels leaving the floor.

As she embraced her baby, she thought, *Everything is changing, and I don't know how to protect her anymore. Henry will explode. I'll settle him down, and then he'll agree to pay our little girl's tuition, room and board, or Heaven help the man. Little Sophie... if only she doesn't allow her blind determination to cloud her judgment when she leaves the nest....*

The ride home from town the following Thursday, like every week, had clinched Jake's empty gut, like a twisting fist. Once more, he scanned what he could see of the beat-up old dirt farm in the dusky light—all forty-two acres, forty of it tillable—because that's what it was —a beat-up old farm. But it was the Hardt home place. He had grown up here. With the farm, he had inherited four old cows, all now past their prime, but still decent milkers, along with three decent hogs. His six chickens included four hens of near-laying age, with a fifth that was almost as close. Oh, and one cranky young rooster constantly sounded off with his serious inferiority complex. His daddy bequeathed it all to him. He and Mom passed two years earlier. It was all his. At least for the next twenty-eight days. Jake had also inherited Daddy's fantasy that this farm would provide more than just debts. After the end of the month, well....

Once he stashed his provisions in the house, he returned to check on Queenie in the barn. He brushed her out before hooking her up in her open stall. Smiled at her, rubbed her velvet nuzzle, palmed her the half-carrot he'd stuffed into his trousers pocket earlier, and left her nickering, bobbing her head.

The wind swirled a small drift—more brown than white— a good six feet into the barn where doors should be hanging, not just twisted hinges. Daddy never told him what happened to those doors. He smirked. The faded barn used to be red. *Has mighty fine bones, this old barn, just needs some buttoning up.* If he could make the last and next payments to old Silas, he'd be around long enough to build and hang some new doors. But that'd take lumber 'n nails.

As he came out into the crisp starlight, he looked up over his left shoulder. The open haymow door up near the roof's peak dangled down toward the missing doors. *A whole lotta empty up there. But the weather will turn for the better, come Spring. Has to.*

JAKE SAUNTERED FARTHER OUT INTO THE YARD. His thoughts rambled on as he stared at Mom 'n Daddy's turn-of-the-century house that offered the barest hint of fancy trim— what was left of it, anyway. They called that folderol ginger-bread. Sections dangled in disrepair. Like the rest of the old pile. Daddy—God rest his soul—hadn't been big on mainte-nance. Neither was he. Who had time? He indulged in reflec-tion. *Sure could use some paint. Maybe a woman's touch inside too, now that Mom's gone.* In spite of the guilt that washed through him, he cursed the god to which his parents had devoted their lives. That god took them from him summer before last. *Sumbitch, I should hate this place.*

He gazed to his right toward the dirt driveway that wound in from the north-south county road a hundred yards off to the east. The barest hint of snow had failed to cover the musty odor of County 14's dust, even here in the yard. A line of naked cottonwoods hugged the ditch on the south side of the driveway, with a doddering old snow fence just to the north. Well past its prime, less than half its length still stood. The other half drifted over, flattened by tired snow. The driveway split. The lesser-used right fork circled around to the front of the house. The fork most everyone used—the left one—ran near the house's back door which faced the well, hardpan yard, and the spot where he now stood near the barn.

Off to his right and behind him, a large chicken coop squatted from the weight of its swaybacked roof. *Might cave in some day, eh, plow hand? That'd squash them hens and that sassy rooster. Yup, gotta fix that too, somehow. Nobody else will. That's for sure.*

These outbuildings were soldiers standing guard over a patch of gray dirt as if it were hallowed ground. "It *is* hallowed," his daddy used to say, "as long as a Hardt works it." Like most farmers, Daddy was big on leaving a family legacy. He served up guilt pretty well, too. There was a time Jake dreamed of this place as his own. Even thought maybe old Silas Hummel might sell Daddy or him another forty acres. Yep, there was a time.

Jake usually pasted on a ten-dollar smile of anticipation that pinched his puppy dog eyes. Some said he reminded them of a balding John Wayne, only shorter. Jake had said, "Who?" But that smile concealed a steely determination. He *knew* he was destined for greatness. He *would* claim more than plains grit, crankcase grease under his nails and countless layers of callouses and scabs that caked his rough-hewn soul. Some day.

A white-hot flame deep within him tempered his strength not measured by any mortal scale. He tasted the truth of it, even more than he could taste the gray ice crystals swirling up from an easterly gust laced with leftover smut. That little dust devil snaked its way into the yard, and around the chicken coop from the prairie beyond as it blew across the length of the rectangular hog pen. *At least this hellish breeze is carryin' the hog stink away. Maybe it'll blow some luck this way. At least it ain't that turkey farm stench like up north of George!*

Daddy used to say they were blessed to have electric out here this far south of George. He called it the brighter side of town, even though they were six miles out. Electric this far out was rare, but with Klein's grain elevator south of town, and the Hummel place just north of their own place, all that money bought electric poles and lines out this far, even farther. Daddy had thrown in with Silas Hummel and Lester Klein back when crops still grew. Now, because of Daddy, Jake's place had electric when so many other farms did not. That meant a few lights, but that was about all Daddy could afford. Mom hoped for one of them fancy refrigeration appliances, tired of salting meat and throwing away rotten eggs. "Maybe later," Daddy had said.

The yard light hung near the top of a once-tarred pole that used to stand straight up. It would cast a yellow glow. That old light did its best to guard the yard against darkness and night critters. But shadows still claimed at least half the yard every dusk—even when he could afford to pay the electric. Otherwise, no night anywhere was as black as an Iowa farm six miles out. Tonight, darkness and doubt and critters would prevail. At least there was a full moon.

Jake glanced at the hogs he tolerated. He liked them on the dinner table well enough. Eating them instead of selling them, though, would not help his all-too-thin stash of cash— mostly coins—buried in a hole in the barn for safekeeping under a small section of planked floor. Some day he'd save enough to pay off the place.

But there was just no money. Since a couple of seasons

ago, an angry prairie victimized most all the crops. Silas came through with a private loan, no doubt as a favor. He and Daddy were once fast friends before their falling out—something about a disagreement over the use of Silas's bull stud, although neither could really remember.

By moonlight, Jake shrugged and shook old snow off the upside-down tin pail that covered the stumpy well-head and its pump handle. Stalks of stale straw from the bales surrounding the pump to protect it from freezing had somehow gusted their way onto the bottom of the up-side-down pail. After a dozen pumps to get a decent prime, water came up. Pumping also shook loose the thin icicle hanging on the spigot from pumping that morning. After covering the pump head again with a second pail kept nearby for that purpose, he lugged his half-full pail toward the rear of the house that faced the barn. He swore that someday the old place would have a pump right inside the kitchen.

He missed *her*. Already. A farm without a family made for a cold and lonely life, no more so than in the dark of winter. Solitude also made it damn hard to work the land, even when God wasn't so pissed.

That's when he heard Queenie whinny—not once, but twice. *What the heck?*

❧ 6 ❧

❧

Ignoring persistent shivers, Jake set down his pail halfway to the house, turned and hurried back into the barn. "What's the matter, old girl?" Queenie bobbed her head. He spun around to a rustling behind him. He dismissed the thought that it might be old Jesse, his prize milker, shifting in her stall. That's when he caught sight of a ghost approaching from the deep shadows of the empty stall next to Jesse's. Jake blinked to confirm he wasn't hallucinating.

A knife glinted from the ghost of a man's hand as he shuffled forward in the dim light, dragging his right leg. His ragged breath clouded his face. He trembled either from exposure, malnutrition, or something worse. No wonder. Scarecrow rags hung on his emaciated frame. And the young man's big toe protruded from his right shoe—no socks. At least not on that foot. Gaping from under a flimsy jacket and a buttonless tatter of a shirt, his ribs cast spidery shadows on his milk-white chest.

"I'm taking your horse, mister."

Jake struggled to understand what was happening. The demand in a voice fierce with determination came out thick and hoarse. And quavering. Jake held up his hands, his palms facing the intruder. He flipped from fear to pity.

"Look, brother. I have some food. We can sit by a warm fire for a while. You can even spend the night. But you ain't takin' my horse. That'd kill my farm."

"I gotta get home. I *am* taking your horse. Now move." The knife jabbed at the air toward Jake, its tip still three feet away. The ghost's hand and blade shook with a series of involuntary tremors.

"Alright, alright...." Jake side-shuffled out of the young hobo's way. He had never seen such desperation up close. The man now divided his attention between Jake and unsnapping Queenie's halter. *No way he can get up onto her. Not in his condition.* Jake backed to the far wall of Queenie's stall. With slow deliberation, he reached behind him. While keeping his eyes on the hobo, his fingers closed around the handle of the shovel he knew was there. The man now stood in front of Queenie's head, unsnapping her halter.

In a clear, calm voice, Jake called out, "Queenie."

His favorite girl jerked her enormous head around in response, colliding with the stranger's face. He stumbled back from the blow, his nose now suddenly an open spigot, a fountain spewing blood that appeared crimson in the twilight.

Jake swung the shovel downward. The measured swing— not hard—struck the man's knife hand with a metallic clatter. What looked like an old kitchen knife dropped to the floor as the scarecrow spun in shock to collapse in a defeated heap. His energy spent, he lay where he fell and bawled like a baby, bubbling blood and phlegm and despair.

Jake dropped the shovel and kneeled at the young man's side. Yanking a hanky from the back pocket of his town trousers, he gently applied pressure to the kid's nose, now a mixture of blood, tears and mucus.

"C'mon, little brother, let's get you inside."

"Sorry, sorry, sorry...." The nearly indiscernible words gushed out between sobs.

Half-carrying the wasted soul across the yard to the rear of the house, Jake said, "Look, mister, I don't know what your story is, but we're gonna get you some help, okay?" Twenty feet from the mudroom door, the kid collapsed with a gasp. Jake carried him the rest of the way like a newborn calf from a ditch to the barn. The poor kid smelled of urine and feces and... something else... rot? Maybe just old puke and body odor, he hoped. Jake prayed to the Almighty he wasn't carrying the sickness. He propped the sorry soul into a straight chair near the wood stove in the kitchen.

First things first. Back in the mudroom, Jake kicked off his oxfords, and slid his feet into the tattered slippers he'd owned since he was a teen. Grabbed two fistfuls of tinder and a few stringy chunks of box elder out of the worm-scarred wood box. Threw it all into the stove where a few coals still smoldered from this morning. *Praise the Lord.* His mom had called this old stove Blackie. When stoked, Blackie kept the kitchen and adjacent bedroom warm. He wondered how many thousands of meals and pots of coffee and rescues of wayward hobos this stove had witnessed. *Now, to tend to this kid.*

Jake peered into the young man's empty eyes. Chin on his chest, semi-conscious, shaking and blinking, his nose had stopped bleeding. "What's your name, pardner? Hey! What's your name?" Slapped the side of his leg to get his attention.

The kid struggled to lift his head. "Um, Peter."

"Where's home, Pete?"

"Um, until a few weeks ago, a Hooverville outside Omaha."

The last few years, shanty towns had popped up all over the country to house the destitute. They called them "Hoovervilles," named after the president that nobody supported anymore.

"Okay, Pete. You hang in there, buddy. Gonna warm you up some."

Like magic, the tinder took, and the fire crackled. The chill surrendered to Blackie's radiating heat. Jake held his breath and started peeling off Pete's wet shoes that were mostly rotted away. *Oh, Lordy, grant me strength here!*

7

Lyon County Sheriff Billy Kershaw survived the Great War. But just barely. The gates of Hell had opened and swallowed him, along with a bunch of other fellas and much of France in early October 1918. Six companies of the three-hundred-eighth Infantry Regiment—including his—later known as the *Lost Battalion,* became isolated. They captured a ridge near a place called Charlevaux Mill in the heart of the Argonne Forest. The bitter fighting with the Germans all around them lasted a week. Felt like a year. Billy's battalion suffered heavy losses until the seventy-seventh Infantry Division relieved them. But by then, the bloody hand-to-hand fighting changed Billy in frightening ways.

Corporal Kershaw met the devil, spit in his eye, and lived to harbor a tale that would forever remain untold. He would never talk about the blood ponds deep enough to drown in at the bottom of countless foxholes, unrecognizable body parts, and tripping over yards of intestines of his fallen brothers. Nor about the shit- and urine-soaked mud he breathed in and spit out as he elbowed through on his belly. Or about trying not to puke at the stench of raw and rotting meat. Or feeling guilty when the charred flesh of a buddy smelled appetizing to his shrunken stomach.

Billy knew he wasn't just anybody. Nothing fazed him. Not the prospect of certain death. Nor losing friends to battlefield carnage. Especially not the countless teenage Krauts whose lives he ended while he watched their hopes and dreams drain from their eyes inches from his own. If only he believed that lie as much as he thought he did. His fire-brand recklessness even earned him a couple of medals that now collected lint in a drawer in his lonely Rock Rapids bungalow. *Or did I give those damn trinkets away to them church ladies?*

His teenage wife always wore a camphor necklace and a mask everywhere—for all the good it did her. While Billy fought abroad for her safety, the damn Spanish Influenza robbed him of the joy that gave his worthless life purpose. Losing little Alice broke his heart worse than combat. He suffered a near-fatal crisis of faith. Shunned his childhood religion. Even pushed away old church friends, what few he had. Took to strong drink in a big way for more than a few years. And he never forgave the god that ripped such a gaping hole in his soul. Little Sophie Bairns down in George reminded him of his irreplaceable Alice who he hoped could rest in peace, like she never could in life.

Well, enough lolly-gaggin'. Time to get back to work. Darkness had crept into the Lyon Sheriff's office unnoticed. Hadn't turned on the lights yet. The phone ringing on the wall behind Billy shook him loose from his day-dreaming. Flipped on his desk lamp, stood, and grabbed the ear piece off its hook, stared at the smelly mouth piece and the ringers above it.

"Sheriff Billy Kershaw here. How may I serve?"

"Hello, Sheriff. This here's Jake Hardt. I'm on a farm six miles south of George. Didn't know who to call. Got a fella here needs some help. Can you stop by in the morning?"

8

൭ൠ

The new day at the Hardt farm felt like new hope. Jake sat across from Peter, his gaunt friend from last night. He still stunk like a newborn calf who's momma neglected to lick off after birth, but he had thawed out. They nursed their mugs of coffee. The sun lit up the kitchen table between them. Turned out Pete wasn't just cold, he was hurting, in pain, ill. But not from the sickness as far as Jake could tell. He'd heard stories of people addicted to drugs. His daddy used to talk about the Chinese railroad workers who brought their opium addictions with them to America. But he'd seen nothing like that up close. Not in little Lyon County.

"So, what is it you need, Pete?"

"Gold. I need gold." As he brought the mug to his dry lips, he splashed the hot black coffee, dousing his hands and the tabletop. Jake rose, rounded the table, and took the cup from him. Set it on the table, and settled into the chair to his right.

"Yeah, buddy, don't we all."

"No, Mr. Hardt, you don't understand. I need a drink. *I need some Black Gold! Just a sip or two. Please!*"

Peter had settled down after a strong cup of yard mud—farm coffee, the way Mom used to make it—just kept adding water and grounds. Always on the boil. Jake held the cup for him while he gulped. But now he was gettin' all riled again.

"Okay, Pete. Not sure what Black Gold is, but we'll ask the sheriff to help you out. Okay, pardner?"

"Sheriff? Oh, God. No, we don't dare do that." He started fidgeting, and Jake's level of concern ramped up once more. Wrong thing to say.

"Look, he doesn't need to know about the whole knife thing in the barn last night. Just between you and me, okay, Pete? But I can see you got some problems you can't solve by yourself. Level with Billy, and see what we can work out for ya. Fair enough, friend?" Using the first name of a sheriff he'd never met seemed to inspire a little trust. After a few beats, Peter stopped fidgeting, leaned back, and nodded. Jake fed the kid another sip of mud.

"What's goin' on, little brother? What are you tangled up in?"

"Shucks, all happened so sudden-like. Working on my papa's homestead over Omaha way. Bored, ya know? Went to a party. Tipped a few," Peter cleared his dry throat, like the memory brought up some dehydrated phlegm, "and everybody was drinkin', havin' a high old time. Went home around midnight. Papa'd whoop my butt if I was late. But I couldn't sleep, ya know? Sat up fidgeting all night. Got real thirsty, but drinkin' water didn't help. Then, next afternoon, I got real tired, fell asleep in the barn. Pissed off Papa cuz I didn't get my chores done. That's real important to him. And I done the craziest thing. Got real mad, ya know? Got up, and I done hauled off and hit Papa, right in the mouth. Real hard. First time I ever raised a hand. Layin' on the ground bleedin' all over, he looked up at me standin' over him. Tore my heart out. Told me to clear out. About old enough anyway, and said he didn't want no ruffian livin' with him and Momma.

"That was more 'n a month ago. Been goin' to parties where I could drink away my thirst, ya know? But I ain't got no money, so I done odd jobs. Dunno, Mr. Hardt. It's real bad now. Real bad."

A motorcar rolled into the yard. A peek out the kitchen window confirmed it was the sheriff.

"Pete, you wait here by the fire, buddy. I'm gonna bring in Billy. He's a good guy. He'll know what to do." He patted Peter on the shoulder, traded his slippers for his boots in the mudroom, threw on his favorite old fedora, and strode out to meet the sheriff. Rubbed the back of his forearms against the morning chill before jerking down on his shoved-up long-John sleeves.

"Mornin', Mr. Hardt. Billy Rhett Kershaw." Touched the front of his brim. Jake didn't expect him to be so tall. Had to be at least six feet. He wore a black cowboy hat, thumbs hooked into his gear belt in front of a holster stuffed with a revolver on his right hip, a leather pouch on his left. Straw-colored hair poked out from underneath that tall-crowned hat. Covered the top of his ears. Not at all spit-and-polish, that was for sure. A real good-looking guy, though. All smiles, hard around the edges.

"Mornin', Sheriff. I'm Jake. This here's my place." Said that with more pride than he might have thought. He thrust out his hand to meet the sheriff's.

"Just Billy, Jake."

"Okay, Billy. Found a stray in my barn last night. Christian

35

name's Peter. In a rough way. Didn't offer up a family name. Real desperate, but sick-like."

Billy's eyebrows raised under his Stetson. Dropped his arms to his sides, spreading his fingers like he was stretching them gettin' ready for a quick-draw. Interesting. Jake quickly added, "No, I don't think it's that. Looks more like a drug thing. Keeps talkin' about needing black gold."

Billy relaxed. "Huh. I saw some of that drug stuff during the war. Could be a new name for some addictive sh—, ah, substance. Don't see many junkies 'round these parts. Just wandered in?"

"Yup. But other than his, um, need, seems a likable sort, like maybe a good kid got tangled up where he shouldn't oughta. Can you do something for him, Billy?"

"Well, at a minimum, take him off yer hands, for sure. Get the young fella back to my office in Rock Rapids. Find his family. If he's been drinkin' the laudanum, though, I might run him over to the hospital in Spencer. I'll let ya know. Appreciate you callin' me, Jake. Right Christian of ya." The sheriff was even more handsome when he threw a crooked smile.

9

ᘒᕈᑐ

The sickness—one of them—had struck millions, among them was Sophie Bairns when she was six, but she was a survivor. The infectious disease had deformed her left foot and misshaped her right hand. It also weakened and deformed her spinal column that resulted in a noticeable forward slump. Acute cramping plagued her. They were the worst, conquered only by will and by time—they seldom lasted less than an excruciating half-hour when they struck, sometimes longer.

An infectious virus called poliomyelitis—polio—swept the land. But Sophie was lucky, branded "only" with atrophy and partial paralysis. Forever. Thousands had died horrible deaths as their own bodies suffocated them. Doctors were at a loss. But Sophie's strength of spirit told her she was perfect, despite the restrictive undergarment she wore all the time, without which she could neither sleep safely, nor sit nor stand, much less walk. Was she not perfect? She believed that despite evidence to the contrary.

Her parents' affluence proved ineffectual in fighting the infection. At least the Bairns afforded the best treatment and equipment. Only the strength of their faith and mutual affection carried the family through Sophie's darkled childhood pock-marked with pain, disappointment, and a near-paralyzing fear of dubious tomorrows.

Then Sophie met Jake Hardt. Well, she hadn't actually met him. She'd known *of* him since elementary school. Her far more adventurous friend, Edith Everniss, four years younger but already more worldly than she, told her a month ago. Jake was smitten with her, but shy.

"Oh, Edie, you always exaggerate. Yes, he's awfully cute, but really? Jake Hardt? Don't you think he's a bit, well... dangerous?" She'd heard rumors.

The uneven path scraped clean of snow alongside the street challenged them both. The huge branches overhead shed flakes from last night's fall, showering them here and there as an occasional gust coaxed some of them loose.

"I'm telling you, Soph, he watches you with those puppy-dog eyes, like you have him on an invisible leash." Sophie's blank stare was her only reaction.

Edie continued with impatience. "Well, what are you going to do about it?"

"Do?"

"Oh, for Heaven's sake, Sophie. Next week when he comes to town—you know, every Thursday like clockwork in case you hadn't noticed—when he finds you, like he *always does,* wave to the poor guy! Toss him a bone! Why not? There's nothing *else* to do in this one-horse town."

"I could never—" Sophie's cheeks flushed like twin roses blossoming in June.

"Sure, you could. And if you don't—"

"Edith! You wouldn't!"

But Sophie knew Edie was right. She *had* noticed. Sweet

Jake. Slender, not that tall, and at the same time, larger than life. And that perpetual smile, at least whenever she noticed him nearby. Surely too grand for a sharecropper, or whatever he was. She considered him an admirer from afar at first, then as her personal protector. Adorable. His shy spirit shone like the sun in the bleakness of her small world. And that smile... suggested something more than an indomitable spirit. There was also... something else.

A WEEK LATER, SOPHIE TOOK EDIE'S ADVICE, SAW JAKE across the street as she left Edie's house—alone—intentionally, despite the considerable risk. And there he was. None too subtle, way too casual, he did his best not to stare. She turned, already knowing he was there, and... waved. Just a tiny wave with her good hand, down low, by her hip.

Jake's eyes widened as he jerked his hands out of his pockets. He had been leaning against a light pole and stumbled as he untangled his crossed ankles with some difficulty, like his shoes were longer than he realized. He read Sophie's tiny wave as an invitation, recovered from his shock, and bounded across the street, like a schoolboy to a free lollipop. Adorable.

Oh, God, what do I do now? Please, Lord— Sophie unconsciously cocked her head sideways, dropped her chin, tugged her left ear lobe with her good hand, and responded with a coy smile to his awkward body language.

"Hello, Sophie. I'm Jake. Can I walk you home?" Eager, like a puppy ready for a walk.

"Oh, well... I don't see why not."

"Let me give you a hand..."

"Oh, dear, well, sure. It *is* very slick." The hazy sun glinted off the sheen of thin ice dusted with dry snow underfoot. Without Edie as an escort, Sophie had taken a very real risk to be here alone, and approachable. Now, she realized a fall would be a high price to pay for meeting a boy.

Not waiting for another invitation, and seeing her nervous glance down at her shoes on the shiny ice, Jake grabbed her arm, a little too abruptly. Her eyes widened for a moment and she flinched, almost upsetting her balance, before she realized Jake's excitement had just gotten the better of him. She welcomed the stability he offered.

"Uh, sorry. Don't want either of us to fall, now do we?"

And there it was. Sophie basked in the glow of that devastating smile. What *was* she doing?

Oh my... that odor.

✹ 10 ✹

৩৯৯

The morning haze penetrated the Lyon County Sheriff's Office on Main Street in Rock Rapids, the county seat. But it left shadows spraying more than half of what looked like a storefront with windows that could be cleaner. Billy's young deputy, Jimmy Lenert, stood by the phone he'd hung up moments earlier. Jimmy grimaced as if he'd just bitten into a fresh lemon and some had squirted into both eyes. "Sheriff?"

Distracted, Billy had yet to look up at his deputy leaning against the wall with his chin on his chest. The sunlight could not reach him. When he did raise his gaze, he watched Jimmy clench and unclench his fists while pummeling the sides of his legs. Then Billy saw Jimmy's twisted expression.

"Old Silas Hummel down George City way discovered a body in the ditch out south on County Road 14." Jimmy's voice quavered, his eyes now misted over completely.

Still sitting at his desk, Billy had been filling out a stolen bicycle report, more likely just lost. A silly report. His desk sat far enough away from the front windows off to his right that natural light alone didn't cut it. They did not turn on the ceiling lights until sunset, per the county budget office. He worked at close range under a bright candescent desk light with a green glass shade. His forty-eight-year-old eyes no longer worked so good, even with the fancy spectacles from the VA.

When he heard *body in the ditch,* however, he jerked up his head so fast to meet Jimmy's eyes, a soft snap in his neck signaled an old injury was about to flare up. That's when he saw Jimmy's face in the dim light as he approached, as if in a funeral march.

"Settle down, son. Accident?" He already knew it wasn't. Jimmy's reaction....

"No, Billy. No car, nothing around the body out in the middle of nowhere." Tears rolled down both cheeks.

"Oh, *thee hell*, you say."

Fifteen years had passed since Billy had seen a body not from an accident. And that was his buddy Stevie's, or what remained of his upper torso, right next to him in a half-frozen mud hole. Could have been yesterday. Stevie was a good kid. Blue eyes, hellacious breath, runny nose. Krauts blew him up on his birthday.

"Well... let's get on out there, Jimmy." Billy was already swiveling in his chair. Jimmy remained frozen, now standing too close for the sheriff to get up, as if he needed to get something else out before Billy stood. His eyes now twin waterfalls. Spots appeared on his beige uniform shirt.

"Sheriff, it might be Roddy." Billy shot to his feet, pushing Jimmy back, tipping his heavy swivel chair over backwards. His holster had snagged the chair's wooden arm. The keys on his equipment belt jangled with annoying insistence because he was bouncing around like a boxer on the prowl. Jimmy stumbled, recovered, looked like he was a cat in need of another life, no limit to his own nervous edge since he had hung up the phone. Billy saw all of that now, the veins in Jimmy's temples bulged and pulsed. Couldn't hear his teeth grinding but saw his jawbone making that happen. Jimmy didn't dare move. Unsteady.

More buried memories of the war threatened to erupt. Then... silence. Billy froze too. Roddy Braddock wasn't yet twenty, way too eager to be Billy's newest and most gung-ho deputy. Not much younger than Jimmy. He realized that it's different when you've known the victim his entire life. And his parents. And his new wife. Especially a murder right down the road from where Roddy and he both grew up, although a generation apart. *Instead of in a field sopping with mud and cow shit and blood and guts and urine and vomit on the sorry side of the Atlantic. That was bad, but....*

"Oh, Jesus, Jimmy. Roddy didn't report in after his shift yesterday, did he? I thought he mighta just took his cruiser home for the night. He does that sometimes. He was patrolling south on County 14 between George and west to the Nebraska line—"

"That's right, Sheriff, according to the duty log. Old Silas thinks he recognized him, even though...."

"Thinks?" Everybody knew Roddy. He was a real sociable kid. *Thinks?*

"About all he'd say on the phone, Billy."

Both still frozen, standing in place, they gazed out the windows together. Jarred from their morbid brooding, Billy jolted them both into action. "Get your ass behind the wheel of your cruiser, Deputy, and get us out there. Right now, dammit!"

43

❦

As a German businessman for the last fifteen years, and no longer an elite soldier, Hans Graber thought more than once that he would not survive the intense period of training for this new mission. Covert training was geared toward much younger recruits. But motivation, reinforced with patriotic fervor, fueled him to complete his new mission for which he was uniquely qualified.

As a result, he now felt quite at home in the enemy camp, even though no formal declaration of war defined who that enemy might be, but there was no doubt. Especially for a veteran stormtrooper—one of the elite troops who ravaged their enemies on the Western front in the last desperate days of the Great War fifteen years earlier. They executed blitzkrieg maneuvers with stopwatch precision.

These infamous *sturmtrupplers* raced through trenches, attacking the enemy's soft spots. Moving in small units, firing light machine guns, bypassing enemy strongpoints, they'd head straight for critical bridges, command posts, supply dumps, and above all, artillery batteries. All by themselves, these stormtroopers could decide the outcome of a battle in its first thirty minutes.

Yes, those were glorious days. And then his wounds took him from the action during the last days of the hundred-day offensive—the largest and bloodiest battle—against the Americans in 1918. He'd known the war was already lost by then, but not his courage, nor the fury of his passion.

Now was his chance to serve once more, to help restore Germany to her former glory, even greater. They had learned a great deal since the Kaiser's foolish march to personal glory and defeat at the expense of Germany's people. Now they would win an undeclared war without firing a single shot. They'd not hesitate to use Americans to kill other Americans —icing on the tart.

Herr Graber had fought for the Kaiser before retiring to the private sector, and thought his usefulness to the Fatherland might have ended when the Americans destroyed and humiliated the German Empire on the world stage. But that was only a temporary setback. Every loyal member of the Second Reich knew that.

Now, far from home, entrenched in the filth they call New Jersey, he would seed his revenge, not for himself, but for the Fatherland. A sympathetic corporation from Britain had secured an untraceable lease for this invisible warehouse nestled in the heart of a dilapidated industrial park south of the city they called Newark. Its one-year lease should provide more than enough time for him and his *kameraden* to bring America to its knees.

Hans took inventory as he scanned the warehouse's dim interior: a loading dock and commensurate equipment to accommodate six trucks at time; ten-thousand square meters of sheltered storage space; electricity; a small fleet of a dozen panel trucks emblazoned with "Swiss Miss" logos parked inside and out of sight until needed; and under a field of canvas tarpaulins, two hundred bales of US dollars—new twenty-, fifty-, and hundred-dollar bills in numbers too vast to count—and they were perfect.

Indoor plumbing graced the small flat and adjoining office next to it with a desk, chairs, a telephone, and a room hidden behind a row of filing cabinets containing a full complement of state-of-the-art radio communications gear. An acre of flat roof concealed an elevated long-wire antenna to ensure maximum radio range. Just another old warehouse in a broken-down industrial area with almost no traffic anymore. Perfect. Soon, the Reich would send scores of carefully chosen employees. All was in readiness. The honor of being *der Vorhut*—the advance guard—was his.

Herr Graber licked his lips, tense with excitement. He jerked his right arm aloft toward nobody and whispered with intensity for fear that someone might overhear, "Sieg Heil!" This would be a glorious victory for Germany. And the Americans would pay for the terrible scarring that covered forty percent of his body. The pain was harder to hide than the scar tissue. But his legs hurt the worst, because the Amerikaner had blown them to shreds. He had left everything below his knees on the banks of the Meuse River in France, courtesy of the American Expeditionary Force. He could, however, still serve *das Vaterland* from his wheelchair—from within the enemy camp. After all, once a *sturmtruppler*.... Glorious.

❦

12

T hat it was cold didn't matter. Sheriff Billy and Deputy Jimmy flew south on the rutted road at almost fifty with the windows rolled down to suck the stench of death from their imagination. Billy tugged down hard on the brim of his black Stetson to hide his misty eyes.

"Son of a bitch. What in thee hell going on, Jimmy?"

He didn't expect an answer. Jimmy offered none. Who would kill an innocent young deputy who didn't know shit from Shinola? For all he knew, it could have been an accident, but not likely. Where was Roddy's cruiser? Stolen from the scene after the fact? Also not likely. Not in these parts. What, then?

The unspoken question he had been afraid to ask haunted him as they flew toward the scene. "Jimmy, why was it hard for Silas to recognize Roddy?" He wasn't sure he should ask, but better now than later. Just in case.

"Silas would only say that most of his face—"

"Aw, fer cripesake!" Billy thought of all the cuss words he *wanted* to howl, but saw no point in punishing Jimmy like that. He wanted to pound the dash in front of him, but did not for the same reason. He was sure that ditch would stink like blood and maybe shitty half-frozen mud from leaks and loosened bowels, robbing Roddy of every ounce of dignity. More haunting memories of the Argonne threatened to flood over the monster dam he'd built many years ago now, and spent a lot of energy maintaining to this day.

Clenching and unclenching his fists on his lap, Billy's stomach lurched at the thought of informing Roddy's wife and parents, but first things first. He needed to examine the scene to the extent he was able. Sure as shootin', somebody was gonna pay dearly for gentle Roddy Braddock.

WHAT THEY FOUND IN THAT SHALLOW DITCH SURPRISED Billy as much as shocked him. The body—that's all they found—lay at an odd angle at the bottom of the shallow ditch where it had been dragged, dusted with gray snow. Just once-white long-Johns, socks and one boot. Dried and frozen blood spots blossomed everywhere on the body. Like lethal measles. Or budding blood roses. Not a square inch, from clotted hair to shredded socks, escaped some sharp and piercing instrument of death.

The killer wanted the body found, but not too soon.

Billy stuck to business after drawing a shaky breath. He ticked off a couple of conclusions to his young deputy, though he was no homicide investigator by any means. "Okay, Jimmy, we got a job to do. We gotta catch the assho—, the perpetrators who done this. They didn't kill him here. With his face and skull and everything messed up like that, there should be lots more blood, and other, uh, matter." He'd debrief Jimmy later. Billy was pretty much flying blind, but Jimmy needed to be aware, this being his first homicide and all. *Mine too, truth be known.* "He's missing his right boot? Why one damn boot? Where's his uniform? And where's his damn cruiser?"

Jimmy ran a few steps away so as not to sully the scene with his vomit. *Good presence of mind, that kid.* Billy scratched his square chin that felt like grit, now under a two-day growth. Or was it three? Done misting up, now just pissed off, Billy pushed his hat up. Rubbed his forehead. Fingertips came away greasy. Jimmy got back to business taking notes. Both of their guts churned. Right now, Jimmy looked like he felt—tired beyond physical exhaustion, and older than his years. Wasn't even noon yet.

Billy whispered, as if in reverence while resting his hand on the body's cold shoulder, "So, somebody beats Roddy all over with a, what? A club—maybe a fence post—wrapped in barbed wire? Undresses him, puts one boot back on, and moves him here in a car or truck? No, a car. A truck's open bed is too obvious. But why?" He got progressively louder as he spoke, his diaphragm pushing his hoarse vocal chords through his anguish, farther into anger. Then he backed off, saw Jimmy getting too jittery.

The kid still wiped puke from his chin on his right sleeve. "Great questions, Billy. We're gonna find out, aren't we?" Jimmy's now-angry voice quavered and had gotten loud. He suddenly looked self-conscious, like he was surprised at his own nervousness and intensity. He lowered his eyes.

"Darn tootin', Jimmy. Yessir, we are." Even though the kid sported his game face, Billy could see from a yard away his guts still churned, like he was gonna throw up again, like his hand pressed against his gut could stop it. Couldn't blame him. He was still more than a mite unsettled himself. *This is some strange shit right here. That's fer sure.*

Standing there looking down at Roddy, Billy decided to consult a friend, Officer Dwight Spooner of the Worthington

City Police Department. He'd worked as a homicide dick in Minneapolis before the war. After he returned from France, he resigned from the MPD for unspecified reasons. Nobody questioned his unusual decision to become a small-town beat cop.

They used their fancy new radio in the cruiser to relay a message to Doc Gustavsen over in Spencer. An hour later, Doc Gus arrived in an ambulance to collect the body. Billy and Jimmy drove back to the office. Took most of an hour. Neither Billy nor Jimmy spoke a word all the way back to Rock Rapids as Billy formulated his plea for help to his old combat buddy, and what he would say to Roddy's pregnant bride.

❧

13

Roddy and Sara Braddock kept a small apartment around the corner from the sheriff's office one block off Main above Kierkegaard's Modern Home Furnishings, the only furniture store in town. Roddy had told Billy in confidence that he and Sara were looking to buy a house on the southern edge of town near Dawson's Farm and Implement. Until then, the apartment above Kierkegaard's was cheap, and allowed Roddy to sock away most of his paycheck for a down payment. But it was going to take awhile longer than they expected with the possibility of a "bun in the oven" now. That was okay. They weren't going anywhere.

Billy trudged up the long flight of stairs to Roddy and Sara's apartment in the alley on the north side of the store. Today, it was not long enough. He dreaded reaching the top and that last step that would be the first step to ruining Sara's life. What would he say? He rehearsed a few lines, but they all sounded lame. He'd just wing it.

Billy knocked. She looked even younger than he remembered. Especially now. *She's just a child. Roddy too. Dammit.* "Hi, Sara." He tried to sound neutral, but failed in epic fashion. A gust of wind grabbed his hollow words and swept them to some cold place. In that moment, she knew. Her eyes swelled into large dark pools. She knew.

"Oh, God. No. Please. No!" Billy helped her helped her into the once cheer front room where she crumpled onto the worn sofa. He looked away. It wasn't cheery anymore.

"I knew when he didn't come home last ni—" The place seemed cheery. It wasn't. Not any more.

She said, "How?" Neither dredged any words from within their mutual sorrow for what seemed a lifetime.

Finally, Billy said, "Sara—"

Her tears now spent, her eyes now flashed with anger. "Billy, tell me, dammit!"

"Somebody murdered him. Some time yesterday. Jimmy and I just discovered his, his.... We don't know who or why, yet."

"Oh, sweet Jesus." Then, she grew resolute. And stiff. She stood and pointed to the door. "Billy, please leave."

"Sara, I—"

"Don't you say another damn word, Billy. You *know* he worshipped you, and you, you just went and got him killed, didn't you? Please. Just go. Okay?"

He didn't say another word. What *would* he say? What *could* he? Billy hung his head, slapped his gloves on his leg, turned on his heel, and slumped out, misty eyes and all. *Shit on a damn shingle, Billy! You handled that real good, didn'cha? I guess it's time I went and did my damn job.*

BILLY'S DESK IN THE ROCK RAPIDS SHERIFF'S OFFICE THAT some smarmy politician named the Lyon County Law Enforcement Center backed up to the building's small side window and a door out to the south alley. Escape routes had been important to him since the war. In front of him and to his left, two desks that faced each other. They sat closer to the back wall and to the cells than to the front windows. Seemed safer. Both were empty. Jimmy's neat desk sat vacant because he was out cruising. Roddy's desk remained in disarray because the kid hadn't yet learned to organize. Like his boss. Now he never would. Neither he nor Jimmy had the heart to clean off Roddy's desk. Not just yet, anyway.

"Son-of-a-BITCH!" As hard as he could, he hurled the clay jar of pencils that sat on Billy's desk. They crashed through the bars of cell number one twenty feet away. "And STAY there!" At least those damn pencils couldn't escape. "I need a damn killer to lock up!"

Billy didn't spend all that much time in the office. Not much of an office, anyway. Not like they'd put any actual money into it, other than a couple of bolt-in cells. Three desks in a store front was all they needed. They had four, including a nice desk in a separate glassed-in room toward the back of the... *LEC*. That was supposed to be his office. He called that unused room the fish tank.

Two four-drawer filing cabinets contained stacked folders on the few arrests, convictions, and envelopes for all complaints received and processed over the years across the county. Several of those eight drawers held nothing but coffee supplies, Christmas decorations, a few boxes of ammo for the department's handguns and for the three rifles in the gun rack on the wall back by the fish tank. Oh, and all the stupid forms they were supposed to fill out. He'd been meaning to purge, clean and organize the drawers with actual hanging folders for months, but that job never seemed to reach the top of the heap. Other duties always intervened. Besides, paperwork and filing were for deputies, not sheriffs.

❧❧❧

14

Edie just loved Sophie. The two of them met when Edie's momma had taken in the Bairns' laundry for a spell. But Momma needed to make more money. They both went to work for Zach Mutter at his speakeasy, six blocks from their house on Bern Road. Less time to play with Sophie made those days harder.

Zach opened his watering hole in the garage behind his bungalow. Called it *The Joint*, although he posted no sign. Zach's lack of creativity was legendary in George. Accessible only by alley, the half-dozen regulars knew to park in back. Some of them walked over from their homes, or from work if they had jobs. Nobody cared about his little enterprise, not even the sheriff up in Rock Rapids. Except those pious church ladies from First B over on Harms Street always tried to stir up trouble. They'd rant, "The devil's winning on that side of the tracks."

Old Zach and his regulars all liked both Edie and her sassy

momma, Maud. Bud—Edie's stepfather—the one-eyed troll? Not so likable, but still, he was a good spender.

⚜

As was their habit, Edie walked Sophie to and from a regular visit to her house on Bern Road and across the tracks. Crossing those rough tracks made for a few yards of tricky stepping. They left this afternoon when her parents started squabbling—a real donnybrook. Edie couldn't bear Sophie witnessing that abusive spectacle. Again.

"Sorry about that, Soph."

"No worries. A little scary, but... hey, I appreciate you walking me home. I truly enjoy this, especially when you fetch me from Father's dealership. Now that you're working for Zach, we don't get to do *this* as often." With her right arm occupied by Edie's guiding left arm, and her left hand grasping her bad one, Sophie only nodded back and forth to punctuate what she meant by *this*.

"Me too. Plus, I never miss a chance to get away, especially from home." She didn't really want to talk about this, but....

"Happens a lot, doesn't it?" It seemed to Edie it happened every time Sophie visited. Maybe *because* of Sophie's visits? Like her own parents didn't want her to have Sophie as a... no, not that.

Determined to shut this down, Edie said, "Yeah. Bud's not a bad sort for a step-dad, I guess. When he isn't tippling, which is most of the time. Momma and me just try to stay out of his way." Eager to change the subject, Edie chirped, "Hey! Saturday night, there's this whoopee party up in Rock Rapids. You should come."

Sophie's inquisitive expression drew Edie on. She grew animated, waggling her free arm overhead, gesturing expansively. "You know. Friends get together for a good time, have a few drinks, and before long, somebody hollers, 'Whoopee!' It's fun."

"Oh, dear. I could never," Sophie blushed, like she'd just heard a raunchy joke, "besides, aren't those your high school friends?"

"Well, Ritchy'll be there," now it was Edie's turn to blush with excitement, "but also his older friends from all around. A mature crowd. Like you, Sophie." Edie paused, realized she sounded like a schoolgirl trying to appear all grown up by putting on airs. She stumbled on a slick patch, but recovered, preventing them both from taking a tumble. She pushed away thoughts of the party. She would *not* be responsible for injuring her frail friend.

"I've heard you speak of Ritchy before—"

"Yeah, you know, Ritchy Winkels. One of your dad's mechanics. Handsome, popular, two years older than me. He graduated last year. Not that he's stupid or anything, they held him back a year on account of football, and not enough time hitting the books. Not that he's stupid or anything, he's just focused. You've seen him around, haven't you?"

"Maybe. At the dealership. Tall, dark, dimple in his chin, broad shoulders?" Was Sophie fantasizing about *her* Ritchy? Edie grinned.

"Yup, that's *my* Ritchy, alright. I'm guessing your dad pays him pretty darn well. He drives a nice motorcar, and buys me some to-die-for clothes, including a dreamy flapper that I'm dying to show you. Wants me to look pretty. Plus, he knows where *all* the parties are—Rock Rapids, Sioux City, even up in Worthington. Anyway, how about Saturday night?"

"I don't think so, Edie, but I do appreciate the invitation." Sophie sideways-glanced down at herself with one eyebrow cocked, as if she was self-conscious about her... problem. Edie would not embarrass her friend by pushing it. She suspected

Old Iron Hand just wouldn't allow anything other than a church social.

With a cheerful dismissal, Edie said, "Okay. So, you and Jake Hardt? Dreamy! You do it yet?"

"Edie!"

❦

15

"What? Oh, dear God. Alright, well, thank you for the call, Doc." The Lyon County Sheriff sagged in his desk chair. Deputy Jimmy sat at his own desk in the early morning shadows, glanced ahead at Roddy's empty and still-messy desk silhouetted by the window's haze. The sun bathed his desk in a hazy veil that would lift later. He worried about his boss. Gave him a sideways glance. And now this call. He worried, now more than ever.

❦

"What can I do, boss? You look for shit." Sometimes Jimmy threw in the occasional swear word to butch-up his post-pubescent image. Billy might reward him with an appreciative smile under any other circumstance.

"Remember that kid I picked up from the Hardt place south of George? On the way, he seemed all twitchy and was obviously hurting. The kid suffered from some sort of nasty withdrawal from a very addictive substance. I was afraid he might get *real* sick. I was headed back here with him, but instead, took him over to Doc Gustavsen at the Spencer Hospital.

"Told me he was a drinker, Jimmy. Something called Black Gold was his hooch of choice. In fact, he would drink nothing *but* that stuff. He even said, 'why even bother with anything else?' Said he couldn't sleep or think straight. Couldn't eat, or feel anything at all. That does not sound like he was *just* a drinker. I asked old Doc Gus to figure out what the kid was using. Doc said whatever it was, he was taking it orally. That's consistent with the kid's story. He was drinking something real addictive.

"He was more'n just hung over, then, Sheriff?"

Billy swore it was like the kid wasn't listening, or this addiction stuff was completely out of his field of experience, as if he couldn't quite grasp the concept.

"Jimmy, Doc said he was suffering from *severe* withdrawal and malnutrition from not eating much, if anything, for *weeks*. Not only that, he suffered some sort of psychotic break from long-term use of a powerful stimulant, maybe like cocaine ingested orally, along with something else. When I asked Doc about laudanum, you know, an old-fashioned mix of opium and alcohol, he said that while that's sure addictive as hell, that ain't no stimulant like what this kid's been swillin'. But he said the kid was suffering from what looked like opioid addiction, *like* laudanum, but somethin' else too."

"Well, what do you think the kid was into, Billy?"

"The doc thinks there's some kind of new hooch somebody's brewing. Looks to be both toxic, very addictive and with longer term use, can make folks kinda crazy. At least that's what he thinks is the case with this kid. If that *is* the case, we got a real problem. Some nasty shit out there,

Jimmy." Billy placed his hands firmly on the arms of his wooden desk chair as it to boost himself up, but stopped cold in mid-motion and mid-thought.

"How nasty?"

"Pretty nasty, I'd say. The kid just died. Jammed a pencil all the way into his own ear and into his brain."

❧ 16 ❧

"Henry, the boy has been walking her home every Thursday afternoon. I thought you should know. She's at a tender age."

"She's twenty-three, Hildie. Who's the boy?"

"Jacob Hardt, that farm boy from the old Hardt place out south on County 14."

"Oh, dear. That will never do, now will it?"

"Henry—",

"Hildie, not on a party line. When?

"Last week it was at half-past four o'clock."

Click-click.

Now, Henry Bairns paced near the window in the front room of the house he and Hilda had built twenty-five years earlier—one of the few red brick homes in George. The handsome cottage whispered of money. He had first seen the plans advertised by an exclusive builder in one of the trade magazines at the dealership. He just had to have it built, despite the mortgage. Today, Henry had come home early, which was unprecedented. Hilda had called him off the show-room floor—she was never to do that—before dropping this bomb in his lap.

WHEN SOPHIE AND JAKE APPROACHED HER HOUSE, THEY could see her father standing outside with his arms crossed over his chest. No coat, just trousers, a white long-sleeved shirt with cuff links, suspenders, and a broad tie. Beads of water distorted the mirror finish on his Oxfords.

He must be freezing. Maybe that's why he looks so cross. But Jake didn't have to guess. He wasn't good enough for Mr. Bairns' daughter. As they approached the three steps up, he released Sophie's arm as she negotiated the first step trailing her stiff left foot, just as Mr. Bairns reached down to grab her good hand. The steps were shoveled, salted and sanded, but a sheen might still be too slick. Both men worried.

Jake looked up, met Mr. Bairns's eyes and simply muttered, "Sir."

Henry Bairns said nothing, only offered a slight nod of begrudging gratitude for this dirt farmer seeing his baby home. Nothing more.

Sophie turned to offer Jake a goodbye wave, but her father was already hustling her inside.

Jake sauntered down the long, narrow sidewalk back to the street. He muttered, *Well that went just fine, didn't it, you idiot! I can only imagine what the old boy is warning Sophie about right now.*

Regardless of that cool reception, Jake made it his mission to ensure Sophie got home without incident from her weekly visit to her friend's house every Thursday afternoon.

AND SOPHIE MADE VERY SURE SHE VISITED EDIE EVERY Thursday, even if she didn't feel like it, even if her parents were fighting, as usual. Edie could be an emotional handful, but they both needed a friend. She'd need to be careful, though. The first semester of nursing school began in March.

❧ 17 ❧

J anuary 1933

❧❧

THEY WALKED ARM-IN-ARM DOWN THE STREET. BEFORE
they turned the corner onto Sophie's street, they stopped.
Their eyes locked. Two hearts beat as one.

Jake thought, *Oh dear God, is this it?* He drew her in. She
did not resist. So warm, so soft, so small.

Time skidded to a stop. Her dry lips never parted during
that gentle kiss, nor did they even embrace. They held both
of each other's hands as if together they feared destroying
something too precious to risk. But the glow that engulfed
them as their innocent lips drew away after just a second cast
an enchantment that was sure to last a lifetime, an eternity.

With an abruptness that shocked them both, as if she'd
been shot, Sophie jerked away. Her suddenly wide eyes saw
something only she could see. Jake's eyes were still closed,

still lost in that almost-embrace, when he felt everything change. His eyes popped open as Sophie stiffened. He felt her hands clench. Had someone attacked them? Or shot his new love in the back. Those eyes darkened and became dangerous. Nobody hurt Sophie, not now, not ever. He pulled away, his eyes on the hunt, scanning the street for the source of her sudden panic. He perceived nothing out of the ordinary, he grabbed her shoulders, ready to shelter her away, to shield her with his own body.

"Sophie! What is it?"

"Jake, this is a mistake."

Not what he expected. At all. No danger? He was almost disappointed, now more afraid than he'd ever been in his sometimes-adventurous life, even when he disappeared from the farm for a year. He tried to gather some sense from her words.

"What? No! I love you!

"Jake, I start orientation for nursing school in St. Paul next month. I'll be leaving. What will happen? Wait, you *love me?*"

"Sophie—"

"My dearest Jake, I can't do this, not to you. Oh, dear God, help me, I do love you so, but—"

"This is not happening."

༄

THEN SOPHIE SAW SOMETHING IN JAKE'S EYES THAT SCARED her, a side of Jake she saw for the first time. She could only imagine the cauldron of primal anger about to boil over. But then he softened almost before his alter ego surfaced. She had misread him. His hands had dropped uselessly to his side. Now he grasped her narrow shoulders once more.

"My love, if that's what you need to do, I'll drive you up myself. I've waited my whole life for you. I can wait a little longer. Somehow."

Oh my Lord, he's crying.

As tears rolled down both of his stubbled cheeks, she wiped them away from his left cheek with her crippled hand —the brush of a butterfly's wing. He grasped that soft claw of a hand with care, held it to his cheek with some desperation. This time, they fell into a deep and hungry embrace, as close as they could cling to one another, fearing it would end all too soon.

Am I really going to leave this precious man? Now?

THEY SAID NOTHING FURTHER. THEY BOTH SOBBED silently, as if any sound would seal their separation, as if they feared sharing their despair. Pulling apart, it became impossible to look each other in the eye. They resumed strolling toward Sophie's house with downward-cast gazes, every step a desperate quest. Upon turning the corner, they spotted Henry Bairns standing on his stoop, awaiting his little girl's return, as usual.

As they approached, a small smile on his face surprised Jake. But the smile transformed into something else, something dark, as Sophie's father spotted the deep sadness sculpting their faces. Jake simply passed Sophie's good arm to her father's waiting hand, and said, "Goodbye, sir," turned and slumped away.

"SOPHIE—"

"Not now, Father. Please."

For the first time in recent memory, home seemed dim, empty. Henry Bairns was at a loss. "Hildie!"

❦

18

S tanding at the telephone on the wall, Billy banged on the hook a few times with the fleshy side of two fingers. "Mabel, kindly connect me long-distance to the Worthington City Police Department for a private call." That meant he expected Mabel, the local operator, to unplug the rest of the party line and to remove her headset until his light went out. A law enforcement perk.

"Official business, Sheriff?"

"Mabel—"

"Of course. Sorry."

After a delay, he spoke to the WCPD desk sergeant. He hailed one Officer Dwight Spooner, who was indeed in the building. He said in a somber tone, "Hey, brother, it's Billy."

"Billy! It's been too long, brother! What can this lowly cop do for the esteemed sheriff of Lyon County? How do you like being an elected official? Never thought of you as a politician. You—"

"Dwight, among other stuff that's goin' on, somebody murdered one of my deputies."

"What? Oh. Murder? In Rock Rapids? Shit, Billy. How can I help?"

"Yeah, down George way, to be more accurate. I could use a consult. You game?"

Nothing but static on the noisy line—for five seconds, ten seconds....

"You there, Dwight?"

"Yah, man. Still here. Billy, I don't do that anymore. I—"

"Look, Dwight. I'm sure you got good reasons for that, but I need your help. Somebody attacked *my cop family!*" He chastised himself as his voice shook with emotion so profound that he choked, then cleared his throat. It sounded contrived, but surely Dwight realized it was not.

"Dwight—"

"Okay, brother. How about if I commit one afternoon? I'm taking tomorrow off, anyway. Best I can offer right now. Otherwise, it's, well, too much."

"You sleepin' yet, Dwight?"

"I'll see you tomorrow after lunch. Your office?"

"Thanks, man. Sorry about this."

"No, you're not. Just feeling guilty."

You can hear smiles, even over a scratchy telephone line, especially in times of sorrow.

☙❧

WITH BACK SLAPS AND MAN HUGS OUT OF THE WAY, Officer Dwight Spooner of the WCPD sat in Billy's guest chair the next day. He looked right smart in his gray wool slacks and matching belt—no suspenders—slick Oxfords. And he wore what Billy thought of as one of them big-city shirts. No hat, just a light coat he slung over the back of his chair before he sat down.

"I can't thank you enough for comin' down, Dwight."

"Can't say no to a brother, Billy. Got photographs?"

"Shit!"

"No worries. Describe the scene for me."

"Found him yesterday about two PM. Victim is my twenty-year-old deputy of just six months, Rodney Braddock. Everybody calls—called—him Roddy. A local farmer on County 14 found the body, west side ditch, about four miles south of George. In his long-Johns, socks and one boot—the left one—laying right next to the body, half on, half off. No uniform, badge, or gear belt, and no right boot. What the hell does all this—"

"We'll get to conclusions in a sec, Billy. Autopsy? COD?"

"We sent the body over to the hospital in Spencer east of here. They got a decent ER doc over there who specializes in such proceedings. What's COD?"

"Sorry—cause of death. They get back to you on that?"

"No need, Dwight. He was cut up real bad. Face and skull bashed in so's it was hard to even recognize him, 'cept for them fancy boots Roddy was fond of. And them colorful argyle socks, and his general gangly build. Plus, he's the only person reported missing in Lyon County. Oh yeah, his damn cruiser's missin' too. He was bloody from scalp to socks, lots of little slices. Looked like somebody beat him to death with a club or a post wrapped in barbed wire or somethin'. We didn't find nothin' like that, though."

"Had rigor set in?" A blank stare met him.

"Billy, was the body still warm to the touch? Cool? Or downright cold and stiff?"

"Oh. Cold and stiff and kind of bluish gray." *Gawd. Poor Roddy.*

"Was he laid out all nice and straight, or did it seem like

he'd been tossed there? Did you notice any broken bones or fingers, like that? Somebody that had a beef with the kid?"

"Well, struck me he was laying at an odd angle, but we saw drag marks, like maybe he was dragged there by one foot. No real obvious bones or fingers broken, but hard to tell. Roddy was always clean as a whistle, kinda gung-ho, wanted to do a good job for me. He only got married last Fall, told me last week Sara's pregnant, they think. Not like we make a lot of arrests around here, and he hadn't made a one yet. Cited a few traffic stops, parking violations, like that. Cripe sake, anyway."

"Anything else, Billy?"

"Aw, heck, Dwight. I dunno. Different from combat, ya know? Close to home, somebody who grew up right down the road, His parents—good church-goin' folk...."

"Nah, I mean motive?"

"Oh. No idea, although we got this new hooch makin' the rounds. Sounds like it might be laced with coke and some other downer shit that makes it both toxic and real addictive. I don't see any connections to all a that. But who knows? We got a regular little crime wave goin' on down here, Dwight."

"A big reason I got out of the Mini-apple, big guy. Gotta dig through a vic's life like nobody else can or should. But nothing harder 'n losing a friend, except family. Yah, sucks wind, brother. Okay, let's talk conclusions we can jump to with what we know right now."

Dwight ticked off points on the fingers of his left hand. "Obviously a homicide. You already know that. Killer took trophies—his uniform and such—after doing the deed elsewhere, at least a day before you found him. He was dumped, not thrown, dragged out of a vehicle feet first. That got him to the dump site. A passerby spotted him from his vehicle, as if the body was meant to be found. Could be the killer, or killers—most likely male—didn't care if he was found, or maybe that was the point."

"Why most likely male, Dwight?"

"Most killers of violent crimes are male because they're more likely to overcome a victim, especially a male victim, and statistically, men are most violent—physically, anyway. The fact that this killer overcame not only a man, but a law enforcement officer, points to a real hard kind of criminal. Or even a professional, or a career hooligan, sure enough a brutal one. That goes to motive, and may lend some weight to your booze/drug connection.

"Sounds like a very unique weapon too, Billy. Why not just shoot him? Might even be part of a message. Not sure. Maybe like a club with something sharp embedded in it, like blades or broken glass. Barbed wire would puncture more than slice. If true—and I bet your doc over in Spencer can figure that out—I've heard some big-city gangs use something like that. They make 'em themselves. Ask your doc to check for pieces of razor blades in your deputy's—"

"Roddy. His name is Roddy, Dwight."

"Sorry, yah, okay. Have your guy check for pieces of blades snapped off in Roddy's wounds. Here's what we don't yet know. Why the trophies? A random psychopath? To obscure the scene, or slow down an ID? Send a message? If so, to who and why? You? Somebody else in the community? Or more likely, your guy saw or heard something he shouldn't have.

"Each of these questions needs to be investigated, run to ground. Together, they paint a picture of what could have happened. That can lead you to suspects. Then you eliminate the suspects with alibis until you're left with your most likely. That leads to an arrest, an indictment, and, if you're lucky, arraignment and conviction. What you gotta be asking your-self right now though, Billy, do you think this is something a member of your own community could have done? If you don't think so, any strangers around that you should look at real hard? But you can't rule out anybody. Yet."

"Good Lord, Dwight. Where do I *start?*"

"Well, brother, you start with the simple stuff and work toward the harder stuff. Talk to everyone Roddy knew or came in contact with recently. First, his family. Each time you learn something, you revise what you think happened. Talk it over with someone else you trust, like a deputy. Cast a wide net, as they say—talk with the other sheriffs and PDs down here. See if they can help you find, um, any suspicious characters, agendas, and Roddy's cruiser. Gotta be somewhere. Might give up a clue or two. I guess you can call me too as you get into your legwork. Fill in enough pieces, you get the bad guy. It's a process.

"But statistically, Billy, odds are not good if this is just some traveling madman. He's already long gone. You gotta do the gumshoe work, put in the time. Make lots of lists and take lots of notes. Make a list of who you gotta talk with, and then just work your way down the list. Jot down notes during every interview, and keep going over them to look for little things that didn't jump out at you at first. List the suspects, their families, friends and acquaintances who might have enemies, or who just might know something. It's usually something small that breaks a case.

"My gut tells me you should also make a list of everyone you know who keeps secrets around here. The bigger they are, the more likely they have something to do with your case —with Roddy's case. And the harder they'll be to squeeze out. Listen to rumors and gossip and conflicting stories. They can be especially important in a small or rural community like yours. Might turn up something that just doesn't sit well. Ask everyone if they've seen any suspicious activity or strangers in the area.

"Then put the high-level stuff all in one place where you

can stare at it, like a decent size notebook, or better yet, a big-ass sheet of blank newsprint. I'm sure you could get some of that from the newspaper office. We called that a *case book* or *case sheet* at MPD. Write everything down about the case, all in one place—notes, diagrams, ideas, you know, anything and everything. And keep staring at it. You just keep adding stuff, or crossing stuff out—as you get answers, and add or eliminate clues, motives, suspects, or suspicions. You'd be surprised.

"My gut tells me this was a hardcore kill by somebody from outside your community. Might not be a pro, but almost surely somebody who's killed before, like an enforcer-type. Assume this could be part of a bigger picture somehow—like maybe your drug thing. That's a crash course on homicide investigation. Make sense?"

"Jeez, Dwight, no wonder you left Homicide!"

ॐ

DWIGHT JUST SMILED. VIOLENCE WAS MUCH MORE straightforward back when this country sheriff and he shared a foxhole and faced a battalion of the Kaiser's troops coming out of the trees in the Argonne Forest. They tried to kill both of them. He and Billy returned the favor. He owed this big handsome lug. For more than just pulling his unworthy ass off that killing field outside of Charlevaux Mill. The Germans fired two slugs into his gut. Corporal Billy Rhett Kershaw gave him back his life. He still suffered from stomach and intestinal problems because of damage from those hunks of lead. If Billy called again, he'd darn sure help. Hell, he'd leave his job and work for Billy if he asked.

Might be time for another change, anyway. Worthington is a bigger town than I thought. May be time to downsize again. If Billy asks.

19

Ritchy Winkels grew up with natural advantages, like his height and chiseled good looks, plus some of his own making—his physical shape and attitude. While his parents gave him everything he wanted, he always felt like he had to scrap for everything he needed, or was owed. He was always the biggest kid, the tall one with the broadest shoulders. Most thought that made life easier.

But he was the one that everybody wanted to take down a notch, the guy to take a shot at, usually from behind. At some point, maybe in the sixth or seventh grade, a light bulb blinked on. Instead of waiting for somebody to take a shot at him, Ritchy mastered the pre-emptive strike. Hit 'em hard while they're still *thinking* or *talking*. Maybe even before that. No talk, just a fist, or a body slam. Set the tone. Pretty simple once he realized that's how the world worked for big kids, for the strong. Saved a lot of time, and beatings.

He lived in the garage behind his parents' house. That two-story four-stall garage was bigger than the house, and stood back a good fifty feet, accessible only by one of the alleys so popular in George. The garage's quadruple swing-open doors admitted not only his 1932 Cadillac V8 Town Sedan, but was also a place to have the barrels delivered and picked up.

Ritchy's parents remained oblivious. He slept out there too until the weather dipped below the fifties. He needed seclusion more than fancy *inside* furniture. And the apartment over the garage, though not heated, afforded him privacy and comfort.

His arrangement with Roy Dillworth provided him with a lavish lifestyle without depending on his parents and their ridiculous rules. The information he shared with the Ford dealer from Worthington City about the inner workings of Bairns Motors here in George seemed to be worth a lot. He'd get two barrels of Black Gold each month he supplied information to *Mr. Ford*, as he called Mr. Dillworth, not that he ever called him that to his face. Most of that hooch went to Zach Mutter's speakeasy for a handsome price—demand far outpaced supply, these days.

But he reserved a few dozen gallons for his own use, which Mr. Dillworth fully endorsed. Much of that kept the parties he sponsored supplied with the good stuff, and added to his stash of cash. And *that* is how they grew their business, and his own popularity. Didn't hurt to swing a pretty little thing like little Edie Everniss on his arm at parties, either.

❧ 20 ❧

S ophie and Hilda Bairns sat side-by-side in the parlor
at an angle, just staring into each other's eyes. Sophie
broke the comfortable silence. Their discussion
sounded more like two close friends rather than daughter and
mother.

"Mother, I've decided there will be time for school later.
I'm in love with Jake and I want to marry him. Am I crazy?"

Hilda knew this was coming. Mothers know. She felt
blessed that her daughter had come to her. Sophie could be
fiercely independent, and usually was. She had already
decided her future, and this was her diplomatic way of
sharing her plans.

How will Henry take this news? So many changes....

"Oh, Sophie, I thought you wanted to be a nurse. Have
you thought this through? You won't resent Jake and regret
this decision later?"

"Well, Jake supported me, whatever I wished, and for that
I'll be forever grateful. Besides, it's just a decision to defer

school. I'll always be thankful that you and Father supported me. There is time."

They both fell into the morass of their own thoughts. And then....

"Sophie, you're not crazy. Love is the most powerful force on Earth. Shall we see where that takes us, takes you?"

They smiled and embraced like two friends, two sisters, mother and daughter, mentor and mentee. But Hilda thought, *who is the mentor now?*

🐟

21

"**S** on-of-a-BITCH!"

Two weeks had passed, and Billy was no closer to solving Roddy's murder. He was going through all the useless motions Dwight Spooner suggested. After making a dozen stupid lists and interviewing everyone who might even be remotely associated with Roddy or the department, Billy slumped at his desk, defeated—couldn't even identify by who. What was he to do? He'd call Dwight, that's what.

"Brother, I'm at a loss. Make me feel better." Dwight would know what his old friend needed. And what came next would confirm that.

"Got any openings in your department, Sheriff Kershaw?"

"Wait, what? You want to come work for me?"

"You askin'?"

"Hell, yeah, I'm askin'!"

"Look, Billy, I can't promise any more progress on Roddy's case by coming down there, but I'd rather work with you. I'm... it's... going fine here, but I'm, well, empty right now."

"Dwight, when can you start? I'd like to swear you in tomorrow."

"Hell, they'll hardly miss me here. Give me a couple of days so I don't burn too many bridges."

"Deal!"

And that's when a brick crashed through one of the four Law Enforcement Center's plate-glass windows. Sounded like a shotgun blast. It was a big window. Billy dove for the deck behind his desk, left the phone's earpiece swinging. Head down and gun drawn, he screamed, "Son-of-a-BITCH!" He just caught a flash of red and black as a motorcar sped off.

"Billy? *Sheriff!*"

22

ⅭⅩⅫ

Circumstances at home with Sophie and Hildie distracted Henry Bairns, but he needed to sell just one more automobile by month's end to meet yet another short-term commitment to his Chicago investors. A rough bunch, it seemed. Without one more sale before the end of January, his deal to purchase four other Chevy dealerships in Iowa and Nebraska would fail—ridiculous terms, he'd realized in retrospect. Yet another carrying fee. If he forfeited now, he'd lose substantial up-front fees already paid and his earnest money—a large piece of two years' profits and the remainder of Sophie's treatment fund. Noon had come and gone. He thought, *Lord, please help me help myself!*

And that's when Silas Hummel trundled into his show-room smelling of cash. He rushed to the door to greet the old farmer and to shake his hand, but not until he closed and latched the entry door behind him. Still, a nasty gust of wind and a few flakes billowed in around them. For the hundredth time, he considered installing a double-door entryway. But that wouldn't fit his building's clean lines, would it?

After a few minutes of shivering, talking weather, and how they thought the winter's thin snowfall might affect the upcoming Spring planting, they got down to business. Silas had *finally* finished stomping his feet on the coarse entry rug in nervous anticipation. The stove's warmth drew them in like magnets to pig iron. The two of them hunkered near the pot-belly stove in Henry's showroom. Silas rubbed his hands together before extending his palms to within inches of the hot stove.

Henry kept a brass spittoon near the stove. It was expected for some customers. Silas issued a long spit of black juice in its general direction. Some missed. Beaded on the floor's beeswax. He immediately stuffed a new chunk of chaw into his right cheek, and started working it. His clothes reeked of it, and Henry spotted more than a few stains on the old man's coveralls under his now-opened wool overcoat. Stained his white beard too. Filthy habit. As he thawed out, the landowner flipped up the earflaps on his wool cap. They hung like drooping wings.

The stove sat in the center of the large space. It was freshly painted and fully stoked with seasoned oak. Even though the coal-black pot belly and stove pipe were on the verge of glowing red, it barely kept the temperature above fifty degrees. A slight odor tickled their noses—of sintered stove-black and burning metal—as they huddled to warm up. The pipe shot straight up into the showroom's tin ceiling with its tight geometric pattern. The intense heat had discolored the fresh coat of white paint around the chimney pipe. Or was that soot? A few dried rust stains that had dribbled down the upper pipe signaled a less-than-perfect seal against snow melting on the flat roof.

Another Alberta Clipper swept through northwest Iowa

as if avenging some past iniquity. Knee-to-ceiling glass along the entire western-facing store front transmitted the near-zero temps inward like that's just what those windows were designed to do. In the summer, that wall of glass performed equally well at the other end of the mercury. The summer sun treated the street-facing showroom like its personal hot box. On the best of days, those windows bathed the showroom in a natural glow; however on most days, as Henry's mother of good German stock always said, "Vanity must suffer pain." A wise woman. Henry had suffered through the pain of paying a king's ransom for those magnificent windows.

The heavy wood-planked floor gleamed with a fresh coat of beeswax. The place was spotless, as usual, except around the spittoon. After all, Bairns Motors clung to its sterling reputation as *the* premium automobile dealership in Lyon County and beyond for over twenty years. And Bairns was the only dealership in the town of George, population now over nine-hundred. Once away from stove and spittoon, the showroom smelled of new metal and fresh paint. And a little grease. And oil. And cowhide. A man's showroom.

With the thumb side of his right fist, Henry Bairns massaged his fifty-year-old nose reddened from the chill, smudging the right lens of his circular wire-framed spectacles by accident. Again. The thumb of his other hand hooked into the armhole of his imperious vest—gray wool, of course. The suit's jacket hung over the back of a chair in his office, despite the showroom's cool interior. Meant to appear dressy casual when dealing with the farm folk, and it worked. Most of the time.

Was this the old boy's fourth visit this week, or his fifth? Each had concluded with Silas saying, "I'll think about it," or "gotta talk to the wife." *Time to nudge him off the fence and close this deal.* Once more, Henry guided the landowner toward his latest-model four-door sedan, less than fifteen feet from the stove and farthest away from the windows. The sweet spot. The showroom lights weren't bright enough to make the car's paint gleam, but bright enough to sparkle its massive chromium trim.

"Look, Silas, I've been selling automobiles since before the Model Ts and As. Before I stepped up my game, I even sold a few horse-drawn carriages. I'm a Chevy man all up and down the line now, and for good reason. Just look at her. This is the car for you. See her lines? Fully enclosed. She even features a heater that'll keep you and the missus warm even on the coldest mornings. She'll go like sixty if the road's smooth enough."

"Yup, Henry, she's fine, alright. But six hundred dollars is a heap a cash."

"Well, you don't get what you don't pay for, my friend. Don't you and Erna deserve a little comfort? Isn't that why you work like a dog? That's what success like yours is all about—comfort. You can stick with your "Fix-Or-Repair-Daily" farm truck out there, not that I'm against Fords, mind you. But consider stepping up to a Chevrolet sedan."

As if to emphasize *stepping up*, Henry stood high on the generous driver's-side floor board that connected the flared front and rear fenders in one clean swoop. His right arm embraced the long straight roof line, even though the cold metal further chilled his hand and forearm. The old farmer stood enraptured in front of the object of his obvious affection.

❧

SILAS STARED AT THE GLEAMING HEADLAMPS, EACH THE SIZE of a watermelon, the running lamps the size of footballs, and the twin tubes of her chromium bumper sparkled. But his now-naked gaze of desire rested on the massive rectangular grill topped with that distinctive and prestigious hood orna-ment—the Chevrolet wing. He admitted to himself this coach got his blood boiling, even on a wintry day like today. He imagined this sleek crate could fly. But it was time to horse trade. "Henry, no wonder you got an indoor heated showroom and all, with these prices."

❧

"Silas, I won't try to pull the wool over your eyes. Business is good, even though times are tough for most. But when I deal in quality products and treat my customers right, *that's* what got me this showroom. Why, we can fit five auto-mobiles in here and still offer plenty of walk-around space to dream big. Right now you see only two because they're selling faster 'n Detroit can ship 'em to us." He pronounced it *DEE-troit*. Wanted to impress the old farmer with his knowledge of geography, as if he had personal contacts at General Motors, the premium automobile manufacturer. Even though this new model was assembled in St. Louis.

"I know for a fact you're still getting over top dollar for your corn from Lester Klein down the road, Silas. And you got the finest bull stud in Lyon County, not to mention all your milkers and renters. You can afford this Series AD Universal. Think of driving this beauty back to the home place to pick up Erna for a drive."

That earned him a sideways stare. "You are very well informed."

Henry's voice remained low-key, almost conspiratorial. It was as if he didn't dare allow the only other customer in the showroom twenty feet away to hear that he was selling this particular automobile to his friend. Henry knew what appealed to farmers, but also to their wives who often made the most important decisions. Rich landowners were his

85

bread and butter, although their numbers had been deci-
mated since the crash.

He'd already swung up and latched open both jet-black
hoods. Looked like a giant eagle's wings half-unfurled for
flight. "I ask you, my old friend, what would you think of
taking home this new stovebolt one-hundred-and-ninety-
four-cubic-inch straight-six? And don't you worry about any
of that first-model-year folderol. First year for the AD, sure.
But you're looking at the tried-n-true Series AC motor that's
been selling like hotcakes since twenty-nine. But this baby
features bigger intake valves and smaller exhaust valves, along
with a brand new manifold. Bumped her up from forty-six to
fifty horses. And I'll tell you this, Silas, with her new
hydraulic shock absorbers, you'll be floating on a cloud, even
rolling down County 14. This here's a new decade, old son."

"Not sure the missus 'd go for it, Henry, other than all the
finery. She does look right pretty."

"Silas, show her *this*. C'mon around here with me." He
curled his right forefinger and waggled it at Silas over his
shoulder, beckoning him to the promised land.

They too-casually strolled around the front of the huge
auto with Henry leading the way to give Silas plenty of time
to stare, and to relish her fit 'n finish. Like two generals
inspecting their troops. With a flourish, Henry swung open
the front passenger door—the ladies' side—and planted his
right foot on the heel-friendly running board. He bent
forward so his head was well inside the cabin. He drew in a
long noisy breath through his nostrils before exhaling
through his mouth with a long noisy sigh, like he'd just
enjoyed a huge Thanksgiving dinner. With his right elbow on
his upper thigh, Henry peered back over his hunched left
shoulder, where Silas hovered. Henry pointed at the innova-
tion nestled dead center in the elegant dashboard panel. He
knew he had a sale when Silas stuck his head inside, almost

pushing Henry out of the way, and heard the farmer draw his own deep inhale.

The scent of new leather gets 'em when nothing else will. Especially the farmers. Get 'em under the hood and into the cab, and they're good-and-well done.

"Looky here, Silas. Fuel gauge right there on the dash, my friend. Your Erna doesn't even have to step out into the cold to check her gasoline at the tank filler. You can leave the fuel stick in your truck. Doesn't get any better 'n that, does it? Now press the palm of your hand down onto that premium calfskin." And with that, Henry backed away to leave Silas alone for a private moment of intimacy with this black beauty.

"Will ya take five-seventy-five?"

"For you, my friend, I'll take five-eighty-five, and I'll throw in a full tank, an orientation drive for you and Erna, along with a basket of the wife's legendary crullers. You ever bite into one of Hilda's crullers? Put 'er there, Ford-man. It's official. You are now a Chev-ro-let pilot!"

He knew Silas would jump at his counter-offer, and it didn't hurt to get the old boy feeling good after the sale, too. This landowner would now be repeat business for years to come. Besides, that old Ford truck parked out front was close its last gasp. Not that he needed to tell old Silas that. He'd be replacing that at Bairns Motors too.

👁️🗨️

SILAS INDULGED IN HIS FIRST GRIN OF THE DAY BEFORE IT once more lost its running battle with worry. He could afford it, couldn't he? In his mind, he spun up one hell of a whirlwind. *The next growing season just has to go right, and Lester'd better still treat me good at the elevator come harvest time. My renters and mortgagees had all better make their payments on time too*

—*either in cash or crops.* But those were worries for another day. Moments later, that grin won his face back as both of Henry's hands shook both of Silas's in congratulations. *Today, me and the missus are riding in style, assuming we don't get this new carriage stuck on old 14.*

Henry shouted back to Violet, his office manager, "Ring the bell, Vi. We have another proud Chevy pilot!" The wood crackled and popped in the stove's belly fifteen feet behind them as the bell clanged.

Silas needed to spit or swallow. He dripped onto his bibs. Again.

❦

HENRY NEEDED TO VOMIT. HE'D BE ABLE TO MEET HIS commitment to his banker—this week—but just barely. Plus, he worried about his little Sophie with her long face when she walked home with *him* yesterday. If that Hardt boy had hurt her, there would be holy Hades coming due.

🦋

23

Billy crumpled up the county commissioner's budget memo that had been occupying his rapt attention. Threw it like a fastball, without a windup, toward cell number one, but it fell short. There it stayed. He thought about the boarded-up window without looking at it. Wracked with uncertainty over why somebody was trying to intimidate him and his department, or was it just a vandal? He thought about resigning—for about one-tenth of one self-pitiable second. Then he hoisted a wolfish grin. *Well, I guess they almost succeeded.* Budget or no budget, brick or no brick, he owed it to *all* the folks in Rock Rapids, across the county, and to himself, to pull his sorry carcass up by his boot hooks, and do his damn job.

War memories had come close to paralyzing him after that brick came flying through his window two days ago. The only progress made on that front was to board up the hole against the cold and to question his reasoning for getting into law enforcement. What was he *thinking?*

It was ten AM. Dwight was due in from Worthington after lunch. A hell of a way to welcome his new deputy. Instead of grabbing a bite at the Lucky Domino down the block, as was his custom when in town at lunchtime, Billy slumped at his desk. Not hungry. Instead, he thought about service and honor and commitment.

The door swung open and closed. Billy tensed. Kept the palm of his right hand on the butt of his holstered thirty-eight revolver beneath the desk. He hadn't told Dwight about the brick yet. Or the note. He would do that now before Dwight drew his own weapon as Billy observed him scanning the darkened office with alarm. His eyes darted and he swiveled in a crouch, like he was entering an active crime scene. Right now those eyes looked like smoldering lightning in the dull reflected light. Then he spotted Billy transitioning from stiff to slack, as he dropped the elbow of his gun arm and hung his head close to his desktop, looking like contrived casual.

"Okay there, brother?"

"Uh, yeah, Dwight. You're early. C'mon in."

"Looks like a little excitement here. Thought so after you hung up the other day after cussing and then saying it was 'nothing'. Thought maybe you dropped a stone on your foot or something." Dwight also spotted a few shards of glass where the tile floor met the knee-wall below the boarded window. Like someone had swept it up in haste. Billy noticed he'd caught all those details.

"Not a stone. Some asshole chucked a brick and a note tied to it with a piece a twine." After Dwight strapped the retainer back over the revolver's hammer on his right hip, he dropped into Billy's guest chair and recalibrated to a half-casual pose—also contrived. Billy showed him the note by skittering it across his cluttered desktop.

"Special delivery, eh?" He perused the one-word note. "Someone accusing you of being a *Communist?* So?"

"So? What?"

"Well, *are* you?" The smirk that crept over his face signaled he was trying to lighten the murky mood. Any thicker and you'd choke on it tryin' to chew, forget swallowing.

Billy said, "Gotta be misdirection or a distraction, right? This close to Roddy's murder?"

"From what, though? Maybe you're onto something."

"Who the hell would think such a stupid stunt would...? I'm just sitting here feeling sorry for myself. Huh. Maybe it's working. A little. Regretting your move yet?"

"Hell, this here's already a lot more interesting than parking tickets, brother. Big news at WCPD? Gotta write ten percent more tickets all around. Naw, I'm glad I'm here, Billy."

"It's just that I'm nowhere catching Roddy's murderer. I don't even have a motive. All the interviews turned up squat."

"Look, boss, when you're done with your little pity party, I'm here to work. What say we do *that?*"

A flash of annoyance passed over Billy's face, but disappeared almost before it reached his eyes. Billy threw a tired smile Dwight's way. "Shit, brother, I mean Deputy. When you're right, you're right. I could use some inspiration over here."

The next two hours flew by. Billy reviewed all his interview notes with his new deputy, and Dwight stood over the table with one of Billy's big-ass sheets of newsprint. They listed all possible suspects, underlined the folks Billy thought might be hiding something based on body language—and his cop's gut—asterisked those who might be worth another visit. This time, Dwight would interview, and Billy would take notes. They'd listen for deviations from the initial interviews.

Billy flipped on the overhead lights and they continued to talk.

"Dwight, it just seems what somebody did to Roddy went way beyond anger, even brutality. Never seen anything like it. Not even in combat, ya know?"

"Billy, during my time as a dick in Minneapolis, I worked on a federal task force for a couple of weeks with some feds and a Chicago gangland undercover name Seamus O'Shaughnessy. They tasked him to knock down a running beef between a couple of bad-ass gangs on the South Side. A Mick gang made a move on a WOP neighborhood. That's what started it, anyway. Lots of blood. That was my last gig after the war before punching out of MPD."

"Mick? WOP?"

"Sorry. Shorthand for *Irish* and *Italian*," he pronounced it *EYE-TAL-yun*, "but never call any of 'em that to their faces."

"And why does that matter here?"

"Dunno. Maybe it doesn't. But here's the thing. Those Micks, they were a very brutal bunch. Seamus provided us a brief because it was rumored that as they gained strength and influence, we might see 'em headed toward the Twin Cities. Said they were maybe spreading as far west as Omaha. Now these Micks, most immigrated to New York or Chicago from Dublin. That's in Ireland. Some of 'em ran with a crowd the Mick cops called the Animal Gangs."

"What, Dwight? They use animals?"

"No, brother, they *were* the animals. Even the cops didn't go into their territory in the heart of Dublin. Nastiest stuff you can imagine, and then a whole lot more. Even had their own informal uniforms—black shirts with white buttons. But most of the have-nots in the worst neighborhoods loved 'em. Some kind of Robin Hood stuff, they say. Anyway, Seamus told us some of 'em brought their old ways over with 'em. Like they use these clubs embedded with razor blades to send a message, like Mick holy writ or somethin': 'Nobody messes with our turf.' Shit like that. Sound sorta familiar?"

"Oh, man. Yeah, it does. Send a message, huh? To who?"

"Well, that's the question, Billy. Find that out, and we'll find the *what,* and then, maybe the *who*—our killer. Got any Micks moseying around?"

"Dunno, but now we got some different questions to ask."

By suppertime, Billy smiled big again. They had a plan. He realized how much he needed an experienced deputy now that his county had graduated to drugs and murder. A new decade. Tomorrow, more interviews.

❧

24

Jacko Ulster took as his family name—his only family—
the province in Ireland he hailed from. Until then, he
had no last name. Grew up on the streets of Belfast.
Most from that city were Protestants. But this had
nothing to do with religion for him, only that he wasn't a
Catholic, like most of the boys from The Pale, like his boss
Finn Malone—a Dubliner. That both he and Finn were Irish
is what held them together—mostly—here in the new
country.

The narrow but deep red-brick building on the north side
of Chicago was near the lake. Jacko sat at the tiny desk in his
tiny office at the back of his big motorcar repair garage, Elite
Carriages. They catered to an upscale crowd who had made
their money in the streets and escaped the filth and stench of
downtown proper to live in gentrified lakeshore neighborhoods farther out. Life was fine here because of Finn Malone,
even though he hailed from The Pale. They shared an uneasy
friendship.

On the phone, Ulster said, "Finn, I don't like it. What do we know—"

"Boy-o, all ya need to know is the Windy City is only the start. Yer boys are already spread thin outside a downtown. I'm payin' these new lads to back you'se up 'round yer turf, and beyond as we go wide. Outside a that, nothin's changed, 'kay?" An awkward silence ensued. "I said, 'kay, Jack-o?"

Ulster realized the foolhardiness of pushing the fiery Finn too hard. But he'd be dealing with dozens of strange faces—soldiers of fortune from the cut of their cloth. This was not how they'd always done business. A small voice inside told him that in this game, without personal trust based on one-on-one relationships, ya got yerself and maybe others dead.

But Finn seemed so sure, and that would have to do, wouldn't it? "Sure look, boss. We'll watch fer your boy and the head of the new crew to get us started on this fancy new hooch. Goin' with a new cooker, and all this talk about more turf—a *lot* more turf? Why of such a sudden, Finnster?"

"Timin', boy-o. We got this chance at the brass ring. Pieces are fallin' into place. Now, any more quizzin' fer me, Jacko?"

"Naw, just feelin' a might woozy over here. I hope to all the saints ya knows what yer doin'."

"Aye, me too, boy-o. New lad's name is Dillworth. Got a recipe with a proven record out here in the boonies'll make us all richer 'n all of the Kings of Ireland. He's bringin' ya the plans to get ya started. Be ready. Tell your boys, 'kay? Gonna be big, boy-o, bigger 'n big. A lot more swillers out beyond them city limits. You 'n yer boys will own turf from Chicago to New York 'n down to Miami, friend. Ya *are* still me friend, yeh, Jacko?" Click.

So then, why did ole Jacko sniff desperation in the boss's otherwise steel-on-stone voice? Was it fear? Or just a greedy eye forward? Either way, for Finn 'twas never enough, was it? Be the death of 'em, for sure.

❦

25

I t had been weeks. They savored their walk today, despite the brisk February weather. Sophie always dreaded crossing railroad tracks. Though she minimized the degree to which her stiff leg affected her mobility, walking —limping—across those tracks was the most dangerous part of the four-block trip home from Edie's house. But with Edie's help, she relaxed a bit as they crossed them.

"You and Jake, huh? I am so happy for you, Soph."

"Thanks, Edie. But what about you and Ritchy? You just disappeared single and came back married."

"Yeah. We drove to Nevada. Sorta romantic. Right now we're living in the guest apartment in the garage behind his folks' place. Even got a new oil stove for heat. Looking for our own place. Ritchy's talking about buying a house. I'm glad we got married, I guess. I thought it would be different...."

Sophie would need to be catatonic to miss the clues. "Alright, sister, what's going on—"

"Nothing! We're doing fine. Just that, well, Ritchy sometimes likes it rough, and—"

"What? Edie! You—"

"Oh, no. Don't get me wrong—"

"You don't mean—"

"No, not really. Sometimes we just misunderstand each other. I hate to disappoint."

"You guys just seem like the perfect couple. Successful, two of the most beautiful people I know...."

"Yeah, Sophie, well, almost perfect. But it's really fine. Really."

"Okay, then." But she didn't believe *almost perfect* for one second. "If you ever—"

"No, yeah, I will. Thanks, Soph. So, when's the big day?" She clapped her tiny hands together like a little girl getting ice cream, eager for that first lick.

"Well, Mother planned the whole thing for next month. Father even helped. I think he's molting a little around the edges, though. And Jake is very sweet about it. Says he doesn't give 'two hoots and a holler about such goings on' as long as he and I can be together. But I think I'd like to honor his wishes for a small wedding. He's so... country, isn't he?"

And as if they had rehearsed it, they sang out in unison, "Men!" They both shared a badly needed laugh. But Sophie worried about her young friend. She wore an extra-heavy layer of foundation on her right cheek.

❧ 26 ❧

M arch 1933

❧

JAKE AND SOPHIE MARRIED, HE FOUR YEARS HER SENIOR.
They exited the First Baptist Church on heavily wooded
Harms Street, with their few witnesses and guests. Sophie
had insisted on a small wedding.

Jake helped his blushing bride board his old work truck
out front. Sophie's friend Edie and her rowdy friends from
high school had decorated it with old shoes and tin cans tied
to the bumper with twine. Jake started the engine, and as
they rolled toward their future together with cans clattering
behind them, Sophie asked her new husband about a honeymoon with bright expectancy, albeit with little genuine hope.
She thought that in the coming days they might at least drive
up to Worthington City to the confectionery for an ice
cream. Jake purred with patience, "There is no time, *mein
seelenfreund*. I have to milk the cows. I need to plow and get

ready to plant now that the field is thawing. Gotta feed Queenie, there's hogs to slop, and—"

"It's fine, Jake." That's what she said, but she was thinking that the work out there seemed endless. The message was clear: *Jake needs to be there, and he needs me to be there with him, with my man.* What more special honeymoon could there be than working shoulder-to-shoulder with her soul friend, her *seelenfreund?* She was ready.

STRAIGHT FROM THE WEDDING, WITH HELP FROM TWO OF her father's mechanics—both Owen Bunn and Seppel Tolley now nursed broken hearts—Sophie moved her already-loaded dowry from her parent's house to Jake's weather-worn hovel. The new couple followed the overloaded panel truck borrowed from Bairns Motors. At a crawl, the two vehicles traveled the six long miles beyond the town's southern reaches. Beyond the grain elevator, dusty Lyon County Road 14 was barely two lanes wide and three ruts deep between shallow ditches. Both northbound and southbound carriages, buckboards and motorcars shared the center rut. Passing an oncoming vehicle, though rare, was always an adventure. Sophie felt as if she had just crossed the border from one country to another. She had visited Jake's farm many times over the past few months. Still, all seemed foreign out here now that it had become very real, now much more than a romantic notion. She felt this was a one-way drive. That was silly, of course.

Jake's farmhouse and forty acres challenged her sensibili-ties, starting with the most uneven ground she had ever tread —the caked and cracked yard! But she told herself all that did not matter. She and her dearest Jake were together—at last. Nothing could change that now, except maybe a few immutable circumstances she tried not to dwell upon. And nursing school could come later, but would it?

She imagined herself a child bride even though she was almost twenty-four. Starting that day, Sophie asked herself a hundred times a day, as days creeped into weeks and months, *Can our love survive out here? Should I have gone away to school first? Can I adapt until one of Jake's grand visions takes root? And will I ever grow accustomed to this smell!*

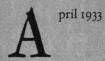

27

April 1933

THE HOUSE RUMBLED LIKE THERE WOULD BE NO TOMORROW
—more than thirty people laughed and drank. They even
overflowed out onto the front porch and into the small back-
yard, despite the brisk air. This would not have worked in
George, but on the outskirts of Rock Rapids, nobody cared.
Scotty, a well-heeled bachelor and owner of the house, said he
had warned the neighbors of a loud whoopee party. Besides,
they were all invited, and the drinks were on him.

Ritchy Winkels knew Scotty was grateful—even at
Ritchy's steep prices—for the silky but crisp booze that
tasted like something between vodka and a decent blended
whiskey. The Volstead Act turned a lot of places very dry, but
not the parties Ritchy sponsored. Now, it was all about
supply and demand. They would vote out the local sheriff if
he made too big a stink about neighbors getting together to

blow off a little steam. Scotty said, "Ritchy, this hooch is *the best,* even though it tastes and looks, well, different, but in a good way. Sends ya right over the moon! Worth every penny, my friend."

"Tell your friends, Scotty. I can get more, but prices are goin' up. And its dark amber color comes from its very special —but expensive—distillation process. Black Gold, my friend."

"Hey, how come you're not drinking, Ritchy?"

"I got a long drive ahead of me back to George yet tonight. Enjoy, friend."

RITCHY GOT A PERSONAL TOUR OF MR. DILLWORTH'S FARM —the distillery—an impressive operation. Between that and his Ford dealership in Worthington City, Ritchy admired the hell out of Mr. Dillworth, his hero. During the distillery tour, which was a real honor, he expressed a concern to Mr. Dillworth. Folks kept drinking, but they got cranky. Even mean. He had explained, "Son, this is how you develop a market."

"Sir?"

"Ritchy, it's no different from Coca Cola's approach at the turn of the century when they spruced up their product with something called cocaine, produced from all-natural coca leaves. Gave their product the zip their customers loved. In fact, that's how they came up with the name they still use today. Just business, son. Same with tobacco. Same with coffee, yes? Business doesn't get any more American than that. You see, it's all about developing and expanding an excellent product's customer base, and *Gold* is just the ticket. We're gonna be rich, son. Then you can tell your daddy to go pound sand. You like the sound of that, don'tcha, boy?"

Took about a second. "Hell, yeah, Mr. Dillworth."

"Just call me Roy, son. Now go help your friends get wide.

And don't forget, I need the interior dimensions of old Henry's warehouse by Monday, including the height and width of all the doors, and a list of the equipment supporting the loading docks, alright?"

That discussion left Ritchy with a gleaming notion concerning his side job. He still worked for Bairns during the day as a mechanic. That's how he got the *Gold* that he sold to his friends and to Zach Mutter's speakeasy. *Gold* in exchange for information. *Gotta love America. God bless Prohibition.*

28

M ay 1933

❦

SATURDAY MORNING ARRIVED AT THE HARDT FARM. Everybody loved Saturday mornings. Still the same chores, but Sophie baked. She had grown to love Saturdays too, especially when she enjoyed the luxury of flour and butter on hand to bake with. The entire house exploded with a yeasty bouquet. She had just pulled a couple of "mile-high" loaves out to cool. Laid her heavy cotton mitts aside and stood back to admire her handiwork. The steaming loaves perched on the well-worn oak counter top, uneven and scarred from decades of culinary abuse. She basted a sliver of melted butter on top of each loaf with one of her mother's old brushes. The twin loaves shone like mirrors in the mid-morning sun that gushed in through the open window just above them.

The origin of her almost imperceptible grin came not from admiring her handiwork, but from the memory of Jake's pride when he presented her with a burnished butter churn. He had bartered something-or-other of value. Now they could churn their own butter from Jesse's cream. But then he realized with only one good hand, she'd need him to operate the charming appliance. His open-faced embarrassment at this oversight rewarded him with her deepest affection. He didn't think of her as handicapped at all, only in need of a compassionate partner. So, they sat together last night in the kitchen by the fire. He churned while she read to him her favorite passages from the epistles of Mark, Luke and John. There had never been a sweeter batch of New Testament butter.

Her left index finger challenged the crust. It dented a little, then sprang right back. She licked the butter off and rolled her eyes as she wiped her wet finger on her apron— Edie's apron. Yup. Perfect. Wave after wave of fresh bread fragrance washed through the kitchen as the breeze tickled the loaves. Not a lot of dust in the air today. *Praise the Lord.* While that confounded breeze was a delight, it coated everything with a sheen of infernal dust—even today.

With the wind drifting in from the open front room window, the kitchen curtains fluttered out the back window toward the yard. Might as well have rung the dinner triangle. That bread's aroma beckoned to Jake and Walt, all the way out by the hog pen. She could hear them kibitzing out there, now hiking toward the house with a momentary spring in their step. They talked of tasty toppings as they approached the mudroom door propped open with a field rock to keep it from banging in the breeze.

"You boys better be kicking off those boots. Or no jam and butter for either of you, much less half of one of my mile-high loaves washed down with a strong cup!"

She heard them chuckling under their breath, no doubt horsing around in anticipation, muttering about the old ball and chain. She was certain those were Walt's words—their voices sounded similar, but not what each said. Jake would *never* say that about her. She smiled. *He wouldn't dare, nor would he want to, but cousin Walt, well....*

Sophie didn't allow hogs in the house, of course, or dogs, or *any* livestock. And she made sure the boys knew there would be proper hell to pay if they failed to swing shut the glass-panel door between the mudroom and the kitchen. They knew the house rule—quarantine the stench of those filthy boots. They entered *her* domain now. No livestock, no smelly boots. She feared she would never get used to the relentless barrage on her sensitive nose.

What I endure for love! She couldn't help but smile.

She fiddled with the wobbly damper handle on the stove pipe for the third time in as many minutes. Her eyes stung from a tiny tendril of smoldering box elder that snuck up around the edge of one of Blackie's warped hot plates. That evolved into a haze that hovered near the high ceiling before surrendering to the swirling breeze. Maybe the darn flue needed clearing again. Maybe the wood in the firebox was wet. It smelled a tad sooty. And she could never purge a perennial haze, even with all the windows flung wide. Yes, she had learned a great deal in just a few months—especially how her hyper-sensitive nose loathed the stench of wet box elder smoke.

In this moment, Jake seemed in jovial spirits. "Mother, that bread smells mighty good!"

Sophie sang out, "Well, praise the Good Lord for butter and flour and this breeze, and that *you're* smelling bread instead of *me* smelling chickens and pigs."

Jake sat down with a guilty smirk, as if he needed to apologize for the fragrance of nature, but wasn't sure if he wanted to. Without thinking, he tugged and tucked the sock through which his big toe protruded seconds before, and folded it underneath and between. Sophie spotted the all-too-common remedy and scolded, "Now you make sure that sock finds its way into the darning pile, okay Jake?" He said nothing. No need. Not even a nod. Why waste words? He smiled. Thought he had gotten away with it. Fat chance.

The boys plopped down into the straight chairs at the round table between the stove and the window. Both maintained a clear view of the bread at all times. They knew the wacky cake—made without eggs, but with baking soda & vinegar instead—behind them on the high counter was for supper. They dared not ask. Bread *and* cake on the same day? The Lord had indeed provided his bounty on this day—once in a month of Sundays—even though it was Saturday.

Walt mocked in a tone worthy of Amos 'n Andy, "Yes indeed, sister, praise the Lord and slice that bread, if you please! And is that Old Judge I smell?"

Sophie offered Walt a patronizing grin as she fetched her bread knife from a sticky drawer. Closed it with a bump of her hip which drew a frown. That cuss-ed hip. "Yes, Walt, fresh-brewed Old Judge, and we thank you for bringing us those fancy tins of coffee. A skosh bitter to my taste, especially the way you boys like it boiled for a week. You could strip paint with this yard mud. Jake! For Heaven's sake, get your filthy mitts out of that jar of preserves! You go right back out and get those hands washed. For Heaven's sake, were you born in a barn?"

"As a matter of fact—"

"Stop, mister. You know what I mean."

Jake glanced at Walt with a playful smirk and said, "Town girls, ya know...."

"Jacob Hardt!"

Sophie sounded stern under a beetled brow, but her heart overflowed. Jake offered her an almost tearful glance over his right shoulder. He padded across the planked floor to the mudroom, draped in weariness but ripe with anticipation for a few slices of Sophie's bread slathered with jam. Jake had to know her mother had snuck that jam out to her, but he said nothing, even though she knew that was a source of scorned pride for him.

He tugged his boots on again with the laces still loose to traipse back out to the pump and the half-barrel in the yard. She watched him through the window. Her own little big man roiled up a small cloud of ankle-high dust in the desiccated dirt as he shuffled toward the pump under slumped shoulders. He looked exhausted. She felt a pang of guilt. Dear God, how she loved her balding hero.

"Hey, Soph! How about a slice?"

"Hold your horses, mister. Wait for your cousin. Enamel mug alright?" He nodded without looking at her. Walt also followed Jake's trajectory toward the pump. Why did *Walt* look worried? What did he know that she did not? Walt always seemed so... complicated. Based on his history that Jake had shared with her, Sophie wondered if he had pulled the plug out of the jug again. Thought she might have caught a whiff of gin underneath stale smoke as she handed him his coffee. She knew whenever that happened... well, she knew more than she let on. A multitude of conflicts within this complex man...

Jesus, be with us, oh Lord! Hear my prayers....

꧁꧂

29

The next Thursday, Jake brought cousin Walt to town for supplies. Figured Sophie could use some time to herself. She was still getting used to the idea of having Walt around. And she was still sore at Jake, although she had warmed up to his cousin. But the guilt from not consulting with her before taking in Walt stuck to the roof of his mouth like morning's bad breath. It felt good to do something nice for her by getting the two of them out of her hair for the day.

They strolled through the front door of the General Store. Something seemed different. "Howdy, Marvin, S'here's my cousin Walt. He's bunkin' with us for a spell."

Marvin seemed jittery, gave Walt a friendly nod as he asked Jake, words tumbling out, "Remember that murder back last December? Front page, Lyon County News. Then, and again now. Sheriff Kershaw is asking if anybody has any information. They're still comin' up dry."

Jake said, "Don't have much time to read no newspaper,

Marv. Murder? Yah, we heard old Silas found the body not far from our place, but we keep to ourselves, ya know. Must be some new news there somewhere."

ॐ

MARVIN UNDERSTOOD. TO FOLKS LIKE JAKE AND THAT cousin of his, newspapers were an unaffordable luxury. But Marvin went on, eager to gossip. This was still big news right here in their own county. Besides, Marvin prided himself—he was almost always better-informed than the paper.

"Yah, a sheriff's deputy, no less. You didn't know Roddy Braddock from up Rock Rapids way?"

"Nope. Don't think so. A deputy." Seemed like Jake was keen to change the subject, but Marvin was just getting started.

ॐ

WALT'S EARS PERKED UP AS THE OLD STOREKEEPER described how the deputy had been found. It seemed the paper re-ran the bulk of the December story. It's as if this wasn't the first time today Marvin had exercised his gossip muscles over this case. "Election's comin' up, ya know. Sheriff's few enemies makin' hay over no progress. Sayin' piss-poor law enforcement can't even take care of their own. I know the family. Roddy was a good kid. Beat real bad, and cut up all over. Left him in the ditch. Paper didn't say much more 'n that, other than old Silas Hummel was the one what found poor Roddy. He was in here t'other day. Said he couldn't recognize Roddy at all, was bashed up that bad. A real grim memory for Silas. I felt real bad for him."

After digesting all this while rubbing his chin, Walt tugged on Jake's sleeve and pulled him aside with a furtive glance at the storekeeper, ignoring Marvin's wary expression. Walt whispered, "Jake, d'you know this sheriff?" They whispered, but didn't care that Marvin could still hear.

"Sure. Billy Kershaw passes through George two, maybe three times a week. A decent sort. Why?"

"I got a hunch, Jake, maybe even some useful info about this killin'. I'm not crazy about cops, but I hate criminals even worse. We should call him, set up a meet, okay?"

"Um, sure, Walt." Now Jake's forehead wrinkled in worry. *My cousin has useful info about a **murder?*** In that moment, he couldn't help but mentally re-evaluate everything he knew about Walt with almost no new information.

"Let's go, Jake. We gotta find a phone."

"Hold on." Now louder to Marvin, "Hey, Marv, can we use your talkie? Private like?"

৩১৪৩

"JAKE, NO NEED TO SHARE MY LAST NAME WITH THE sheriff, alright?" That drew a slantwise glance. He had already asked the operator to connect them from Marvin's back room.

"Sheriff, this here's Jake Hardt. You'll recall I live just south of Silas Hummel on 14 down George way."

"Howdy, Jake. Any more strays lately? Hey, you're the lucky guy married Sophie Bairns. I know the Bairns family real well."

Jake wasn't sure he liked the sound of *real well.* He remembered the sheriff's rugged good looks. "Yup. I'm a lucky guy, alright. No more strays. Thanks for helping with that kid Peter, though. A shame what happened. Listen, Billy, my cousin Walt is bunkin' with us. We may have some information for you—" Party lines being what they were, the sheriff jumped in.

"Where you boys at—*right now?*"

Startled by the interruption, and the sheriff's brusk tone, Jake said, "At Marvin's General Store, in George."

"You hang up. I'll call you back, forthwith." Click.

Walt said, "So he's gonna call right back?"

Unsolicited from the front of the store, Marvin piped up, "My ring is two longs and two shorts." He'd obviously been listening. The old boy's hearing was pretty good.

They did as they were told and waited right by the phone. Less than three minutes later, the sheriff called as promised. Jake snatched the earpiece off its hook while the twin bells still vibrated from the striker between them and he spoke close into the mouthpiece. No doubt Marvin would be trying to overhear at least part of the conversation. Jake wasn't sure why he cared who heard them.

"Boys?"

"Jake Hardt here, Billy. I'm putting you on the phone with my cousin, Walt." They shifted where they stood. Walt held the earpiece so they could both hear.

"Howdy, Sheriff."

"And your last name, Walt?"

"Uh, okay. It's... Weller."

"Okay, Walt. What you got for me, son?"

"Maybe nothin', but old Marvin here was telling us what he read in the paper, and what Silas Hummel told him from discovering your deputy's, uh, your deputy. Turns out I might know somebody who might know something."

"What? Spit it out, son. We're on a private law enforcement line here. And I sure could use a lead."

"Well, I've spent some time up at the casinos in Rapid City, and, uh, there's talk, you see. About an enforcer who uses a bat that cuts you up." He fell silent, awaiting a reaction.

Finally, "Name?"

"I don't have a name, Sheriff, but I know he's Irish, and they say he's from out east."

❧

Bingo!

Sheriff Billy Rhett Kershaw smiled, clenched and shook a celebratory fist. "Okay, Walt. Just call me Billy, okay? Listen, me and my deputy, Dwight Spooner, are gonna come down tomorrow and talk with you and Jake. Just to see if you can remember anything else, okay?"

"Uh, sure. I guess so, Billy. If it's okay with Jake." He shoved the earpiece Jake's way. Mouthed the sheriff's request.

"Okay, Billy, you coming down tomorrow? That's fine. South of George on 14, Fire sign six. On the west side."

"I remember, Jake. Thanks. Til tomorrow, then."

❧

"Walt, why you nervous talking to a cop? And the last name thing? Jeez! Something I should know?"

"No worries, cuz."

30

৩৯৫

The next day, Finn Malone, erstwhile leader of the most infamous Animal Gangs in the notorious Liberties neighborhood near the heart of old Dublin, held court. His frontier residence while *on safari*—he'd heard about great white hunters somewhere—was at the prestigious Dayton House on the outskirts of Worthington City, Minnesota. His immediate staff included Sticks Leary, backed up by a pair of unsavory but silent types in expensive suits and callous attitudes, rather like decorative gargoyles.

On behalf of his boss when they first arrived, Sticks negotiated an unspoken agreement with a fistful of greenbacks placed in the right palms. He reinforced each negotiation with a suggestive pat of his unseen ivory-handled pistol. That cannon produced a very visible lump under his right armpit. And his leer could not be mistaken. Mr. Malone was to be afforded every courtesy during his extended stay this summer. That included exclusive access to the entire covered porch on the east side of the establishment, around the corner from the south-side entrance. The owner and the staff tolerated this seasonal eccentric and his staff, along with their unusual affinity for fresh air. They could ill afford not to.

MALONE RELAXED IN THE LARGER OF TWO WICKER loungers—his throne. He sipped excessively sweetened iced tea, what he considered to be a uniquely American frivolity. A nervous Roy Dillworth perched in the other padded lounger positioned at an angle to the first. They both faced the spacious lawn. A copse of giant white sycamores guarded its distant edge at the bottom of a genteel slope.

Elbows on knees, Roy kept his hands folded in supplication, and to camouflage their trembling. The porch's shake-shingled roof cast them both in the afternoon's cool shade. Roy's tumbler of tea sat untouched on the glass-topped wicker table between them, alongside his distinctive olive-drab hat with a quartet of dents in its crown, not unlike the hats worn by state troopers.

"So, then, Mr. Dillworth, now din't ya promise me a twenty-five percent increase in production if I supplied ya with sufficient additives?"

"Yes, sir. In fact, by next week, we will have increased our production from seven gallons per hour to ten. That exceeds your goal." He knew this should have pleased this brutal criminal, but he was already two weeks late in achieving the new quota.

"That mean yer producin' two-hundred-forty gallons per day, Mr. Dillworth?"

"Well, no. You may recall that we can run the distillery flat-out eighteen hours a day. We require the other six for maintenance. Otherwise, both the product and the equipment will suffer and erode production rates. But we also transfer product from the production tanks to barrels for shipment within that six-hour maintenance interval. Plus, our ability to receive used barrels must depend on your customer accounts returning them promptly. We can speed up the supply of incoming barrels by supplementing used barrels with new ones from our suppliers, but we'd need to source additional—"

In mid-sentence, Malone slammed his tea down onto the table hard enough to crack its thick glass surface and to produce several dark spots splashed onto his beloved chapeau. Startled, Dillworth just stared at the crack and his hat slantwise, not daring to look Malone in the eye. In a soft voice, Malone said, "Soundin' like a bag of excuses, boy-o. Tell me what yer producin' and shippin' today, and what yer doin' startin' next week, three weeks past yer dead line." He placed cold emphasis on the word *dead*.

In a halting voice, Dillworth said, "Uh, yes, sir. Today we ship, uh, six-hundred-seventy barrels a week. Starting next week, we'll be shipping one-thousand-eighty barrels per week. That's an increase of almost sixty percent. We've been able to increase our production schedule from six days per week to—"

Then came the sing-song lilt. "Was that so hard, boy-o? That's all I want to know, ya see. Now I want ya to change the additive. Increase coal tar codeine five percent 'n decrease the coke five percent. Let's see how that, cooked in with yer ninety-five proof juice, plays with our customers, 'kay?"

"Sir, you also wanted any news of that Weller mongrel. One of my boys says he's been hanging around with a local who farms down in Iowa, maybe even staying with him. Name's Jake Hardt, six miles south of George on County 14." Dillworth heard this from his boy, Ritchy Winkels, who got this from his young squeeze.

"Good boy, Roy. You'll be movin' into yer new dealership

in no time. And we'll have a bang-on warehouse in a wicked location for the goods goin' west. Now let's see that production increase startin' *this* week instead a next. Don't banjax this fer me, boy-o."

The meeting is over? Just like that, with a smart-ass wave? Won't even look at me? I'm busting my ass, and not even a thanks for my trouble. Just threats and demands. How did I get in so deep with these Irish animals?

As if by magic, Malone's henchman hustled Roy Dillworth out with a soft chuckle.

And this bug-eyed son-of-a-bitch is laughing at me!

꧁✿꧂

31

Later that same day, with Jake in tow, Walt had met with Sheriff Billy and Deputy Dwight in the shade of Jake's barn.

All eyes were on Walt. "There isn't much more I can tell you about this Irish mook that was all the talk up in Rapid, other than his reputation for brutality cuz of what those who owed him looked like after he got after 'em with his razor-sharp club. Oh, and they say he's from Chicago." Walt squirmed as he spoke, like he had worms in his pants.

Billy wrinkled his nose, kept scratching at the side of his forehead with the tips of all the fingers of his right hand. Moved his head, not his fingertips. Pushed his hat back and squinted while Walt spoke. Looked over at Dwight. The deputy just sat there on a bale of hay staring at Walt, like there was something wrong.

"Okay, Walt. And how'd you come across this mutt? Exactly?" The suspicion in Dwight's voice was the reason Walt didn't like cops.

"Well, I spent time in a couple of the casinos up in the Dakotas. Where there's money and talk..." That seemed to satisfy Billy, but not Dwight. "Mr. Weller, do you know a man named Finn Malone?"

Shit! "Yeah, heard of him. Who hasn't?" Why did he feel so damn nervous? He was just trying to help here.

"We heard he's hanging around up in Worthington. Got a few of his boys with him."

"Well, news to me. But that ain't good." Walt watched his poor cousin sitting there on another bale trying to figure out just what the heck was going on. *Poor guy must think I'm a hoodlum myself.*

Billy asked Dwight, " Malone's from Chicago, isn't he?" Dwight glanced first at Billy, then at Walt.

Walt just dropped his head and started shaking it slowly, side to side. *Blasted cops are the same everywhere, aren't they?*

⚜

THAT NIGHT, JAKE AND SOPHIE SAT IN THEIR SMALL kitchen near the stove, a.k.a. Blackie. Jake decided not to burden Sophie with the details of the sheriff's visit. Just that Walt was trying to help with an investigation. She just smiled. *How does she do that?*

Supper preparation and a chill in the evening air called for a fire even though the early summer heat seared their feet in the hardpan yard during the day. Generous cushions on the seats of two straight chairs faced each other at an angle with their feet closest to Blackie's firebox. They shared a low footstool. This made their little alcove seem like a simple but significant guilty pleasure. The odors from the mud room just a few feet behind them seemed a small price to pay for their little haven.

Jake would have reveled in their companionable solitude if

Sophie's forehead wasn't all squinted up right now. Walt, the diplomat, spent as much time in the barn as he could—like tonight. He even set up a cot, slept out there instead of the upstairs bedroom, weather permitting. Sophie admitted that he seemed a tolerable house guest alright, in his rough but amiable manner—most of the time. But there was something else on Sophie's mind. Something that had her massaging her bad palm with her left thumb. Something was up. Plus, she wasn't looking him in the eye. *Oh-oh*.

❦

SOPHIE WATCHED THEIR BUDGET. JAKE APPRECIATED THIS. He lacked that skill. She met his worried gaze and explained, "Jake, dear, there is no money left. For anything. Not even for food or ice." She could see this was a source of immense shame. Sophie said they'd plan—not for the future, but for tonight, for tomorrow.

Together, the three of them would forage dandelions for greens from the yard tomorrow. Jake and Walt would butcher a hog. That would leave them a boar and a sow. Her mother had sent her on her way to the farm with three dozen Mason jars she had yet to press into service. They were still in their case. Sophie would salt the pork and can most of it in some of those jars. The boys would dry the rest into jerky from an old recipe Sophie had discovered in the house, in Frau Hardt's elegant hand.

There was no money for lard, but after every meal, Sophie would save bacon drippings to cook the next meal. At least the four cows—a big part of Jake's inheritance—kept them in milk with a few gallons left over to sell. Jake could use that milk to barter with Marvin at the General Store for salt and coffee. Maybe Marv would throw in a few planting potatoes. Old Silas lived just a country mile north. He might also barter, or less likely, pay Jake to repair his tractor. That old tractor always needed some fixing. Jake could fix anything. Besides, debts aside, farmers stuck together when times got tough.

They went to bed feeling better than an hour earlier, and that created tired smiles.

THE NEXT MORNING, SOPHIE STEELED HERSELF FOR HER daily trek out to the hen house to collect the morning's eggs while the boys culled out the lucky boar. As always, the yard remained devilishly lumpy. *Please don't ask me to suffer a fall, Lord.* She uttered such silent prayers throughout her day. Someone to talk to, if not with. Thus, her faith carried her through many a rough patch.

She would not admit to herself how difficult this simple chore was, with her arthritic right hip and bad left foot conspiring against one another. Caused a sideways wobble with each cautious step. She didn't doubt that her pronounced limp caused the infernal fire in her hip. *We all bear crosses, don't we, Lord? Reminders that life is fragile and precious.*

She also vowed to find a suitable wicker basket to carry the eggs from now on instead of in this steel pail lined with wash rags. A basket would be much lighter, but Jake had always just used this darn pail ever since his hens started laying. They would need to find the money to buy a basket. That's all there was to it.

After making her way to and from the hen house, Sophie washed the day's seven eggs, grateful for each one. Jake filled that washing pan every morning for her. *Maybe there's even a double-yoker in this batch—for luck*, as irrational as she knew that sentiment to be. When she collected sufficient eggs to barter with Marvin, most of his customers expected washed eggs. As did she, an artifact of growing up in town. Now she could hear squealing coming from behind the barn. She had asked the boys to do their killing back there. She couldn't bear to catch sight of that process from the hen house or from the kitchen. *Oh, Lord, please put that poor hog out of his misery swiftly.*

Sophie's young friend Edie had sewn her an apron with little needlepoint hearts around its hem. As she looked down at it, she smiled. She needed a pleasant memory. Edie was a woman now, too. She remembered their walks arm-in-arm in town a lifetime ago, even though it had only been six months, and how Edie had teased her about talking to Jake the first time. Now, he was out there providing for them. *You were right, Edie. I only wish you were as happy, sweetheart.*

Sophie still took to calling her friendly old stove in the kitchen Blackie, like Jake's mother used to call it. "From when times were good," he'd said, "and there's some doubt how long this contraption has been here." But Sophie harbored no doubt it would last forever and a day—maybe even until the rapture. She had never met Herr und Frau Hardt. Jake still found it difficult to speak of them.

SOPHIE SPENT TIME BY HERSELF. SHE LEARNED THAT WAS the lot of a farmer's wife much of the time, at least until children arrived. She conversed with the only person in the room —most often in the kitchen—herself. Or the Lord. Or the stove.

Well, Blackie, you can't hold a candle to Mother's porcelain enamel range. Oh, how that stove is the proud centerpiece of her kitchen, eh? But you just squat here against the wall staring at the mudroom door, you old relic. Blackie, you work just fine even though you aren't Kalamazoo Emperor Blue. Nor do you have a glossy splasher back and twin warming closets up top like Mother's Blue

Zoo. The practical difference between you two, though, won't buy anybody any bacon, will it? Even without a thermometer in the oven door, you still whip up an airy cake and a mile-high loaf, alright. Worthy of blue ribbons at the county fair, too, aren't they? That is, if she had had time for such tom-foolery, and if they hadn't canceled all of that again this year. She just needed to attend to the changing aromas coming from within, *and that serves as well as any thermometer, doesn't it, Blackie?* And who doesn't have a nose?

Sophie snickered. Funny how a good long spell on the farm adjusts one's idea of what's important, and with whom you'll strike up a conversation. She wouldn't worry too much, however, until Blackie answered her.

32

June 1933

❦

THROUGH THE KITCHEN WINDOW, SOPHIE WATCHED THE stranger wheel into the driveway, stopping his fancy motorcar near the rear of the house. She used to observe her father drooling over Duesenbergs when nobody was watching, like that was a sin. After all, Father was a Chevy salesman.

The rather tall man seemed too well-dressed for a Watkins or Fuller Brush man. In fact, Sophie thought he looked more like a confidence man. She'd heard of such characters roaming the countryside, preying on farm wives.

He stepped out onto the huge auto's running board, stood tall, and did the oddest thing. Instead of coming straight to the house, he performed a slow pirouette as if to scour the yard and the out-buildings, looking for something, or someone.

The stranger's frame filled the doorway as he approached.

He was a tall and slender sort with broad shoulders. They spoke through the mudroom's flimsy screen door which doubled as the house's primary entrance, opening into the kitchen. Nobody used the house's front entrance. As a town girl, Sophie found this a strange practice.

"A fine mornin' to ya! Finn Malone's the name, ma'am. A pleasure, to be sure."

"Mr. Malone, a fine morning indeed. How may I help you?" She admitted she found his Irish brogue fascinating. Hadn't met too many foreigners in her young life. He looked chagrined—embarrassed about something. Scratched the back of his neck, which pushed his perfectly placed flat-brimmed Fedora lower on his forehead. Gave him a, what? A sinister appeal? That beautiful hat looked brand-spanking new.

"Well, ya see, I travel the countryside selling my tonic—"

"Oh, we can't afford such finery—"

"No ma'am, I'm not here to sell ya anything."

"Then—"

"Ma'am, plain 'n simple, I'm as lost as a tick on a hound, and I sure could use some directions."

He spoke country, but she heard city. The hairs on her neck prickled. After he told her where he was headed, she gave him the best directions she was able. She knew Worthington City was north of George. *Way* north. All the way across the Minnesota line, for crying out loud. Peculiar that he'd end up here south of George without someone redirecting him. Peculiar, indeed. But maybe....

"Just you and your husband, ma'am?"

"Yes, well, and his cousin. The three of us work the place."

Sophie knew she should be concerned by this stranger's intrusion, but the farm was a lonely place. And a friendly word or two was never a bad idea. However—

"Never farmed me-self. Seems a good deal of hard work."

"It is, but Jake loves it. His cousin? Not so much."

Sophie had been about to invite this polite man into the kitchen table for coffee, but something about him now made her skin prickle. Those slitty eyes... And did he have his brows plucked and shaped? Surely not. She decided to send him on his way.

"Well, it's a big change for Walt, more than most, I would imagine. Mr. Malone, I don't mean to be short with you, but I should get back to my kitchen. The boys will be here any minute expecting lunch. You understand."

"A'course, ma'am. I thank ya fer the directions. Don't know how I coulda got this turned 'round."

"My pleasure, Mr. Malone. Good day to you," and without uttering another word, she closed the storm door inside the screen door with a firm push. Even though it was ninety-two degrees according to the mercury just outside the open window. She gave the skeleton key in the lock a gentle twist with her good hand as quietly as she could and backed away without turning.

Gauzy curtains covered the windows in that door, and she could see him still staring at her through the curtains for several seconds. As if he had had more to say, before he turned and strolled around the yard, like a prospective buyer of the place. At last, after sliding in behind the wheel of that giant auto, he coaxed its big motor back to life. Made a few J-turns to maneuver back out of the driveway toward County 14.

Sophie shivered, but got back to packing lunch for the boys in the field. She decided it was nothing. She would not worry the boys. And she only felt the slightest guilt for the little white lie she'd told the stranger. *City folk!*

❧

33

Dust blew with merciless insistence, carried on a nocturnal wind. It felt as if another storm was brewing, but they knew only wind and more dust were likely. The closed windows denied entry to most of it, but that also made for a stifling night of sleep. Early June already felt like mid-August.

Sophie always wore her whalebone-staved corset to bed for fear of injuring her delicate spine from which recovery would be unlikely, or at least, lengthy. That's what she was told by Father's expensive specialists up in Rapid City. That meant even during moments of the utmost intimacy with her precious Jake, she wore her girdle. That dear man even said he found the garment "alluring," but he would say no more about that. He incorporated what he called "her helper" as a playful part of their little "dance of romance." His words—a carry-over from his past. After all, *actual* dancing was verboten, wasn't it? That made their private little ritual a taste more risqué. But nobody needed to know that, did they? And she refused to allow guilt to intrude.

Jake would flirt with his fingers around her helper's edges. He treated it like Sophie's second skin. She adored him for small kindnesses such as these. While the garment mandated a certain inflexibility to their amorous adventures, they discovered delightful work-arounds. Together.

Then, that very night, Sophie called Jake into their darkened bedroom from the kitchen where he labored over a drawing. Their double bed with its creaky old headboard was just visible across the small chamber from the open door. She could see Jake silhouetted in the door near Blackie.

JAKE TURNED AWAY FROM HIS DRAWING. FROM HIS CHAIR IN the kitchen, he could just make out a swath of milk-white within the shadowed bedding that remained. Most of the covers were on the floor. Sophie lay there looking so vulnerable, like fragile porcelain. No words were needed or wanted. She was offering herself to him—*without her helper*.

From the kitchen table he carried a lantern turned down low. Setting it with care on her tiny bedside table, he couldn't help but notice her soft eyes broadcast both allure and fear and... something else. Wonder?

Jake mumbled, "I don't... what... won't you...?"

The corners of her mouth puckered her cherubic cheeks. "It's okay, my dearest. We'll go very slow. No sudden movements, alright? And you'll help me after."

Tears rolled down his cheeks. She could just see them glinting in the lamplight's amber wash. Without even touching, they had already shared a new pinnacle of intimacy. She guided his every child-like movement, his every sensual touch, as if both feared she might shatter, or melt. Each gesture became both intentional and intense. They achieved and sustained an extraordinary quiet, as if Sophie's parents might hear their intimacy from the kitchen, or the front room. Sophie's whispered commands were those of a lover and a mentor, and Jake, the humble and grateful apprentice.

THE NEXT MORNING, JAKE HOPPED AROUND SOPHIE IN THE kitchen like a jack rabbit on hot sand. He attended to her every wish, which weren't many... just enough to satisfy his desire to be helpful. They had both survived their adventure with aplomb. Walt had enduring sleeping in the barn during last night's minor storm, per Sophie's insistence. Jake had wondered about that until... she was *such* a planner!

❧

AS THE TRIO NOW SAT AROUND THE KITCHEN TABLE IN THE relative cool of an early Iowa morning in June, sipping Old Judge, Walt tried hard not to grin into his half-empty mug. But his heart was full. So was his hair—of dust. Sophie's eyes explored the depths of his own. He was definitely growing on her.

"So, what are we doing today, boss?"

Sophie knew Walt called Jake that to impress upon her that he was taking his farm duties seriously. Despite her after-glow, it wasn't working.

❧

JAKE APPRECIATED WALT'S LAME ATTEMPT. THERE WAS NO way to disguise the spring in his own step, not that he cared to even try, but for Sophie's sake.

❧ 34 ❧

❦

That afternoon, Jake faced Walt as he sat on the bale opposite him up in the barn's haymow, the one place where Sophie could never climb. The cavernous space engulfed them as a whale might swallow plankton, especially in the conspicuous absence of hay, but for a few bales. Jake said, "Okay, cuz. Your mysterious past is tearing Sophie apart. I'm more than a might curious myself. I need to know, and then I'll decide what to share with her."

Walt fondled his considerable girth, as if it were a baby anxious to make its grand entrance into the world despite slim odds of survival. Then he sat down, his demeanor suddenly serious, before he spoke in a soft voice.

"Here's the thing, cuz." Back hunched, elbows on knees, Walt cocked his head lopsided to silently stare up into the depths of his cousin's soul. Or at least as deeply as he could from below the low-slung brim of his own threadbare fedora.

He swept the old hat off his head to better look Jake in the eye with surprising solemnity. His pitch-black hair dully shone in an errant ray of summer sunshine that invaded the haymow through an insignificant hole in the roof. Dust motes in the air lit up that beam, as if God himself were pointing down at cousin Walt's head. If Jake believed in omens....

"No surprise I've been known to take a tipple." Jake's involuntary reaction, a snigger and a good-natured nod reminded Walt he remained a storied master of understatement, but he ignored the well-deserved jibe and pressed on. "I've gotten myself into a pickle on more 'n one occasion, but it ain't as sour as you might think." What he didn't say was that he would reveal much here today, but not all. Without another word, Walt gathered momentum by leaning forward. He stood up and started undressing.

Another involuntary reaction. "Whoa, cuz, what the Hell is this?"

"Hold on. Don't be so impatient, Herr Hardt! And don't worry. You ain't my type." As he snickered, he unbuttoned his shirt to reveal a yellowish-white undergarment snugged about his torso, as plain as an old bandage. Hard to miss all the stains, though. Walt seemed only somewhat embarrassed at the odor wafting from the garment as he unraveled a bow knot under his left arm. The tie came loose and fell away, along with the strange wrap that looked a lot like Sophie's girdle, but with lots of padding and without the staves.

Walt grinned as he observed Jake's deepening perplexity, which gave way to a look of full-on shock. Walt was cadaver-thin under the garment, as if he had shed twenty pounds of soft bulk in the blink of an eye.

"Jake, it's the strangest thing. When I drink, some instinct kicks in. I don't get stupid or mean or sloppy, or even giddy like most drinkers. I become an exceptional gambler. This here's the fruit of my labor." He dropped onto his hay bale again, as if a deep exhaustion had just set in. As he spoke, the strange girdle now lay across his lap beneath his slender torso. His now-oversized shirt lay in a pile next to him on the bale. A sleeveless cotton undershirt remained, turned a mottled gray from too few washes and maybe advanced age. Walt drew open a small zipper that adorned the entire length of the wraparound garment. Inside, Jake could see rows of compartments on either side of the zipper, now exposed. Each burst with a bundle of... cash?

"Holy Hell, Walt, there must be *thousands* in there!"

"Yeah, on the tall side of ten. See, the thing is, this kinda money don't come without a price. Not only am I banned from every casino and back-alley craps game from Chicago to Denver—not because I cheat, mind you—but because I *win,* I've made a few enemies. Your cousin's kinda famous." He rewarded—or punished—Jake with one of those infamous family smirks. "What that means is that I'm on the lam from some bad mooks until they get bored looking for me. And they will. But I got this cash that *I* can't spend, but you and Sophie *can.* Besides, I got nothin' to spend it on.

"Walt, I—"

"Shut up, cuz. Here's what we're gonna do, and do *not* insult me with any of that churchy crap here, okay?"

For the next twenty minutes, Walt convinced Jake to conspire with him about how they would spend some of what Jake considered ill-gotten gains—with care. But he spent at least that much time convincing Jake these were not the proceeds of any immoral venture, and that this was a loan, not a gift.

What *was* a gift was Walt's ability to shift the grift. He explained why Jake dared not spend too much at one time. This would only draw unwelcome curiosity. They made a spittin' vow to bury the money beneath the barn floor and treat it like their own little bank. Jake agreed, having been levied the sternest warning and the strongest assurances. For any expenditure, he would first consult with Walt, who seemed wise in the ways of under-the-table finance, like Jake never could be.

※※※

WHILE WALT DRONED ON, IT WAS AS IF JAKE WAS ONCE again just meeting this now-gaunt blood of his blood for the first time—twice in as many days. He knew Walt liked the hooch, but this traveling gambler side of him? And his extensive knowledge of hole-and-corner banking? He had had no idea. Sitting in the barn, though, making financial plans without telling Sophie? This tore at Jake's heart strings. Out of necessity and strangled hope, he resigned himself to a begrudging finality born of desperation: this was now who he was. Only because it seemed the only viable alternative to losing the family farm and becoming homeless—or worse, accepting a handout from Sophie's father.

With this much money he could both fund his loco-baler and buy the farm back from old Silas! But not now, Walt had warned. Not until... when? Jake didn't like how this windfall made him feel. Life seemed a lot cleaner thirty minutes ago.

❧ 35 ❧

Jake and Sophie had not only started their new life together unceremoniously, they already weren't talking about muddy undercurrents caused by cousin Walt moving in with them. Sophie didn't yet understand that's what farm folk did—they took in family, no matter what. But Jake had ushered Walt into their small home without first discussing it with her, despite their money problems, especially considering Walt's mysterious past. Now *this*. She looked him in the eye across the kitchen table. A brilliant day and the hot breeze passing through the house did not thaw Sophie's frigid mood.

"Jake, I'm not blind. And I'm not so stupid as to miss Walt's sudden miraculous weight loss. Yesterday we couldn't pay Silas for last month. He threatened to evict us and take the farm. Today we're square with him. He's too mule-mean to forgive a debt. You took money from Walt, didn't you? And worse, you did it behind my back. I don't know you at all, do I?" Her look of pain at his betrayal ripped through him like a dull sickle through dusty weeds.

She would not relent. "You'll take dubious money from your cousin but not honest help from my parents, or even consider working for my father?" That was not a question. He just kept croaking the words, "We're fine, dear." But deep inside, his own anxiety grew by the minute from within the anguish he felt for lying to this woman he did not deserve. This is not how he envisioned starting their life together. They hadn't even been married ninety days.

He always thought his invention would launch their future —his steam-powered baler, his *loco-baler*. He also thought he would go to business school to learn success, and Sophie would manage their wealth. To make matters worse, Sophie had sacrificed her dream of nursing school for... this. He peered around her at the old kitchen, the old stove, the old door to the old bedroom and their old maple headboard. At least that dredged up a small smile—inside. A bright spot on a dark stage that he dared not acknowledge right now.

SOPHIE, WHILE TOLERANT TO A FAULT, ESPECIALLY FOR Jake's moldering dreams, had at last grown impatient at these notions. "Jake, are you listening? I love that you feel inspired all of the time, but that does not feed us. And now, I'm not sure how what you've just done will affect us." But she would never ask him to reverse a decision, despite the worry.

JAKE FELT SICK, AND NOT JUST IN HIS STOMACH. HE KNEW she wasn't just concerned about the implications of accepting what she considered dirty money—she had called it filthy lucre. It was as if she could see into a dangerous future. Sometimes he believed she had, well, abilities that nobody understood, least of all him. *What have I done?*

But they were okay now, weren't they? What was the old saw? *Tell yourself a lie often enough, and you'll soon believe it.* He could only skulk out to the barn to attend to something important. Though he didn't look back, he could feel Sophie's pitiful glare burning holes in his untrustworthy behind.

❦

36

S ophie needed a distraction—chores. She acknowledged she found something satisfying in caring for critters that provided them sustenance. She navigated the parched yard without incident between the pump and the chicken coop with a half-pail of water. That alone always kicked up a small sense of pride, and ankle-high dust. The new batch of chicks was a testament to the natural desire for, and renewal of life. Without a single doubt, smile-worthy. Chicks needed fresh water the most, especially in this steamy weather, and protein. They couldn't afford fancy poultry feeds from Marvin's, but since all their grown chickens were now productive laying hens, Jake taught her they too needed lots of protein, like the chicks. She scattered their own mixture of grit and table scraps, which made the coop reek. Jake cleaned it out at least once a week to keep it from growing too ripe in this heat.

As she finished dumping and filling the water trays, spreading their home recipe of layer feed, a motorcar pulled into the driveway. Setting the now-less-heavy pail down, she turned, with some care. She dared not stumble. She stared at the fine new car she didn't recognize. It lurched to a startling stop in a cloud of dust. Sophie froze as she recalled the dubious city slicker's visit a while back.

The slender woman who extracted herself from the car's cockpit was bundled in a gigantic overcoat that reached her ankles. Even though a mid-June sun battered the yard with a midsummer scorch. The bulky but stylish coin-cheek scarf looped around her neck dwarfed her head. A snug-fitting cloche hat with its generous brim cast her face into shadow. The woman's hands fidgeted with the twin tails of her long scarf in front of her as she scanned the yard before spotting Sophie working near the hen house.

Whenever someone visited the farm, Sophie vacillated between excitement and apprehension. If it was someone new, apprehension often won out, like now, until the woman made her precarious way across the lumpy yard toward Sophie in her fashionable but high-risk heels. With her head down to avoid tripping or falling, she picked her steps with care. Sophie could not yet see the woman's face, but found her general demeanor alarming. Her gait was anything but straight or steady, which seemed incongruous with her elegant attire, and she appeared... what? Frail? In distress? Who could this be? So far, neither had spoken, even though a mere fifteen paces now separated them. There was a familiar air about her. Sophie wiped her hands on her apron and glanced downward. It mortified her to receive company in dusty shoes, dirty stockings and homely dress only appropriate for working in the yard. Anything but fashionable.

At last, the young lady stood before her, and raised her head. The first thing Sophie noticed were the black stains under each eye that descended past the corners of her puffy lips. Crying had demolished her heavy makeup that now did nothing to hide the pain in those huge doe eyes, both swollen half-shut. And it was now impossible to miss the bruises. She was still the prettiest girl Sophie knew, but Sophie had never seen her in such... disarray—nay, anguish.

"Edie? Edie! Oh, my goodness. What *happened* to you, sweetheart?

Several sobbing and halting inhales preceded Edie falling into Sophie's arms, now bleating like a gutted goat. The weight on Sophie's legs almost brought them both sprawling. It took all of her strength to support the bulk of Edie's what, eighty or ninety pounds, *at most?* She was an absolute rail.

After about thirty seconds of hugging, patting, and separating, Sophie hoarse-whispered, "Let's go inside for a cup, okay, dear? You can tell me all about it." Sophie grabbed Edie's right arm and interlocked it with her left. The opposite of what Edie once did for her during their walks together in town. That was back when Edie was a squeaky-fresh high school girl trying to tempt Sophie into allowing the "dangerous" Jake Hardt to court her. Now Edie's frail frame and spiked heels on treacherous ground, not to mention her alarming mental and physical state, made *her* the handicapped one.

THEY MADE THEIR WAY INTO THE KITCHEN THROUGH THE mudroom. Sophie was the only one who got away with not changing from outside shoes or boots to inside shoes. That was because she needed Jake's help into and out of her relentless orthopedics, without which she could not venture a step. That rendered a small but significant inside-smile of gratitude. She would not ask Edie to shed her elegant ankle-strap heels either.

"Here, sweetheart, you sit at the table. This chair's the most comfortable with the best cushion. I'll pour us a cup."

Edie still had not spoken an intelligible word. She didn't have to, but Sophie knew she would. She hung her head, gloved hands folded in her lap, palms up, like she didn't know what else to do with them.

The kitchen sweltered from the eighty-eight degrees outside, although a gentle breeze blew through open windows. Old Blackie had kept the coffee warm, not hot, with a smoldering fire that would need tending in an hour or two, but also contributed to the kitchen's oppressive heat. Sophie glistened from head to toe. She could only imagine Edie's condition under that bulky wrap.

"Would you like to take off your coat, dear?" A small sideways jerk of Edie's bowed head answered, although she unraveled the scarf's double wrap with some difficulty. Silence reigned in the kitchen. Their only rooster was young and still learning to crow. He practiced every few minutes with the most laughable ruckus throughout the day, except at sunrise. No doubt when *he* still slept. Otherwise, the kitchen remained country quiet. A burned coffee odor, along with the mudroom's undeniable bouquet, prevailed. They sat next to each other at a right angle, each with a mug of yard mud in front of them. Edie's gloved fingers twitched as she tugged on their tips, one after another. Then, frustrated at the futility of doing this, she laid her hands back on her lap, palms up, useless. She fell into a listless trance.

"Okay, girl, spill."

After a full ten seconds of waiting, Edie spoke in a haunted tone. Sophie leaned in close in order to hear her. "Oh, Sophie, I'm not sure I wanna go on."

This was *not* the Edie she knew. What had *happened?* "Just tell me. Is it Ritchy?" Momentum built as Edie launched into her confession. Nobody else in the world had heard this. Only Sophie. She needed to be here now, nowhere else.

"He was good to me, at first, Soph. So handsome. Bought

me nice things. For the first time in my life, I felt... special."
Now sobs convulsed through her birdlike frame until she
withdrew a huge white hanky from her left coat sleeve where
she had stashed it. Dabbed her eyes, blew her nose, then
clutched that folded hanky in both hands like it was her life-
line. Sophie laid a gentle hand on her right forearm, but
stayed silent. Edie slowly settled down once again, until she
could speak once more.

"He *uses* me, Soph. At all the parties in Rock Rapids, Sioux
City, even Rapid. Early on, they were great fun, ya know?"
Sob, sniffle. "Everybody loves Ritchy. He brings the booze.
People pay him. He parades me around like a doll, ya know?
Gets me drunk, and I do stuff that isn't me. Awful stuff. I
dunno. For him. Or for more Black Gold. Said I didn't want
to do that, ya know? At first, just a little slap or poke, here
and... down there. I figured he just liked it rough. But he likes
others to watch, too. Some men are like that, but you
wouldn't know that, my sweet Sophie. Not with sweet Jake."

She fell silent. Then, halting and silent sobs punctuated
everything she could croak. Sophie waited. Nodding. Locked
onto her sad eyes, stained with more tears and caked makeup
now so utterly demolished, it looked... clownish. Sophie
waited some more.

"I drink every day now, Soph. Not just at parties, and not
just at night. He slaps me when I'm sober, and slugs me when
I'm drunk, like it takes that to get my attention, or to make
sure I dish up enough, um, obedience. Like I'm not doing
enough to.... Oh, Soph...."

Still, Sophie said nothing, but thought she might grow ill
at what she was hearing. *Can't let it show. She needs me just to be
here, and to be strong. Somehow.* Sophie nodded as she
continued petting and rubbing Edie's arm. Like this girl was a
lost puppy in need of a rescue. For the first time, she noticed
Edie's tremors. It was as if every abhorrent thought incited a

sideways jerk of her head. Almost non-stop. So small they were almost unnoticeable, unless you were staring at her. Same with her hands and arms. Sophie could feel those jerky tremors only because her hand rested on Edie's arm. Small muscles convulsed. Her cheek muscles twitched. And that caused her lips to gyrate into unnatural shapes. Frightening. Manic. And they became more visible the longer they sat there. She should call someone, but she dared not move even an inch away from her dear frail friend. Sophie saw something frightening in her mind's eye that cartwheeled her stomach.

She started speaking slowly, but sped up until her speech was a stuttering staccato. "Soph, I drink to forget. But I can't pass out. Can't sleep. Can't think. Can't stop. Can't go. I don't dare go home. I don't trust myself behind the wheel. I don't want to hurt anyone. Not that I even care. And I've burned all my bridges now. Except to you, Soph. My parents won't speak to me. You're my only friend." Suddenly, she paused, every word carefully chosen. "I took this from Ritchy's bedside table. I think I need help."

She drew a huge handgun from her large left coat pocket and laid it with care on the table next to her untouched mug of coffee. Sophie's eyes widened. They both stared at that malevolent presence now. It suddenly consumed their thoughts. As if they were one. As if they both worried that its inherent evil could and *would* seep into their consciousness. Despite their mutual fear of it.

Sophie spoke for the first time since sitting down. But not before shoving the pistol away from both her and Edie with a slow scraping push, to a neutral location on the otherwise empty table, except for their mugs. That blue-black *thing* was heavier than Sophie would have guessed.

"Edie, no."

The distressed girl's next words crept into the recesses of Sophie's spirit like acid dripping on lace. "My dearest and only friend, I've lost hope. I'm empty. Used up. My shame is complete. I now just need it to stop." As if these thoughts triggered some obsession, Edie reached into her right pocket. She pulled out a silver flask, and unscrewed the cap that was attached by a small silver chain. She poured as much brown liquid into her coffee as the mug allowed. Secured the cap. Set the flask on the table between her mug and that gun. Picked up the mug, downed its tepid liquid in one series of contiguous gulps. Coffee and liquor leaked from the corners of her mouth onto her scarf. As if this sequence of actions were self-evident, she said, "You see, Soph? That's the only purpose I now serve and am faithful to. That's it. Me and Ritchy and Black Gold. I love you, Soph."

With calm deliberation, she reached over. Picked up the pistol in her left hand. Sophie froze in the paralysis of disbelief. Like she was watching a moving picture. Edie cocked it with the heel of her right hand, which required considerable effort. She placed the end of the barrel into her beautiful mouth. Pulled the trigger.

IT OCCURRED TO SOPHIE THAT IF SHE HAD BEEN SITTING ON Edie's opposite side, with her bad hand closest to her friend, what happened next would not have been possible. In retrospect, she should have predicted Edie's desperate gesture, and chastised herself for not having done so. Her good hand still rested on the tabletop next to Edie's right arm. When she saw the gun ascend to her friend's mouth and enter it, she swept her arm upward without thinking. She would learn later the abrupt movement broke both of Edie's front teeth. The aiming sight at the end of the pistol's short barrel caught behind them on its way out, also ripping a nasty gash in Edie's upper lip. But the bullet punched a hole high on the kitchen's north wall instead of in Edie's soft palate and brain pan.

Sound ceased. Time stalled. Only ringing remained. Both were stunned. Not sure if either of them were alive for a few horrific moments. The blood then flowed from Edie's mouth as her head rebounded forward after Sophie's blow. They both watched the blood from her damaged mouth expand into a small but expanding pool on the tabletop. The empty coffee mug had disappeared, but the flask stayed put.

Edie stared straight ahead, not sure what reality had snagged her. Sophie gazed first at her friend, then sought the gun. She tried to stand in order to reach her friend's left hand, now below the table. But Sophie fell back into her chair—insufficient momentum. Instead, she grabbed what she could reach—Edie's shoulders and upper arms. Her dear, crazed, suicidal friend. Hugged her from her seated position, best she could. That gun might still be in the hand she could not see or reach. Both cried as if their lives depended on that simple human response useful in so many situations. They cried together, because they still could. After a half-minute-long eternity, Sophie heard the gun clatter to the floor below the table, and then she cried in gratitude and relief. Edie shook as she sobbed and gasped like a little girl again.

That shot would bring Jake. She needed her Jake—right now—to get her little Edie some help. *Praise be to the Lord for delivering my friend into the arms of providence!*

❦

37

A week had passed since Sophie's friend had attempted suicide in their kitchen. Sheriff Billy joked he would just patrol past the Hardt farm for regular pickups. Called that gallows humor. Said he'd read about that somewhere. Though Jake's first impression of Billy was that of a rather coarse older guy who showed little emotion, he now realized Billy's hard shell hid his mushy insides. With his young deputy's help, Billy had transported Edie over to Doc Gustavsen in Spencer. Mentioned that the contents of her flask would be important evidence. *Interesting. Must be that Black Gold junk that young hobo Peter and Sophie's friend Edie both craved—more than life itself. Terrible business—rotten to beat all get-out! Dear, brave Sophie....*

Jake worried about her after that ordeal, but he need not have. Seemed the more trying the circumstance, the more resolute Sophie grew. But was she just hiding how Edie's crisis had affected her? He and Walt took care of the farm, even meals and coffee, while Sophie spent time at the hospital over in Spencer. She wanted to stay close until Edie stabilized. When she returned home, Jake asked, "Edie doin' okay, Soph?"

"I think she'll be fine as long as she stays away from that poison and her even more toxic husband. You should have seen her in the days after she stopped drinking that stuff, sweetheart. It was awful."

"I'm more worried about you right now, dear."

"Well, I must admit, that whole thing shook me up, but with a little time...." She drifted off into some memory. Or was she praying? Either way, Jake kissed her forehead and left her in the kitchen to commune with Blackie, or whatever.

Now, a week later, the farm's rhythm returned to its normal harsh beats, more or less. Not long after that nightmare, Jake started chasing his own dream again. He had built and tested a small model of his loco-baler, but small was a relative term. The darn thing weighed an awful lot—he guesstimated over two-hundred pounds—and ended up the size of a three-foot cube, not including gadgets that stuck out in all directions. He'd reconsidered whether loco-baler was the best name. But since steam powered it—just like a loco-motive—he liked the clever name. Chief told him what loco meant in Spanish. Maybe the name *still* fit.

Jake hoisted the model into the back of the old stake-side truck with an assist from Walt and Queenie using some blocks and tackle suspended from the barn's peak above the haymow door. He loaded and strapped down the model on its platform—a rough-hewn table he found in the back of the barn under a pile of dusty old horse tack. Hauled the contraption from the farm to the tractor meet at the Lyon County Fairgrounds up in Rock Rapids. Time to show it off. Walt said he had some business up in Rapid City. Jake didn't ask.

Jake was pretty sure his working model's oak platform— that table, supported by four-inch-square legs, now up in the truck's bed—could handle the weight of his mechanical marvel. The bumpy roads between the farm and fairgrounds would be the test. He hoped other farmers would each kick in a grubstake. That would enable him to start building a full-size prototype of the contraption. He'd heard that fancy word somewhere—prototype. Folks would believe he knew what the hell he was talking about as an inventor.

Upon his arrival at the fairgrounds, Jake's confidence rose. He saw a multitude of curious stares, and more than a few familiar faces. He picked his spot for maximum foot traffic, parked, pulled the stake sides from the truck's bed—now a stage—leaving his baler model unfettered sitting atop the old table.

The machine smoked like a tiny locomotive a half-hour after set-up. Time for the demonstration. A small cadre of curious farmers and a few suits gathered around the miniature column of wood smoke rising from the model. On one end of the machine, closest to the truck's cab, he'd bolted a small ramp. He piled long grass scythed from the ground around the truck upon his arrival at the bottom end of that ramp. This grass simulated mowed hay to be bundled—baled. A rotating belt with small spikes gave the grass traction, and conveyed it up that miniature ramp into the eager maw of the baler's front end. He cleared his throat to answer questions not yet asked.

"Gentlemen, this here is a one-eighth-size prototype of a fully automatic machine that will get your baling done lickety-split. Yup, I said fully automatic. You see here these little twigs in the fuel hopper up top? They represent firewood used by the full-size machine. Gravity draws them down into the firebox, as needed." He made deliberate eye contact with every farmer to ensure they knew what that implied—an *automatic* feed.

Then he pointed to another bolted-on steel component

on the scale model—a framework that housed a heavy two-gallon glass bottle. "And this here's the water tank that'll be steel on the real deal. A valve just knows when the boiler needs more water so it can boil it and turn it into pressurized steam. Your standard steam engine." He pointed to a steel canister with clamps around the top. "A jet of steam from this pressurized tank turns the power takeoff, or PTO, and that, my friends, makes everything work. Kind of like a steam loco-motive, but with fewer moving parts since not near as much power is needed as a locomotive. That makes it real reliable. Once you build up a head of steam, there'll be nothing to stop it, except you, the operator. You're in complete control of this little darlin'."

"Hey, Jake, is that Sophie's pressure cooker you butchered to build that boiler?" The crowd rewarded Aaron with a smat-tering of chuckles.

"Sure is, Aaron. But don't go telling Sophie, okay?" That raised a more boisterous round of guffaws from the crowd. "You all know a boiler does the same basic job as a pressure cooker. But you won't find no rutabagas inside this one," a few more knowing laughs, "just water turnin' into steam power to drive the baler mechanism via that PTO."

"Jake, that's all well and good, but I ain't gonna stop in the middle of my field to stoke no fire. No offense, son."

He pointed down at the questioner with an exaggerated gesture, like he was tryin' to snap a booger off the end of his index finger. "Clarence, no need. That's the beauty of this here design. You chop your own wood ahead of time, from your own land at no cost other than some of your own sweat. How about you cut and split that old gray ghost that's been standin' proud in your tree line for years? That'll fuel this baby for a few *seasons.* And you can store enough wood up top here for a whole day of baling. Same with water to feed you steam. Fill 'er up at your well-head in the morning or the night before, and you're good to go. You light your fire before leavin' the yard, and by the time you reach your field, it's all automatic."

"So, then, how do the bales get bundled and tied?"

Before answering, Jake pulled a lever and belts started moving with a series of tiny screeches as they picked up speed. A perpendicular set of tines rotated as they approached a pair of curved pressure plates. Jake had already positioned a handful of his fresh-cut grass at the base of the intake ramp. The steam engine picked up speed, and smoke billowed from a tiny stack.

"Well, Eugene, you see, that's the heart of this time- and labor-saving machine. These two sets of right-angle tines scoop up and compress the mowed hay into a tight bundle at the baler's front end. The first set of tines scoops up a loose bundle and compresses it from underneath, against this here curved pressure plate. And the outer tines facing inward rotate the compressed bundle as the twine feeds around it under tension, tying it in two places, near each end. Now here's the cat's meow. See those two spools of string that I stole from Sophie's sewing box? That's where the twine waits to be drawn around each squeezed bundle - two per bundle. And this contraption here is the knot-maker, done with a twist, a tuck and a snip. All automatic. The only way you untie *those* knots is with a sharp knife. Good and secure."

The little steam engine chuffed away. And sure enough, a couple of twigs drew down into the firebox, all by themselves. Smoke rolled out of a round chimney the size of a toilet paper roll. Looked as if Jake had robbed it off a miniature locomotive, complete with a spark screen. Smelled like a steam-powered locomotive too—a hot campfire in a summertime washroom. The water tank bubbled as a float valve opened. The need for more water to generate more steam had just been satisfied. Straight belts and belts twisted at right angles high on both sides connected the steam engine's PTO to the drive belt that handled the hay tray. The machine hummed and wobbled with a satisfying harmony. As long as Jake fed cut hay (grass) into the front end, the machine compressed and tied the grass into neat round bundles. Opposite the intake hopper, toward the back of the truck, a conveyor drew the hay bundles up and over the edge of a miniature hay wagon.

"Hey Jake," someone in the crowd of a dozen onlookers, "what about the ragged ends on them bales?"

"Yup, they get chopped off before they're conveyed up into your hay wagon. I didn't know how to model that, but that'll be in the regular-size loco-baler, patent pending."

He wasn't sure what that last bit meant, but he'd heard it somewhere. And it sounded real official. Anyway, farmers appreciated a hard-working piece of equipment, even better when it was complex and looked serious, but only if it worked.

"You tow this behind a team, Jake?"

"Yup, you can, although it'd work better behind your tractor—more consistent speed gets more bales done faster. But either will work. You just tow your hay wagon behind this baby, and swap out wagons when they fill up. This lever lets you stop and start. If your horses need to stop for a drink or to put on their feed bags, you just drop this here lever until you're ready to go again. Same when the wife delivers coffee and sandwiches for lunch. Kinda like the emergency brake on your truck. Easy."

He pulled a lever toward the front of the machine down toward the ground. All movement in and around the machine stopped with a few soft screeches as the pulleys under the belts stopped quicker than the belts. But little puffs continued skyward from the chimney, along with a hiss from the steam tank's pressure relief valve. Both slowed in frequency.

"Oh, and if you're out in the back forty, this here will signal the missus you're ready for some chow."

With a devilish smile, almost boyish, he yanked on a tiny chain and all hell broke loose. The shrieking steamboat-style whistle spooked nearby horses. Every farmer within fifty feet jumped before they covered their ears and squinted and hunched over to stave off the onslaught. Jake held tension on that spring-loaded chain for a good five seconds before relenting and grinning. Those closest shook their heads, wrung their index fingers in their ears.

"Good Lord, son," Clarence declared before staring at Jake and his devilish grin, then at his neighbor Eugene. Both broke out into hearty guffaws, as did most of the rest of the men. Many were slapping their thighs or their neighbor's backs. Jake seemed a bit of a showman.

"Yeah, that'll get the sandwiches and java run out to the field at a gallop, for sure!"

Jake said, "You betcha!" He stooped down on the truck's bed to slap Clarence's shoulder, who stood below him at the front of the small crowd.

Several of the farmers seemed to believe this loco-baler was a real fine idea. Most also agreed Jake might want to consider a name change for his invention. As hard up as everyone was, some saw the wisdom of easing the burden of harvesting their hay and straw with some automation. When there were crops to harvest. That would mean more profit, especially if it were possible to harvest more acreage when times and weather took an up-tick. Successful farmers were nothing if not visionaries. Once he built his baler, Jake even promised to come bale fifteen acres of hay for them for free. But only once. That brought the tinkle of change and even the swish of some folding money descending into the one-gallon pickle jar Sophie contributed to the cause. She wanted it back, though.

Jake overheard a couple of old boys as they strolled away, as if reluctant to leave. "Young Jake is a likable sort, and if he builds that machine, how about we go in on one together?"

"Yeah, might work."

He raised almost twenty dollars on the day. Even Henry stopped by and dropped a whole dollar into Jake's jar. He suspected that was Sophie's doing. Her father had stood nearby through the entire demonstration, watching the crowd grow. Afterward, he even raised both eyebrows and offered a deliberate nod and slow blink of approval after the whistle gag. Jake thought he might have impressed the old war horse, at least a little. And that meant a lot, coming from a veteran sales hound like Henry Bairns.

෴

38

Riding high from his successful showing at the tractor meet the previous day, Jake had secured his baler model in the barn for further tinkering. But play day was over. His least favorite task, feeding the hogs and cleaning their pen after neglecting this important task for almost a week, occupied most of his morning. He had shoveled a wheelbarrow of soupy hog manure and trundled it out behind the barn, where he loaded it into his makeshift manure spreader. That's when he heard the alarm.

Sophie's custom was to only ring the dinner triangle that hung from the eaves outside the mud room door for regular meals and snacks. She'd clang the inner sides of the triangle with an even, rhythmic toll. This was not that. The triangle rang with a sporadic urgency, without rhythm. Alarm! Then it fell silent.

Jake dropped the heavy wheelbarrow where it stood, slopping juices over the rim and onto, well, everything. He sprinted around the barn's north side, the fastest but roughest route to the rear of the house. Even after stumbling twice, it took Jake only seconds to gain a sight line to the mudroom door. He only saw the triangle swinging with the striker dangling below it, but no Sophie in sight.

Didn't bother with the boots, hog shit 'n all. Flew straight through the mudroom into the kitchen to find Sophie leaning back in her favorite straight chair with her right elbow braced on the tabletop. She stretched her legs out as straight as possible, spread apart, favoring her right hip. Her left hand clutched her left thigh like a vise.

"Soph!"

"It's bad, Jake. I need you. Now."

"Okay, okay!" Per their routine, he grabbed the small padded foot stool from its place under the table. With a quick but gentle motion, he lifted her left foot. Placed it on the low stool. Just at the ankle. This allowed her foot and the heel of her shoe to hang over. Unlaced her orthotic shoe with practiced haste. He tugged it off with care by its stubby three-inch-square heel. Set it down. Didn't bother to remove her knee-high silk stocking, a town vanity. Jake massaged her foot in just the manner prescribed by Doc Gus, guided further by Sophie's strained whisper, hoarse around the edges.

ONE CONTINUOUS CRAMP CONSUMED HER. SOME PITILESS force pounded a dull but white-hot stake through the top of her left foot. She could think of nothing else but imagine, *Is this what Christ felt when they nailed him to the cross? Is this for **my** sins?* She grew vaguely aware of Jake's presence now. *Praise the Lord!*

She spoke to him. She was sure of it. During the first few

minutes, Sophie couldn't help but resort to a moment of self-pity. *The word* **cramp** *will never do these episodes justice. More like the relentless agony of a hard-core charlie-horse, multiplied by a thousand. But self-pity is a vice you would not expect of me, Lord, is it? Forgive me.*

Through Jake's efforts, the pain abated after several minutes. Otherwise, she'd be no good to anybody for at least half an hour, or more. On his knees before her, she now noticed the top of his old hat, replete with bits of straw and what she suspected was a generous spattering of hog manure, judging by the distinctive odor that suddenly flooded her sensitive nose. Her heart swelled despite the residual discomfort in her foot.

SOPHIE'S CRAMPS RESULTED FROM THE PARTIAL PARALYSIS and atrophied deformity of bone, muscle, and sinew from her childhood affliction, made worse by the severe correction forced by her custom-made shoes necessary for her to walk. Polio conspired to plague her with a lifetime of these horrific episodes. Hilda had passed this baton to Jake, and that immeasurably endeared him to her.

Today, Sophie made it into the kitchen to collapse into a chair before falling. *Any* fall for her could mean incapacitating agony, or even a lethal injury. Such a possibility made every single day on the farm her next heroic adventure. Jake's words, most certainly not hers.

Such was just one cross she bore without complaint on her journey toward the heavenly gates. Yes, as corny as it sounded—she did not care one wit about how such comforting sayings sounded—Sophie viewed life as preparation for an eternity of service to the Lord. Jake had translated that homily to militaristic terms: life was boot camp for

Heaven. Such was the strength of her faith; however, Jake remained a serious work in progress.

Gazing once more at the top of her dirty rescuer's filthy fedora—and feeling the life-renewing strength coming from those rough hands—her Jake sent a visceral thrill through her entire body. The profound relief she now enjoyed in her deformed foot was but a small part of the flowing gratitude that engulfed her. Every time this malady consumed her foot, her worldly savior came to the rescue. Unconditionally.

❦

NOW, AFTER TEN MINUTES OF AGONY, JAKE SENSED THEY had weathered the worst of this storm. He saw and felt the more relaxed and less contorted shape of Sophie's twisted foot. She even eased her death grip on the edge of the table. Jake now took the time to peel off her semi-sheer stocking. He now more gently tugged and rubbed each deformed toe, each calloused spot. Focused much of his energy on those reddened cald calluses where her shoe, with relentless purpose, contained the foot's shape necessary to support her walking. He worked up around her ankle, and when she sighed, signaling the pain had passed at last, he worked the slippery stocking back into place, just so. She would want to get back to preparing dinner. And he had hog shit to get back to. He smirked at the weird pleasure he gained from comparing the two very different parts of his day.

❦

THE AFTERGLOW OF EACH ONE OF THESE PAINFUL BUT loving episodes had become a source of profound joy in Sophie's life. And she knew he loved making her pain go away, delivering not just relief, but pleasure. This had become a sensual act for both of them—the near-biblical contrast between her acute pain and a simple joy they both relished. Unique in all the world, they'd say. Like them. Even though this was just boot camp.

39

The bone-jarring drive down from Worthington City, plus the anticipation of setting in motion their plan, launched Finn Malone into a flighty mood. Might be just what he needed. He'd been too long away from the incomparable comforts of his white stone in the recent expansion of Chicago's North Side near Lake Michigan's shore. The mob boss missed his tree-lined Lake View neighborhood within the elegant Surf-Pine Grove District in his adopted city, where everyone that mattered feared and respected the name of Finn Malone. He missed that more than anything. Anonymity—acceptable to lesser mortals of limited power and means— gnawed at him like a rabid alley dog. But ever devout to his business expansion, one did what one must, even suffer the pains of country living, at least temporarily.

The Dillworth farm on filthy Route 60 came into view, with its familiar plume of smoke spiraling from the red brick smokestack into a hazy sky. Seemed the atmosphere out here remained in a perpetual haze—or worse. *The feckin' frontier*....

As his childhood friend and lieutenant pulled the huge Duesenberg into Roy Dillworth's winding driveway, Sticks Leary glanced to his right and said, "House or barn, boss?"

"Sticks, how many folk d'ya reckon are in our paid employ?"

"Here, or all about?"

"All about. Chicago to Denver."

"Mmm, I reckon topside of five hundred, countin' labor, management, 'n vendors."

"So, we're providin' a service in tryin' times—and a heap a jobs—yeh?"

"Sure, boss. Doin' a fine thing. Doin' our part."

"Smoothin' bumps along the way ain't free. But a fine thing, a sure. To the house. Sound the trumpets, if ya please."

Leary happily lit up the magnificent half-dozen electric horns festooning both forward fenders of the big Duese—a trio on each side, and each a full yard long, more or less.

It would seem not only was Roy Dillworth in residence, but he'd been waiting. He appeared on the ornate porch of the sizable house, even while the trumpeting still echoed off the enormous barn, house and sundry outbuildings. With a circular wave, he invited his guests to maneuver the red and black motorcar around the circle drive. The Duese crunched to a stop in the covered driveway's shade.

⚜

ROY DILLWORTH FEARED HE WOULD SHIT HIS PANTS. THIS was an important meeting solicited by Mr. Malone himself after his own production manager called in the weekly numbers to Malone's management team. Said they needed to come down to talk of the future. His "farm's" production of

Black Gold had exceeded all expectations. At almost eleven-hundred barrels a week for the last three weeks, they'd experienced one hiccup last week where they fell below a thousand barrels. Roy had been almost three weeks late increasing production from their earlier six-hundred-seventy barrels a week to one-thousand-eighty barrels. With the loss of almost a hundred barrels to the bad batch, *and* wasting Malone's expensive additive to support that batch, they'd learned an important lesson. That meant this meeting could go either way. *I just wish he'd leave the weasel in that fancy motorcar. Fat chance.*

As the unsavory pair slithered out of the huge Duese, Roy waved yet again. He thought about having one of his own lieutenants at this meeting, but everyone except him working production in the barn provided better optics. Besides, Roy didn't need one of his own underlings watching him suckle on Malone's Irish teat. He'd ensured his housekeeper had Malone's favorite ready and waiting, a pitcher of sickeningly sweet tea and three glasses of ice. She had already made herself scarce. Smart woman.

THE THREE OF THEM GRABBED COMFORTABLE CHAIRS surrounding a circular table in the shade of the massive porch. The white house almost looked like one of those antebellum estate homes that once sprinkled the deep south. Roy was very proud of his old house. Malone spoke first, signaling their formal start. "Roy, can ya tell me what happened last week?"

"Sir, we learned a valuable lesson for a future premium product line. As you know, we use the standard process of boiling, cooling, and fermenting the mash—our raw material —before filtering and distilling it. Since we increased our output by over fifty percent three weeks ago, recent batches were presenting a subtle but noticeable aftertaste. Bitter. To prevent that, we filtered the mash *before* boiling, cooling, fermenting and distilling. It's called lautering, a technique used by high-end distilleries in Europe. That improved the taste, but reduced production output. I decided that was not acceptable. We reverted to the previous process. We could, however, adopt this early filtering process to produce a premium line of less-bitter liquor in the future. Charge more for the better product to justify the slower production process. Your call, Mr. Malone."

"Good judging, Roy. Forget a premium line. We're a volume business. Folks are swillin' this product just fine, yeh? So, here's what we're goin' ta do next. We're goin' national—coast to coast. If you don't have your process and production plans written out yet, get 'em that way by the new moon. We're goin' to duplicate your little operation here to a dozen distilleries feedin' a hundred coast-to-coast distribution centers inside the next two years, 'kay?"

Roy sensed this meeting was going well, but this! He stammered, "A dozen. Two years."

"That's for starters, lad. This Volstead banjax be goin' away in a year or two, and we're taking the trolley to the village square, boy-o."

☙ 40 ❧

❦

Jake had put every spare penny into building his invention—the loco-baler. Including some of Walt's ill-gotten gains, but not too much, along with what he'd raised at the tractor meet. The full-scale prototype was about ten percent complete, including the custom wagon frame and supports for the boiler. He needed more money and more time to fiddle with the rest of the elaborate contraption. He'd do what any forward-thinking farmer would do. He'd borrow.

Today was the big day. Sophie had packed him not one, but two ham-salad sandwiches in thin layers with the last of their butter between four generous slices of her mile-high bread. She even slathered on a little store-bought mustard. Half the coffee in the dented old vacuum flask kept him alert as he washed down one sandwich during the long drive up to Worthington. Henry Bairns had gifted the second-hand Thermos to them as a wedding present. Jake admitted that old thermal bottle did a right fine job of keeping coffee warm.

He'd test the bottom half, along with the second sandwich, on the way home.

The bumpy drive took longer than Jake expected. He stopped just short of the state line when steam rolled out both sides of the old truck's split hood. He needed to stretch his stiff back, anyway. He retrieved an oily rag and a five-gallon can of water from the truck's bed. Up front, he covered the radiator cap with the rag and twisted. Steam shot up and around the rag. Almost scalded his right wrist. Wasn't the truck's fault. New hoses were expensive. Tempted to use some of Walt's money, he had resisted. After all, they had made a spittin' vow.

Jake recycled some coffee in the ditch after using almost half the water in the can. He could head out again in a few minutes. His gaze transported him across a hundred-acre field of gray weeds—they weren't even brown any more. In better times, colorful prairie grass grew knee-high and flowered right up to the edge of the dirt roads 'round these parts. You could smell 'em a mile away, too, Instead of a couple of feet tall, that pretty grass wasn't more than six inches high, no flowers, and butt-ugly. No matter what, though, nothing smelled like ditch weed to a humble and weary traveler. They had dug no real ditch on this road yet. No need—no rain.

The thought of groveling to a banker churned his stomach like worrying over crops and weather never could. To hell with it—he hogged down on that second sandwich. Two more hours at a brisk pace found him parked in front of the savings and loan in Worthington City—the Farm Federal. The front right tire of his old truck kissed the street's fancy curb at an angle parallel to all the vehicles on both sides of his.

. . .

ALL DECKED OUT IN THE LUCKY DUDS HE USED TO WEAR TO
George City on Thursdays to court Sophie, he looked down
at the ridiculous necktie she'd helped him with. One of
Henry's old ties. Jake raised a stink about that, yet here he
was. His black suspenders held up the wool pants that hid
most of his worn but polished Oxfords. Sophie had even
washed and dunk-starched his only white shirt. Damn thing
could stand up on its own now. Felt harsh, but real business-
like. He looked like some saloon dandy, but supposed that's
the countenance he needed to cow-tow to a loan officer. A
summer wind swirled dust and a few bits of paper. Jake never
liked towns much. He tugged on the short brim of his flat
stroker so it wouldn't take off. Needed to slam the truck door
twice to catch the latch before he climbed that fancy curb.
He gaped at the imposing two-story building in front of him.

The Worthington City Farm Federal S&L financed the
bulk of the farms and businesses in Southwest Minnesota and
Northwest Iowa, an important institution, no doubt run by
smart city folk. Surely they'd see the wisdom of investing in
an innovative machine like his loco-baler. He relived Sophie's
pep talk before he crossed the wide sidewalk that was all cut
with straight cracks to prevent frost heaving. She had told
him with her serious face, "Now Jake, you stand or sit
straight. You look them square in the eye. Show them your
pencil drawings as you describe what your invention can do
for farmers and why they'd be foolish not to invest in your
modern baler. Call them 'Sir' or 'Ma'am,' and don't forget to
smile once in a while. You've got this, mister!" He smiled.
How could she be so strong, yet look so... vulnerable? He
thought, *Now or never!*

THE BUILDING'S INTERIOR FELT DARK AND COOL, EVEN IN
the dog days of June. The shiny marble floors helped. They

must've cost a fortune. Jake knew all about convection cooling. Smart. The front of the building faced Northeast. These parts got hot in the summer. Jake could see only reflected sunlight penetrated through them fancy waist-to-ceiling windows. Twelve-foot up, hammered-tin ceilings with slow-turning fans gave the summer heat a place to settle, up away from customers, and shoved the warm air downward in the winter.

He smelled paper. Noisier than a library, though, but lots of reflected noise—important business being transacted. Reminded Jake of idle banter by worshippers before the Sunday morning service at First B. A sizable chunk of town folk attended the First Baptist Church, including him and Sophie and the Bairns. Almost like family. Yup, this bank sounded somewhere between a library hush and rowdy church gossip.

They invited Jake to pass through a waist-high gate in a fence that separated customers from bank officials' desks. Reminded him of the bar that separated spectators from lawyers and judges and such in a court room. He'd been in a courtroom once. All very official.

They design all this just to intimidate us poor dirt farmers? Darned impressive.

"This way, Mr. Hardt, if you please.
And polite.

"Won't you be seated? I'm Mr. Bannister, your loan officer. I understand you wish to speak of a loan."

Jake tugged on his tie, plopped his sheave of papers on the uncomfortable chair next to him and dropped into one just like it. Sophie made him memorize his next words along with a spittin' vow that he'd use 'em. "It is a pleasure to make your acquaintance, Mr. Bannister."

"Yes, well, likewise, I'm sure. You wish to speak of a loan?" This fancy pants stared at him over the top of his specs, and Jake had never seen a forehead so wrinkled. No doubt, he worried about a lot of important stuff.

The chairs were hard enough to tenderize his butt bones. Made a body sit up real straight. They must not want people looking for loans to get too comfortable. "Yup, sure do. Ah, yes, sir."

"Well, why don't you tell me about it?"

"Ah, you see, I'm a farmer," *did he just frown?* "and farming is changing. It's getting harder as we need to farm more acres to make ends meet." *Shit, this is not going in the right direction!* "Those of us who work the land need better tools to be more efficient."

"You wish to acquire a loan for the purchase of machinery."

"Uh, not exactly. I've invented a new machine to automatically bale hay or straw, and—"

The guy's tone changed. With the abruptness of Sophie's expression upon smelling hog manure on his boots in her kitchen.

"You want a loan to capitalize a new invention." Not a question. More like an accusation.

Jake picked up steam. Now he was on familiar turf. "Yessir! You see, this machine can bale faster 'n ten men. Runs off a steam. I call it a *loco-baler* cuz, see, it runs like a locomotive—on steam—get it? By baling fast with less manual labor, it reduces—"

"We usually don't grant loans for our customers to build untested and unproven inventions, but I am curious. How much do you need? And what do you propose to post as collateral?"

"Collateral? Sir?"

"Yes. Should you be unable to make payments on this loan, what do you offer to the bank in return?"

"Well, once this terrific machine starts selling, I'm prepared to offer a third of all my profits from each sale until the loan is paid in full. Including interest." Sophie had told him to say that last part. "Shouldn't take more 'n three or four sales. I just need a thousand dollars to build the first few units. I've already built a working model that was a big hit at the Lyon County Tractor Meet."

"A *thousand dollars* you say, Mr. Hardt? I *am* sorry. Future profits are not acceptable collateral for a loan, even if they were from a proven product. Now if..."

Jake tuned this dandy out. He rose, collected his drawings, turned, and slumped off. What would he tell Sophie? He felt small. Now, the S&L's interior no longer felt like a library or a church at all. More like a big old cemetery crypt built for one rich guy where nobody else was welcome to view his rotting corpse in one of them fancy coffins. How could they not see...?

Almost four hours later, including a watering stop, he pulled into the yard. Didn't even finish all the coffee. Not even bothering to change out of his go-to-town clothes, he clumped out to slop the hogs. He needed to get good 'n dirty. And that's when he thought of Walt's money under the planks in the barn. What if...?

They would lose the farm. Unless....

JAKE TORTURED HIMSELF. WHAT HAD HE DONE WRONG? HE had been met with hostility and derision from that damn loan officer even before he could present his wonderful idea. Was this how they treated everybody? Or had he made a mistake listing old Henry Bairns as a reference? Henry said he thought the baler seemed a wonderful invention, even though he was no farmer. But he was a prominent local businessman, and his reference could only help his case, couldn't it? Maybe that was wishful thinking. While Henry was no fan of Jake's, he was still his father-in-law.

The crops and the sale of a hog after their own meager expenses had only covered about a third of the loan payment to Silas for the month of June. Walt covered the rest—again. Walt said they dared not spend more. But he said he still had a few more bucks in his shoe to help out— "clean" money, aside from that nest egg they'd buried beneath the barn's floor. Jake was confused, and depressed. At least their sow had given birth to a dozen piglets.

Walt had already helped with the farm's payments since January. Now, though, Jake grew increasingly uncomfortable with exactly how Walt had acquired all that money, what with no visible means of support and all. Kind of like his own situation, but unlike Walt, Jake felt he was an expert at being honestly poor, and at staying that way.

Before heading out that morning, Sophie had suggested one last time that Jake ask her father either for a loan or for a job. But family and business could never be mixed. Everyone knew that. Except with Walt. And his inheritance. And....
Shit!

Besides, Henry worried more about his own situation lately. Something was going on that nobody talked about. Sophie and her mom danced around a topic they couldn't discuss on the party line where everybody listened to everything. But whenever Jake drove Sophie into town to visit her mom, they'd hunker down in a corner with hushed tones. And he knew better than to intrude. Something was going on.

❦

41

"**M**r. Malone, you have a call, sir. Long distance, all the way from Chicago, sir." The bellhop's breathless voice chirped with excitement. Must not get a lot of long distance out here. *Feckin' wilderness.*

"Very well." Finn hoisted his slender six-foot frame from the wicker lounger on the shaded porch of Worthington City's Dayton House. He flipped the kid a half-dollar. As he strolled around the corner, a plume of cigar smoke followed him. Suspected this call was not good news. Finn had given his boys instructions to handle his affairs in the city while he was on safari (he had read that word somewhere). He needed to focus out here.

"Speak to me."

"Mr. Malone, Captain Rock Boyle, CPD. You may recall we've traded favors. It's my turn. You on a party line at your end?" From where Finn stood at the house phone, he caught the hotel operator's eye through the open door behind the check-in desk. He waved a twenty, and she removed her headset.

"No, I am not, Captain. What ya got fer me, boy-o?"

"Your boys didn't want to give me your number, but I told 'em this might be hot. You decide. One of my dicks asked me why we got an inquiry about the modus operandi for one Aghaistín Leary from some hick sheriff in Iowa. I believe that's your boy Sticks. That interest you, sir?" Silence and static on the line popped and crackled as Finn digested this information.

"Mr. Malone? Still there, sir?"

"Yeh, mate. I am interested. Who's be askin' 'bout m'boy?" Finn heard paper shuffling before the police captain answered, "One William Kershaw, Sheriff of Lyon County, Iowa. Says his office is in a burg called Rock Rapids. Also says he's working a case involving the murder of one of his deputies." Pause. "But, um, one of the Boy Scouts in the division here passed on some info he found on file before I got wind of this. Sir, this could get sticky. Want me to do anything on this end?"

"Captain, suggest you get that Boy Scout on board. Follah?"

"Yes, sir. I follow. Anything else?"

"Not at the moment, Captain. Ya did good, boy-o." And he hung up with a small beckoning wave to the hotel operator, who came out to retrieve her windfall. Malone crushed the twenty up like a ball of waste paper and flipped it to her with a disarming smile. She caught it and blushed.

That feckin' copper's name keeps comin' up!

❧

42

Poor folks didn't possess a monopoly on worrying. Silas Hummel harbored suspicions. The air around his line of trucks in the open-ended tunnel where they offloaded at the base of Lester Klein's grain elevator raised a dripping sweat on Silas's neck and shoulders that trickled down his back. His discolored hat band was already sopping. The musty grain dust and chafe itched every square inch of exposed skin. But most of all, it smelled and felt like money.

Silas sold all the corn he could still grow with the dirt drying up faster than an August tomato left too long on the vine. But Lester Klein, here at the George Grain Elevator five miles up the road from his biggest farm, was paying him way too much.

"Now, why are you offering twenty cents on the bushel above market and forty cents above anyone else, Lester?

"What's the matter, Silas? I'm fetching a good price, and I'm passing some of that profit back to you. Plus, I don't want you selling to somebody else. Pretty simple—supply versus demand—and supply is drying up. As we've talked, though, the only condition is that you keep this to yourself. Now no more questions, okay, Silas?"

"Sure, I guess. No problem. I appreciate the good price, Les. It's just that—"

"You're welcome, my friend. Besides, you gotta pay for that fancy new ride I hear you bought from Henry Bairns, right?" *Does everybody know about that?*

As Lester handed over the cash—literally on a barrel head, counting the big bills out one-by-one—Silas sensed Lester glancing up at him after every fifth bill or so. He had come to a private decision that must have shown in his eyes. Silas picked up the thick bundle, folded it, and stuffed it into his most generous pocket—chest high—in the center of his bibs. Silas had transacted this type of business for fifty years. This arrangement was more than a little unusual, but business was business. Just seemed too, what? Conspiratorial? But theirs was a straight-up trade: cash for crop. Still, something scratched at Silas's conscience, besides the itchy dust. So be it. For now.

❦ 43 ❦

❦

Finn Malone relaxed in one of several cushioned wicker loungers on the far end of the wrap-around porch at Dayton House in Worthington. Deep in long afternoon shadows on the covered porch, he gnawed an unlit Charles Denby Invincible that claimed a bite-proof head. He'd mutilate any other cigar in a matter of minutes. Preferring a ten-cent pure Havana, he stuck with his Invincibles, not because they were half the price, but he grew annoyed at spitting out splintered stogies. He peered up at his lieutenant. Sticks Leary stood before him leaning against a porch post with one bony hip hoisted atop the porch's railing.

"Sticks, pay old man Bairns a friendly drop-by in George. I'm told he missed a payment on his up-front candy again this week." The Heeb sharks in Chi-town called it *vigorish*, or just *the vig*. "That feckin' Kraut agreed to pay our fees by installments, and he's layin' mental anguish on me soul. Aye, time to take the bloke to school."

"Sure, boss. How friendly?"

"Just tickle the maggot. He needs a reminder. Take the Duese." Sticks smiled. He loved that monster.

"And boy-o?"

"Yeh, boss."

"Lay off the product before yeh got no chompers left a'tall. Lookin' real ragged from the crystal, they are."

"Aye, boss."

The gunsel wheeled in slow motion like he didn't care. Finn knew he preferred the less friendly visits to clients, but it mattered little if he got to drive the grand roadster. He loved that car.

⚜

THE TIME HAD LONG PASSED WHEN HENRY BELIEVED Malone Investments was nothing more than an exclusive private lender. This, despite what Lester Klein told him in confidence at a George Chamber of Commerce meeting a year ago. He had trusted Lester's judgement who said he'd used Malone's money on more than one occasion to expand his grain elevator operation. But almost immediately, storm clouds swirled.

Malone's congenial veneer chipped the first time Henry was a day late. The man's true colors had since become all too obvious. Gangsters wore many colors, and this one, well, aside from the man's black shirt—with white buttons, no less —Henry realized too late that his own greed had clouded his vision. *If something appears too good to be true, it no doubt is. But I didn't see it.*

Henry knew he should have spotted the signs and steered clear. But lower-than-average interest rates drew him in, despite penalty clauses for every eventuality. And most telling, in retrospect, Malone Investments required several up-front fees to be paid before they even approved the loan.

Plus, none of the contract documents he signed offered any physical address, only a Chicago Post Office Box. He had been sure he'd turn around the troubled dealerships he was buying while at least staying afloat with their current sales. That's not what happened. And now....

For the past several weeks, Henry smoldered. After arriving at home late each afternoon, he watched the street shadows lengthen from his favorite chair in the front room through Hildie's lace sheers. Today was no exception. A few hours later, as he feared against all hope, Malone pulled up in front of his house! He had sheltered Hildie from all this madness, but that would be unlikely now. He saw his own dream car driven by the devil himself park on the street in front of his house. Two of its huge whitewall tires sank into his manicured grass next to the street. Henry's stomach churned. He thought he might vomit. That beautiful nine-teen-and-twenty-nine red and black Duesenberg Roadster with a beige suede top was Malone's personal auto.

Henry grabbed his coat and made his way down the front steps. It surprised him to see not Malone slide out of the cockpit, but that foul-mouthed weasel, Sticks Leary. He inter-rupted Leary's approach on the sidewalk leading up the gentle slope to his house, blocking his way halfway up. He tried to sound not cheery, but not confrontational either.

"Mister Leary, what brings you by?"

"Now that's funny, right there, boy-o. All polite 'n all, right here in front of yer fancy little neighborhood, out here in the chilly night air. Almost as if ya didn't want the missus ta meet me. I be offended." Leary snapped the back of his middle finger off his thumb onto Henry's chest with a forceful *thwack*.

"Look, Mister Leary, I don't transact business at home. I thought I made that clear to Mister Malone. What can I do for you?" He backed up half a step. *This kid needs a dentist.*

"Oh, now that's rich, ain't it? What can you *do?* Well, Finn tells me yer doin' okay on yer principle and original interest, but comin' up short on yer weekly carrying fees. Not very business-like. And *that's* not healthy."

With those words, the shorter Leary shifted most of his weight to his left foot in order to peer past Henry's right shoulder. The weasel cast a menacing gaze toward the house as someone inside turned on several lights. Henry shuddered as if an evil specter had just stomped on his future grave. What had he gotten himself—and now his family—into? And for what? An easy loan to expand his holdings?

"Okay, the problem is, Malone keeps escalating those *carrying fees* beyond our original agreement, and—"

"Shut it, maggot. First, it's *Mister* Malone. And second, we not be negotiatin' here, boy-o. Follah?"

The little man's voice had raised an octave to a tight screech, but kept its soft conversational tone as he leaned into and up toward Henrys face with his eyes bugging out even farther than usual. He came across far more frightening than if he had shouted. The man was demented. And his breath watered Henry's eyes! Leary wielded that stench like a weapon.

"Yes, I follow. Alright, alright. Please tell Mister Malone his payment will be forthcoming."

"*Forthcoming?* What the shite does *that* mean? You still owe us five hundred last Monday. The same next Monday, and every Monday, or..." Leary began slapping an imaginary baton held in his left hand into his right gloved palm while sneering at Henry. He threw another contemptible sneer toward the house and the now-visible silhouette of a woman in the front window. After about fifteen eternal seconds, and without another word, Leary wheeled on his heel and returned to the driver's side of the Duese. The auto rolled slowly away, like a hearse.

Shaken, Henry returned to the house, his shoulders slumped even more than when he had come outside five minutes earlier. His life had just grown dangerous, with no end in sight. Anger came next.

Henry Bairns had never been one to ask *anyone* for help.

I need help.

❧ 44 ❧

✣

"Sophie, can you make sense of this? I'm not sure what this means, but it looks serious."

She had poured a mid-morning mug of Old Judge for the two of them. Set them on the kitchen table, and plopped down next to him, her last six inches a controlled fall. As always. And every time she got up, she'd first scooch to the front of her chair. Sophie dared not even try rising until she had rocked back and forth at least three or four times to collect the right momentum. Then, at least one hand on something solid always assisted her escape from the same gravity that got her seated. Now on her feet again, she peered over Jake's shoulder with one hand resting on it.

"Let me see, sweetheart." Sophie took the watermarked and notarized page from him and read to herself the large ornate script at the top: *Foreclosure and Notice to Vacate*. Handwritten on the brown envelope from which it came, it said *Served June 19th, 1933 by Lyon County Sheriff William R. Kershaw, Officer of the Court.*

Sophie smiled and said, "Looks like Billy and Silas are having some fun. I wouldn't worry about it. We'll call Billy this weekend." Jake was brilliant in many ways, but paperwork was not one of them. He had never been a strong reader. Even when not distracted, he saw only what he wanted to see. He muttered, "Whatever you believe best, dear." He went right back to sketching something or other, now on the very envelope that had contained the fancy paper Sophie already folded small and stuffed into her bosom. *Bless his innocent heart. Time to attend to business.*

WASTING NO TIME, SHE GRABBED THE KEYS FOR THE TRUCK that hung by the mudroom door. Jake didn't notice. She drove the whole long way to the Law Enforcement Center in Rock Rapids. She left the beat-up old step-stool she used to get up into the truck back at the farm. This was going to end today.

Sophie parked the truck out front on Main and marched in, paying no attention to the boarded-up window and the office's darkened interior. Wobbled at a quick pace—for her —to stop in front of the sheriff's desk lit by a small lamp with a green glass shade. He was all alone. When he spotted her standing there, half in silhouette with the sun behind her, he stopped shuffling the papers in front of him and jumped up.

AT FIRST, SHERIFF BILLY RHETT KERSHAW THOUGHT IT was his dear deceased wife, Alice, somehow risen from the grave. But that wasn't possible. "Sophie! You here all by yourself? Are you okay?" He jumped up and walked around the desk on the verge of alarm. He remained off balance. Watched her reach into the neckline of her dress, an awkward maneuver since she favored a high collar, but he could tell it was for effect. He did not care. Sophie withdrew the folded eviction notice from her bosom vault. Unfolded it, and sailed it to the precise center of the sheriff's disarrayed desk, even though he now stood right next to her. A little too close.

"Billy, you need to be straight with me, and I mean right now. Please." She threw one of those doe-eyed expressions at him, something between a flirt and a threat. Billy could not hide his soft spot for this young lady, even though he was more than two decades older, never mind that she was now married. Reminded him too much of his own Alice, gone sixteen years next March 15th.

He didn't look at the heavy beige paper with the distinctive border of green scrollwork. He knew what it was. "Look, Sophie, I don't want to get between Jake and your dad—"

Her eyes widened and her jaw dropped before she recovered. "My *father?* But old Silas Hummel holds Jake's note." She retrieved the now-rumpled document from the desk and shook it in his face. Her husky half-whisper hissed at him. "Wait, you're telling me that my father put Silas up to this, and you're doing their dirty work?"

"I did not tell you that, Soph. Well, I didn't mean to. I shouldn't have." He cowered in front of her, tried to slump down to her height. Failed.

࿐

SHE TOOK PITY ON THE BIG BRUTE AFTER A DEEP BREATH. He was a good man. "Not your fault, Billy."

"Aw, I'll just come clean with Henry. Tell him you forced it out of me. He'll believe me!" She did not show her amusement, but thought, *He has such a charming smirk.*

Sophie further softened her tone, now that he was talking. "Any idea why he would do such a thing, Billy?"

"I think it had to do with getting you to give up the farm

life and come back to town. At least that was my impression. To his credit, Soph, your daddy thought if the farm failed, it would be a way for Jake to save face and come work for him at the dealership. Jake's a great mechanic. Henry says everybody knows that. Henry just wants to help you and Jake with a house in town. And you'd be closer to your momma."

"Oh, for goodness' sake. Of all the hair-brained schemes. He thinks killing Jake's dream is a way for him to *save face?* My father is still just trying to rescue his helpless little girl."

Billy issued a spontaneous chortle. "You? Helpless? You gotta be shi—, kidding me. You're a tougher interrogator than me, Miss Sophie. And I can more 'n hold my own with some pretty rough characters."

"Well, you can bet Father and I will have words. Thank you, Sheriff." Sophie knew he loved her calling him Billy. Now she wanted him to suffer—just a little—for agreeing to be part of this darn-fool contrivance. She limped off before he ingratiated himself further. Billy was a proud man. He followed her as she stormed out of his office. She spotted his shadow tailing her and growled, "Help me up into this darn-fool truck, Billy."

THE SHERIFF DIDN'T SAY A WORD. JUST DID AS HE WAS told. And was glad to do so. Sophie left him standing in a cloud of dust as she backed out, tire spinning, and headed south on Main, back toward George. *Old Henry doesn't have any idea the Hell that's about to rain down on him. Poor cuss. But that Sophie....*

THE OLD FARM TRUCK WASN'T SAFE OVER FORTY MILES PER hour. Carried Sophie from Billy's office to her parent's house in George in almost record time. A little-known law of nature: rage makes old farm trucks go faster. An even lesser-known law of nature: old farm trucks with bad hoses dare not strand enraged young women on the side of the road.

It took Sophie some effort to exit the truck in front of her parent's house. She slid down the side of the driver's seat where stuffing hung from the torn upholstery. The bottom of her corset caught on that cuss-ed tear, which did nothing to improve her mood. Without her step-stool, this was the only way to reach the ground without hurting her back and hip.

With the decent head of steam Sophie had stoked-up on the drive down from Rock Rapids, she made her way to the front door. Didn't bother knocking. Charged in, knowing her father would be home by now. Henry dropped his opened newspaper into his lap when he heard her distinctive gait. "Sophie, dear, to what do we owe this unexpected—"

"Don't you 'Sophie, dear' me, Father. I know all about your cockamamie scheme with Billy and Silas. This is what you are going to do. You'll call Silas. You'll tell him to back off this new foreclosure tack he's on at your behest. Then you'll call Billy and tell him to tear that notice right up. I left it with him. After that, you'll call Jake. You'll tell him the whole dad-blamed story about how you thought he'd *save face* by working for you *after* losing *his family's farm by your hand*. And you will apologize to that fine young man for all the heartache your malarkey has caused him over the last few days. Further, you will do *all* of this *today*. Or I might find it in my heart to forgive you about the time your youngest grandson is old enough to kick your conniving butt to Kingdom Come. Do we have a deal? *Father?*" Sophie spat out that last word like it tasted bitter on her tongue.

· · ·

HENRY NOW SAW JAKE'S TRUCK OUT FRONT FROM WHERE he sat.

"Sophie! You drove to Rock Rapids all by yourself? You could have—"

"Father!"

Henry Bairns, an accomplished businessman, looked up at her, sat there dumb-founded. He never imagined his little girl could be so... forthcoming. Instead of looking hurt, or insulted, or even chastised, he stood up so fast the newspaper took flight. The movement startled Sophie as her eyes darted back and forth between the falling paper and her father's eyes, but she stood her ground. Not that she feared her father would ever strike her. But he *was* an imposing figure.

Henry's face transformed. He stepped up to his little girl, a full foot shorter. Grabbed her by the shoulders, and said with a sudden grin blooming, "My little girl has grown up! Put 'er there, partner. Deal." He stuck his left hand out like he'd just sold a new car. Sophie extended her own good hand with slow deliberation, under a furrowed brow, and they shook on it.

This was a high compliment. Father was a master negotia-tor, and she had just earned his respect—*on his playing field!* Then she realized he had designed this compliment to disarm her. Nothing doing.

"Fine. But I'm still upset, and will be for at least... another day or two." She rewarded him with just a small smile. "Look, Father, I know your heart is in the right place, but for mercy's sake, you should *not* manipulate *family*. We're not *customers*, after all. Promise me you'll never do something like this again, especially to the fine man who is my husband, and your son-in-law. The truth is, I spared his innocent heart from your little scheme. If he knew about this, he'd have been here himself. While he respects you, you might not be wearing a smile right now if he had discovered this on his own."

"Jake's a lucky man, Soph. I do promise. I should have known better. And Heaven help anyone who crosses the wrong side of *your* path." She thought, *Lord, he has a winning smile, to be sure. Better than Billy's.*

Then, he grew serious. "Sophie, as long as we're leveling with each other here, and this is not an excuse, you're just not safe out there."

"Oh, Father, I—"

"Sophie, *listen*. You do not understand." The sudden solemnity in his voice, and the granite expression that had transformed his handsome face in an instant, gave her cause for new concern.

"What do you mean? Safe from what? We're—"

"There are forces at work—"

"*Forces?* Father, what on earth is going on? What else aren't you telling me?"

The subsequent look of anguish on his stalwart face pierced her heart. Anger forgotten, he had genuinely frightened her. She had backed this proud man into a corner, And for that, she felt some shame.

"Sophie, I'm in trouble—financially. I owe money to some fearsome folks. I must ask you this. Have you seen any strangers visiting the farm in recent days? Anyone you don't know?"

Only a second or two of worried thought retrieved the troubling memory of the hard man who presented himself as a traveling salesman. "Just one, maybe a week ago. The man sounded friendly, but there was something about his eyes. And no salesman I ever encountered drove a car that grand or dressed that well, like a big-city slicker, maybe.

"Dear, what kind of car was it?"

"It was huge. Red and black with a soft beige top. Had the longest hood of any car I've ever seen with lots of horns on each front fender."

"A Duesenberg?"

"I think so, Father, like the kind you used to dream about, you know? I thought of you when I first saw it. He asked if I was alone. Can you imagine? For a moment, I feared for my safety. That's when I told him my husband and his cousin were due in from the field at any moment for lunch. Funny name, too. I can only recall his first name. It was unusual. I remember, it was Finn—"

"Malone?"

"Yes! How—?" She stopped when she saw the strongest man in her life—until three minutes ago—transformed into a frightened child.

۞

HENRY FREE-FELL INTO HIS ARM CHAIR, LIKE A BLACK ROCK dropping into a dismal swamp. "Oh, alright. No worries then." The sudden thin syrup of his sing-song voice, combined with his deflated demeanor, shocked her. His face grew ashen. "Sorry, dear. Now I need to make a few telephone calls to fulfill my promise to you, and to myself."

"But—"

"Later, dear. I will explain everything later. But for now, can I do anything else for you? No? I'm glad we talked." He was now extremely distracted, he stood up with some difficulty and hustled her to the door like a nervous corpse. Endless scenarios flashed through her mind. All of them ended in imagined disaster. He led her out to the sidewalk, knowing she'd need a boost up into the truck. And that was that. Didn't say goodbye or offer her a peck on the cheek. Nothing. Slammed her door, walked around the rear of the truck back toward his catacomb. He had never behaved like this with her before.

Sophie's state of mind edged toward madness. *Dear Lord, I need to talk with my Jake.*

❦

Charles-Royce Hugo's parents denied him nothing, except the use of his legs. An auto accident seven years ago left him a paraplegic—his spine severed. He was the only one injured—a source of guilt for his parents. Charles-Royce told himself it was not their fault he'd never walk again. But he retained full use of his upper torso. Now fifteen, Charles-Royce clung to an upbeat attitude from the seat of his wheelchair, and filled his life with amateur radio, his surrogate for a real childhood.

Self-taught and proficient with Morse code, he owned and operated a sophisticated radio station at his parent's bungalow in Lakehurst, New Jersey. They lived near the naval air station where his father worked as a civilian contractor. Charles-Royce watched other kids his age playing stick ball under the streetlights from his bedroom window. But his wheelchair didn't translate well to streets with drainage ditches and uneven ground. Instead, he watched. And he listened. To his radios. Mostly at the edge of night when the frequencies he most enjoyed really opened up.

One cool and clear twilight, Charles-Royce encountered some suspicious radio traffic, in code, and in German. *Someone is hiding something.* His mother was American, but his father's family immigrated from Germany in the late 1890s. Because they often spoke German at home, and because he could copy Morse code at a lightning-fast forty words-per-minute, he understood the traffic, albeit cryptic. As a conscientious citizen, he called the FBI.

✺

ONE OF THE FBI's SISTER AGENCIES AT THE US Department of Justice had published a Law Enforcement Bulletin to be on the lookout for anything mentioning the phrase *Black Gold*. The Newark, New Jersey FBI field office then contacted the ATF agent listed in the LEB, one Milford Langford Eubanks, on assignment in Rapid City, South Dakota. A secure telephone interview between Agent Eubanks and Mr. Hugo took place the following day, with permission from, but the exclusion of, Charles-Royce's parents. The young man sat in his radio "shack" in his bedroom. The dapper federal agent reposed at his desk in the federal building in Rapid City, South Dakota, eager to conduct this interview.

"Tell me what you heard, Mr. Hugo."

"Please, call me Charles-Royce. Well, sir, I knew I was listening to proficient fists—"

"Fists? And please just call me Lang."

"Okay, Lang. A fist is someone who transmits code—"

"As in Morse Code—"

"Right. You can tell a lot about a guy by his fist, his style of keying code and the device he uses. For instance, though more modern devices now exist, like semi-automatic iambic —or dual vertical squeeze—paddles, these guys were both using old-school straight keys, that is, a single horizontal paddle that is fully manual. You know, like in the old Westerns. I could tell. Straight keys are slower but require more skill. Tells me they're older guys. Like you, maybe."

The young man couldn't see Lang smiling over the phone.

"Plus, they still both ripped along at thirty-plus words-per-minute and never made a mistake, which tells me they've been doing code for a long time. I also heard a formality to their transmissions. Very efficient. Not a single extra tone. Almost no pauses between their exchanges. I'd guess military or ex-military coders. And I'd guess English isn't their first language, but not just because they used German. They knew each other's fists pretty well, which means they communicate with each other a lot. Probably on a *sked*, that is, a predetermined schedule on a radio frequency and contact interval agreed-to ahead of time."

"You ascertained all of that from listening to a series of dots and dashes on your radio, Charles-Royce?" Lang didn't need to feign admiration for this young man's skill and insights.

"Oh sure, Lang. But phonetically, we call 'em dits and dahs. I chew the fat—that is, I enjoy lengthy conversations—with lots of guys over in the United Kingdom and Europe. And from a lot of states all the way to the west coast. Even connected with a guy in Hawaii once. I'm guessing both these guys are European, or recent immigrants, but they were both broadcasting from within the states. And given their very different signal strengths and directional vectors, they broadcast from different parts of the country.

"Lang, I just happened across their frequency when I was spinning the dial looking to connect with someone, anyone. By convention, they're supposed to use only the bottom one-hundred kilocycles of each amateur radio band, or frequency range, for code. But they worked code on a little-used part of the *voice* spectrum on the eighty-meter band. That's a long-distance band between 3.5 and 4.0 megacycles that, with the right conditions, can reach a few thousand miles. Not illegal to send code on a voice frequency or anything, but it's kind of unusual. All together, Lang, this was just way too weird to be on the up-and-up.

"Oh, and these frequencies require a serious antenna, like an elevated horizontal wire over a hundred feet long. With the right weather, you can really bounce your signal off the reflective ionosphere fifty to four-hundred miles up. And if you pick the right time of day—because the sun influences radio waves—you can talk to any other serious ham just about anywhere in the world. Well, almost."

Lang appreciated the young man's hyperbole, but the kid had convinced him long-distance radio communications were possible and practical. He had skills. Charles-Royce continued. "Eighty-meter is one of the bands where you hang out when you want to communicate long distances."

"You divine a great deal from these radio signals. Any chance you can tell me where I might find these two suspicious, ah, hams?"

"Sure, in a general sense. Based on signal strength, time of day, and the orientation of my own antenna, I can tell you this with some confidence. The powerful signal, with no skips —meaning he was really too close for this frequency—is north of my QTH, my location here. Could be up toward Newark. That's NG2AO. But the other signal, based on propagation behavior for that time of day on eighty meters, I would guess is way west of here. Say, between five hundred and fifteen hundred miles out, and likely farther south than north. That's the guy using the W2MQX call sign."

"Like Chicago?"

"Naw, I'd say farther south."

"Iowa?"

"Let me check a map and a propagation chart." Lang waited for almost ten seconds. "Yup, Iowa's a definite maybe."

"Excellent. You copied down the entire exchange, right, Charles-Royce?"

"Oh, sure. Already in my logbook. Including date, time, frequency, and text copied, along with signal strengths and some other stuff I'd guess you don't care about, like gray wave propagation, and—"

"Right." Lang smiled. This young man continued to impress him. "What did they, ah, say, so to speak?"

Charles-Royce said, "I'll translate this into English and expand on the Q signals, or ham shorthand, which wouldn't mean anything to you. Here goes..."

Lang poised one of his perfect pencils over his omnipresent leather-bound notebook as he propped the phone's earpiece between his ear and left shoulder.

"W2MQX this is NG2AO, Flour in the kitchen?'

"2AO this is W2MQX, Yes. Start baking bread.'

"Label?'

"Schwarz Goldmedaille.'

"Spice?'

"On hand.'

"Delivery to all bakeries?'

"End of summer. Latest.'

"Alt-hotter recipe?'

"Imminent.'

"Tree blossoming.'

"Shade good.'

"Dit dit.'

Charles-Royce took a breath before continuing. "That last phrase is a bit of radio humor used by veteran operators, in English-speaking countries, anyway. But it translates to any language anywhere based on worldwide ham tradition. Remember the old jingle, 'Shave and a haircut… two bits?' Two dits? Get it, Lang?"

"Yes, brilliant, Charles-Royce. I assume the German phrase you left in there means—"

"Yup. Black Gold. But I have no idea what that or the rest of it means."

"Charles-Royce, I congratulate you. I cannot divulge what I've gleaned from this dialogue, but rest assured, my young friend, you may have just helped buttress our nation's security. For that, I thank you. Now you must keep this to yourself. This is a matter of utmost gravity. You dare not even share this with your parents. Do you understand, and do you agree, Honorary Agent Hugo? If so, raise your right hand and respond in the affirmative." Lang smiled as he dabbed the moisture from his forehead with his pressed kerchief. He grasped the implications of this cryptic message, and it terrified this seasoned field agent.

The kid's enthusiasm grew to epic proportions. His prepubescent voice broke as he squeaked across at least two octaves, "Yes, sir! I do!"

How could one not feel great affection for this young man? Their liaison would continue throughout the summer of 1933.

❧ 46 ❧

enry drove straightaway to Rock Rapids for a visit
with Sheriff Kershaw, the late hour
notwithstanding. It was now all too clear that Finn
Malone was a ruthless gangster. Threats, intimidation, extortion, and God knows what else were this man's stock-in-trade.
It was time to seek a very different conversation with the
sheriff. Maybe it was also time to share his personal burden
with others who might help. If Billy wasn't at his office, he'd
visit his bungalow.

Henry had never been to the Rock Rapids Law Enforcement Center, other than reading about it in the Lyon County
News. Billy had always visited him at his dealership. He was
underwhelmed. The place looked like a half-closed half-vandalized general store. His confidence rose after he
entered. Spotted the barred cells in the dim light, the gun
rack, and Sheriff Kershaw consulting with a uniformed
deputy who appeared as weathered as the sheriff.

"Mister Bairns? To what do we owe the pleasure? Oh, this

is my newest deputy, Dwight Spooner. Dwight, Mr. Bairns is the most prominent businessman in George."

"Sir, an honor. Bairns Motors, right?"

"Ah, yes, Deputy. A pleasure. I read of your appointment in The News. Welcome." Henry shifted his gaze back toward Billy. "Sheriff, might we speak in confidence for a moment?"

"Of course. Won't you join me in the fish tank, ah, the private office I never use?" He smiled at the small joke. Henry did not. Dwight tossed a casual half salute toward Henry and made himself scarce. He decided to walk a beat.

Settled in the glass-walled office with the door closed and the overhead lights on, Billy stood behind the desk. Henry stood in front. The sheriff spoke first, appealing with up-turned palms. "Mr. Bairns, I'm sorry I got you in trouble with Sophie. It's just that—"

"Billy, don't worry about that. Finn Malone, who *is* this fellow?"

"Who, Mr. B?"

"I borrowed some money. To expand my business. I heard of this Chicago financier—Malone Investments. Companies like Malone's—a lot fewer of them these days—lend money to promising businesses at reasonable rates. Or that's what I thought. Turns out this fellow makes more demands all the time, and backs them up with intimidation, or, I suspect, much worse. Now, instead of allowing me to pay back the money I owe him, he's levying outrageous *surcharges*. And now that I'm falling behind his escalating demands, which are impossible to meet, he's threatening to call it all due. If I don't produce the amount of the original loan, plus all his additional charges by the end of the month, he's going to take Bairns Motors from me.

"But worse, Billy, while nobody's laid on hands as of yet, he's threatened me and my family in no uncertain terms. He sent his muscle to my house last night, and he's even been to

Jake and Sophie's farm. Caught Sophie alone, scared the living daylights out of her. That's the long and short of it. You are the only person I've told. I am in way over my head here."

"He threatened *Sophie? Sumbitch!* Where do I find him, Mr. B—Henry?"

"Billy, it's not that simple, I'm afraid. He employs a small army of thugs. One sneaky little bastard named Sticks Leary is always with him. A nasty little piece of work. Know him?

"I might, Henry. These boys real Irish-types, are they?"

❧ 47 ❧

Sophie smiled. Though she couldn't yet see it, or so Jake thought, Walt had saved their bacon since January. Or that Walt had seeded some financing for Jake's full-size loco-baler. Nor did she know Jake struck out with the S&L in Worthington City a month earlier. When she asked, he said the loan would take some time. In fact, she *had* seen through his ruse, but did not press it. A man's pride is a sensitive and fragile thing. Especially Jake's.

JAKE WORRIED ABOUT WHERE WALT'S MONEY CAME FROM, that he hadn't grasped the specifics. He suppressed that anxiety, stuffed it down deep. Now this week, Sophie's dad discontinued his negativity campaign. Jake did not understand Henry's dislike for him to begin with, and grew even more perplexed at this sudden cessation of hostilities.

Sure, he admitted to some blind spots, especially for business. That's why it made sense to attend the two-year J. Hildebrand College of Business over in Rapid City. But there was no money or time, and everybody told him that was a fool's errand, anyway. Nobody articulated why, other than with generalizations that made no sense. Other than the money. What the hell was he working hundred-hour weeks for, anyway? They barely afforded food, much less made any progress.

And then Walt confided in him that his past might catch up with him. While working up in Rapid City last winter, he'd fallen in with a rough crowd. The jug wasn't Walt's only vice. Gambling caught him and would not let go. He won some money, but lost a lot to others. In return, he had done some favors. Told Jake he didn't want to know. Since then, he'd left town after town before coming to live with Sophie and him, arriving on foot, no less, wearing all his worldly belongings.

And if those revelations weren't shocking enough, ever since Jake had been indebted to Silas Hummel, and his father before him. the old man had always taken a hard line on his loan payments, much more so recently. Jake suspected Silas cozied more up to Henry lately. And, well, Henry thought little enough of Jake, didn't he? But now Silas softened, just like Henry, and the sheriff called to tell them the eviction proceedings were all a big mistake.

What in the world is going on?

48

T he small farm looked like an Amish post card—all white, red and green that was now brown, but absent the apparatus and odors of keeping live-stock. Dan Rustywire—everyone called him Chief, or Chief Dan—didn't raise or eat animals. But he loved and respected his horse, Kona, which meant *friend* in Lakota Sioux.

Young Chief Dan didn't much like most men, especially white men. There were too many. They had done his people no favors—quite the opposite. How much of America's native culture did the white man bother to learn, much less respect? How much of the language did he speak, or even try, before he dismissed it as irrelevant, as little more than heathen drib-ble? And how legal was his rape of the land by mass-slaugh-tering bison just to starve the red-skinned savage?

He killed our children, raped our women, murdered our defenders, before he took our land as if he had a god-given right to do so. And he forbad teaching our true heritage to his children. Even overlooking all of that not-so-ancient history, how much of the white man's culture still dismisses our nation's native history in favor of a fabricated history that still defines America to this day? Its religions, holidays, persecution, slavery...? The victor of any conflict writes, rewrites, or erases history.

But Jake Hardt befriended Chief, respected him *and* the dream. Unlike most white men. Jake was a friend. He respected the old ways and always asked questions. Yup, he could be friends with this white man.

Chief Dan's white mother of Irish affluence married his father, a tribal elder of the Lakota Sioux from North Dakota. Their respective families then ostracized both for marrying "outside." His mother had her own money. Both of his parents made every attempt to preserve their son's Lakota heritage.

That did not mean Chief wore his hair in a long pony tail, or exploited beads and such. Most of the time, he just wore dungarees and a chambray shirt, leather belt and boots. But no hat. Ever. In fact, he looked more like a town cowboy than a country Indian. Chief shared his father's coal-black hair, burnished skin, and high cheekbones, but with his mother's Irish curls atop a slender nose and face. He looked... different. Exotic. And that was okay with him. He celebrated differences *and* commonalities. He considered himself all-American for all those reasons. Mother came from money and Chief inherited her little-used country estate, small but bountiful. At least it was.

Though a neighbor to Jake and Sophie, Dan did not socialize. But like Jake, he wasn't afraid to field his visions when asked about them. Though everyone called him Chief, he was never a tribal elder himself. He didn't encourage that moniker, nor did he discourage it. Truth be told, he rather liked it, even though that would mortify his now-estranged tribe. He wrote his own history while preserving theirs.

CHIEF'S MOTHER WAS A PIONEERING WOMAN, BUT NOT OF the prairie. Annie Cavendish—before she became Annie Rustywire—was a child of the sea before she fell in love with her *Injun*, the love of her life—Bear Rustywire, Chief's father. She even named her sailing yacht a most fitting Lakota name: Taku Skanskan. It fit: a capricious and chaotic spirit who is master of the four winds and the four-night spirits - Raven, Vulture, Wolf, and Fox.

Because Annie Rustywire loved sailing at night, Bear learned to love it. On long offshore voyages, nights on the open ocean were their favorites. Bear and Annie could not have been more different, yet they grew to be more compatible and more in love than most couples. Their differences, and an abiding admiration for those differences, defined their passion for one another, for life. They passed that universe of contradictions on to their only son before they were both reported lost at sea while sailing aboard Taku Skanskan with their crew of three. Chief had never been very close to his parents, but his fascination and respect for them knew no bounds.

IN HIS BARN, CHIEF LABORED ON HIS OWN VISION. NOT FOR monetary gain—he needed little, and his inheritance left him quite comfortable—but to explore all the world offered, like Annie and Bear. They had bequeathed to him that gift of curiosity and the means to pursue it. His airship gave him a unique perspective of his world. For that, he overflowed with gratitude. He still wrote his own history in honor of his parents.

Chief grew no crops on his forty acres other than a large

subsistence garden. In better seasons, when its table crops proved plentiful, his parents had shared the fruit of that garden with neighbors. Now his garden withered. It seemed the land was angry, and not without cause. Chief prayed daily to Wakan Tanka—the Great Spirit—to offer thanks, to remain humble and true to nature's balance. He often prayed for guidance in using his talents to battle imbalance because of trickster spirits. But he vowed to always do so with honor and dignity.

He'd converted his gigantic barn into a hangar with what he guessed must be the tallest and widest set of doors in the Midwest. The Rustywires had no need for a haymow. And like him, Kona needed little. Consequently, the interior of the barn was cavernous. His beloved dirigible employed hot air in a huge triple-sectioned silk bag overhead to develop lift. A pedal-driven propeller provided forward thrust, and a set of overlapping horizontal sails offered auxiliary vertical thrust. The sails also allowed the airship a degree of controlled descent—in theory—should the hot air bag suffer a catastrophic failure.

During flight, the hull of a fourteen-foot flat-bottom "boat" with a seven-foot beam hung below the hot air bag that some would describe as a chubby torpedo almost fifty feet long. This bag provided enough lift to skid the airship out of the barn, and featured Chief's custom design for droopy "wings" on either side—toward the bag's top. They wouldn't inflate with additional hot air until the airship was free of the barn-slash-hangar. These voluminous wings provided extra lift and must be deflated before skidding back into the barn post-flight. They were deflated separately from the main hot air bag for rapid descents if necessary.

While the boat's bottom was flat from side-to-side, it sloped upward at the bow and stern. It appeared smooth except for countless tiny scratches. A light wooden frame supported the thin silk skin of the main bag overhead from inside and below until hot air filled and inflated it. When there was no fire to plump her up, you could see hints of her skeletal structure inside, also suggesting faint shadows here and there from an intricate web of twine cross-strutting inside—except immediately above the firebox's chimney. She sat on her hull's bottom when the lightweight firebox on deck was cold. Spider-like stanchions, reinforced with more twine struts, kept the silk structure—that contained heated air during flight—and its internal frame from falling onto the boat hull that Chief called *the car.* The entire affair seemed... precarious.

But when Chief stoked the flames in the sleek firebox amidships, a flue-constrained stove pipe directed the heat up into the torpedo-shaped bag overhead. Packets of wood chips automatically fed into the firebox as needed—they burned fast and hot. With enough of this fuel onboard for a two-hour flight, the buoyancy of this hot air bubble—lighter than the surrounding air—lifted the car's flat bottom enough to allow her to slide across the straw-strewn barn floor. Chief would then sit on a bench in the car, aft of two pairs of bicycle-style pedals which powered a six-foot three-bladed propeller aft. Its vanes also comprised sails of silk stretched across a hardwood exoskeleton—the only hard-wood in the entire craft. Chief had constructed the rest of the airship from light but stout cedar. The vertical prop, as wide side-to-side as the overhead hot air bag, nestled between the bottom of the bag above and the ground below when moored inside the barn, with just a few inches to spare.

Behind this sail-vaned propeller hung two barn-door-size rudders of ultralight balsa-wood slabs. They directed the prop's air for steering the ship. Pivoting on vertical cedar shafts through their centers, the pilot controlled them via thin flexible wires led around pulleys to the hollow-spoked ship's wheel in the cockpit.

Once out of the barn, Chief pulled a lever that would further open the stove pipe's flue—or hot-air control valve. The increased flow of heated air into the overhead bag. Flaps between the main bag and the droopy wings opened or closed via control lines led to the cockpit. Opening these flaps caused the auxiliary "droopy wings" of the airship to inflate, and they would gain altitude. He might choose to deploy the outboard sails for further maneuverability and lift, or he might not. If so, a system of fine wires and small winches in the cockpit at the ends of the pilot's bench allowed him to spread these sails like a dragonfly's wings.

⁂

JAKE MOST OFTEN WORKED ALONGSIDE HIS COUSIN WALT on maintenance tasks around the Hardt place, like fixing fences. Not that Walt needed constant supervision, although the slightest diversion would distract him. He'd say he was thinking of numbers between Aces and Kings. They needed some chicken wire to repair the fencing around the hen house. Jake boarded his old stake-side truck and rattled four miles south on County 14 to the Rustywire place.

Chief Dan lived there alone in the enormous house left to him by his parents, who he'd lost, just like him. Chief always had most everything on hand. And he seemed friendly enough, even though he did not socialize with anyone—at all, at least not intentionally. This was pretty clear after just a few not unpleasant encounters in Marvin's store in town and a couple of amiable conversations sitting on Marvin's store-front porch. Jake would sit down, nod, and after nodding back, after a few pleasant words, Chief would leave. Just like that. A few Thursdays like that convinced Jake that Chief was likable, but very private.

Yep, Jake liked Chief. As he rolled into his yard, he spotted the young man just walking toward his strange behemoth of a barn. He approached, extended his hand and greeted Chief with one of the few Lakota Sioux words the Indian had taught him, "Hau." Chief responded with a grin, "Taŋyáŋ yahí. Let me show you something, Jake."

They weren't even inside yet when Jake spotted the monstrosity lurking up in the shadows of this barn's cavernous bowels. As he observed Chief's huge contraption, it appealed to his own airy sense of wonder. The entire affair reminded him of something both reminiscent of the past and in anticipation of the future. He forgot why he had come.

"Chief, you're a genius! An aerial vessel? Does it fly?"

"Of course it flies, white man. You don't think I'd go to all this trouble for a fancy decoration that fills my entire barn, do you?"

Chief took pride in his mixed heritage, and to call his friend *white man* delivered a not-so-subtle jibe as a reminder. "Want a ride, Jake?"

Well, that was like taunting a pissed-off bull with a red flag drenched in heifer-juice. "Hell, yeah!" *And I accuse old cousin Walt of becoming distracted. He'll understand, won't he? Besides, I'm the boss. Now Sophie understanding? A different ball of twine, right there....*

"Then let's stop jackin' our jaws and go punch a hole in the sky. Okay, *kona*?" Jake tucked that word, meaning *friend* in Lakota Sioux, away for future reference. He was trying.

"Hey, isn't that the name of your horse?"

"Yup. I guess I now have two friends." Chief smirked and slapped Jake's back, a little harder than he intended.

On the car's side, Jake noticed two words painted in small letters: *Cik'ala So'ta*. When Chief saw Jake scratching his head at the words, he explained, "In Lakota, that means *Little Piece of the Sky.*"

"What are the pedals for? Whose bicycle did you butcher?"

"They get us out of the barn and headed in the right direction. I can operate this little ship by myself, but it's easier with crew." Wink.

The top of the car's low railings were less than two feet from the barn's floor. They stepped over and onto her deck, but they hunched down to avoid bumping their heads on the hot air bag and its frame close overhead. The entire affair felt flimsy, like it might all just break. After Chief explained the necessity for ultra-lightweight construction as hot air could only lift limited weight, he said, "Have a seat."

Jake plopped down onto the low bench just behind the pedals. He noticed a vertical sprocket in the middle on a horizontal shaft that connected both sets of pedals. A chain over that sprocket disappeared into the deck. Chief saw Jake's appreciative smile. Told him the pedals, chain and gears to a shaft just below the deck drove the big propeller behind him. The bottom third of the spoked steering wheel also disappeared into the deck at their feet—for clearance, Jake guessed.

Chief went about retrieving a bundle of packets wrapped in newsprint and tied with light twine from a hatch in the deck beside what had to be a firebox amidships. He accumulated a small pile of those cylindrical packets by the stove's door that faced aft. He then stacked those packets in a chute that fed down toward the firebox. Chief had wrapped the stove in what looked like yards of copper tubing. Jake observed it all with keen interest—nay, naked fascination.

The chimney disappeared up into the bottom of the bag less than six feet above the deck through a hole thrice the diameter of the smallish stove pipe. The firebox occupied a good portion of the car's deck amidships forward of the helm. Chief already had kindling glowing and the start of a good flame. He tossed one of the cylindrical packets into the box, and the flames flared. He explained those packets contained wood chips that burned hot and fast. As the flames flared and a few more packets gravity-fed down into the upper portion of the firebox, Chief shut its door. The heat quickly plumped up the bag overhead. He told Jake, with no small amount of pride in his voice, about his additional plans for Little Sky.

"You see this thin copper tubing around the fire box? That leads back to those horizontal tubes aft" He pointed to the rear of the car beyond the transom where the horizontal pipes pinched, then flared." Some day soon, heat from the stove will turn water from a reservoir atop the firebox into pressurized steam. That will be directed into those tubes which I'll enclose in an insulated jacket. The steam jets will provide additional forward thrust to help us peddlers. But I haven't yet figured out how to make all that work in a light enough package."

"And that'll enable Little Sky to go faster?"

"Naw, but it could enable longer distance travel with less peddling. Still needs a heap of work. What do you think?"

"Like I said, Chief, genius!"

Chief knew of Jake's affinity for steam power, and that nobody in Lyon County knew more about that than him. He'd need some serious help to get that part of his design to work. Jake was about to comment when a sudden movement jarred the car's deck as it shifted under the now-lighter-than-air bag overhead. His sudden look of panic amused Chief.

"Relax, white man, that's just Little Sky's version of fore-play. The car is settling into place as we're now suspended under the bag instead of sitting on the floor holding it up."

Now, the somewhat suspended car jittered in response to

their every movement—like a small boat afloat, but still partially aground. Chief settled onto the padded bench to Jake's right and grabbed a spoke on the starboard edge of the steering wheel between them. "Let's see if we have enough lift to sled out the door." Jake was ready to be out of the barn. He now felt waves of heat radiating off the firebox and smelled hot metal. Lightweight construction, silk and wood and twine in close proximity to open flames, and the prospect of leaving the ground in this thing? What could possibly go wrong? Exhilarating!

Both men peddled—slowly at first. Then they applied more energy. Nothing much happened, other than the wind-vaned prop now revolving behind them generated a low-throated warble as it drew and expelled air. They could feel the turbulence it caused as it swirled around the barn's interior. Some straw on the floor took to flight, but not them.

Jake shivered in anticipation. Chief warned they didn't want to generate too much lift too fast or they'd never exit the barn. He reached through the slender spokes of the wheel to fiddle with a knob on the side of the post to which the wheel's hub and horizontal axle were mounted. He called that post the binnacle, whatever that meant. Jake guessed it was a nautical term. He'd heard a few stories of Chief's seagoing mom, Annie. Chief explained that the linkage to that knob controlled the chimney's flue, and throttled how much heat found its way from the firebox and up into the bag. He pulled on the knob a fraction of an inch with two fingers. For precise control, he rested his wrist on the padded bracket affixed to his side of the binnacle—the pilot's side. A small ship's compass sat on top.

"Let's try for more thrust. Now peddle wakinyan—like thunder beings."

This time they felt the car's bottom scraping across the barn floor as they accelerated toward the double doors swung wide. Jake noticed the doors behind them were wide open too. With less than a few feet of clearance atop and on either side of the overhead bag, they slid forward. Just as the scraping sound from below ceased, the airship found open air. Jake felt the slightest sensation of vertical acceleration. They were flying!

He couldn't wait to tell Sophie of his excellent excuse for not finishing the repairs to the chicken coop. But would it be a good enough excuse? Walt would slap him on the back for seizing this opportunity, because he'd already be napping on two end-to-end bales in the haymow, seizing his own opportunity, probably dreaming about aces and kings.

❦

49

Three months ago, Walt recalled one of his least favorite days in recent memory spent with a most interesting fellow in the unlikely employ of Uncle Sam. Serious men had pulled Walt out of his almost-favorite Rapid City casino, Black Jack's, most unceremoniously, while he was on a winning streak at the poker tables. They even smelled like feds. They must all use the same soap. But he hadn't been rousted in a while and had started to feel down-right anonymous. At the time, he thought he might even get a free lunch out of the deal.

Walt had heard the minuscule Federal Building in Rapid City, South Dakota, was a most unimpressive pile. He was not disappointed. Rumor suggested it had been a stable in the not-too-distant past. Still featured the faint scent of road apples under the stronger odor of fresh paint and turpentine.

Milford L. Eubanks, diminutive in stature, presented a striking figure. Walt knew of Eubanks by reputation. People in his circles talked. He was said to be a meticulous field investigator bestowed of a middle-management title within the Bureau of Alcohol, Tobacco, and Firearms, an agency within the US Department of Justice, along with its fledgling sister agency, the FBI. ATF had risen to prominence since the beginning of Prohibition thirteen years earlier. Eubanks was a senior special supervisory something-or-other.

Agent Eubanks seemed more like an obsessive accountant than a top government cop. Told Walt he had learned, almost as if by serendipity—he didn't believe *that* was likely—of an insignificant item in the Lyon County News, a rural Northwest Iowa newspaper. Someone within the DOJ had directed him to an innocuous announcement of holy matrimony. One Jacob Hardt had taken one Sophiena Bairns as his bride. Her family name rang a small but insistent bell in Lang's mind. That was his preferred moniker—Lang. Said they listed Jacob Hardt on some government score card as a "known associate" (that is, a relative) of one Walter Weller. Eubanks had explained that the groom had sent his cousin a wedding invitation, General Delivery, to the Rapid City Post Office. From there, it became a simple surveillance job. In retrospect, Walt remembered wondering, *Is he trying to impress me with his prowess as an investigator? I wonder why?*

Iowa remained a frontier region regarding Prohibition. Citizens out here treated Volstead as more an act of volunteerism or religious fervor than as the law of the land. At least for the time being. And the hooligans that slaked their thirst could spot Gs coming over the horizon. Since the rule of law was Lang's Holy Grail, to a fault, Walt recognized what was coming.

He couldn't see the high ceiling cloaked in deep shadow. He guessed there would be rough-cut beams up there. Two lights hung just six feet above floor level. The rectangular table that separated him from this dandy looked like a relic from the last century, like beat-up old kitchen furniture. The cops must've snagged this beauty from a local auction. This snappy G-Man looked *really* out of place.

"Why am I here, Mister—"

"Eubanks, Mr. Hardt. Milford Langford Eubanks. You'd honor me by calling me Lang." Of course, Walt already knew who sat across from him, but giving that away wouldn't be any fun. He'd seen a headline with a picture somewhere. Not to say this guy was a glory hound or anything.

"Okay, Lang. Why am I here? I've done nothing wrong."

The shit-green walls in that smelly "interview room" screamed of cheap paint. Just meant to cover the planked walls of this six-foot by nine-foot windowless shoe box, about the size of a horse stall, maybe.

Walt patiently watched this unusual little man unwrap a gray silk hanky he'd withdrawn from his right inside breast pocket with his long bony fingers like it contained the crown jewels or something. Unfolding it on the table in front of him revealed four yellow-orange pencils, all sharpened and of identical length. All the erasers had seen identical use. Walt took pride in his own fastidious attention to detail at the tables—poker, roulette, *and* interrogations. But this!

Lang then pulled an ivory-clad pocket knife from his left vest pocket and laid it on the hanky next to the pencils, parallel to them. Just so. He picked up the leftmost pencil before peering into Walt's eyes. Yup, Lang verified that Walt witnessed this bizarre little ritual. Walt gave him nothing. Lang laid his chosen pencil on top of and perpendicular to the rectangular cover of a small leather-bound notebook in front of him, yet to be opened. *Jeez!*

This mope could have just changed out of his Confederate uniform after the war of northern aggression. His mellifluous tones rolled off his tongue like warm Kentucky honey dripping from a dulcimer. And that double-breasted hundred-dollar suit of creamy gray wool lacked for nothing but war ribbons, insignias of rank, and shoulder boards, plus a medal or two for meritorious pencil sharpening. A lesser agent brought in... a tea service?

"Sir—" it came out *suh,* "it has come to our attention you owe a considerable sum in back taxes to the federal gov'ment on your, ah, income. Do you know of what I speak, Mr. Weller?"

Shit. But why the ATF? "Well, Lang, why don't you tell me what you think you know and I'll see if I know of what you speak. Fair enough, pardner? And since this is just a friendly chat, it's just Walt."

This cop was talking about his ignominious winnings, but confessing to nothing remained at the top of his own list.

"Tea?" Lang diverted his attention to the wooden tray with the clay teapot, mugs and a small... what? Honey pot? Walt saw the handle of one of those grooved honey drizzlers sticking out of the dark honey in the pot. Quaint. Lang then retrieved a tiny paper packet, that had been folded with precision, from his inside left breast pocket. He explained, "Once distant from my native Atlanta, I find regional allergies problematic. I have discovered that my particular physiology responds well to a custom blend of Japanese Sencha and Chinese Dragonwell tea leaves. I've blended this mixture with herbal echinacea to stimulate the immune system. Local honey offers some defense against local allergies. At least, that is the lore. May I offer you a cup, even though these *urns* aren't what I would consider civilized fare?"

"Uh, I'm sure it's the bee's knees, Lang. No thanks. But I thank you kindly for the offer. Right white of ya." Walt found this little dance of social graces and obsessive behavior inter-esting, even revealing. Why did he already feel like he could trust this weird little guy? He watched as the tea leaves went into the pot of hot water. Gave off a faint smell of what, perfumed gunpowder?

"Alright then, Walt, you've quite a reputation in every casino and private game of chance from Chicago to Omaha, plus a few as far west as Denver. According to our records, you've accumulated unreported winnings in excess of ten thousand dollars. Your official state of residence is Illinois. That means you owe Uncle Sam at least two thousand dollars and another one thousand two-hundred dollars to the state of Illinois. I'm sure this has been a mere oversight for an itinerant gentleman such as yourself. But to be blunt, and more to my point, Walt," Lang paused to smile at his pun-infested humor, "I'm only concerned with the federal tax burden for which you are in arrears. That sounds more civilized than federal tax evasion, does it not? The government requires either remuneration or incarceration. Are we as one? Walt?"

"What's the deal here, Lang? How much hot water am I in?" *I'm sensing a deal here with Mr. Honey Pencils and Oriental Tea Allergies.*

"Work for me, and I pay your tax bill. It's that simple. The alternative? Pay what is due right now plus late penalties, or go to federal prison."

Walt's wheels turned. He knew this guy had copped the goods on him, but seemed a straight shooter and a whole lot sharper than most tree stumps posing as feds. He could pay the bill, but why give up twenty percent or more of his hard-earned winnings, plus who knows how much more in late fees? Besides, the world had become very dangerous, and a partnership with a G-Dandy in return for... what?

"What would I have to do, Lang? And who are you, again?"

"It is all quite simple. We need ears on the ground from a total government outsider, but an insider into, ah, certain circles. Our agents can't seem to pass muster in either quarter. That makes your qualifications unique, Walt. I am but a humble employee of the Bureau of Alcohol, Tobacco and

Firearms, a relatively obscure agency of the federal government. We often partner with departments within the FBI and the new Internal Revenue Service. But I might suggest you'll find ATF more understanding of your tax transgressions than some zealot within the ranks of these IRS upstarts. Well?"

"Oh, golly, let me think. I assume you already know I'm not a stupid man, whatever else I may be. Of course, I'm in. But I have a few stipulations of my own."

And for the last three months, good old *Lang* had been true to his word.

50

Edie found it difficult to contain her excitement. She felt giddy as she pulled into the Hardt yard. Girls only, like it used to be. Better times. She struggled with her addiction, and likely would for the rest of her life. It had taken some time and some serious counseling with good old Doc Gustavsen over in Spencer. But she now clung to one thought for sure—she did not want to die. Armed with the certainty born of her near-death experience, continuing to tumble down that Black Gold hell hole would indeed bury her. If it hadn't been for her dearest friend in the world—dear little frail Sophie....

Edie had even grown hopeful enough for the oral surgeon up in Rock Rapids to fix her up with two temporary front teeth. It was expensive, but after she threatened to visit Sheriff Billy, Ritchy paid—and then some. The bastard. And her lip was almost healed, too. She was almost beautiful again, but with *some interesting mileage*, she was told.

Doc Gus, bless his cantankerous old heart, had put her

onto a Christian organization called the Oxford Group who specialized in such things. She'd have to travel some and admit she would go to any lengths to get and stay clean and sober. Ritchy agreed to pay for that, too. Almost like he felt guilty or something. He was hurting too, and that was too bad. She'd pray for the prick.

With her Chevy sedan—also paid for by her soon-to-be ex-husband, or more likely, his daddy—she maneuvered to within twenty-five feet of the mudroom door at the rear of the house. With caution, Edie navigated the rough yard in her town shoes. Might have been a mistake wearing those. Spotted Sophie through the kitchen window and they waved to each other like a couple of school girls. It was to be a frivolous afternoon of silly girl talk, something neither woman had indulged in for months.

☙❧

SOPHIE GREETED HER FRIEND IN THE KITCHEN. THE MUD room was too small for both of them to hug or for once-overs. Sophie didn't bother to ask Edie to remove her shoes. Town dust didn't stink, and with no rain, no mud. Not outside, anyway. Besides, she was company.

"Welcome, sweetheart! How about some coffee? But I'm warning you, Edie. This isn't town coffee, this is stout farm brew. We call it yard mud. Remember?"

☙❧

SOPHIE OFFERED HER THE SAME KITCHEN CHAIR WHERE SHE had tried to kill herself less than a month ago and had gulped down a cup of coffee she had diluted with that poison before pulling that trigger. Edie retained her grin and rewarded Sophie with a knowing look at that chair, like it was okay, but she still wrinkled her forehead and widened her huge eyes for a different reason. Jake arose from the chair next to hers, offered his hand. The callouses and warmth dealt her a tiny thrill.

"It won't be just us girls, Soph? Not that a handsome man is ever unwelcome." She blushed.

"Girls only, as promised! Jake is waiting for someone who also loves my coffee. They'll drink it outside, though. Won't you, dear?"

He grinned. "Sure thing. Not often we have more than one beautiful woman right here in this old kitchen. And Edie, Soph tells me I have you to thank for putting her up to waving at me that perfect day last January."

Edie still blushed, but that remark escalated her rosy cheeks into full bloom.

Dear God, that smile. No wonder Soph fell hard for this lug.

"HELLO, THE HOUSE!" CHIEF DAN HAD ARRIVED. WALT intercepted him in the yard coming from the barn, and hollered to make their presence known. Chief's idea of calling ahead. Walt and Chief had spent a few minutes getting acquainted before the two of them rambled through the mud room into the kitchen. One of them was smiling as they talked. But time did a funny thing at that moment. It stopped. For two, at least. Their jaws dropped. And they stared. At each other. It was if Edie and Chief were alone in that kitchen and the rest of the world faded into insignificance. They failed to hide what each was thinking, though they tried, as if considering something forbidden.

"Um, Chief...." Jake vied for his attention, but failed.

"Edie, this is...." Being a conscientious hostess, Sophie tried to introduce her friend to the other men that frequented the Hardt farm. But she drifted into silence, realizing that her friend and Jake's friend were sharing a significant first moment. You know, the type that you glance back at and remember, months or years later.

Walt, however, wasn't that sensitive. "Hey! Chief, this is Edie, uh, what's your last name, kiddo? Edie?"

Jake said, "Shut up, Walt."

A few more moments passed before Chief spoke with a velvet tone. "Hi. I'm Dan Rustywire," and he extended his hand toward Edie, their gaze still unbroken. Not like he intended to shake her hand, but as if to lead her somewhere, perhaps into a new life.

As she accepted his almost-delicate hand with only the slightest hesitation, she half-whispered, "Rustywire? What a lovely name. Unusual. I'm Edie." And just like that, the two of them strolled out the back door into the yard together, not speaking further—locked into a life-altering gaze.

After they left, Walt blurted, "What the hell was that?"

Sophie smiled. "I'm guessing my friend has met her knight in shining armor. Oh Jake, this is perfect! Edie is such the damsel in distress. Ritchy is nothing but toxic, and your friend seems such a gentle soul."

"And Chief looks to have overcome his resentment of white folk, at least for a few." He chuckled and winked. But in sudden concern, Jake reached over to grab his bride's hand. "Honey, are you crying?"

"Tears of joy, my love." She reached down for a handful of apron—Edie's apron—to dry her eyes before reaching out to him. She snuffled, "Now, does *anyone* want some fresh coffee? It's not very thick yet, but—"

"Hell, yeah. Got any cream? How about cookies?" Jake and Sophie couldn't help but grin at each other over yet another of Walt's outbursts, tender moment notwithstanding. He seemed oblivious, *or* keenly aware of the desperate need for some levity. With Walt, ya never knew.

Ten minutes later, the young couple wandered back into the kitchen, holding hands.

With an embarrassed expression, Edie said, "Soph, I'm sorry. Dan and I are getting acquainted. Is that okay?"

"Yes, yes! I'm pouring coffee. Want a cup? Sit down. Walt, go fetch that extra chair from the front room. It's a party!"

As they shuffled the chairs so all could belly up to the round table, Sophie fetched her "company cups," cookies, and cream. Jake helped. With this sudden flurry of activity, Jake mentioned over his shoulder, "Edie, Chief—Dan, that is— built this wonderful airship. Tell her about it, Chief."

A man of few words, Chief nevertheless emerged from his cocoon, spread his fresh wings, and became a loquacious butterfly. He described it with increasing enthusiasm as he watched Edie's face light up, as if he were dialing up her sunshine.

"Oh, can we go for a ride together some time, Chief? Is it okay that I call you Chief, like everyone else?"

"Sure. That's fine. I would love to fly with you, Edie. I'm just four miles south of here."

"I've never told this to *anyone* before, not even you, Soph. I've always *loved* aviation. Amelia Earhart is one of my all-time favorite heroines."

⚜

SOPHIE'S SURPRISE WAS PALPABLE, AND SHE WASN'T SURE IF Edie was just shining Chief or not. But her enthusiasm was unmistakable. She did know who Amelia Earhart was. But her next questions of Chief convinced her beyond all doubt— Edie was indeed an aerial enthusiast.

"Chief, how do you generate lift?"

"Hot air."

After the briefest of thoughtful pauses, "And that's enough?"

"Well, with sufficient volume. That and extremely light-weight construction."

"Thrust?"

"Bicycle-style pedals power a propeller with directional airflow forced over twin rudders. In the future, I'll provide auxiliary horizontal forward thrust with pressurized steam. Maybe. Some day. With Jake's help."

"Vertical thrust?"

"I control the temperature of air in a large hot air bag through a flue-regulated stove pipe up into the bag. And I can deploy horizontal sails, like wings, if the wind is right, which are also a fail-safe against catastrophic bag failure... in theory."

"Brilliant!"

Walt soon grew bored, downed his cup while demolishing three huge oatmeal soda cookies, and tromped off into the yard. Jake followed. For a while, Sophie sat on the far side of the table—basking. But she excused herself too, off to the front room to attend to some urgent sock darning.

❦

NOBODY NOTICED WALT FIDDLING WITH THE PUMP equipment outside the open kitchen window. Nor did they notice that his fiddling took place closer to the house than to the pump.

"Chief, you should know I'm suffering through an awful divorce." It was obvious Edie expected him to cool off and excuse himself. He didn't.

"He's been hitting you." Not a question. He pointed to her left cheek, almost touching it. She'd tried to conceal it.

She suspected he also wondered about the not-quite-healed gash in her upper lip. At least her teeth looked good, maybe a little too white. Edie lowered her huge eyes, embarrassed. Chief read that and said, "You don't deserve that, nor do you deserve to feel shame for an animal you can't control. Edie, *he* doesn't deserve *you*."

Chief realized he may have said too much and clammed up. Lowering his own eyes, but not in shame or embarrassment, he reached for her delicate hands folded in front of her as if she were praying. He enclosed both in his own. "Edie, tell me about him."

"I'd rather not." One tear escaped, adding to her embarrassment.

"Please?" He gently brushed the tear away with the back of his index finger, large against her tiny cheek. Edie did not pull away. Instead, she mustered her courage.

"His name is Ritchy Winkels. He works for Sophie's father. We started out great. He makes a lot of money, but more from his side business than from Bairns Motors."

"Side business?"

"Yes, well, it's not strictly legal, but everybody winks and nods at Prohibition. You know. Ritchy buys and sells something they call *Black Gold*, a quality liquor that is all the rage these days. When he drinks, Chief, he gets real mean. Otherwise, he's a pretty nice guy, like when we met in high school. Trouble is, he's drinking more often than not these days. Chief, this brand of booze is bad news. It almost killed me. But I'm on the mend. I just thought you should know." Upon hearing this, the young man's blood boiled, but he clung to a calm exterior. The depth of his emotions surprised him.

"I see. Do you have a safe place to stay while—"

"Oh, I'm fine. Really. I'm staying with my folks, although they have their own troubles." Chief deciphered that as code for an abusive situation there as well.

Not sure at all what came over him, not like him at all, he spat it out fast before she could cut him off. "Come stay at my place, Edie. I have this big house. We'd almost never run into each other. No obligation. Free of charge. It's just me and my horse, my friend, Kona. What do you say?" Silence. Yup, he just blew it. Even *he* thought that sounded creepy. Then....

"Oh, gosh, Chief, we just met and all. Let me talk with Sophie about this, okay?"

"Yah, sure. You're right, of course. But if you take me up on my offer, I promise *nobody* will mess with you. Nobody messes with my friends, Edie. I don't have many, but the few I do have know that." And he meant it. "Look, I gotta go take care of some farm business with the boys outside." As he stood up, he let go of her hands with some obvious reluctance, and said, "I haven't had this much fun in a very long time. In Lakota Sioux, I wish you Wakan Takan kici un, which means, May the Great Spirit bless you, Edie.

She just blushed again. Chief turned in slow motion to leave, turned back, then wheeled to leave as if he were doing so against his better judgment.

Walt hurried away from the open kitchen window.

WALT STOOD AT THE PHONE ON JAKE AND SOPHIE'S kitchen wall. They were all outside, saying goodbye to Edie. Chief had already left, like it was the hardest thing he ever did, poor kid. Another one bites the dust.

"Lang, this is Walt. Got a tidbit for ya. A kid named Ritchy Winkels, one of Henry Bairns's employees in George, is distributing Black Gold around here. He's using the stuff himself too. Makin' him mean. Hitting his wife."

"Who's your source?"

"His soon-to-be ex-wife, Edie. She opened up to Jake's friend, a Lakota Sioux named Dan Rustywire."

"*What?* We think Rustywire is Malone's Black Gold cooker."

"No, that's wrong, Lang. No way. Don't know where you got your info, but it is dead wrong."

"Okay, what else?"

Walt heard Jake and Sophie returning. "Gotta go." Click

"HEY, WALT, WHATCHA UP TO?"

He made for the stove. "Got any more coffee?"

❦

51

The Dayton House porch in Worthington City was worthy of a Swedish sauna today. Two well-dressed gentlemen sat beside each other in the shade, in the still air. Finn Malone and his top lieutenant, Sticks Leary, both dripped perspiration. It leeched through their starched cotton shirts. Even their silk ties showed dark stains. Caused their wool suit coats to radiate a musty dead lamb odor, but it never occurred to them to shed those coats, or their drooping fedoras. This was business. And stubborn male pride.

"So, Sticks, m'boy. Why're ya actin' the maggot? You were to tickle ole Henry Bairns to make his obliges. And yet, he's still b'hind. Must not be ticklish. Warn't he impressed by yer stern countenance, lad? Did ya not throw yer customary passion his way? Why have ya failed me, boy-o?"

"Finn, I thought I was bang-on with the old gent. Fairly ate his head off, but guess I made a right bags of it, I did."

"Well, let's jump to the morn, me boy-o. The plike must

be thick as a plank to doubt yer true, yeh? Remember our days back in the Liberties? I miss the Pale. You?

Leary was relieved his boss and friend was backing away from what could have become a violent reaction to his failure with Bairns. Instead, his reflective mood back to their days in the notorious Dublin slums allowed him a temporary sigh of relief.

"Sure thing, Finn. We did some solid goods together..." Leary chuckled, almost to himself, before mustering the courage to continue. Finn was the only bloke alive who could put the dire dread on him. "...'member the old greens-grocer down Church Street what was rousted by that feckin' guard? Like his badge and that bat give him every right to take half the old bugger's meagers ev'ry week. You called him out 'n he give chase. From around a corner I bang on 'im a right taste of me stick, yeh? Feckin' scum. Done in one, yeh? The rest was fer fun. Not much left fer the other coppers to collect."

"Aye, Sticks. Bangin' days. Done helped more 'n a few, we did. When them tenements collapsed, we was also right in there pullin' out the ones what still squirmed, staunchin' the bleedin'. And we hunted down and squashed that bug of an inspector what just declared 'em safe, the watery shite. Them old piles should of been flatted a decade afore. Put that piker's head on a stake for all the 'hood to see, we did. We was heroes, Sticks. We crawled out of them corporation projects like we was supposed to be thankin' the man. Put it right back to 'em, din't we, Sticks? Specially them blusterin' IRA pussies. Solid good days, m'friend. Are ya glad we hopped that boat and made our way over? Are ya?"

"Well, lots more space for the guards to watch over here, means more for us 'n ours. Ain't been feeling hollow fer a couple of years now," he rubbed his full belly, "so, we suckin' the best of the juice, yeh?"

"Aye, indeed. Now go do your feckin' job, 'kay, boy-o?"

❧ 52 ❧

S heriff Billy sat at his desk in Rock Rapids. He splurged by turning on the overhead lights first thing this morning, a departure from his habit of only turning them on after dark. He needed light, dammit. And this next call wasn't one he relished making, but it was time to take advantage of a little help from the feds. He stood and sidled up to the telephone. The county was too cheap to get him one of them fancy desk phones. Asked Mabel at the town's switchboard for the federal field office up in Rapid City. She got him connected to the right guy for a speakeasy raid.

"Agent Eubanks, we got a little joint down in George that stays pretty low profile, and I cut 'em some slack. No harm, ya know? But now they're serving this Black Gold shit, and I can't have my constituents being poisoned. Gonna raid the place, and I could use a couple of your agents to back me up. I only got one experienced deputy and he's working a murder.

Don't wanna be bringin' a knife to a gunfight, although I doubt it will come to that. Interested?"

"Certainly, Sheriff. I heard about your young deputy's murder, and I am very sorry. Back to current affairs. Enforcing Volstead is central to our charter. And while I can't condone your laissez-faire attitude toward its enforcement, I understand that position as part of your social contract with your constituents. Can you give us twelve hours? Or is the situation more pressing?"

"Tomorrow's fine. The joint is open around the clock. Should be the fewest number of patrons around ten in the morning."

Billy even went through the formality of getting a warrant from old Judge Simmons.

ZACHARY MUTTER'S GARAGE WAS THE ONLY PUBLIC HOUSE in George. But that was nothing new. There were no bars in George, even before Prohibition. The church ladies went wild when they found out through their gossip circles that Mutter had opened for business. But there were enough customers, law or no law. Sheriff Billy hadn't raised a stink over it. Now, it was different.

The raid—scheduled for ten the next morning with an assist from one of Agent Lang Eubanks' two-man teams—shouldn't have been a big deal. Billy planned to serve old Zach with the warrant. They would perform a search and confiscate all contraband materials found on the premises. They'd post the cease 'n desist. He'd take Zach into custody for a Volstead violation, even though he'd likely be out the next day. And there'd be one less place for people to buy that poison. Easy cheesy. But that's not at all what happened.

. . .

THE THREE OF THEM APPROACHED ZACH'S GARAGE—HIS joint—from its alley side. Two trucks and a sedan occupied half of parking spaces on what used to be Mutter's lawn behind his modest cottage out on Bern Road in George. Billy walked into the dim joint first, followed by two feds in full tactical gear over their suits, toting Thompsons.

"Zach, it's Billy Kershaw. We're comin' in. Got a warrant, old buddy."

Billy hadn't seen Zach for a few months, at least. No reason. They weren't friends. Barely knew each other. Zach had always carried an extra hundred pounds of heavy living on him. Not anymore. His gaunt appearance shocked Billy, at least from the waist up, since he stood behind his bar. But he found Zach's eyes above his sunken cheeks most disturbing— hollow in their sockets, searching, darting around. This man appeared manic, even from fifteen feet away.

"Billy, get out of here. This here ain't no place—"

"Zach, this ain't a social call. Like I said, I got a warrant which gives me the legal right to search your garage and to seize any contraband. *Do you understand?*"

"This ain't no garage, Billy. This here's my place of business. Now you turn right around—"

"Can't do that, Zach." He noticed the man's hands were no longer visible on the bar. "Lemme see your hands, Zach. Like right now, dammit!" He hadn't meant to raise his voice like that, but he was nervous too, although not as skittish as the two ATF agents. He risked a glance back toward them. They stood by the door—one covering the three patrons sitting at two flimsy card tables, and the other trained his Thompson submachine gun on Zach. They looked mighty tense, too. Customers looked like just a couple of farmers and a towny.

But something was off. From what Billy knew about this Black Gold crap, they all were likely real nervous. He could see Zach was on the edge of doing something idiotic, as if he had no choice. "Zach, I mean it, man. Get your hands out here! I got a couple of real twitchy federal agents right here behind me. What's your plan, old buddy? We just wanna look around, okay?"

"You ain't takin' my *Gold*, Billy. Get that right outta your head."

"Zach, I'm done talkin'. Get your ass out from behind that bar." Calling it a bar was generous. Two stacks of pallets supported the ends of a couple of rough-sawn two-by-twelve planks, side by side, not long off the mill. A blue-and-white checkered tablecloth thumb-tacked along the customer side hid shelves of... what? Bottles and jugs? Maybe a shotgun or a revolver down there too? Add four kitchen stools in front, and you got one makeshift speakeasy.

Well, the next few seconds whizzed by in a blur. Billy was almost sorry he'd asked for ATF help. Those serious boys were done talking too, even though neither had uttered a word so far. The bulked-up monster covering Zach hollered at a decibel level rivaling a locomotive engine whining down a steep slope. "Get your face on the floor right now or you're eating lead, asshole! NOW!" His volume and ferocity shocked even Billy.

Well, it was clear Zach wasn't in any shape to follow orders. He brought his hands up above the bar like he was going to surrender, but his right hand held a revolver. Swung around to face Billy and to the agent who called him an asshole. Providence rained hell down on poor strung-out Zach. He dropped like a ninety-pound weakling from half a pound of lead. Dead.

Billy hit the floor. He didn't relish getting shot in the back. When the shooting stopped, he crawled back to his feet with ears ringing. He was pissed. "Aw, c'mon, guys. Was that necessary? Couldn't you have gone for anything but center mass with a full drum? Shit!" Billy was beside himself and didn't like what he saw. Two of the three regulars, now stretched out spread-eagle on the floor, whimpered like wounded pups, but they were okay. The third, though, collected what was left of his wits and charged the agent who killed his friend. A full body slam and a swat-down later, the second agent had him collared. Said he was going to prison for attacking a federal agent. "That's major felony-weight, shit-head!"

This was not at all how Billy envisioned this simple search and seizure. He didn't blame the agents. God only knows what they had seen and found necessary during this whole stupid Prohibition facade. Another damn political football.

But now, with this poison wasting away normal people, turning them into felons, or corpses, there would be no more winking and nodding. This must stop. *And* he'd use help from the feds more judiciously in the future.

53

Roy Dillworth both thanked and cursed Malone's master cooker for coming up with their most profitable hooch recipe yet. But without the Indian's personal touch, his guys hadn't been able to duplicate that recipe. They missed something about the guy's complicated process. The first few shipments proved downright awful, both in taste and in potency.

They'd made some progress since those first putrid batches by reverting to more traditional distilling techniques. What made their recipe unique now were the additives recommended by Malone's experienced cookers from out east. But those additives turned their clear product into the color of watery diarrhea. But like they say in car sales, *if you can't fix it, feature it.* They branded their label Black Gold. They replaced what they lost from the now-missing master cooker—everyone just called him the Indian—with an opioid called codeine made from domestic coal tar. Nasty stuff used to preserve railroad ties. And they also added some raw cocaine to keep 'em awake. They'd stay awake more, and drink more, and keep coming back for more. The soup they now produced and shipped in volume was a winner. Customers couldn't get enough of the stuff.

Why, then, was Malone still acting the fool, trying to find his old master cooker? *Gold* was a great product, and he had personally ramped up its production. Even going national with it. Was there something else going on there?

54

It didn't take long for ATF Agent Lang Eubanks to figure out that their Rapid City field office was a remodeled stable. But that was not the reason he spent little time here. Nor was it the subtle but unmistakable fragrance of nature that permeated these premises. An office that he swore was a refurbished horse stall had been his home non-stop for the last nineteen hours. Somebody took pity on him and brought in food. Unrecognizable as it was, he showered his benefactor with thanks.

Walt Weller had proven an invaluable informant. Once more, Lang congratulated himself for recruiting the drunken gambler. He admitted, though, he'd never seen the man tippled. And having discovered a low-level distributor of *Gold* was useful, but they already knew Malone was involved.

Lang had also collaborated with local law enforcement, per protocol. He learned that Weller, on his own initiative, reached out to one Sheriff Kershaw of Lyon County, Iowa, concerning the murder of one of his deputies. Weller provided the sheriff with a critical lead—the modus operandi of the deputy's killer matched the known MO of an Irish enforcer from "out east."

Pieces were falling into place. Sources in Chicago confirmed the Irish mob in their fair city has used the sort of tactics they now saw exhibited in this little corner of the Midwest. Lang could only come to one conclusion: the Irish mob from Chicago—Finn Malone et al—were undertaking an aggressive westward expansion. Further, this rural area was witnessing the early harbingers of that expansion, maybe even as a test bed for their newest product.

What worried Lang most was this new product's addictive properties, along with non-trivial levels of toxicity. This combination not only proved very habit-forming, but produced self-destructive behavior with longer-term use, likely attacking the areas of the brain that govern psychotic tendencies. But longer-term use with this substance meant weeks, not months or years. The stuff was addictive *and* psychopathically poisonous.

Sheriff Kershaw, the charming man who insisted on being called Billy, provided information concerning two personally disturbing incidents. Both Volstead abuses were likely related to an illicit drinking establishment within his jurisdiction. He closed it down with an assist from ATF.

The two incidents that Billy had witnessed evoked deep emotional responses from the use of this substance—one suicide and one attempted suicide. On these two separate but recent occasions, Billy had escorted both to an area hospital. He described their behavior while en route, which was consistent with a later chemical analysis that revealed this Black Gold product contained both strong depressants—some toxic —and powerful stimulants, a dangerous combination, to be sure. In a word, *poison*. The former was a young man wasted away after prolonged use of Black Gold. He then jammed a pencil into his brain through his ear canal, while under medical supervision, no less. The latter, a slip of a girl just out of her teens, had placed a pistol in her mouth and pulled the trigger. She did this in the company of a friend who came to her rescue at the last moment.

LANG'S INTUITION, SUPPORTED BY THE EVIDENCE, screamed at him. These animals were in the early stages of implementing a nationwide manufacturing and distribution strategy. If that happened, this would become a widespread public health hazard and a threat to the security of the United States of America. Were there other unseen forces—international forces—at play here, too?

Agent Eubanks anticipated that possibility a month earlier. He had asked his contacts at the FBI to issue an official Law Enforcement Bulletin to their field offices nationwide. That paid off and resulted in his interview of a young man named Charles-Royce Hugo in Lakehurst, New Jersey. He referred to his notes to refresh himself on the following unconfirmed intelligence points:

1. An expansion plan to manufacture and distribute Black Gold on a large-scale basis is already underway, perhaps even nationwide.
2. The plan is to complete that expansion plan by the end of this summer.
3. Chatter about some "hotter recipe" worried him too. Might that be the aviation fuel derivative of Black Gold?
4. Code names of two operators are yet to be deciphered. One likely in the Midwest, possibly

Iowa, code-named Shade, and the other, likely in New Jersey, code-named Tree.

And *that* is why *Federal* Agent Lang Eubanks had spent the last nineteen hours in a converted horse stall in Rapid City, South Dakota, USA.

❧ 55 ❧

❦

Sophie's kitchen: a gathering place, a warming place, a place of renewal three or more times each day en route to a tough-as-nails job, and no less, a confessional. This kitchen—the center of many little universes within the Hardt orbit—gave much, but asked little in return. Not unlike most country kitchens. Today, this particular kitchen would ask for no less than the whole truth, and nothing but the truth.

Sophie sat stiff. Like always. But today, hers was a stern stiff. She had asked Jake to fetch Walt for her and then directed her husband to go out to the barn. Or anywhere but the kitchen. As he left Walt standing at the mudroom door before running for cover, Jake thought, *God help the poor man. I'll say a prayer for you, cuz.*

"Hi, Soph. What's up? You okay?"

"Come sit next to me. But before you do, pour us a cup."

He asked over his shoulder as he sidled up to Blackie, the

huge iron stove, to fill the pair of mugs already set out. "Sure, Soph. Milk?"

"Do you enjoy living here, Walt?"

❦

HE STILL WORE HIS WORK HAT, AN OLD FEDORA THAT USED to belong to Jake. Sophie bet dollars to donuts it still smelled like her Jake. Before answering, taking a moment to analyze his situation, he tossed it toward the hat rack by the mudroom door seven feet away. Of course, it landed right on target at the very top, with a quarter spin. He glanced over at Sophie when he set her cup down as if to say, *Yeah, I'm lucky, but I'm good, too.*

"Um, yes I do enjoy living here, Sophie. Family. More important than I'd have thought. And you and Jake, it's great to see how good you guys are together. Fun to see that, and to be a part of it."

"Thank you for saying that. Family *is* everything. And loyalty. The tougher times get, even more so. What do you boys talk about up in the haymow, the one place you know you have all to yourselves?"

A cloud swirled through Walt's brain. He now saw where this inquisition was headed. "Jake told you about the money."

"Walt, you're a generous soul. Or you're afraid. Either way, or both, I hope you know what you're doing. Do you know how almost impossibly independent Jake perceives himself? Do you think maybe you're sacrificing that part of him on the altar of easy money? He's like a child in many ways: petulant, lofty, and breakable. Walt, you're a good man."

He thought to himself, *This is not at all what I expected, gawdammit. Shit!*

"Jake, profanity is never called for, nor is blasphemy."

"You're a mind reader too." Not a question. *I am so screwed!*

"No, Walt. But I am a face reader. Jake rationalizes that he's trading your help for room and board. But *we* should pay *you*. You are good for Jake, *I* should pay you. And you're a joy to have around, as ridiculous as some things you say. Walt, we love you. I only ask that the secrets stop."

❧

SOPHIE DID NOT ASK FOR A RESPONSE. SHE ONLY STRUGGLED to stand—it took a full three momentum-building motions forward and backward, leaning on the chair's arms, then on the tabletop, to get to her feet. She limped over to stand behind Walt. He was smart enough not to help her or to get up, warming his hands on his tepid mug of mud. She boxed his ears, the good hand harder than her right, and asked, "Want more coffee, you bad boy? And Jake, you can stop eavesdropping. Get back in here to warm up over a cup with us." *My other bad boy!*

Walt roared with laughter loud enough to startle the rookie rooster out in the coop into a practice crow.

After the three of them settled down, Jake lit a lantern for the middle of the table against the waning light. Sophie made it clear she was not yet finished, not by a long shot.

"Okay, boys. Spill. Where is all this filthy lucre coming from? Details!"

The boys did indeed spill their guts while Sophie fetched three small plates, a knife, a loaf of bread and a Mason jar of her mother's canned preserves.

❦

56

On a rare trip out to the Hardt farm early the next morning, Hilda parked Henry's Chevy in front of her daughter's house. Equally rare, Sophie greeted her mother at the *front* door, which nobody used. Except Hilda. A town habit.

"Mother! You're here! And you're driving Father's car!"

"He didn't go into the dealership today."

"What? Ah, please, come in, dear. Is everything alright?"

"No, sweetheart, it most certainly is not."

After an awkward moment and a shaky embrace, Sophie and Hilda seated themselves next to each other at the kitchen table. A small fire defeated the damp chill. Hilda described the red and black Duesenberg convertible at their house, and the intense exchange she had witnessed through the front window, but could not hear what was said.

"Sweetheart, that shook your father—to his core. For the first time in twenty-five years of our marriage, I saw Henry cry. After that huge auto roared away last night, the poor man clumped into the house and dropped into his chair. Sophie, his eyes burned with shame, and *fear*. It was as if that frightening little man had electrocuted him. He sat in the front room, staring out the window, scanning up and down the street. For *hours*. I dared not even speak to him. I have never seen this strong man so scared and so... small. He wouldn't speak until I threatened him. At last he said, 'Hildie, I'm a damn fool. I've placed us in danger, and for the first time in a very long time, I don't know what to do!' Well, then it all came tumbling out."

For the next ten minutes, Sophie held both of her mother's hands in both of hers and listened. She dared not reveal that she already knew much of this—her vow to her father. With the secret revealed, she understood the unusual request her mother then made.

"Mother, now I understand why you need to leave town, but, well, you and Father can't stay here."

"Sweetheart—",

"They know about this place too."

"Oh, my...."

"Last week, some city slicker knocked on our door. Said he was a salesman. Asked a lot of questions. Drove the same car. Can't be more than one of *those* monsters around here."

"But dear, Henry tells me the man threatened his *family*. That includes *you!* Oh, Sophie—"

"Mother, stop. Here's what we'll do. Right now, we're safer here—together—with Jake and Walt. Jake's not here right now, but Walt is out back working. Let me fetch him."

"You're going to tell all this to him, dear? Is that necessary? Henry will be very cross."

"Yes, Mother, it is necessary. Cross is better than, well, most any other alternative. Now let me pour you a cup and I'll return straightaway."

Without another word, Sophie gathered her momentum,

gained her balance, arose, poured a cup from the always-simmering pot on Blackie, and left through the back door. Five minutes later, she returned with Walt in tow.

⚅✦⚅

"MOTHER, MEET JAKE'S COUSIN, WALT WELLER. HE'S bunking with us."

"Hello, Mrs. Bairns. Honored."

"Mr. Weller." She suppressed a wrinkle in her nose at the overwhelming wave of farm odors that followed this rough young man in from the yard.

"Just Walt, please."

Sophie summarized the gist of Hilda's story for Walt. He furrowed his brow and growled with some intensity in his voice, "Did this car have a beige convertible top? Red sides? Black hood and trunk?"

"Well, yes, Walt. That describes it perfectly."

"Shit—"

"Walt!"

After Sophie's admonishment, "Sorry, ladies. Was the mook—ah, the man—that drove the car and conversed with your husband short with bug-eyes?"

Hilda said, "Yes!"

"Sh—, ah, okay. That's Sticks Leary. The stories say he's from the worst Dublin slums, a member of the Irish Animal Gangs."

Sophie first appeared shocked at the implication, but then perplexed. "That's not who showed up here pretending to be a salesman. Same car, but a taller sort with slitty eyes, smooth handsome face. A mean-looker with an Irish accent.

"Oh crap on a post. That sure sounds like Finn Malone. That big Duesenberg is his car. He's Leary's boss. He was *here?* This is *not* good."

Sophie swallowed hard. "Walt, um, I might have mentioned your name. But just your first name," as if to soften the blow. But she knew from Walt's earlier confession this would devastate him.

"What?! Oh, Sophie. Okay, we need to get out of here. These boys don't play around."

"Alright, Walter Weller. You tell me *now* why these thugs are coming after both you *and* my father. And I mean *right now!*"

Walt looked like a mouse caught in a knotted bag of cats thrown into the creek. "Um, okay, Sophie, but let's get Jake over here first. That way, we only need to do this once, okay?" His sheepish tone carried no weight.

"No, Walt. I suspect he already knows your entire story, anyway. I thought I did as well. Now spit it out, mister!"

So, for ten minutes, he laid it all out for Sophie and her mother. That's when Jake walked into a perfect storm in his own kitchen.

๑๛๑

As Jake strolled in, the sight of Mrs. Bairns in his kitchen surprised him. Not to mention seeing Sophie glaring at him all the way to the table. And his contrite cousin, with hat in hand, all he saw was a stupid expression pasted on his reddened face. He reached the only logical conclusion. *This cannot be good.*

"Mrs. B... Honey?"

"Sit!"

"Oh, golly—" He looked over at Walt standing behind Mrs. B between Blackie and the still-open mudroom door, like he was about to make a run for it. Walt shrugged, looked at his hog-manure-covered boots, and shook his head from side to side. Jake thought, *Sophie doesn't even mind he's wearing shitty boots in her kitchen? This is really bad, isn't it, plow hand?*

"If we didn't have more pressing problems right now, Jacob..."

Jacob? Oh, golly galore!

❦

57

After Sophie caught Jake up to speed, her tone mellowed from frustrated anger at Walt and Jake to measured anger. These mobsters were attacking the three most important men in her life. She said, "We need to circle our wagons, but not here, and not in town. Suggestions?"

Eager to mitigate his wife's foul mood, Jake offered his best ideas. "Well, we should get Sheriff Billy in the loop. Meantime, I'll drive over to the Rustywire place and see if Dan can put us up for a few days. Nobody knows about that place except me. You ladies and Walt drive into town to pick up Mr. Bairns. That big Chevy sedan will be cozy with the four of you, but better safe than, well, sorry."

Mrs. Bairns spoke in that definitive half-hoarse whisper she shared with her daughter that everyone could hear, even across the large table. "Look, Jake, it's about time you called us Henry and Hilda, don't you think?" She followed up with a warm and demure smile. Jake imagined he was looking at his angelic wife twenty-five years into the future.

He nodded with appreciation. Now if only Mr. B—Henry —agreed. Last time they spoke.... "Sure. Thanks, um, Hilda." He swiveled his intense gaze. "While you all are in town, Walt, ask Henry to call up to Billy in Rock Rapids to make sure he's at his office. Do not take no for an answer. If Billy is there, drive up to talk with him in person. We can't trust the damn party line."

"Jake!"

"Sorry, Soph, Hilda. Walt, lay it *all* out for Henry, and then for Billy—both your thing *and* Henry's thing, no matter what Henry says." He glanced over at Hilda for her tacit agreement. A faint but definitive nod emboldened him to toss an affirming nod toward Walt in return. He continued. "If Billy agrees, bring him back. With some hardware. He'll bring his cruiser."

"That'll be pretty late tonight before we get back, Jake."

"So be it. Make sure both Henry and Billy know we can't afford to fool around here, or our lives won't be worth a hill a beans. Stop here on the way back. If we're gone, head on down to Chief's place four miles farther south on 14. He's on the west side. Kind of hard to spot his driveway through the trees, though, especially in the dark. I'll set a lantern where you should turn right. Once you're all in, bring the lantern in with you. Sound about right?"

Walt piped up. "Good plan, cuz. Long night ahead, but we need to stick together. At least for now. These are very dangerous mooks. Henry's right to be spooked. I know I am, but I had no idea he was tangled up like this too."

WITH NO FURTHER DELAY, JAKE NODDED ALL AROUND FOR one final assurance of the plan before snatching the keys to the work truck on the hook by the mudroom door. He had just placed them there twenty minutes earlier. He was off to twist Chief's arm.

After Jake left, Walt said, "Sophie, I need to find out if Sheriff Billy is in his office. Where's your directory?"

"In the drawer right under the talkie." She pointed to the small stand under the telephone mounted on the wall between the mudroom door and the kitchen's rear window. "Mother, why don't you and I go talk in the front room?"

"Yes, dear. I'd like that."

"Walt, let us know when you're ready to leave."

They settled into the small sofa under the front room window, side-by-side.

"Mother, when Walt's done with the telephone, you call Father to let him know you're on your way home. Say nothing else. That's important."

❧

"HELLO, LANG? JUST YOUR OLD GAMBLING BUDDY HERE."

"Yes?"

"Fins are circling Bairns Motors in George, Iowa. You should also be leery. That's all for now."

"Thank you. Goodbye."

❧

JAKE SAT IN CHIEF DAN'S KITCHEN. CHIEF'S INCREDULOUS reaction spoke volumes. "C'mon, Jake. You want me to put up a bunch of snooty old *white* folks? In my *home?*" Henry's reputation preceded him, thanks to Jake's sour-pussing during their first flight together earlier in the week.

"They're *family*, Chief! Plus, it would do you good to cozy up to the county sheriff. Besides, Billy's a really good guy. My cousin Walt, too. And, well, I'm terrified for the women in my life. Maybe Edie too." Jake knew that was a low blow.

"Whatever. Sure, I guess. The house might be a bit dusty. I mostly sleep in the barn."

"Injuns!"

"Hey!"

They both turned dour faces into grim grins.

"You're a good friend, Dan."

"That's 'Chief' to you, white man."

JAKE HAD BROUGHT ONE OF THE FANCY TINS OF *OLD JUDGE* Walt gave him upon his arrival at the farm. He and Chief knew it would be a long night awaiting the gang from town. They sat together in the large kitchen, drinking the strong black brew and brainstorming. Even talked steam power for awhile. When they heard gravel crunching in the driveway a few hours later, they walked out front to watch two sets of headlamps circle into the yard in front of the big house. Sheriff Billy Kershaw led the way in his cruiser with the Bairns' sedan close behind. They pulled up behind Jake's truck.

Several car doors opened and slammed. Under the glow of Chief's yard light, Billy appeared from the driver's side of his official vehicle and went back to help the ladies. He carried the still-lit kerosene lantern Jake had left at the driveway's entrance. Walt and Henry were already on the job helping the ladies. Jake rushed out, too. Sophie was formidable indoors, but less sure-footed on loose gravel outdoors at night, though the yellow glow of the yard light helped. But even its brilliance could not fight off the tiny ground shadows that sprayed the pebble drive. He need not have worried, though, as he saw Henry to her right and Walt to her left, with Billy trailing right behind, escorting Hilda. The ladies were in excellent hands.

After Jake performed cursory introductions all around, they worked through a moment of head-bobbing silence, after which Chief blurted, "Well, unless you like gettin' sucked dry by mosquitos, I guess we oughta get inside." He led the way. The six guests followed their host in silence, each consumed with their own doubts and fears.

58

Chief's spacious kitchen could absorb seven bodies, but his kitchen table just four. They drifted into the even more spacious formal dining room between the kitchen and the front room. A sizable parlor was visible through a pair of doors housing panes of elegant water glass.

They sat three on each side of the long dark wood table with Chief at the head end. Sophie's friend Edie drifted into the room like a ghost haunting this elegant old house. Sophie couldn't help but notice a glow emanating from her as if she were a bottle of sunshine. Edie offered a demure nod to her and the others, almost like the lady of the house. She had accepted Chief's offer of sanctuary, even though Chief still slept in the barn. He was a gentleman, to be sure, but also a creature of habit.

THE SPACIOUS OPULENCE OF THIS INDIAN'S ABODE surprised Henry and Hilda. It's state of neglect, however, did not. You could see the ladies were already planning their frontal attack on the dust plaguing every surface, the cob webs taunting them from every corner, and the profusion of rich dark crown moldings above raised paneling badly in need of oil. It was the least they could do.

Henry seemed to be less in shock than he was after Sticks Leary's visit to his house yesterday. After everyone sat down, and yet another awkward silence ensued, he stood and faced Chief at the head of the table."

"Mr. Rustywire—"

"Just call me Chief, Mr. Bairns."

"Of course, Chief. And I suggest that since we're now engaged in an intimate enterprise together, how about first names all around? Allow me to be the first to thank our gracious host for accepting us into his home. Thank you, Chief."

"Sure. Wasn't my idea."

"Yes, ah, alright then."

Jake took a turn. "Look, I asked Chief to put up with us for a few days. This is all pretty strange to him. Am I right, Chief?"

"Yeah, it is, but it's fine. Make yourselves at home. I'm just not that great with, you know, people. And other than my horse, Kona, Jake's about my only friend. No offense."

Sophie arose from her chair, scraping it on the inlaid wood flooring. Limped around to the end of the table in her slight sideways wobble, stood behind Chief, and threw her arms around him. She said nothing. No need. Caught the poor guy by surprise. After a small flinch, not knowing what else to do—other than maybe bolt from the room like his curly black hair was on fire—he just patted her hands resting on his chest. Then he smiled. Sophie raised her hands to rest on Chief's shoulders from behind and said, "Okay, folks. We have a problem. What are we going to do about it?"

THOUGH SHE DIDN'T SHOW THAT SHE NOTICED, ONE PERSON at the table cast an admiring eye toward Sophie. He watched her standing up there, hitching her giddy-up around her bum leg and damaged wing, now leaning forward, bracing her good hand on the table, speaking with authority. She shone blazing courage, despite the obvious danger. She took charge as if this were her personal crusade. As far as Sheriff Billy Rhett Kershaw knew, little Sophie had no idea how much of a crush he had always had on her. Even though he was more than two decades her senior. He found it especially hard to hide that tonight, even sitting at the same table with her new husband.

THEY TALKED ALL NIGHT. NEXT MORNING, BILLY USED Chief's telephone to check in with Deputy Jimmy. Billy asked him to keep an eye out for that fancy Duesenberg. As his most experienced deputy, Dwight held down the fort. Told Dwight he'd be out cruising for the day, where in actuality, he'd be spending time with Sophie's little gang. He preferred to think of them as his posse, but recognized it was Sophie who held them together. What with Jake and Henry still sparring under the table, he having a crush on her, she and Walt staring each other down now and then, especially when she spotted Walt's eyes searching, smacking his lips, as if he would dry up and blow away. And she was the stabilizing factor for her frail friend, Edie, who now seemed to be an item with their host, Sophie's neighbor. Yeah, this was

Sophie's gang more than his posse, and he was just fine with that.

The big house sprawled with only three large bedrooms, but all found suitable accommodations in their new hideout. Chief offered Henry and Hilda the large bedroom at the head of the stairs. Chief had already offered Edie the smaller bedroom at the far end of the upstairs hall. Sophie and Jake claimed the smaller one on the main floor at the far end of the hall behind the parlor. Walt camped on the antique sofa in the parlor. Per usual, Chief slept on his cot in the barn, close to his beloved airship, and to his horse. Besides, Jake had told Billy that Chief just could not bring himself to spend much time in the house still haunted by the specters of his parents, gone four years now.

Chief had not offered Billy a bedroom, nor was one expected. When the sheriff wasn't sitting at the kitchen table drinking coffee and scratching notes in his little notebook, or daydreaming about Sophie, he walked the well-lit yard, just pacing. Billy lamented that vicious criminals had good people hiding in someone else's home. In his county. *There will be hell to pay,* he thought, simmering in his own juices.

He disappointed himself by dozing a bit while sitting in his car, jotting down a few more thoughts in his ever-present notebook. Just after sunrise, he strolled around the yard once more. Wandered out near the barn to check on their host. The Indian kid seemed a good sort, but.... Aw, who was he trying to kid? Billy knew why he had such a hard time with his sort. He'd lost a great aunt to a band of roving Sioux back in the day. How many decades ago was that now? Maybe that was it, as irrational as he knew that notion to be.

"Mornin', Sheriff." He jumped. The kid startled him. Everybody was edgy.

"Hey, Chief. Ya know, feels funny callin' you that, me bein' so much older than you, ya know?"

"Yeah, I get it. Thanks for watching out for my friend."

"You known Jake long?"

"Just since his folks passed almost two years ago now. Lost mine two years before that. They asked me to keep the farm in the family. Same as Jake's. I was their only kid. Guess they were always just too busy to have more."

"You and Jake—"

"Yup, he barged right in to introduce himself not long after I moved in. Just two lonely bachelors. 'Course that's changed now. He's got Sophie, and, well, I just met Edie. We still get on just fine."

"Yep, Edie's had a hard row to hoe. Sweet kid. You moved in from...?"

"I had just graduated from the U of M—"

"*Thee hell* you say!"

Chief tilted his head back and stared slantwise at Billy across his wrinkled nose. "What? You surprised a dumb redskin has an advanced degree? Two, in fact. Mechanical Engineering and Chemical Engineering."

The chagrined sheriff said, "Aw, no, Chief, well, I just didn't know."

"It's okay. Nobody expected me to... least of all my parents. Pissed off my dad. Not sure what he expected of me, other than maybe become the tribal constable on the rez up in North Dakota."

"You mean he wanted you to be a lawman?"

"Does that surprise you too, Sheriff?"

"Jeez, I'm not doin' so good, am I? Look, you seem like a good shit, Chief. I'm maybe not so good with people either, okay? Do me a favor. Just call me Billy, like everybody else."

"No sweat. Listen, you know anything more than what we talked about last night?"

"Matter of fact, my deputy radio'd me a few minutes ago just before I wandered over here. Said he spotted that big-ass Duese haulin' east on State Road 18 through Boyden, just southeast of here into Osceola County. Followed him a ways, but hung back at the county line. Lost him. Must've turned off, maybe up 60. I'd sure like to know where he was headin'. Was thinkin' about goin' for a drive. Wanna come?"

Looked like Chief was deciding. Then, he said with mischief in his voice, "Wanna go for a real ride, Billy?"

59

A bout that time, Jake strode up, having overheard Chief's offer. He knew full well what Chief had in mind. "Ya don't want to pass up that offer, Billy."

"What?" Looked at Jake, then at Chief.

Chief said, "I can offer you a vantage point that might make it easier to spot that big-ass auto you're looking for." With that, the two younger men led a perplexed Billy into the barn.

"Holy...!" As he peered up at Little Sky's torpedo-shaped canopy with the car underneath that looked like a little flat-bottom boat resting peacefully on the barn's dirt floor, he said, "Does it—"

"Yeah, Billy, it flies," Jake said. Chief just grinned as he climbed aboard and started stoking the fire in Little Sky's belly.

Chief spoke over his shoulder, "Jake, sprinkle some of that dry straw over there on the ground." Jake went to work like an experienced hand at airship deployment.

Billy pulled off his stylish but soiled Stetson by its front brim and scratched his nose with the back of that same hand. "Holy....!"

⚜

TWENTY MINUTES LATER, CHIEF AND BILLY ASCENDED through five hundred feet and peddled with a steady effort. Chief explained, "Now if you spot that car parked somewhere, we need to stay off a ways or we might get spotted. They might not look up, but if they do, we'll sure stand out. That's Route 60 up yonder. We got a tailwind. Going back'll be harder, but we can descend to where there's less breeze. Not too many farms up this way. Most are pretty big."

After another uneventful fifteen minutes, other than Billy repeating, "Holy...," he shouted, "There! What in tarnation? That's Roy Dillworth's farm. What's going on here? Chief, you turn this contraption around, and I mean right now!"

"You got it, Sheriff." Chief turned the wheel left to its stops, and the bulbous nose of the taut hot air bag struggled to turn into the wind. He closed the chimney flue above the firebox to slow the hot air's flow into the bag. They soon lost altitude where they fought less of a headwind. "Peddle harder, Billy."

Thirty minutes later, they descended toward Chief's barn where they saw the rest of their little gang standing in the yard looking up at them in awe. Billy could hear Walt whooping it up at the sight of the airship approaching. He drowned out little Edie's softer, but just as enthusiastic whooping—two octaves higher. They all could tell she was itching to get aloft with who she now called *her Chief*.

Little Sky's creator and pilot navigated toward the back of the barn. Just outside its open doors, he allowed the ship's nose to settle to the ground. Took 'em some time to get the prop to reverse direction with some serious back-peddling, but Chief timed all that well with his barked orders. *Just like a ship's captain,* Billy thought. Billy's hat almost blew off as they threw their energy into some back-peddling action. By now the "wings" had deflated and drooped like big floppy ears. Their forward motion stopped, the ship settled, and Chief said, "Now we peddle forward to get her inside. Okay, Billy?"

"Hell, yeah, but my legs are rubbery from all that peddling. This is the damndest thing, Chief! Holy...."

❦

THE GROUP GATHERED AROUND *LITTLE SKY* NOW IN THE barn, offering to help secure her. Chief declined. He executed his landing and securing routine. Ten minutes later, they stood in front of the barn-slash-hangar. With Edie's help, Sophie and Hilda brought out a large blue-enamel coffee pot of yard mud with a tray full of cups they discovered in the kitchen, badly in need of a wash. A workbench just inside the barn's front door became their buffet. They all stood chittering about the airship. Henry just stared. The ladies passed cups of stout Old Judge all around, and Hilda handed around a tray of her crullers retrieved by Henry from the house in town.

Billy said, "Men, Malone and Leary are at Roy Dillworth's farm over in Osceola County. At least that big auto is. Why, I don't know." At the mention of that name, Henry wheeled around from staring at the airship to make sure he'd heard Billy correctly. "Did you say Roy Dillworth? He's my Ford competitor up in Worthington City! Son-of-a-bitch!"

"Henry!"

"Sorry, Hildie, but—"

"Henry, I have no jurisdiction over in Osceola, but I know Sheriff Graves over there. He might know something. I'll call him. But first, Jake, Walt, what say the three of us take a look-see—from the ground? Consider yourselves duly deputized."

Billy still seemed a little shaken from his first aerial sortie, but offered Chief a good-natured nod of gratitude and a squeeze on the shoulder. "Chief, okay if you hold down the fort for a couple of hours with Henry and the ladies?"

"Billy, no offense, but this is my place, and us *Injuns* don't hold down *forts*. But spending time with ladies, and even you, Henry, well, I'm sort of shinin' up to the idea of havin' some folks around, even if you all are white." Wink.

❧

JAKE ROARED. THE OTHERS FOLLOWED SUIT WITH NERVOUS laughter. Henry smiled. Even he was getting to like this young man, Jake's friend. They owed him a great deal already.

Billy didn't want to be conspicuous in his patrol car. Besides, no jurisdiction. "Henry, okay if we take your sedan?"

❧

HENRY GRINNED, SAID NOTHING, BUT TOSSED HIM THE KEY. He'd never really had friends, just acquaintances. And most of those.... But this strange group, *maybe*. After last night's discussion, and learning from Walt how dangerous these people are, Henry was convinced there was no better place for his family. At least for right now, despite all the awkwardness and inconvenience. He brimmed with gratitude. Now, all his silly business machinations made no sense to him by comparison.

B illy drove, Jake called shotgun, and Walt stretched out on the back seat for a snooze, enjoying the new car. He said, "Hey, Jake. I'm sure your daddy-in-law would say, 'Nothing like that new Chevy smell, eh?'" Walt was trying to lighten the mood. Raised a couple of smiles in the front seat.

They headed south on 14 until they came to a farm road that headed east. Billy turned left. He said, "I think Roy Dillworth's place is the second farm south of Ashton. East side of State Road 60. Me 'n Chief stayed a ways off, and gosh, we was way up there. I spotted not only that big red and black car in the yard. But at least a couple of sizable trucks comin' and goin' too, and smoke rollin' out of a stack upside the barn. Mighty strange. Jake, that machine of Chief's. Hell of a thing. I bet you two are peas in a pod, ain'tcha?"

"Well, he's a smart kid, alright." He smiled, but Billy didn't notice as he kept his eyes glued to the late-afternoon road.

"Did he tell ya he's a college graduate? Says he went to the university up there in Minneapolis."

Jake was just a little surprised. "He told you, huh?"

"Yup. Told me the whole kit 'n caboodle this morning. Comes from money, for sure, and says his mom was somethin' special. Irish, but obviously a very different kinda Irish than Malone 'n his mob. Yeah, us cops have a way of gettin' shit outta people." He swiveled his head toward Jake, grinned, but still kept his eyes on the rutted road.

"I guess there's a lot going on in that Injun's head." Jake ground his teeth, looked out the window. Even though Chief's parents had money, he is still a good guy.

"Yeah, I made some assumptions about him that were all wrong. He's a good friend, isn't he?"

"Yeah, Sheriff. He is, even if he hasn't figured that out, or how to show it." Jake continued his thousand-yard stare out the passenger's window.

"Jake, what's goin' on?"

"D'you mean?"

"C'mon, kid, we've known each other for a little while now. I knew your parents. Somethin's weighin' on ya, pardner. What is it?"

"Aw, Billy, well, I see Dan gets his degree, more'n one, and he isn't doing anything with 'em other than playing around in his barn. That's special alright, but—"

"Listen, Jake, I get it. I think. Greener grass 'n all that. But you got something special too."

"Yeah?"

"In case you didn't notice. I've sorta always had a crush on your Sophie, even though she's way too young for an old soldier like me."

"Yeah, I sorta noticed, Billy. Kinda creepy." They both chuckled.

"Point is, you got a great girl who loves ya to death. You

got friends. You got *community*, kid. And if I ain't way off the scent, you horn dog, soon you'll have a kid or three of your own."

"Billy, it's just that I saw my daddy beat down—by the land. By folks who hate immigrants, especially us Krauts after the war, or by uppity types who look down on farmers. And then a bum ticker slowed Daddy way down before he ever got a chance to go running after *his* dream. Not too long before he died while I was away, he told me he always wanted to be a baker. I don't wanna be my daddy, bless his hungry soul."

"Jake, I've been around. Got twenty-odd years on ya, son. Runnin' toward the horizon ain't gonna get ya what you need. Hang in there, brother. Take yer time. Lots of livin' to be had anywhere if you know what to look for."

They both fell silent. Nothing more to say right then. *Walt's still asleep sprawled in the back seat, isn't he? Hope so. Too much talk. Even Walt's been chasin' his own brand of dreams. But what if Billy's right? Too much stinkin' thinkin'?*

Took about a half hour to reach Route 60 via the rough farm road. They dared not top twenty or thirty, even though Henry's big sedan wanted to give them more. These ruts could flip a buckboard, maybe even bust up a Chevy sedan. Billy turned north onto the smoother-dirt two-lane 60 and said, "Now Dillworth's place is just about a mile up on the right. What say we pull the car off a half mile out and hike through the patch of woods just to the south that Chief 'n I saw from up there?" He pointed skyward.

"Yup. Hey Walt! Get your lazy ass up. We're here."

BILLY HAD SEEN A FIELD ROAD MORE THAN HALF COVERED with grass on the far side of that tree line and field east of Dillworth's farm. He slid Henry's sedan into a well-concealed depression behind the dense cluster of red oaks he'd seen from the air. They closed the doors as softly as they could.

The trio slipped through the woods to the edge of a fallow field, within a hundred yards from a row of outbuildings at the eastern perimeter of Dillworth's yard. They saw the upper portion of an imposing barn and smokestack beyond the roofs of a squat row of out-buildings. Billy edged back into the trees and hiked a hundred yards north for a better angle on the yard behind that barn. Jake and Walt followed. Billy scratched out a map in his little notebook for their use later. Was getting hard to see in the late afternoon light. They saw the tendrils of smoke curling skyward from the rectangular brick stack at the south end of the huge clapboard barn.

Walt said, "Yup, they're cookin' hooch, alright. Sour stink of mash."

❦

61

Billy stood at the wall-mounted phone in Chief's kitchen. He dialed Sheriff Duane Graves of neighboring Osceola County. "Duane, I have information of a major liquor operation in your county."

"What? The hell, you say! Where?"

"Roy Dillworth's farm on Route 60. And that operation has already spilled over into my county."

"Mighty strong words. You got proof, Billy?"

"Seen it with my own eyes. The stink of mash, a big-ass still, trucks comin' and goin', the works."

"Oh, my. Well, I've suspected, and you've confirmed my suspicions. Let's not waste any time. Wanna come over and play with us?" *Interesting. He's both surprised and suspected?*

Billy chuckled. "I was hopin' you'd say that, brother. It would be my pleasure."

"Alrighty, then. Let's not waste time. Tomorrow night? Say, midnight?"

"I'll bring my deputies. Your operation. What's your plan, and how can we help?"

Over the course of the next fifteen minutes, they verbally mapped it out. He wasn't sure why, but Billy said nothing about Malone and Leary, nor that he'd been collaborating with the ATF. And at Chief Dan's request, neither did Billy mention their aerial recon. Dan's gut was talking to him, and Billy had grown to trust that damn Injun. A few phone calls later, and wheels were in motion.

SHERIFF DUANE GRAVES SUSPECTED HIS LAVISH LIFESTYLE was now at risk. Worse, he feared Finn Malone's reaction to this news. He worried about the madman's standard response: eliminate the risk—all of it. No loose ends. *Shit!*

❧

62

Armed with the map of Dillworth's farm scrawled in Billy's notebook, the group sat around Chief's dining room table later that night. An elegant eight-foot rectangular chandelier with geometrical lines bathed the table in a diffuse yellow glow. Though there was still an empty chair on each side of the spacious table, Walt, Chief, and the newly arrived Owen and Seppel, here at Henry's request, stood like anxious cats. They had jumped at the chance for some action. Walt just felt fidgety. Chief didn't sit much. Ever. Another cat.

Owen and Seppel—two of Henry's mechanics and war veterans—seemed joined at the hip. They kept vigilant watch out the big front window down toward the trees on either side of the long driveway fifty yards out. Something about the way their eyes darted, scanning, non-stop. They had each strapped on old canvas belts with revolvers and ammo packs in pouches, courtesy of the wartime US Army fifteen years ago. Both offered to stand watch outside. But Billy said that wasn't necessary. Not yet, anyway. Both possessed eyes that had seen too much. He appreciated their presence, and that they, too, protected Sophie and the rest of this crew. These two boys knew their way around weapons. They still moved like soldiers, even though they were as old as he. His newest and most mature deputy, Dwight Spooner, had also recently arrived in his cruiser, another welcome addition to the posse. Dwight flitted in and out of the house, consumed by his own nervous energy.

Billy started the discussion. "Okay, Sheriff Graves has a larger department, and should be well-equipped to handle these arrests." Jake heard the words, but sensed Billy wasn't convinced. "What aren't you saying out loud, Billy?" Sounded more like an accusation than Jake intended.

"Dunno, Jake, when I called Duane, told him about Dillworth, he didn't sound too surprised. And something else. Like he sounded... scared. Aw, heck, I'm no doubt just imagining things."

"You don't think—"

"Let's just be careful. Duane invited me to the party. I need Jimmy back at the office. We still got the rest of Lyon County to worry about while we're gallivanting east to Osceola. My gut tells me Dwight and I need to be in on this, but we could use some help."

Jake said, "I'm in."

Walt gazed out the window with Seppel and Owen who both nodded with grim determination. Walt wheeled around at Jake's words. "Me too."

"Men, we all need to acknowledge this is a crazy plan, but I don't know any other way to approach this right now. You gotta know this will be dangerous."

Sitting at the end of the table by Billy, Jake piped up. "And so is doing nothing. At least we have a chance of getting through this by taking action."

63

An FBI surveillance team from the Newark, New Jersey field office learned of a series of radio rendezvous between two suspected foreign agents, as reported by a Mr. Charles-Royce Hugo, an informant for ATF Special Supervisory Agent Lang Eubanks. Based on this intelligence report, they monitored 3.614 megacycles within the shortwave frequency band designated for amateur radio use. By confirming bearing and distance vectors, three separate listening posts in the Northern New Jersey area triangulated the likely location of one of their suspects, code-named Mr. Tree. They achieved this by intercepting three separate exchanges between the suspects on the monitored frequency over the course of sixteen days, always on Sunday evenings.

Agent Lang Eubanks had convinced the skeptical Executive Special Agent in Charge of FBI's Newark Field Office, Reece Cobb, that this was likely a critical matter of national security. As such, Cobb authorized a full-scale breach of the suspect's location, comprising twenty elite agents. This breach included the use of specialized weapons and military-style tactics. They weren't taking any chances. Lang stood by his Rapid City field office telephone awaiting news of the early morning operation. He paced more than he sat—a cat prancing on broken glass.

Initial reports indicated they had indeed located a radio communications station at that location. The breach team that engaged in sweeping the dilapidated structure stopped transmitting minute-by-minute updates to their field office. Telephone updates over Lang's open line to Rapid City ceased as well. Lang resisted chewing his perfectly manicured nails while he waited in agony. After seven excruciating minutes, his phone barked back to life. Startled, he listened. The first voice Lang heard was ESAIC Cobb from Newark. The excessive volume splattered his voice. "Eubanks, what in Hell have you gotten us involved in?"

"What do you mean, sir? What happened?"

"I'll tell you what happened. Someone detonated enough high explosives to collapse the entire structure that we raided and turned it into a damn fireball. *That's* what happened. Sixteen of my agents were inside at the time. Only eleven made it out. What frosts my balls more than anything is that radio station in the structure was just a damn repeater, not the source. Your raid cost me the lives of five fine agents and we got shit to show for it. Now you wanna tell me what's really going on here, *Agent?*"

Lang stood at his desk with the phone's base in his right hand and the ear piece in the other. He fell into his chair as if someone just shot him through the heart. The intel they'd received was credible, but they had been deceived.

"Sir, that is truly awful news. I am very sorry to hear that. Sir, we are facing clever adversaries, which only elevates my concern. We identified and raided the right place, but not the *only* right place. You're the on-scene commander. Is that how I should read this, sir?"

Cobb was still hot under the collar from losing good men. But he started to cool down under the influence of Eubanks' calming voice, filled with as much sorrow, but laced with less raw anger and more analysis. "Yeah, we had the right place. I'm pissed we didn't find the explosives on our sweep. It's just that—"

"Sir, I've lost men in the past. There is nothing so emotionally devastating—"

"Yeah, I get it. I don't need a pep talk. Shit! Look, Eubanks, it's not your fault. Your intel was solid, and we confirmed it with our surveillance. Just... who *are* these people?"

"Well, sir, we can surmise they are sophisticated operators, not your run-of-the-mill street thugs like we've been dealing with out here, or even with Malone's mob of bootleggers in Chicago. These people... they feel more like trained intelligence operatives. My source tells me that German is likely their first language."

Cobb was settling back into analytical mode. Devastating losses notwithstanding, he was a professional. "But we won that war. Why Germans? Why now, fifteen years after the war?"

"Well, remember the war ended in a bottom-up revolution. The German populous had had enough of the Kaiser feeding his ego as a conqueror while they starved. At the same time, an entire class of German aristocrats lost everything when representatives of the general population established a quasi-democracy called the Weimar Republic at the end of the war in 1918. Maybe this is a case of the *haves* who became the *have-nots* overnight, at the hands of conquering Americans and their allies, now seeking some sort of revenge. I'm just speculating, ESAIC Cobb," he pronounced Cobb's title, E-sake, "but it's possible we're dealing with German immigrants who blame the American Empire for destroying the old German Empire, and they want some payback. Given their considerable means and strategy, along with other bits of intelligence we've acquired, they may be collaborators with the emerging Third Reich. And that, sir, is a worldwide movement."

"Good Lord. And they plan to use our own criminals to distribute this addictive poison nationwide to enslave and lay waste a significant percentage of the American people? That is diabolical. If that's the case, why don't we just broadcast over all the radio networks to alert everyone not to drink this shit?"

"We could do that, sir, but I fear widespread panic and distrust. There are a great number of German immigrants living across America. The vast majority are loyal patriots. This could undermine their reputations by association. And even if we disassociated such announcements from their suspected German perpetrators, recall how tepid the response has been to the Volstead Act and Prohibition. I fear they might perceive this as a government attempt to falsely claim that 'all liquor is poison,' which could generate other negative repercussions. Worse, we'd scare these perpetrators further underground, leaving them free to continue their nefarious scheme. At least now, we're working several leads out here in the Midwest that we're convinced have a reasonable probability of success. We just need diligence wherever intel presents itself, and continue chasing the leads. I feel this is warranted, given the magnitude of what's at stake. Does that make sense to you, sir?"

❧ 64 ❧

❧

J ake had skidded the dream of building his loco-baler to the back of the barn for now. Same for his running battle with Henry. They set all that aside for the greater good of family and community. The climate had already improved between Henry and Jake as the current crises escalated around them—an alliance forged in the fires of a common threat. Besides, there were now far worse villains to worry about.

But now, Jake's number one demon once again grabbed hold of him and would not let go. The year he'd spent away from the farm at mechanical design school in Rapid City—against Daddy's wishes—developed his natural talent. That experience enabled him to envision the details of how to build his baler. But a bolt of lightning, not his bad ticker, had killed Daddy while trying to secure the cows from the pasture during one of those early hot dust storms. Who knew they made killer lightning?

Worse, Jake later discovered Daddy's journal in the house.

The old man loved to scratch down notes, a habit from dreaming up new recipes to feed his unfulfilled dream of owning a bake shop. One passage read, *"We can't afford the hospital, but Pastor Heinleick saw to it that Doc Gustavsen comes out from Spencer to see Mommy. Said her rash and the pale circle around her mouth looked to him like scarlet fever. She is awfully sick, but Doc gave me medicine she surely needs every three hours, around the clock."* Mom was so sick, and with nobody to check on her for days, or to give her that medicine, because Daddy was dead in a gully, she passed away from a burning fever.

Knowing all of this wracked Jake with guilt—all of the time; although he was pretty good at hiding it. Maybe that's why he loved Sophie so much. She shared with him the worst time during *her* early childhood, and the source of her own irrational guilt and shame. In a private moment when she worried about her husband's state of mind, she had said, "When I was young, like ten years old, I heard the talk, Jake. A school friend told me what her mother told her. She said, 'Cross the street when you walk past a house in the neighborhood where all the children have died of polio. And if we have to walk past it, we should hold our breath and run as fast as we can.' That was before we knew water transmitted polio, not air. You can imagine me *surviving* polio and going to school. The kids treated me like a leper. At first, I felt shame and guilt for even surviving, much less for leaving the house, as if I were putting everyone around me at emotional risk. But then anger replaced all that. I was not a very pleasant person to be around back then. Plus, some of the children made fun of my 'claw hand,' and the way I wobbled when I walked. It took a few years and things got better. But still...."

Jake thought, *Who was it that said 'misery loves company?'*

65

A new moon would make for a treacherous approach across the weedy field adjacent to Dillworth's farm. Billy and his five new Lyon County deputies arrived at the appointed time and waited in the tree line east of the barn's backside. They observed frenzied activity on the far side of the empty field and beyond the three low out-buildings that squatted between them and that huge barn.

Henry's two combat veteran mechanics—Owen and Seppel—carried their old Army rifles and wore their olive-drab gear belts. They had stuffed the pouches in the belts they brought back from the war with ammo. The belts' integrated holsters slung their well-worn but meticulously maintained side arms. Looked like a couple of cowboys. But instead of hats, they wore their doughboy helmets. Their expressions acknowledged this would be no picnic. Billy carried his double-ought-loaded shotgun. Jake and Walt borrowed small revolvers from Billy and Dwight that came with a few words of training, hoping they wouldn't shoot off their toes, or worse. They did not need to borrow courage or resolve.

They were to proceed across the field to the rear of the out-buildings to wait for Sheriff Graves and his deputies who would lead the frontal assault. Billy and his guys were to provide perimeter support to ensure nobody escaped into the field surrounding the rear of the farm during the operation. The plan seemed solid.

🐾

IT WOULD HAVE BEEN MIDNIGHT DARK HAD IT NOT BEEN for the dozen kerosene torches driven into the cracked earth at ten-foot intervals. Their smoky flames danced in the ten knot breeze. They did a poor job of illuminating the area between the rear of the barn whose doors they had flung wide and the pair of enormous trucks. The torches cast even darker shadows between the trucks and the trio of low buildings to the east, behind which they hid. It was as if this area behind the barn was lit just for tonight, maybe otherwise for daylight use only. But tonight looked to be special, like they were getting out of town. Like they got wind of something.

Two trucks received the rapt attention of half a dozen hooligans as they pushed four-wheeled trolleys from the barn's back doors to each truck's open tailgate. Each burdensome trolley transported four barrels. In pairs, Malone's gorillas positioned each beneath the tailgate of a large canvas-covered truck bed and hoisted one heavy barrel at a time to their confederates inside. Those wooden barrels looked to contain thirty or forty gallons each. Had to be hooch, probably that Black Gold crap.

They labored in silence, for the most part, in the dim light. From their hides, Billy's posse could only pick up their grunts and occasional profanities under their breath. The loading process remained bathed in stroboscopic shadows, and what seemed to be a contrived hush. Only the reflected glow from the brilliant yard light in front of the barn reached this surreal scene, as if this was forbidden territory. As if it sensed something horrible was about to happen.

From behind the middle of the three out-buildings to the east, Billy, Dwight and Sep watched Sticks Leary supervising the loading process. He wielded his weapon of choice—a large stick or club—switching hands while twirling it with practiced expertise. They could see bits of torch light glinting off that bat. Billy thought, *The creepy little mutt buried razor blades in that damn thing!* The ER doc over at the Spencer hospital had found brittle pieces of razor blades embedded in Roddy's wounds. *Sick sumbitch. I'm betting we found our murderer.*

The thugs finished loading and prepared the pair of trucks for departure, as if they expected more trucks to arrive and take their place. After they finished tying down the barrels, they hopped down to the hardpan dirt, raised the tailgates, and pinned them. Billy fidgeted. *Where the hell is Graves and his posse? Shit! They're gonna miss the party!* Billy whispered, "Looks like now or never, boys." Grim nods from Dwight and Sep signaled they were ready.

❦

ONCE JAKE SAW BILLY CREEP AROUND THE BUILDING closest to the field, that was Plan B, they were to surround Leary, the six loaders and the two drivers. *But where the hell are the Osceola guys? They're supposed to start this party!* Now committed to the backup plan, Jake led Walt and Owen toward the trucks from their hiding spot behind a building to the north, also at the edge of the loading yard. They could see the east side of Dillworth's house to their right. Illuminated by the yard light, the white mansion sat perpendicular to the barn, but its interior remained dark. Jake ensured their deputized trio kept pace with Billy's advance. He now spotted Sep and Dwight following close behind Billy. All was going according to Plan B until the gravelly voice came from behind.

"Drop 'em! Reach!" Heavy weapons cocked and several pairs of feet shuffled in close. Jake saw Billy look over in their direction in shock just as four goons rushed out of the building behind which *they* were hiding. The surprise was complete. *They knew we were coming!*

❧

BILLY THOUGHT, *If I LIVE LONG ENOUGH TO GET HOLD OF that weasel Graves....* He would not get all these boys shot up right here, right now. He said loud enough for Jake and his guys to hear, "Do as they say, boys. Our time will come." With slow deliberation, he laid his shotgun at his feet. Just then, a high-pitched, warbling laugh—more of a cackle—distracted them. The little creep waving his bat around like some sort of baton-twirling cheerleader looked up at the large man standing next to him with his arms crossed and head down. Billy'd recognize that hulk with that huge broken nose anywhere. *Graves!*

The mutts finished disarming them, even found Billy's boot knife. Pros. Their meager collection of weapons remained where they were ambushed. The heavily armed thugs pushed them toward the torch-lit area between the trucks and the rear of the barn—their would-be killing field, no doubt. They knocked the six of them to their knees from behind with vicious blows to the back of their legs.

"Hands on yer heads, interlock yer feckin' fingers!" Leary strutted over to his prisoners and looked down on them with his bug-eyes and wicked leer. The little creep was enjoying himself. Graves kept his distance: he did not appear to relish what he knew was coming. Leary said, "You," signaling one of his goons with the point of a bony finger, like the grim reaper himself, "fetch me this boy-o's scatter-gun over yonder."

Billy knew this would not end well. He needed to buy some time. "Look, Mr. Leary, I'm the one you want. These boys are just temporary deputies—farmers and mechanics."

"Shut it, maggot. I can see that fer me-self. Shit-scrapers dunna even have proper little copper blouses like the two of you'se." Meaning, like him and Dwight.

"Look, why not just let them go. It's me you want. For the love of God, Duane, tell him!"

"I said, shut it!" And without further warning, Leary landed a vicious left-handed blow with his *stick* to Billy's right arm just below the shoulder. He hit Billy hard enough to knock him off of his knees and his hat from his head. His left cheekbone took a jarring bounce off the desiccated dirt. His arm and shoulder were on fire, almost certainly shattered. And it bled, but not profusely.

SEP TOLLEY WAS FORCED TO HIS KNEES ONLY ONCE BEFORE, knocked there by an arrogant German stormtrooper. A British sniper picked off the bastard and rescued Sep and his brothers. Now he was on his knees again. No sniper around. In fuming contempt, Sep retrieved a mud-caked chunk of snot from his dry throat and launched it at this dirt-bag's face. Too heavy, it failed to gain altitude and fell short, landing on one of Leary's well-shined but dusty shoes. Sep glared defiantly at the mutt. If only looks could kill like a sniper's bullet.

❦

BEFORE BILLY HAD EVEN STOPPED SQUIRMING ON THE ground from the pain, Leary glanced at his goobered shoe—annoyed, but amused. He dropped his club, grabbed Billy's shotgun from his goon, pulled back both hammers with the heel of his left hand, raised and swung the business end toward Seppel, and said, "Ya got stones, maggot, but I dunna like the look a yer glare." Leary unloaded both barrels into the center of Sep's chest at close range. A casual gesture. Turned back to gloat at Billy before Sep's body had even thumped backward into a tiny cloud of dirt, as if to say, "this one's on you, copper." But did Billy see something else, looking up into the mobster's eyes as time slowed to a gripping crawl—a flash of regret? He could imagine the countless souls this monster had murdered, but also could imagine that each one took a bite for themselves. Then his own vision grew misty as time spun back to normal. Billy's sight became tinged with a scarlet vignette, an aperture that threatened to close in a cloud of dust, but he dared not pass out. Not now.

"No! You—" Billy had no more words, only wracking sobs. What had he done?

Sheriff Graves turned his back, shrunk away.

BILLY ROLLED ONTO HIS OWN BACK, SINKING INTO A PIT OF paralyzing anguish, realizing they never had *any* chance of defeating these experienced criminals armed to their teeth. *What was I thinking?* Now Billy realized he might be the cause of the death of all his friends—to his own damnation—not to mention his failure as a lawman. But there were still innocent lives here. He'd gotten them into this mess. From within his growing hatred, he glared up to see twin reflections of a nearby torch in those dead black eyes. The wheels turned again to buy precious seconds. "Why d'ya have to kill him, Leary?"

"Who, boy-o? That little grease monkey with the fancy helmet?" He nodded toward poor Sep and his shredded upper torso. The powdery dust still tried to settle around him in the gentle breeze. Meanwhile, the uncaring torches threw shards of light to bear witness.

Between sobs that now cadenced his bitter anger—and what must come next—Billy said, "Sep was a soldier. He knew the score. I'm talkin' about my deputy. He was just an innocent kid, for cripe sake."

"Not all that innocent, Constable. Twas a copper what saw more'n he was supposed to. 'Sides, don't need much of a reason to snuff a copper, yeh?" Another subdued cackle punctuated his casual declaration.

"But why strip him?"

In a low but malevolent voice Leary said, "Won't say it again. Shut it, ya proper wanker."

ROY DILLWORTH STOOD NEARBY, BETWEEN A TORCH AND the line of intruders—four still on their knees, one bloody corpse, and Billy laying on his side. Billy was in disbelief when he spotted Roy. *That sumbitch is really the largest producer and distributor of corn liquor in this part of the Midwest? The Worthington City Ford guy?* Billy could only see him in silhouette, but the large man's fidgeting broadcast his nervous demeanor. And he'd recognize that stupid hat anywhere.

DILLWORTH PULLED LEARY ASIDE AND ASKED IN A LOW voice, "Why *did* you take the kid's stuff, Sticks?" not caring that their prisoners heard him as they were already dead. They just didn't know it yet. As soon as Finn arrived to give the word, though....

"Insurance, boy-o, along with your bloody jacket from helping me load the stiff in to the sheriff's carriage. So's you don't get no fancy ideas, ya slippery git, in case ya decide to act the maggot 'round these culchies—you and that feckin' big-spendin' sheriff a yers." He nodded toward the line of prisoners. "I don't fancy they's yer grand besties, but just the same, insurance."

"What? And what the hell are *culchies?* Oh, farmers?"

"Aye, boy-o. Ya daft?"

Gawd, these Mick mutts frustrated Dillworth. *Why can't they speak American!* But he knew the threat was real enough. Untrusting runts. Must have sensed his second thoughts about their alliance. *This is getting way too serious. If it weren't for Mr. Shade's private assurances....*

Dillworth said, "Look, Mr. Malone funded this operation, his chemist designed the process, and built the still. My boys and I make the product. You load, guard, and transport to your joints in Omaha. You get me Bairns Motors when the old man can't pay anymore. That was the deal. We all make money. I don't know about all this other bullshit you've sucked me into. A deal's a deal, Sticks."

Dillworth didn't push it any further when he saw the stare of glazed crazy coming off of Leary in a fierce wave before he started pacing again. He just turned away before *he* got bludgeoned with that nasty bat.

⚜

THEY HALF-WHISPERED, BUT BILLY HEARD EVERY WORD. ***That's*** what this has all been about? Henry's loan? The threats *against his family? Roddy's murder? All for shipping poison and stealing a dealership? The pitiless bastards. Who thinks like this?*

Sheriff Graves was no longer anywhere to be seen, but his betrayal was complete. Billy wondered what he got out of all this. Didn't matter. Graves was as much a criminal as these devils. Worse. *Betrayed by a brother lawman! No matter,* Billy thought, *I'll be dead soon enough, and dead men tell no tales. Unless....*

AS STICKS LEARY WAITED FOR HIS BOSS'S ARRIVAL WITH growing impatience, his crew finished loading and buttoning up the second truck, along with some paperwork. Circumstances convinced him the time had arrived to burn the house down. This Dillworth culchie was bang-on delivering the goods to replace the loss of their Minnesota cooker. Even better, but now the git had become a liability. He could smell the thick of it on him. And their bestie cooker, the Indian, had disappeared. Aul Finn didn't give two hoots about that auto store over yonder in yet another shite-bit town, but losing his bestie cooker? That's more 'n a wee bit a trouble, that is. *Just need leverage on Dillworth—a right git, turns out.* He thought, *This melter's now as useless as a chocolate teapot, he is. And he's a bloody pain in me bollocks! But did he know where to find that cooker? That'd be Finnster's bloody button, fer sure.*

66

The red and black Duesenberg roadster—the Emperor's chariot—crunched the pebbly driveway under its three-ton heft in the otherwise cemetery silence. It wheeled around the northeast corner of Dillworth's barn. With the trucks loaded and nothing more to be said, the only other sound was the subtle crackling of the foot-high torch flames in the breeze. The yard reeked of their coal-oil smoke. The huge auto rumbled to a stop. It dwarfed the dapper slicker who slid out of the cockpit. Finn Malone himself. He did not look happy, but would have been more unhappy if he hadn't received the call, given the situation.

The drive down from Worthington City in the dark after being beckoned had notched up his anxiety, more than normal. Sticks decided at the last moment he should be here. Malone took in the situation in five seconds after eyeing the row of prisoners, nodded to Leary, who then jerked his exotic handgun from its shoulder holster slung under his right arm. The holster's leather creaked in protest, but relented. Several of his thugs took their boss's cue and levied their weapons at their prisoners.

❦

AT THAT MOMENT, A HUGE CONCUSSIVE BLAST OF HOT AIR diverted their attention, and the ground quaked. Jake nudged Billy's foot with his own. Both nodded. Billy said just loud enough for the other prisoners to hear, "Now." On cue, their little group still on their knees flopped flat forward, face down, with their hands covering their heads. This was where they'd put their lives in Chief Dan's hands.

Within a few seconds of the first blast, a second fiery explosion collapsed the huge roof of the barn in slow motion. The combination of these two concussions in rapid succession knocked Malone and his mob off their feet. Billy saw that at least two would not get up again, impaled by flying shrapnel.

The ground shook with a third explosion on the far side of the barn. The trio of flashes heated the surrounding air in an instant by a good forty degrees, at least. Another concussion of equal force shook the earth yet again. This time, the flash from the explosion was much brighter as the interior of the now-roofless barn partially combusted. Everyone knew that in seconds the flowing flames down into the barn's volatile interior would detonate the storage tanks of alcohol and the remaining inventory of barrels full of ninety-five proof alcohol, the ones not already exploding.

Whump! The remainder of the vast roof and the upper perimeter of the barn's walls descended into Hell itself. Tons of bricks that comprised the tall smokestack chased the barn's now-collapsing south wall down onto what remained of the thirty-foot-tall still. Flames followed the plumbing leading to the row of five-hundred-gallon storage tanks.

Whump! Whump! Whump! Panic reigned. The sky and the air all around them glowed white-hot. With their prisoners forgotten, the dozen gangsters, including Leary and Malone, skittered away from the roiling flames. Now arcing out onto the loading zone's periphery, secondary explosions reverberated from within the now-half-razed barn. *Whump! Whump!* Before they ducked for shelter behind the storage building north of the barn, in case the trucks exploded too, airborne fireballs engulfed a few of them. Barrels of hooch relieved of gravity's burden launched upward, outward, and downward, like lava bombs. One of the corpses incinerated still clutched an ugly bat with embedded razor blades locked in the death grip of one hand, and an Ivory-handled pistol clutched in the other.

ONCE THE LOADING ZONE CLEARED OF CRIMINALS, BILLY, Jake, and the rest of their posse bolted for the open field to the east through which they had come. Billy grabbed his boot knife where it had fallen, and the others followed suit, risking precious seconds, to retrieve their treasured weapons. They'd return later for poor Sep's body. Nobody took chase. The bad guys now focused on surviving an attack from an unknown superior force.

CHIEF DAN GLIDED IN STEALTH TWO HUNDRED FEET ABOVE. He had dropped gallon jugs of gasoline, with smoldering wicks stuffed down their necks. Each jug also contained a stick of Silas's stump-blowing dynamite. He had dropped two on the large barn's roof, one in the yard to the north of the barn, and one in front of the house. That was supposed to hit the barn too, but... didn't. Chief held two more jugs in reserve, but he'd already risked incinerating his friends laying prone behind the barn. Too close.

The group of hooligans now hiding to the north of the barn still had no idea Chief was up there. Good thing, too. He spotted at least two weapons that looked like distinctive magazine-fed selective-fire automatic weapons. Some called them machine guns. White men! Hard to miss those distinctive circular drums, pistol grips under their shoulder stocks, and extended barrels, even from the air. Those Thompsons would tear him and Little Sky into heavier-than-air chunks of debris, not to mention ruin his best flight jacket, leather helmet and favorite goggles.

His friends had fled to the field. Now he could see a caravan of automobile lights racing south toward the farm on Route 60. Chief would not risk dropping any more bombs. Just a bunch of silly white men squabbling, anyway. But if those criminals headed for his friends again, he'd light 'em up, for sure. Yeah, *his friends*. Besides, fiery debris now climbed wave after wave of super-heated air, and were coming way too close to his silk air bag. Time to climb and disappear into the night. He'd left a triangle of torches burning behind his own barn. Now to dead-reckon a course home.

✥

67

Billy, Dwight, and the rest of the deputized crew lay prone in the field, observing and waiting for the situation to develop. Billy had provided Walt's G-Man friend, Agent Eubanks of the ATF, precise directions to the Dillworth farm the previous day. He instructed them to lie in wait a mile to the north until they spotted Malone's big Duese pass by, not before. But navigating these county roads at night was not for the faint of heart. He had also instructed the ATF guys to *follow the flames in.*

✥

THOUGH THAT UNUSUAL INSTRUCTION PUZZLED AGENT Eubanks, he didn't ask Billy to explain. He hungered for a chance to catch Malone and his Iowa mob in deep guilty with the goods—maybe even his master chemist, one Dan Rustywire, a.k.a. Chief, if he was lucky. Eubanks was quite content to follow the locals' lead out here, and he appreciated the precision of the plan. He'd owe Walt Weller a debt if this mass apprehension panned out.

An hour earlier, they had parked on a dirt field path amid a copse of box elders. That positioned them a mile north of what Weller called the Dillworth farm on the east side of Osceola Route 60. Being a stickler for details, Eubanks had reconnoitered this hide earlier in the day.

After Malone's distinctive automobile thundered passed, as predicted, they waited the prescribed five minutes. They then aimed their trio of agent-filled vehicles south onto 60 with their lights off—a warranted risk. Malone was a slippery character, and Eubanks would not chance premature discovery, or the notorious mobster might just keep on driving and disappear like he'd done in the past.

Then they spotted flames—of war zone magnitude. The signal. As promised. They turned on their lights and followed the flames in at as high a rate of speed as they dared.

❦

68

Roy Dillworth broadcast abject fear in his voice. They shouted over the wind noise. "Mr. Malone, where are we going?" It seemed a heavy long-wheel-base car like the Duesenberg could navigate rutted dirt roads at speeds well in excess of what was possible in a lesser motorcar.

"Settle down, boy-o. Setbacks are part of this business, like the gobshite at yer farm just now. Yer me number one cooker now, and yer goin' to Chicago."

"But—"

"But what, boy-o? By now, the bleedin' Gs locked ya out a yer own money and yer business, plus ya just watched yer grand house and property burn. Like it or not, me aul lad, I'm all's ya got left. We leg it to our stronghold, 'n point our heads at the next gig. Will make the last one child's play, 'twill."

He thought Dillworth might cry, the great git. "Yes, sir. I guess you're right."

"Well, 'kay then. We crack on by first losin' this grand

ride. We find somethin', well, less grand, 'n less scorched, yeh?" The convertible top had been completely incinerated by the flames, and the interior was considerably worse for wear. But the paint survived. "Then you meet up with me boys on the North Side. Get ya set up. Earn yer keep. Here's yer bonafides." With that, Malone passed a card to Dillworth with a name and an address on Chicago's North Side, along with Malone's distinctive signature scrawled on the back."

"You're not coming?"

"There's a sound lad. I'll be along after a wee bit more business hereabouts."

AND THUS, ROY DILLWORTH'S EDUCATION PROCEEDED. HE never imagined it would take less than thirty minutes to devastate his future, and thirty seconds more to steal each of two cars. But Malone left the keys to the battle-damaged Duese on its seat, parked next to the Chevy he stole for Dillworth. The Ford coupe next to the Chevy he hot-wired for himself. He called it fair trade. Dillworth guessed even animals followed a certain code of ethics. Said he was bored with the big car, anyway. They transacted these transfers in the first town sizable enough to not get noticed on the spot— a place called Mason City. And just like that, Malone sent him on his way. Alive.

MALONE FIGURED BY DITCHING HIS DUESE FAR ENOUGH east, the coppers might think he'd hightailed it back to Illinois. With the setback at Dillworth's farm, Malone reflected that at least he and Dillworth escaped, but not his oldest friend, Sticks. Went up in flames, he did. Bastards would pay.

No sense tellin' the culchie cooker he sent the Indian's old roommate to Utah to prepare for their western expansion. Malone remained hell-bent on honoring his contract with Mr. Shade: to capture the Indian and make good on the fuel deal, as well as their Black Gold expansion plan. Now to set all that in motion....

❦ 69 ❧

❦

One night and two days had passed since the raid on Roy Dillworth's farm. Walt and Jake stood in Chief Dan's front yard on the circle drive, staring at the darkening horizon over the tree line to the north. They speculated on what the source of a large column of smoke might be. In their hearts, they knew. They said nothing, only shared misty-eyed glances.

❦

ACCOMPANIED BY THREE OF HIS MOST TRUSTED ATF AGENTS, Lang Eubanks visited *the George gang,* as he now thought of them, at Chief Dan Rustywire's farm. He already knew of Rustywire's history, including corrective revisions, which was another reason for his hands-on approach to this affair. The news that Rustywire had left his term of forced servitude to the Malone mob—long before this Black Gold phenomenon—came as a pleasant surprise. And when Walt informed him Chief Dan had provided air support for the Dillworth raid, it further pleased his sensibilities. Walt explained the real reason Malone wanted Rustywire back was to complete his aviation fuel formulation. Chief Dan Rustywire's safety had now become a national security matter. All of the pieces now fell into place. This dovetailed with the "hotter recipe" chatter his youthful amateur radio informant in New Jersey had picked off the airwaves. Lang Eubanks flipped from a desire to apprehend Chief Dan to a desire to recruit him, and to protect him at all costs.

The ATF contingent wound their way through the woods lining both sides of the Rustywire farm's driveway before breaking into the spacious yard. Sheriff Kershaw stood alongside his two uniformed deputies. He recognized his own consultant, Walt Weller, but not four other men he assumed were the sheriff's deputized locals, and three women, all awaiting his arrival. They stood in front of the sprawling prairie-style house—a severe but elegant two-story Frank Lloyd Wright design. The house's sophistication surprised and pleased the agent's penchant for eclectic architecture. Less for the immense structure to its south, however, that appeared to be a hybrid between a barn and an aircraft hangar.

AS THEIR LARGE BLACK SEDAN CRUNCHED TO A STOP IN THE pebbled drive that circled around the front of the house, Agent Eubanks slid out of the passenger's seat. Walt remembered this curious little man, but still blinked twice at this dandy's duds and fluid motion. Could have been the subject of a painting, this guy. Who wears an ascot and carries an umbrella during a multi-year drought? He could feel the others looking over the eccentric agent once, and then a well-deserved double-take. Walt thought, *Ya just don't see duds and attitude that fancy and that perfect out here. I hope the boys don't give him a hard time. We need this G-Man as a friend right about now.* Walt was mighty glad nobody ventured beyond polite stares and casual nods.

THE ATF AGENT OFFERED A PRE-INTRODUCTORY NOD TO the assemblage before turning to Billy, recognizable by his bearing, his badge, and his battered condition. "Sheriff, despite your injuries, I am delighted to see you alive and well. It would seem, however, unfinished business remains." He took a moment to acknowledge the sling on Billy's right arm, along with cuts and bruises from his beating and from the "bombing." Lang offered his left hand.

"Well, Agent Eubanks, that's a right genteel way of sayin' we screwed the pooch over at Dillworth's. Close, but no cigar. We let the head mobster and his top supplier slip away. Our fault as much as yours. I trusted that shit-head sheriff over Osceola way. At least *he* got what he deserved, and one of our own didn't."

"Yes, well, aspersions aside, your Deputy Weller here—" Lang offered his right hand of gratitude.

"Jeez, Lang. Just Walt, okay?" Walt took his hand with a grin.

"Ah, yes, of course. Alerting us to that operation proved invaluable." He ticked off their victory points on the bony fingers of his left hand. "We've interrupted the Chicago organization's supply chain to Omaha. A corrupt county official has been taken out of play. And a significant alcohol production site has been, ah, decommissioned. Not a bad evening's work." But Eubanks saw this was perhaps an inadequate summary of events. In haste, he added, "and I am sorely saddened by the loss of one of your own."

Billy muttered, "Sep."

"Sorry?"

"His name was Seppel Tolley, Lang, a helluva mechanic, a fearless combat veteran of the Great War, and a good friend."

"Yes, I am truly grieved by the loss of Mr. Tolley. What say we formulate a plan to minimize further losses and complete the task we started? Now I suffer from an old wound that requires me to sit down straightaway. Might we repair to a suitable venue in order to continue our conversation, Sheriff?" Lang leaned on his umbrella like a cane.

Billy looked over at Chief. "With your permission?"

"Sure. Agent Eubanks, my name is Dan Rustywire. This is my house. Let's hunker down in the dining room." Chief stuck his hand out. Lang gratefully accepted it.

"I thank you, sir. Your hospitality is much appreciated, and your reputation precedes you." That raised a few eyebrows, but the moment passed.

Chief shrugged. "Well, beats lettin' these good folks get shot up in town."

"And with informality the theme du jour, please just call me Lang."

"Right white of ya, Lang. C'mon in, everybody." Lang just smiled and followed this interesting young man into his beautiful home.

❦

70

The three feds that arrived with Lang stood perimeter guard along with Owen who said, "No way I can swallow another sit-down. Need space." Besides, he grieved better for his friend in solitude and out in the open. He offered to stand watch, concealed near the end of the drive with his trusty old M1903 Springfield that chambered a thirty-aught-six slug and fixed a nasty bayonet. Looked nasty, but he and Sep had found that thing too damn long for killin' down in the mud holes of Cambrai, fighting the Krauts with the Brits. That old rifle had saved his and Sep's bacon in trench combat more times than he cared to admit. He kept that pig-sticker razor sharp, but she was best held in a fist all by herself when things got real up-close and personal. He and Sep got so's they'd operate their Springfield triggers with one hand, and slash with their pig stickers in t'other. A course, throwin' the bolt to lock another slug in the chamber took both hands. They'd stick the bayonets in the ground by their heels to keep 'em handy at such times. Sep'd smile at those memories.

※

CHIEF'S LARGE DINING ROOM SEEMED SMALLER, NOW stuffed with Sophie, Edie and Hilda, along with Chief, Lang, Walt, Henry, and Billy, now joined by Deputies Dwight and Jimmy. Billy figured they'd be sitting ducks at the office. He had told the boys to lock it up and hightail it out to Chief's place. Even Silas was there, but still stayed at his own place overnights. Eight of them filled every chair at the long table. Billy sat at one end and Lang at the other. Chief, Walt and Jimmy stood.

※

LANG STARTED WITH AGENCY NEWS. "LADIES AND gentlemen, first, it should please you to learn that Malone just made the top of the nation's most wanted list. We base this on the scope and degree of his felonious infractions, including incitement of extreme violence across state lines and illegal interstate commerce. We've secured a list of more than a dozen indictments that encompass murder of a law enforcement officer, felonious assault of another, murder of at least one civilian, along with a minimum of five counts of attempted murder. And of course, myriad interstate Volstead violations. We're finally able to connect his racketeering activities in Chicago directly to him for the first time.

"That means our agency and others are now pouring vast resources into this case. We estimate a high probability that he is still in this immediate area, however, despite some false trails he seeded. There are now over a hundred ATF and FBI agents between Chicago and Omaha tasked to the direct apprehension of this animal." Lang spit out that last word, displaying uncharacteristic emotion. "We have deployed thirty trained and well-equipped agents in fifteen cruisers between Worthington City and Sioux City alone."

Lang awaited a response, any response, but got none. Finally, Henry spoke for the first time. "Agent—, Lang, those are indeed impressive numbers. But I think what we'd like to hear is a *specific* plan for apprehending Malone before he incites more mayhem. And right now we care most about our own community—not Chicago, not Omaha, nor even Worthington City."

"Yes, certainly that would be your paramount concern. And we are coordinating with local law enforcement agencies to be on the lookout for his automobile. We must assume, however, that he is smart enough to have changed vehicles."

Walt wagged his impetuous tongue. "Well, at least you won't be *coordinating* with that snake Graves over to Osceola, eh, Lang?"

Billy couldn't resist, still smoldering. "Not hardly. No tears shed over that damn weasel." He struggled to let go of the pain of that betrayal.

Lang said, "Yes, I deserved that, gentlemen. They confirmed the identity of Sheriff Graves' corpse at the site of the Dillworth raid, along with the likely killer of your deputy, Billy—one Aghaistín, a.k.a. Sticks Leary. Every available law enforcement official now holds a photograph of Malone and his confederate, Roy Dillworth. We've staked out Dillworth's auto dealership, have seized all assets of Dillworth Ford, Malone Investments, and more than a few of their subsidiaries. However, I'm sorry to say there are hundreds. Wanted posters for these two fugitives are being hung in every post office across the Midwest. And the US Department of Justice is offering a substantial reward for information leading to their arrests."

Sophie spoke for the first time, "Just curious, what is a number-one-wanted fugitive like Malone worth these days?"

"Ten thousand dollars." That earned Lang a few eye rolls and slantwise glances.

Billy said, "What's the bad news? There *is* bad news, isn't there, Lang?"

The agent swallowed, composed himself with a dainty dab of his silken forehead using a folded, starched, and pressed handkerchief before continuing. "Yes. Before we established our dragnet so far from any significant population center, Malone and his thugs moved with what had to be lightning speed. They burned—"

"My farm," interrupted Jake, "the smoke north of here, they burned my farm, didn't they, Lang?"

"Yes, Mr. Hardt... Jake. They burned your barn, but not the house. Some sort of statement, I presume."

Though this confirmed what he and Walt had obviously already guessed, Lang saw his confirmation hit Jake hard. His eyes misted over and he reached for her hand. "Sophie, oh, Gawd. Queenie, the milkers."

Lang swallowed hard. This was the human side of the law enforcement equation, the messy part.

"Stop. We don't know that. Maybe they...." She swallowed a lump. "Dear, it'll be alright. We'll be alright. Just thank the Lord *we* weren't there." Sophie squeezed her husband's hand and threw a grateful nod Chief's way. He returned the gesture, but his face looked like a torn page.

Aw, Walt, the barn...." Jake sent a forlorn expression toward Walt who just shrugged in response.

Lang continued. "That isn't all, I am sorry to say. Mr. and Mrs. Bairns, your house—"

Henry's jaw dropped. "Oh, they go too far! Who *are* these animals, Agent Eubanks?"

Lang folded his hands in front of him on the glossy tabletop. "It may be appropriate to share the dossiers we have on these criminals. Walt here knows some of this. Your little community has made enemies with some of the most unsavory criminals in America. Their leaders and more than a few of their soldiers come from the slums of Dublin, Ireland.

"Malone and Leary, along with their top lieutenants, were members of what passes for law enforcement over there called the Animal Gangs. Their brutality was legendary across the United Kingdom and Europe a few years back. They brought that brutality across the pond with them to New York and Chicago. Malone's criminal enterprises comprise one of the most expansive and sophisticated organizations of violent offenders in America today. Even though he is very much hands-on, we could not tie him personally to any of his criminal enterprises, until now."

Henry said, "Lang, I must ask if you can shed some light on how I came to be involved with Malone. A friend referred me."

"Henry, this is still an active intelligence-gathering operation. That means I am not at liberty to be as open with you as I might wish; however, a relationship exists between Malone and your friend Mr. Klein that goes far beyond the simple borrower/lender liaison he led you to believe. Mr. Klein is not your friend, and he has duped you. Take some small consolation—Henry. Lester Klein is a sophisticated operator. That's about all I can say. I've already shared more with you than I should."

Henry said, "Thank you, Lang." If he had been silent before, Henry now became a ghost who drifted off into a maudlin mood for the rest of the evening. Sophie watched her father through misty eyes.

Billy's newest deputy, Dwight, had listened to all of this, and brought them all back to the bigger picture. "So, Lang, do your guys have a theory about what this Malone character is likely to go after next? I assume you've put your heads together on some scenarios."

Lang only acknowledged his query with a cursory nod and swiveled his gaze toward Chief. "Mr. Rustywire—Dan—could I ask you for a private consult for a moment?"

This brought quizzical expressions to every face in the room, except for Chief's. But for the sake of the room, he just scanned and shrugged. "Sure, why not?"

Lang hoisted his somewhat delicate frame from his padded straight chair, obviously plagued by what he mentioned on his arrival as an old wound. As dapper as he appeared, Lang had seen action. He allowed the taller man to lead him into a smaller room off the far side of the kitchen near the back door, some distance from the dining room. Chief stopped, leaned against the elevated canning counter in what his mother used to call the summer kitchen with its opening window walls, second stove and lots of open-faced shelves.

"Dan—"

"Chief is what everybody around here calls me, Lang."

"Very well, Chief. How much of your history are your friends aware?"

"Almost none of it."

"I think you owe them—"

"Yah, look, Lang. You want we should level with 'em. You're right. For the first time in a very long time, I have friends, like the first ever. I'm a half-breed, don't fit anywhere, and I'm not all that good with words. But these folks, well, you go ahead. Share what you know. Besides, you're more eloquent. And maybe they'll still like me after."

"You *are* a good friend, Chief. And I may even fill in a few additional pieces for *you*. Shall we?"

71

Lang and Chief drew perplexed looks as they returned to the dining room with Lang's free hand resting on Chief's shoulder. Lang said, "My new friends, though we haven't known each other long, I respect your community bond. I'm sure each of you harbors a few secrets from one another. Everyone does. Now I wish to share with you some very private information that your host has given me permission to share.

"You may or may not know that Chief here," a respectful nod, "is an eminent chemical and mechanical engineer, earning advanced degrees in each of these disciplines from the University of Minnesota. More than these impressive academic accomplishments, Chief distinguished himself in the real world with his groundbreaking work on advanced fuel technology."

After he sat back down, Chief never lifted his gaze from the spot he had chosen on the table eighteen inches in front of him. But he could feel the heat of everyone staring at him with incredulity. Nobody spoke. Most jaws dropped and stayed there.

"Chief and I agreed to share his secret with you for two reasons. First, he focused his research not on fossil fuel development, but on plant-based fuel refinement. That's right. Your friend, Chief Dan, produces the finest alcohol in the Midwest, perhaps anywhere in the world. While in school, Chief invented a brilliant distillation and additive process. This resulted in an alcohol with a flash point far lower—that is, far better—than the standard distillation process used almost universally by everyone else."

Walt said, "Chief! You old dog! You *cook*, man?"

Lang continued before the group grew any rowdier at these revelations. "Much more than that, Walt. The result of Chief's process is a superb fuel—for almost any internal combustion engine. But this formulation is particularly well-suited for a new generation of military aircraft engines. And that is why Chief's formula is both important and valuable.

"Now Chief, I don't believe even you are aware of this latest intelligence nugget. We've learned through Malone's Chicago and New York networks that there are foreign emissaries interested in your process. With tensions increasing in Europe, again, you can well-imagine the stakes here have escalated to a concern for our nation's interests on the international stage."

"Holy Hell, Chief!" Billy stood up too quickly, tipping over his chair. With an astounded expression, he rounded his end of the table to Chief in record time. He slapped his new friend on the back hard enough that Chief started coughing. "Oh, shit. Sorry, red man. I don't have any problem calling you Chief now, Chief. I feel like I should salute you, or somethin'." Billy held out his hand and Chief took it, shook it, but did not release it. He looked Billy in the eye, and held his gaze as he said, "Wait til you hear the rest of it, Billy. Then decide." Only then did he release Billy's hand and once again lowered his gaze to the tabletop.

Billy just stood there, confused "The rest of it?" He swiveled his gaze. "Lang?"

"Thanks to Chief's loquacious college roommate and amateur bootlegger, none other than Finn Malone learned of Chief's research. And that's why Malone attempted to hire Chief to distill alcohol for him in the Minneapolis area. For the better part of a year, Malone coerced your friend to be his chief Minnesota cooker, as they say. Another reason *they* call him 'Chief' too."

Billy's eyes grew wide, his hands rested on his hips, instinctively, close to his service weapon. "Wait. You *know* Malone? You *worked* for that mutt? You gotta be shittin' me, son!"

Shame shows a body language all its own.

Lang quickly added, "Now he wants Chief back in the worst way. Chief's *recipe* is worth millions, especially to at least one foreign government. Time to circle our wagons, my new friends. Our most probable scenario? Malone, and likely a small army, is coming here to retrieve their star chef, perhaps on behalf of the Second Reich."

"Oh, shit!" Came out of four mouths at once, all male.

"Watch your language!" Came out of two female mouths at the same time.

Lang's next words tumbled out as if they needed sharing fast, much to his own embarrassment. "Most of you know there is a recent batch of alcohol that has become popular around this region called Black Gold. This poison is a bastardized version of Chief's formulation. Ms. Winkels— Edie here—," Lang offered her an apologetic glance, "can share with you first-hand why it is insidious. Not only is it a fine-tasting but illegal beverage, it is also addictive and toxic because of its additives. The combination of these additives

—both depressants and stimulants—can create a psychotic break in many otherwise-normal users. Malone's objective is to distribute and sell this seductive product from coast to coast to unwary customers. They must be stopped. Your federal government views this as a top-priority risk to the nation's security. Earlier, we believed that this was Chief's recipe, but we now know that was never the case. They created this nefarious concoction long after Chief left the Malone organization—out of a sense of conscience, I'd add."

The room fell into a silent maelstrom of emotional conflict. Everyone looked at everyone else. Henry looked down at his own hands folded on the table. Billy squinted his eyes and scratched his head. Edie's eyes misted over, and Sophie just smiled before she said, "Well, that'll make it easier to find this criminal, won't it? He's coming to us. And Chief, you're here with us, *protecting* us, not there with him. Having come from that life, your being here now is that much more precious to us. We all knew you were smart, but my goodness. Your mother would be so proud." Sophie arose with some difficulty and limped over to Chief as she spoke. All eyes followed her. She threw her arms around Chief's shoulders with a side hug. He just raised one hand to cover hers, still either unwilling or unable to lift his gaze to meet anyone else's.

Lang broke the awkward silence as everyone in the room sifted through their feelings, seeking some sort of equilibrium. "And *that*, my friends, is why there are three armed agents and one of your own just outside right now standing guard at your immediate perimeter. This very moment, thirty more armed agents in fifteen vehicles are patrolling around this point one to five miles out." He jabbed the table with a long index finger, "And more are en route while scanning the roads and towns as they rush to our aid."

Once again, the class clown piped up. Walt said, "Outstanding. We'll nail the bastards by sundown! Hey, Chief, maybe all these G-Men could use some aerial coverage—"

Lang jumped in. "Already en route, Walt. The Army Air Corps has offered to conduct their exercises in this area for the next week. A happy coincidence." Wink. "I'll be returning to Rapid City to focus on our sweeping manhunt and to coordinate with the FBI. Godspeed."

❧

72

Chief reflected on his days in Minneapolis while Agent Eubanks had been droning on about his history with Malone. He remembered how his dorm room had pressed in on him. His parents had offered to pay for off-campus housing, but he'd declined. Carrying a double-major in grad school required constant on-campus time. Nothing else was practical. He enjoyed school because he fit in, often the smartest kid in the room, and was admired for it. Chief found Mechanical Engineering intuitive, and the coursework less than challenging. But his real loves, chemistry and physics, flowed like a symphony.

Incredible memories. Fueled by passion—and lots of coffee—the work inspired Chief to push harder than anyone. And he inspired his assigned dorm roomie, Allan Westerhall. Together, he and Allan influenced the future of chemical compositions and drove each other to the next achievement. Classes became a boring necessity, but in the lab, they did great things, far beyond the splendid dorm room hooch they cooked as a lark. But clearly, Chief was the brains, Allan was his muse.

In their senior year, Chief and Allan—a.k.a. Kookie—tackled an ambitious academic exercise with daring intensity. They created an efficient fuel for internal combustion engines, a plant-based alternative to fossil fuels. Kookie distilled superb but ordinary grain alcohol. Chief, however, with an assist from Kookie, designed an elegant iterative distillation and additive process that produced a revolutionary fuel with a flash point a full forty-eight degrees lower than Kookie's excellent alcohol. *And* it tasted like the world's finest vodka, which didn't interest Chief much. His father's family exhibited strong addictive tendencies. No sense tempting hereditary fate. But fate did tempt them. Their reputation for distilling quality hooch spewed from Kookie's big mouth, propelled by his entrepreneurial spirit. The word spread.

CHIEF SAT ON HIS DORM ROOM BED, WATCHING HIS roommate heading for the door with a huge duffel slung over his shoulder. This would not be a tearful goodbye. "Where are you going, Kookie?"

"Listen, Chief, I love ya, man, but my family doesn't have money like yours. I gotta pay the bills, so—"

"Well, a man's gotta do what he's gotta do. I hate to break up this beautiful relationship." Kookie had grown way too self-absorbed, including the moronic name he'd cooked up for himself and *insisted* everyone use it.

"It's all good, Chief. Thanks for everything." No hand-shake, no man-hug, just downcast eyes, a turned back, a door opening and quietly closing. Kookie walked out of Chief's life. Or so he thought.

. . .

HE'D HEARD KOOKIE TOOK AN OFF-CAMPUS APARTMENT nearby. His ambitions had exceeded his desire to graduate and the volume of hooch he could produce in the dorm. That was the real reason for his hasty departure. He'd made commitments. Besides, it was obvious to him Chief had had enough. Chief learned later that the bathroom in Kookie's new apartment was spacious enough to accommodate a sizable grain alcohol distiller—a still. Collected his product in the bathtub, and ladled it into jugs he sold to a few speakeasies around campus. Not only did he produce illegal corn liquor, annoying his neighbors with the stench of his labors, he extorted the grain he needed to cook from the university lab stores. Felt right to him. Not to Chief. They grew further estranged.

🐲

ONE OF FINN MALONE'S MINNEAPOLIS ENFORCERS NOTICED a few of the speakeasies under their *protection* were buying less product. When pressed, they admitted acquiring a damn good product on the side from a college kid they called Kookie. Malone, who traveled to Minneapolis once a month, paid Kookie a personal visit with some of his local muscle. Gave him a choice—get out of town to preserve his health, or work for him and become a wealthy man. Kookie chose the latter and became Finn's Minnesota cooker.

🐲

MONTHS LATER, WHILE CHIEF FINISHED HIS LAST semester's commitments as a teaching assistant, and placed the finishing touches on his last thesis, Kookie shared with Chief the amazing opportunity he'd fallen into.

"Thanks, old buddy. Not interested. I'm returning to the reservation after I graduate to honor my father's wishes."

"Chief! That is *such* a waste of your talent."

"Maybe, but it's the next right thing for me.

Kookie was smart, but a chronic sycophant. He mentioned his brilliant college roomie to Finn next time he was in town, hoping to curry further favor with his powerful boss.

Thereafter, Finn visited Chief on campus to recruit him before he graduated and disappeared. "I'm honored by your offer, sir, but I need to decline." Chief knew Malone was a dangerous gangster from what Kookie had told him—"but he's still a good guy." Chief's moral code prevented him from getting involved.

"Okay, but I'm not the kind to take no, boy-o. Think about it, 'kay?"

Malone tried to hire him two more times until he resorted to more drastic recruiting measures. "Boy-o, it's not what I want, but yer daddy is just over in North Dakota on the reservation, yeh? Shame if he and his'd come to harm."

Damn you for this, Allan! "My family's got nothing to do with this. Look, Mr. Malone, I'll cook for twelve months. Then I'm done. Agreed?" He convinced himself this would be the honorable thing to do—for his family.

"See? We can deal. Okay, there, boy-o."

But they both knew this would not end well if Chief were to leave. Ever.

At least this'll keep the wolves at bay for now. Kookie, you son-of-a-bitch, you and your big mouth! Chief admitted to himself his friend never was who he thought he was, or hoped he would be. So much for believing in the good inside everyone.

. . .

After a year, Chief said he was done, and prepared to leave. Once again, Finn threatened his mother and father. Malone's Minneapolis mob had sheltered Chief from much of the violent side of Malone's business, including the man's personal proclivity for bloodshed. He believed Malone issued empty threats and departed for the reservation to see his father, an erstwhile tribal elder before he married outside the tribe—a wealthy white woman of Irish descent, no less. He discovered his father had left to meet his mother to fulfill her dream of sailing with him to exotic Caribbean ports of call. *They should be safe*, he remembered thinking at the time.

But he grew concerned when he learned that Malone's goon, a guy named Sticks Leary, visited the rez before Chief, inquiring after the elder Rustywire's travel plans. At that point, Chief feared Malone intended to make good on his threat to do his parents harm. But he remained confident in his father's skill, his mother's means—including their very able-bodied deck crew of three—and distance to protect them. He wouldn't know how to contact them, anyway.

Chief returned to the family farm in Northwest Iowa to await word from Annie and Bear Rustywire. None came. A month later, however, the family attorney and executor of his parent's estate contacted Chief at the home place informing him he was following his mother's directive. It read, "If I do not contact you (the attorney) within any sixty day period, you are to assume I am lost at sea. Failing to reach Bear Rustywire at the tribal headquarters of the Standing Rock Sioux Reservation at Fort Yates, North Dakota, you are to assume he is with me, and is also lost. You are then to contact our only son and heir, Daniel, to inform him we have passed, and that we bequeath all of our entrusted assets to him."

Chief had never been close to his parents. The news of their loss still devastated him. Unsure if this was an act of God or an act of Malone, he was one very pissed-off Injun. But he took some solace that neither Malone, nor anyone else, knew where he was. He contacted the attorney to ensure it stayed that way. If his parents truly were lost at sea, they died doing what they loved together. If Malone murdered them, Chief would avenge them.

BUT THAT WAS NOW OVER FOUR YEARS AGO, AND IT WAS time to deal with current affairs to support his new friends.

73

B ack when the Indian still worked for him, Finn Malone had bragged on one of his Minnesota cookers—he didn't say he was an Indian—that his hooch was so strong, the stuff could fuel any engine invented by man far better than gasoline. Suddenly, investors wanted the recipe. This surprised Finn. *Fuel is worth more 'n quality hooch? Since when? Alrighty, then.*

Kookie, the Indian's friend, supplied Malone with a copy of the academic paper the two college roommates had published, the original reason they invented this concoction. But Malone's guys told him that without the precise process by which the fuel was distilled, the paper was little more than a convincing tease.

One investor told Malone, "Money is no object. I must have that formula." Being a savvy businessman, as well as a pitiless gangster, Malone knew he would do anything to get his hands on Chief again, and his "secret formula." And with their setback in Iowa, now more than ever.

❧ 74 ❧

❦

Mr. Shade and Mr. Tree connected on their regular Sunday evening schedule via their shortwave radio transceivers tuned to 3.614 megacycles, their own little refuge on the airwaves.

"W2MQX, NG2AO, kitchen fire?"

"2AO, W2MQX, bread and oven burned. Chef ok."

"New bakery?"

"In windier weather."

"Deliveries?"

"Slight delay."

"Hotter recipe?"

"In hand this week."

"Falling leaves."

"K. Shade ok."

"73"

"Dit dit"

· · ·

MR. SHADE, A.K.A. LESTER KLEIN, USED THE FICTITIOUS ham radio call sign of W2MQX. He sat in an office chair bellied up to a small desk laden with communications gear. His tiny but sophisticated radio room nested in the little shed that sat high atop his grain elevator on the southern perimeter of George, Iowa. Didn't relish climbing all those steps more than once a week, especially when it was windy. It would seem both he and his collaborator, Mr. Tree, NG2AO in Newark, were under duress, but all was not lost.

The setback on the Dillworth farm, and the assault on Graber's shadow installation in Newark, screamed of a coordinated federal response to their expansion plan. While worrisome, it merely meant they'd invoke their contingency plan. Mr. Tree was worried, but still committed. The money still flowed, and to date, nobody had spotted the near-perfect counterfeit bills among the flood of new government money shipped to banks in recent weeks to bolster confidence in the failing banking system. The bogus bills hid in plain sight. Only he and Mr. Tree could decipher the difference between the counterfeits imported from the Fatherland and the genuine article.

He hoped to assuage Mr. Tree's apprehension over the loss of Dillworth's farm. He assured him they simply relocated the Midwestern production center to the Windy City, along with its cooker, Mr. Dillworth himself. But Klein realized he'd also better deliver the Indian's fuel recipe, so he exaggerated by guaranteeing it would be in hand within the week. But it all depended on recovering the cook himself. War was coming.

He'd pull out all the stops to support Malone's assault on the Indian's farm, now that they knew he was hiding there. And just down the damn road from here. Without the Indian, no hot recipe. That's what they needed, most of all. And to ensure their own survival. Since Mr. Tree was still committed,

Klein put the man's cash to good use. Hired more than a hundred mercenaries with a barrel of hundreds to make their dreams come true. That's one area where America excelled— a plenitude of desperate guns for hire were easy enough to find.

🕸 75 🕸

🕸

It seemed everyone had slipped into their own private reverie after hearing Lang's revelations about Chief's past. Still sitting at Chief's dining room table along with the others, with a cold cup of coffee in front of him, Billy raged one of his many personal battles. *Sheriff Graves was on Dillworth's payroll. A fellow law enforcement officer betrayed me. I trusted that sumbitch, and for that, I got Sep killed. At least my gut— and Chief's—told me not to clue in Graves on everything. That's what got the bastard killed. They thought he betrayed them. Too damn bad. At lease we gave better 'n we got. Boys did good.*

With no real state-level law enforcement, Billy needed to find a way to get more evidence. They needed to be sure of the scale of Dillworth's operation. Had Malone exerted influence elsewhere within law enforcement? Who could he trust other than the feds? Plus, he had to learn more about the pipeline to Malone's speakeasies in Omaha, or wherever. This crap was passing right through his county. And Billy wanted more info on who in Omaha was involved to avoid further betrayals. Without Agent Eubanks—Lang—and the ATF sharing what they had, which maybe wasn't much, how the hell was he supposed to find all of this out? At least Lang seemed forthcoming. But Billy couldn't help but feeling the too-perfect little agent knew more than he was sharing.

☙❧

NOBODY NEEDED TO PAINT SOPHIE A PICTURE. LOOKING around the dining room table, it looked like the last supper, absent the Messiah. She was staring at a blanket crisis of confidence. This collection of drifting souls, on the verge of desolation, appeared so discouraged that it made her heart ache, especially Billy. She could see he was taking the weight of the world on his shoulders. Time to break her silence and do what all strong women do at such times. She turned first to her husband. As she spoke in that forceful whisper, Jake listened hard, as did everyone else.

"Jake, my dear, you've put your dreams on hold. They are not gone. Those monsters burned our barn. So what? It's just a building. We've started making our own life together. We are just beginning, are we not?" She patted his knee before turning her gaze toward their faithful live-in cousin.

"Walt, I'm still not sure what your story is, not completely. You don't strike me as a coward, yet you never stay in one place very long. How would you like to stay here in Lyon County? With Jake and me? For as long as you like? But first, we need to take care of business. Agree?" She didn't wait for a response, but knew what Walt would say.

Then she turned to Billy. "Sheriff Graves isn't who you thought he was, Billy. Get over yourself. And do not dare tell me Roddy died for nothing. You suffered unspeakable horrors during the war, and you lost your dear Alice. I can't imagine. But this is now. You're stronger than *all* of that, and that makes you one of the strongest men I know. I believe in you, Billy, and the citizens of Lyon County do too.

"And Father, you trusted Lester Klein to steer you in the right direction, to Finn Malone. You've known Lester all of your adult life. He isn't who he said he was. There are awful people like him in this world. Always will be. We need them because they test our faith. You need to get past your shame at being fooled, and together we will stop the spread of this poison. Look what it's done to my dearest friend Edie." She looked over at her friend, a mere shadow of her former self, because of Black Gold. Edie dropped her eyes, not in shame, but to reinforce her friend's words. "And all for money? Remember what the scripture says, 'The *love* of money is the root of all evil.' Is there *any* doubt where lies evil here in Lyon County and beyond? Will you let your foolish pride prevent you from helping to stop this evil, Father? I may know you better than you know yourself. You will not. I'm guessing you're concerned about Mother's and my safety, more than your own. But there is no future for *any* of us if we let these bullies continue to beat us, or if we grant them that power over you."

She drew a deep breath as she scanned the small group who had already been through the wringer. "We're strong, and we do not quit, nor will we ask someone else to handle the task at hand. This is *our* fight. Besides, if we do just give up or lose hope, which is what I see in your faces right now, would quitting offer us an acceptable alternative? Of course not. We do not want mobsters in our town, poisoning us for profit or for any other reason. *And* I don't want to see my father lose his business.

"Chief, you ran away from Malone because you recognized him for what he was. Good for you. Now is the time to put an end to your need to run—forever." She first soft-stared at him while she spoke. Then she looked at Edie next to him.

"Dwight, I'm not sure I know what *you're* running from, or whether I'd understand if I did, but you left Minneapolis, and you left Worthington. Now you're here, with us, and for that we are grateful. Do you like it here? If so, it's time to take a stand. With us. We stand with you. Alright, Deputy?" All she got was a solemn nod and a small smile. Had she gone too far?

Ever alert by the door, peering out the window next to it —like a panther about to pounce—stood Owen, with his Springfield leaning against the wall by his left hip. Sophie gazed at him. "Sep died at your side, Owen. Did he die for nothing? No, he did not.

"We all feel like we've been tested, maybe defeated—by our own demons, or by those of others—but we have not. That is *not* who we are. Good *must* triumph over evil, and it *will*. You all think I let this polio defeat me? Look at me! We all have our weak spots. We don't quit because of them, we overcome them, and we become stronger *because* of them.

"Now, let's stay safe, but let's drive these thugs out on a rail—together. Do we still tar and feather folks? Because that would seem fitting. But first, you all need to put on your big boy pants and get this chore done! If not for yourselves, do it for your women, for your families, for your community. I want these... ***bastards***... out of ***my community***. Alright, men?" Sophie flushed bright red with her impassioned plea. She never swore. Normally.

After a five-second period of thundering silence, Walt piped up. "Hey, Sophie, you go to Seminary? Because that was one hell of a sermon." The room roared. Sophie too. She had broken the spell.

A serious dust storm was brewing, moving in fast from the southwest. They were all armed and expecting the worst. Billy glanced at the tree lines that defined Chief's north and south property lines, both to his left and to his right, respectively. He knew two ATF sharpshooters hid on each end of their line in those trees, ready and waiting. Lang had tasked four more agents to guard their flank, concealed in the trees behind the house. But would it be enough?

They had constructed a makeshift secondary barricade of bumper-to-bumper vehicles that extended out in both directions from the garage in the middle of Chief's yard in front of the house. The garage was the tip of the spear. Behind that last-stand barricade crouched Billy's two full-time deputies, Jimmy and Dwight, alongside Chief, Jake, Walt, and Owen, spread out at intervals on both sides of the garage. That's when he heard Sophie's voice behind him. Turned, spotted Sophie at Chief's front door. "Billy, Agent

Eubanks—Lang—is on the line. Says it's urgent!" Billy hustled in.

Once he had made his way to the telephone on the kitchen wall, Sophie handed him the earpiece as he sidled up to the mouthpiece. "Lang, how we doin', pardner?"

"Well, Sheriff—Billy—I'm sorry to say Malone surprised us with the strength of his offensive. He has mustered forces exceeding one hundred strong, traveling at speed, in excess of twenty vehicles, coming in from three different directions, as far as we can discern from phoned-in reports."

"What? How is that possible? And I thought your perimeter would keep that mob away from us! Are you saying you've failed to do so?"

"Not at all, Sheriff." Billy noticed Lang wasn't on a first name basis anymore. "We've contained and apprehended over sixty of these hired guns that have recently arrived in the area from all over the Midwest. Not without paying a dear price— we've lost three agents. But that leaves at least four dozen of these criminals who broke through our line. Most of those will approach your location imminently from both the north and the south on County Road 14."

"That mean we're on our own?"

"No, sir," sounded like *suh*, "not entirely. Our hands remain quite full, detaining this unruly mob in three makeshift detention locations. But I've freed up and dispatched a dozen more of my agents to your location with some specialty gear. They are en route, but are still at least thirty minutes distant. Between your deputies and your friends, alongside the eight agents already at your site, you'll just need to hold your location for a half-hour at most."

"Okay, Lang. We got this. I hope. Just get the cavalry here, quick as you can. Thanks for the warning. Sounds like holy Hell has already broken out here beyond the tree line on 14."

"Understood. My agents inform me they are in hot pursuit of those we could not contain, but to be blunt, they report they are out-numbered and out-gunned. Billy, I am sorry I under-estimated these hooligans. But I've read your dossier. You served with distinction during the war. You already know to keep cover and choose your shots with care. Avoid cross-fire with each other and with my agents. Be advised, your adversaries, well, expect a heavy onslaught of submachine gun fire, but so far, none of these... mercenaries have employed any explosives. I believe I understand the strength of Malone's stunning resolve in this matter—to capture Chief—but I do not yet understand the source of his endless reserves, although I'm awaiting confirmation of my suspicions on both fronts. I wish you and your crew safe hunting."

"Thanks, Lang. Same to you, and hope to see ya soon, pardner. Out." With that, Billy slammed the hand piece onto its hook, startling Sophie, who stood close. He offered her a warm smile before hustling back out to his troops. With some difficulty, he shut out gruesome memories of fallen comrades during the final months of the war. Only this time, those compatriots who never returned from the Argonne Forest appeared in his mind's eye with the faces of his friends and neighbors.

✥ 77 ✥

❧

This entire frontier affair, as Finn called it, had become all too personal. The raid on Dillworth's farm cost him his bestie. *Feckin' culchies took Sticks from me, but not til he give Graves the full force of his little friend, din't he? Maggot got a full measure for his failure. Fair is fair. Now I need that redskin cooker! Aye, make me a richer man still, he will.*

Malone and thirty of the most capable soldiers of fortune that survived the ATF perimeter had broken through to the very farm where he hoped to regain the employ of *his Indian.* He thought, *Hard to hide a redskin in a town of milk-white Europeans, yeh?*

The mobster sent his best into the woods from County 14 on both sides of the driveway with their orders. "They slow you down, you chuck a grenade at 'em if ya can't mow 'em down in the trees with yer spitters. But ya keep movin' forward. The *only* one ya don't dare juice is the Injun in the picture what each a you'se carries, yeh? Now fan out and move in."

Owen crept beyond the barricade, closer to the tree line. He fixed the bayonet onto his Springfield, aimed, and picked off two enemies. Started just like the Argonne.

Pop. Pop.

Then—

Bamma-bamma-bamma....

Lots of mutts come up behind the two he dropped. *And they's packin' Tommys. Too many.* Silas had offered him three sticks from his old dynamite stash he used for blowing stumps out of his fields. He pulled a stick from his equipment belt, lit the short fuse from the embers of the cigar tucked in the corner of his mouth, waited, then tossed it toward the mutts comin' in fast now. As soon as it went off, and shook the ground, Owen retreated. Guerrilla tactics. Thought he saw a bunch of bodies flying. *You want more trouble, ya keep comin', ya shit-bags.*

Just then, fire exploded all around Owen, but when he looked down, he saw no flames, just the ground comin' up toward his face. He remembered the old moving pictures when them talkies first come out. The screen would get dark around the edges and close in until the whole screen faded into nothin' but black. The fire spread, starting in the center of his back before it burned everywhere, just before his movie screen went black. *Well, I gave better 'n I got, din't I? Comin' Lord. Ready for this sorry wrencher? Be lookin' for you too, Sep. Thee End.*

Walt hid behind a larger tree farther in, closer to Chief's yard, along with a couple of ATF agents who had moved up from their flank once they saw where the main force penetrated the farm's perimeter. Didn't gangsters ever hear about things like flanking, or pressing more than one front at a time? This was turning out to be a big-ass street brawl. Walt's was a short-range weapon—a good old twelve-gauge. With number three shot in its twin pipes, he wielded some serious punching power that would throw a respectable eight-foot spread at twenty feet. The wind was coming up fast, and visibility grew worse by the second. Might be an advantage, might not. He slung his mutt-sprayer over his shoulder for now. Instead, he aimed an old service .45 at the first of the mutts that appeared through the cloud of debris still drifting downward on the wind from Owen's grenade. That's when he saw his new friend go down. Had to be a lethal back shot. *Motherfu—*

Bam! One down. *Bam!* Two down. Walt wasn't sure how he felt about taking human lives, until now. These were mad dogs, rabid animals to be put down. But he stopped short in mid-thought as he prepared to pull the trigger a third time.

Bamma-bamma-bamma....

Oh, crap. Am I hit? Walt dropped, his head sopping wet all of a sudden. Nobody saw him go down.

Dust and debris whipped through the trees, reducing visibility to a few yards as a massive windstorm descended like quicksilver over the entire area. The advancing hoodlums tried to cover their noses and mouths with a sleeve, or by hiking a jacket high enough to provide some protection, but they were ill-equipped to defend themselves from Mother Nature's disgust. Visibility worsened faster than the wind escalated—blizzard conditions in June, but with brown dust and airborne dirt instead of snow. Maybe it was appropriate to fight a battle in the throes of a *black blizzard* for a poison called *Black Gold*.

❧❀❧

SOPHIE, EDIE, HILDA AND HENRY HEARD THE CHATTER OF outside gunfire from within Chief's house. All four ducked at each report. More than a few rounds ticked into the outer walls composed of sandstone block on the ground floor. One window shattered, but they had work to do. Sophie kept them going. They had already closed all the windows and curtains in the house, and moved what furniture they could in front of every opening—just in case—except the front door.

Armed with one of Chief's old squirrel rifles, Henry patrolled the first floor. Billy told him the second floor was too exposed. One of the ladies always stayed close to the phone. They took turns while the other two brewed coffee and made sandwiches. No telling how long this chore was going to take, and the boys needed energy.

Sophie remained the strong one. While stalwart, Hilda shook from the unimaginable insanity that seeped into her otherwise unshakable demeanor. And Edie, well, Edie was a hot mess, but followed Sophie's every instruction as if it were holy writ. They all did okay. Though offered handguns, none of the women would touch them. *Besides,* Sophie thought, *where would I carry the darn thing? In my apron?* Not thinking *too* much about it, it did occur to her that Edie's last experience with a gun was an attempt to shoot herself.

Chief had confided in them that his mother had constructed a secret panel that hid a small room as an appendage to the stone foundation. He told them he left the panel open opposite the stairs at the far end of the fruit cellar. Warned them of the scant five-foot headroom and the musty odors down there. Said if worst came to worst, the three of them were to go to the cellar, enter that cubby, and pull the panel closed behind them. Just in case.

❧✿❧

LANG REPORTED IN TO EDIE, WHO HAD PHONE DUTY, THAT they had grounded the Army Air Corps—impossible flight conditions with near-zero visibility. Straightaway, Edie hung up and ran in a full crouch across the yard, nearly tripping on the hem of her skirt, more than once. She would *not* allow her fear to paralyze her, or modesty to slow her down. Not now. She gathered up her skirt around her thighs and galloped like a *thunder being* to relay the news to *her Chief* behind the second barricade before she hustled back into the house, but not before Chief squeezed her hand, and smiled at her courage.

❧✿❧

MALONE'S MUTTS ADVANCED INTO THE YARD, BUT THE BOYS behind the second barricade slowed their progress to a crawl at the primary barricade close to the tree line bordering County 14. Even so, all seemed on the brink of defeat. Against his better judgement, Chief came to a very personal decision. Especially since all his new friends were now in mortal danger. All because he didn't have the courage to walk away from Malone in Minneapolis when he had first approached him.

Rather than risk all of them being overrun by these brutal animals, Chief crept around to the barn's rear doors in what was now approaching zero visibility. He launched his airship in record time out the front, knowing this was almost certainly a death sentence in the horrible weather. But before he did, while in the wind shadow of the huge barn, he tethered Little Sky to an iron ring on the front of the barn with a hundred yards of rope wound around a winch on Little Sky's bow. This should allow him to plumb into the wind once he ascended and fed out rope, like a ship setting her anchor.

As he expected, the prevailing winds carried him out toward the driveway where Malone and twenty or more of his goons were close to climbing their primary (outer) barricade they'd constructed before the battle began. They had pressed Chief's tractor and snow blade into service, stacking his entire Winter's store of firewood, along with some rusted old machinery—Chief called that his "spare parts inventory"— and a jumble of discarded wood-and-wire snow fence across the driveway just where it exited the woods between his place and County 14. This barricade extended well to either side of the winding driveway, which would force Malone's mob to circle around into the dense woods on foot to circumvent the barrier. *Then,* they would have to climb over a row of autos, including Billy's and Jimmy's two cruisers, Henry's sedan, Jake's and Silas's two trucks, Chief's truck, and Dwight's personal sedan.

They did not intend to stop them, only to slow them for Lang's four sharpshooters guarding either end of this line of defense. Or the George gang could more easily pick them off if they failed to retreat or surrender. The rest of Lang's agents had pulled back to flank the intruders, but these ruffians had shown up in numbers and with weaponry that surprised even the ATF boys, and they were a hard bunch. Lang Eubanks had admitted to himself and to Billy this *could* end badly. Chief reviewed all this in his mind *after* he committed to fly. He knew Lang's sharpshooters would be worthless in such poor visibility, neutralizing that advantage.

Once airborne, with a raging fire in Little Sky's belly, with the overhead hot air bag trying to wildly contort to the will of the shrieking wind, Chief reeled out rope from the bow winch until he reached the limit of the airship's ability to withstand the torturous gale. He wore goggles over his eyes.

A bandana covered his nose and mouth. Breathing became almost impossible—he choked non-stop. Could just discern the outer barricade fifty feet below between desperate coughs and gasps. The chance that he might drop a gas bomb onto a friendly was a risk, but one he must take. If spots moving below charged toward the barricades from the road, he assumed they were the enemy. Chief almost failed to light the bulky wick stuffed into a two-gallon glass jar of gasoline that also contained one of Silas's stump-blowing dynamite sticks. The only way to light that wick in this wind was to risk stuffing the entire neck of each jar bomb all the way into the firebox's open door—which faced aft, in the wind shadow of the stove—protected somewhat from the near-gale force winds now screaming in over the bow of his little ship.

Success! With the wick lit, he hefted the volatile jug over Little Sky's railing onto the heads of a pair of invaders. The effect was devastating, just like at Dillworth's farm, but more so. Liquid gasoline vaporized, set aflame, with dynamite propelling shattered glass, combining with airborne dust that combusted? This created a frightening fire bomb that washed outward from its epicenter as if hungry Hell itself had opened its gates searching for lost souls on which to feed.

Malone's two soldiers had no idea what consumed them. But the roiling flames certainly levied a powerful psychological impact. It must have seemed to the ruffians around them that these simple dirt farmers possessed artillery. Chief lobbed a second bomb. A few more bodies fell. That's when the ship shook violently. He feared its skeleton was being torn asunder, or that the car was being ripped from the hot air bag above it. Besides, the thought that he had just taken several human lives sickened him. Working through his nausea, he cranked the handle on the powerful winch that drew Little Sky back down toward the barn door. She was done.

❧

MEANWHILE, BILLY AND COMPANY STRUGGLED TO KEEP A deep-rooted fear at bay as they could hear *and feel* the all-out battle taking place out on County 14 as the ATF agents engaged the mobsters from the rear, and closer in as Owen and Walt engaged the front lines with the eight redeployed ATF agents directing their fire to the area between the tree line and the outer barricade. Then visibility closed in. They didn't know that two of the explosions that reverberated through the ground came from their friend aloft and had taken out several of their enemy's ranks. Nobody could see anything. The wind and flying debris both muffled sound and confused direction.

❧

PROTECTED BY THREE OF HIS MOST BRUTAL GUNSELS, Malone flanked the barricades in stealth through the woods. They made their way to the rear of the Indian's house. With the back door blocked from the inside, they generated some noise breaking in. Henry heard the noise, hollered to the women, "Cellar! Now!"

The girls heard the noise too and wasted no time hustling together to the cellar door in the hallway on the far side of the kitchen. They knew what to do despite almost paralyzing fear. Sophie led the way. But they didn't make it.

❧

THOUGH ARMED, AND DESPITE THE STAKES, HENRY DID NOT possess what it took to pull the trigger of Chief's old squirrel gun, even after four murderers broke through the metal pantry cabinet piled against the back door. Malone savored the moment by looking Henry in the eye with his arrogant smirk in full bloom. Henry dropped his gun to the floor with a clatter. With their weapons trained on him, Malone muttered to his men, "Let's mop up these maggots now and report back to Mr. Shade."

They were about to riddle Henry with bullets when Jake snuck in from the front hallway to the kitchen off to Malone's right. He half-whispered, "Hi," as he intentionally knocked a flower vase off a tall hallway table near his right elbow. As the four weapons swung to train on the party crasher, Jake unleashed a deadly volley from the very illegal but lethal Thompson .45 sub-machine rifle. He had retrieved the huge weapon from a fallen mutt who made it to within spittin' distance of the second barricade before he combusted. The rifle had blown clear. Jake puked at the sight and smell of the body's charred flesh before he crawled out to retrieve the hoodlum's "Tommy gun." Jake used one of Malone's own guns to kill him in Chief's kitchen.

He muttered with a false bravado that only Henry heard, "That's done." Shock shook Jake into shivers, and his eyes teared up. The gun now hung from his right hand as if it had suddenly grown too heavy. It fell from his grip onto the planked floor with a *thunk* and a *clatter*. The message was clear. Jake had just killed another human being—four, in fact—and he silently vowed it was the first and last time. He dropped to the floor beside the deadly weapon, shaking uncontrollably. Sat cross-legged, bowed his head, and prayed for forgiveness. He could think of nothing else. There was no glory here, no honor, no victory, other than he had sent four evil souls away, and four good souls still drew breath. But the price had been high.

Reinforcements had arrived. The ATF not only charged in with a dozen more highly trained and well-equipped agents, they plowed through the outer barricade with what looked like a cross between a snow plow and a tank, catching the remaining dozen hooligans in a deadly crossfire with Billy and his boys who were still taking potshots from behind the inner barricade. Shock and awe—at last.

A sudden absence of gunfire ensued amid the torrent of wind and flying grit as the few bad guys still alive, surrendered. Billy bolted for the house to ensure Henry and the women were okay. He came across Jake slumped on the floor in the hallway, not sure if he had been hit. But saw only vomit splatters instead of blood. When he rounded the corner into the kitchen, sprawled bodies everywhere dripped blood. Blood pooled, blood sprayed on the far walls and ran down. Billy's gut rumbled.

Jake was in shock, muttering and praying. Henry had sprawled into a kitchen chair as if his legs would no longer support him. His chin hung down to his chest. Full-blown shock explained his pasty complexion. Looked like he'd aged ten years in two hours.

"Where are the girls? Henry! Where are the women? Henry!"

"Um, cellar, I think." The man glistened pale. He could not deviate from his thousand-yard stare at the blood running toward him on the floor. He could only look through the carnage before him, not at it.

"Sophie!" Billy ran for the stairs, twisted the light switch, and saw a pile of bodies at the bottom of the stairs in the dim light. "Oh, no!" He stumbled down the rough-sawn treads, bumping his head on a low beam, stopped two steps up.

They were alive! "Oh, God, what happened?"

Hilda tended to Sophie, while Edie hovered over them

sobbing without restraint, her bird-like limbs spread across the heap of womanhood as if trying to protect them from some unseen evil raining down on them. Hilda said in an eery calm, "In our mad dash down here to Chief's secret room, Sophie stumbled, Billy. But just on the last step. I think she sprained her ankle."

Billy stepped over them with care, kneeling and hugging all three with a gentle ferocity born of relief and gratitude. They weeped together. All except Hilda. She was, once again, the crisp matriarch.

JAKE STILL SAT CRUMPLED ON THE HALLWAY FLOOR NEXT TO the kitchen. He raised his head in a cold sweat, on the verge of passing out. Agent Lang Eubanks of the ATF now stood there, surrounded by a small throng of agents that crowded into the hallway and kitchen. Lang kneeled by Jake with a gentle hand on his shoulder. The Tommy gun still lay in front of him, now partially covered with the sparse contents of Jake's stomach he hadn't expelled on the killing field outside.

"Well done, sir. Well done, indeed."

As Lang arose, Jake muttered something that caused him to kneel once more. "What did you say, Jake?"

Jake now regained sufficient presence of mind to swipe at the puke still moist on his chin. "Malone's last words before I.... He said, 'Let's mop up these maggots now and report back to Mr. Shade.' Who the hell is Mr. Shade? I thought Malone was the boss."

"We've heard rumors, Jake. Later, alright, my friend?"

ONCE THE WEATHER CLEARED, AND HE WAS ABLE TO GET Little Sky back into the barn, Chief discovered that he had been too close to the upward convection of the detonations during the battle. The flames had scorched the bottom of Little Sky's car, and had laid the overhead bag victim to more than a few hot cinders. His silk bag, if it was repairable, would now require more patches than he could count. And more than half of his framework was damaged. The bag sagged onto the car. Little Sky looked... sad. He had been fortunate to land her before gravity did. He stopped counting holes and broken struts and started counting his blessings. Used the tractor to drag it back into its nest.

❦

78

Who would suspect the real kingpin behind the Malone organization would be a lowly grain elevator operator in Iowa named Lester Klein? In the flea-speck town of George, Iowa, no less? Nobody, which made it perfect. Klein was the architect for the nation-wide distribution of Black Gold. He provided the brains and money, Malone supplied the brawn.

Herr Klein did not hesitate to order Deputy Braddock's execution because the nosy kid discovered the relationship between himself and Malone while the sneaky little shit skulked around his elevator. In fact, Leary beat the kid to death right behind the elevator before dumping him south of town using Sheriff Graves' fancy new car. Graves was a greedy bastard, and if he got too greedy before he got dead, the deputy's uniform would have shown up in his office over in Osceola. A good thing they had kept Graves ignorant of Klein's involvement. Messy affair, but unavoidable. The message? Don't stick your nose where it doesn't belong—

lawman, or not. The brick through Billy's window in Rock Rapids had been his idea. Diversionary tactics. The sheriff was an edgy one.

Klein got Henry Bairns involved with Malone by design. Klein wanted a warehouse in George as his low-profile Midwestern distribution center for Black Gold between Chicago and Denver. He would create an equivalent center midway between Denver and L.A.—in the small town of Panguitch in Southern Utah—as they continued to expand westward. Their eastern expansion would follow, if all went well, leveraging Malone's Chicago organization as its production hub now, instead of Dillworth's farm. They'd continue to leverage the counterfeit cash from Mr. Tree, another friend of the Fatherland.

Klein looked like a country bumpkin, but his savvy skills as a businessman fueled a naked ambition underneath his *culchie* exterior, as Finn would say. It was more about power and revenge than money, and the delicious secret that enabled him to operate undetected on such a grand scale. Everyone thought, or assumed, that Malone was the mastermind behind Black Gold, and that was just the way Klein wanted it. Besides, that Irish psychopath thrived on his role as the *big boss*—the perfect collaboration. Lester Klein—Mr. Shade—knew he played a dangerous game, but nothing less would satisfy.

Arrogant Americans always under-estimated Klein's German immigrant parents, especially out here, far from any real civilization. He'd always resented small-town life, but this was his lot. His family came from old-world aristocracy, descended from the Holy Roman Empire as recently as 1806 AD, but were forced to live a more plebeian life in America since they immigrated here during the war.

He never tired of his parents' stories of life in the old country, even though he was only twelve when they emigrated from Germany to America. Leuther Kleinschmidt was old enough to remember the vestiges of their previous life, and to understand the significance of what they had forfeited. Their resentment passed on to him in no small measure.

Now, he tried to outdo them even though they were gone. That obsession clutched him by his metaphorical throat and would not let go. Klein was already a successful businessman. But he knew the only way to achieve the magnitude of wealth and influence held by his parents was via illicit means.

They had lived an opulent life in the German state of Saxony, in what some Americans might call a castle—their ancestral home—east of the city of Dresden. The Kleinschmidt family holdings extended as far west as a weapons plant at the outskirts of Leipzig. And other arms concerns as far east as Gorlitz, south to Zwickau, and north to Hoyerswerda. Some say the Kleinschmidts were among the two-hundred-fifty wealthiest families within the German Empire at the turn of the century.

Everything fell apart for the Kleinschmidts in the months preceding the November revolution of 1918. The extreme burdens suffered by the German population during the four years of war devastated them with economic and psychological impacts at the hands of the Allies. Not the least of which were growing social tensions between the general population and the aristocratic elite, with which the Kleinschmidts proudly associated.

These factors conspired against their family fortune and social standing, both of which were stolen from them by the Allies, led by the American conquerors. But the Kleinschmidts, accompanied by their only child Leuther, were crafty in their escape. They concealed means which enabled them to carry into exile a modest portion of their former wealth. Most of their financial holdings evaporated, leading up to the establishment of the ridiculous Weimar Republic.

Democracy, indeed. But they found leaving their social status behind perhaps the most painful.

They emigrated to Ellis Island, NY, where a sanctimonious Baptist church group "rescued" them. They settled them in their new home in Northwest Iowa, the unlikeliest of places. But George was a community that welcomed them with open arms, no questions asked. They befriended many other German families already there, but most were low born, and that was fine. They taught the Kleinschmidts—now just the humble Kleins, with their son Lester—how to behave, how to fit in with these... peasants. It wouldn't do for others to discover his family was of the aristocratic elite of the Second Reich.

The fools in this country were all too willing to enable their pursuit of the American dream, *as long as it wasn't too extravagant*. Never one for limits which his parents had adopted as a matter of survival here, once they had passed, Leuther Kleinschmidt—Lester Klein—pushed boundaries. And Malone's mob, also immigrants, enabled him to push harder than any provincial laws that might try to constrain him.

Lester Klein was a true sociopath, and could dupe anyone into believing what he wanted them to believe. He inherited the small George Grain Elevator from his father. Damn peasant farmers complained when grain prices were too low. Now, Hummel complained they were too high. Offering over-market prices to feed his insatiable demand for local resources that fed Black Gold production may have been a mistake. Made the old man suspicious, and he knew Hummel and Bairns were friends. Worrisome. Well, no help for that now. Hummel might have to be dispatched as well. That would be a shame. He liked old Silas.

Lester remembered sitting around with the other good old boys at the German American Society (GAS) in Sioux

City. They'd visit with others of German heritage—maybe argue which brand of seed would yield the best crop next season—drink German beer and listen to music from the Fatherland. They'd waste time pining for the glory days, although there just was no glory to be had during the four years of war, but before that....

Conversely, Lester's family profited *during* the war, at least in its early years. They sold swords *and* shields. They manufactured various weapons: bayonets, Mauser rifles, armored and weaponized all-terrain vehicles, even naval deck guns. They also sold formidable barricades quickly erected to inhibit the advance of troops and equipment. It seemed obscene wealth was thrust upon their already-aristocratic bloodline. The rich got richer.

But then the short-tempered Kaiser ran out of money and started taking whatever he needed as the Allies overwhelmed his forces. End of glory days for the Kleinschmidts, which never existed at all for ninety-nine percent of the German population, not that they complained. They knew no better. Until 1918. Even now, many of his relatives who remained in Germany after the war were branded war criminals. Even though they had nothing to do with the war perpetrated earlier by the mercurial Kaiser Wilhelm II—a friend of the Kleinschmidt family—or his cadre of warlord generals.

With the emerging Third Reich, Lester was convinced that the true descendants of the Roman Empire would once again command their rightful place in history. These American upstarts started out with the right idea within their own territory during the last century: beat down the savage races, enslave them, suppress their ridiculous heritage, and conquer their lands. But then they softened.

Now, well, he'd open their eyes, bring this arrogant country to its hedonistic knees and back to the cleansing it sorely needed. But that needed to happen without self-righteous Christians coming to the aid of every whelp with a sob story. This was a time for the strong to guide, to manage the weak. Prohibition was the vehicle and Black Gold was the fuel.

When this Mick named Malone blew into town, all high and mighty, Lester seized the opportunity. He told a trusted comrade at a GAS meeting the game had come to them. They'd command a ridiculous margin on an easily manufactured product that was in high demand. Plus, repeat business was guaranteed. But the real froth on the stein? It was both addictive and deleterious to the health of the user. The perfect fuel for another November revolution—in America.

Lester caught a lot of attention when he declared that with a proper national distribution network, this could bring America to its arrogant knees. Before he knew it, a prominent business concern from New Jersey approached him to discuss his plan. Within a month, he gained access to unlimited funds for his Black Gold prospectus from a Mr. Tree, a.k.a. Herr Hans Graber, who used the fictitious radio call sign NG2AO.

Klein had then approached this Malone character and offered him unlimited funding that bore an unlimited profit potential, along with the opportunity to enslave millions of these "arrogant yanks." The mutt drooled over the proposition. But there were caveats.

First, Klein was to be a silent partner—invisible—and that Finn Malone was to be the titular head of this distribution plan. Second, Malone would have unlimited access to profits for growing his Chicago operations as long as it did not interfere with their further expansion in the future. And finally, Malone would provide the muscle necessary to keep their plan on track, including at least a dozen new distilleries and one-hundred distribution centers nationwide by 1936.

The initial influx of funds arrived to prove Klein's bona

fides. It took the form of a trunk the size of a forty-gallon liquor barrel on its side stuffed with new one-hundred-dollar bills. Malone couldn't agree fast enough, and vowed to abide by Klein's conditions.

About six months into their relationship, Klein got wind from his agents within Malone's own network that the origins of this Black Gold concoction might just serve another purpose. This purpose could serve the emerging Third Reich as well. Girded with his family's knowledge of arms manufacture, he knew the importance of an efficient aviation fuel could very well give any nation an edge over the future of warfare: control of the skies. And another war was always inevitable, wasn't it?

Klein commanded Malone to secure the formula for this fuel, an earlier iteration of Black Gold. Malone's own cooker suggested the only way to secure that recipe—*and* the precise process to re-create it—was to secure the services of its inventor, one Daniel Rustywire.

"Rustywire? What kind of name is that, Malone?"

"A redskin. Ya know, one of them Injuns. Sharp kid. Once worked for me, but got all righteous on me. Quit, even though I provided proper motivation. Disappeared. But still in the area, we're told."

"Find him. Could mean another *very* handsome payday, my fine friend."

Malone obviously simmered, but did not boil over. After all, Klein had already made him a wealthy man. But it was never enough.

"Yeh, sure."

Now, inquiries to his own identity had already been reported from within his law enforcement network. They'd located this Rustywire just down the road, south of George. Why hadn't he heard of him until now? Clever savage. The family farm was apparently held in trust under his mother's maiden name. Klein then provided Malone with a hundred hard-as-pig-iron soldiers of fortune, and he *still* failed to capture this cooker. And who the hell called in the G-Men? Somebody would pay.

Brave words, but Klein knew his short-lived empire may be crumbling at this very moment. Right now, he must take stock and acquire information. The Dillworth raid, and the defeat at Rustywire's place, with Malone captured or dead? The time had arrived for a strategic retreat.

Klein called his international contact in New Jersey on 3.614 megacycles via his shortwave radio set. Confidence buoyed him when he reached Herr Graber, an operative for a German business concern with influential contacts in the Third Reich.

After Klein completed these few arrangements for a covert egress from America, he was to immediately drive to Sioux City for a clandestine meeting arranged by his comrade in New Jersey. From there, he'd be provided papers for a new identity and catch a train to the coast. A passenger ship would leave from the Port of New York for England in five days. Then, there would be no stopping him. He would be free and clear with countless resources in the United Kingdom. Klein carried the basics of Rustywire's formula folded and tucked under the insole of his right shoe. That should be worth something to his benefactors. Even enough to keep him alive, perhaps.

It was close to midnight. Klein had packed a single valise at his small but elegant bungalow on Harms Street in George, and walked from his front door to his driveway. He opened the driver's door to his chocolate brown Chevy coupe purchased from Henry Bairns six months earlier. He snickered. The cash he had paid Henry for this car came right back to him through Malone. Delicious irony.

Night-time became daylight. A dozen motorcar headlamps blinded him. Realizing this was now his end game, Mr. Shade pulled a Luger from his coat pocket, aimed at the nearest light, and fired, extinguishing it. In the next moment, his vision faded as a fusillade of bullets perforated his great-coat. One shattered the right lens of his round spectacles. Countless others pinged off every part of his almost-new chocolate brown Chevy coupe and kicked up pea gravel from his manicured driveway. He could hear, but not see. Then, nothing.

❦

79

It saddened Hans Graber—Mr. Tree—that he could no longer serve the Fatherland. The Americans were on to him. The most profound insult of all, however, came from the FBI agent who shot, wounded, and captured him before he could do the honorable thing. Suicide by FBI seemed an appropriate final curtain for this failed performance, but he had been deprived of that. The agent told Graber his location was discovered, not by a skilled government or military surveillance expert. Rather, he had been rooted out by a fifteen-year-old German-American paraplegic with a radio set in his bedroom. He reflected he didn't much care for Newark anyway.

❧ 80 ❧

⛦

Having faced certain death, the *George gang* survivors possessed a new perspective after recent events in and around the village of George, Iowa during the Summer of 1933.

RED CHIEF DIRIGIBLES NOW COLLABORATED WITH A LAB IN Princeton, New Jersey. Two scientists associated with the university there who emigrated from Stuttgart, Germany, contracted Chief Dan Rustywire to aid in the design of a new prop-less aircraft engine. They had made advances designing such an engine, but needed a different fuel formulation. Additionally, their current engine design would not develop sufficient thrust to get a conventional aircraft aloft, but they still needed an airborne development and test platform. This made Chief's hot-air ships ideal for the task, at least until the next generation engine could be scaled up and perfected.

Chief hired Jake Hardt to assist with augmenting the

scientists' mechanical designs, and their implementation. Turns out Chief didn't need the handsome fees paid by the university, but enjoyed the work. Jake, however, enjoyed a regular paycheck for the first time in his life. But this was still just a side job to working the Hardt home place.

As an aside, a thankful government, namely, a particular senior agent with the Bureau of Alcohol, Tobacco and Firearms, launched an investigation into the disappearance of Bear and Annie Rustywire. A crew member of the yacht Taku Skanskan was located in St. Thomas within the US Virgin Islands as a result of a coordinated investigation across multiple departments of the US Department of Justice. A burly crew member of the Rustywire sailing yacht informed agents who interviewed him that the Rustywire yacht did indeed sink during a violent storm at sea near the USVI, and he was the sole survivor. Chief thanked Agent Eubanks for providing him closure.

The love affair between Chief and Edie blossomed. Ritchy Winkels was arraigned on charges of domestic abuse, racketeering, reckless endangerment, and felony violations of the Volstead Act. But he refused to grant Edie a divorce. That is, until Sheriff Billy Kershaw and Federal Agent Lang Eubanks suggested that Ritchy most definitely did not want to earn the scorn of Edie's new fiancée. Chief Dan Rustywire had set half his old boss's mob on fire with gasoline and dynamite because they threatened his friends. Ritchy pled guilty forthwith in consideration for his testimony, and for granting Edith Everniss Winkels an immediate divorce.

JAKE LOVED WORKING WITH CHIEF AND HIS BEAUTIFUL mind on designing processes and building gadgets that could influence the entire aircraft industry, possibly even the next military war effort. But he realized what was most important to him was Sophie and their new baby. Her tumble down Chief's cellar stairs landed her in Doc Gustavsen's office and earned her a full physical. She was at least six weeks pregnant. Together, Sophie and Jake sat down for a serious conversation with Henry and Hilda in their rented house in George while theirs was being rebuilt.

Jake grinned and said, "Gonna have to call you Opa and Oma soon."

Hilda smiled. She already knew—mothers are meant to know such things. But Henry said, "*What!?*" After a few moments of reflection, Henry broadcast his brilliant closed-deal smile and leaped up to pump Jake's hand—for the first time ever. He even hugged him. Farmer or no farmer, it didn't hurt that his new son-in-law was offering him a grandchild, *and* was now a co-signatory on at least three patents—applied for under the company name of Red Chief Dirigibles on behalf of their very own Uncle Sam!

At that moment, it all came together. Jake now realized that there was *nothing* more important to him than his bride and his child. And coffee and sandwiches out in the field. Or smelling and tearing off a hunk of mile-high bread slathered with homemade jam, with Walt and Sophie in the kitchen kibitzing over smelly boots. He relished fixing old Silas's tractor up the road, and going to church with *his family*, and praying to the Lord for a good crop next season. And yes, even slopping the hogs, or putting up with a cocky rooster popping off all the time, except at sunrise. Those were all *big things,* all he needed, and now, all he wanted. He didn't need to leave George to achieve any of them. Nor did Jake need to attend the J. Hildebrand College of Business in Rapid City to learn how to be successful or how to become fulfilled.

But it wasn't too painful to also co-invent innovations that could help his country, just four miles down the road in Chief's barn. Of course, they'd had to construct a new building and take on a few employees. After all, they were now government defense contractors.

The icing on the cake? Not long after their barn burned, Silas Hummel found Queenie and his milkers wandering his pasture, as if they were out for a leisurely stroll. Jake convinced himself Queenie had gotten them out of his burning barn. Finn's thugs would not have released them. They had shot one of his hogs in the forehead and stuffed a store-bought apple in its mouth. The depths of man's evil ceased to shock him. They must remain vigilant. And keep to their faith.

❧

SHERIFF BILLY HEALED, ALTHOUGH HE MIGHT NEVER recover full range of motion in his right shoulder, thanks to Sticks Leary. But it became an ever-present touchpoint for him that there was a price to be paid for freedom, and for justice, *and* that it was worth it.

Billy and Deputy Dwight threw themselves into their jobs, serving the community they helped rescue. Billy vowed to never lose another deputy to violence. He collaborated with Dwight to implement a training program based on the Minneapolis Police Department's Officer Safety Training Program. That was the same program Dwight had completed years earlier as a rookie cop. MPD was only too happy to help with materials and curriculum. Billy and Jimmy would be their first two cadets and graduates, instructed by Senior Deputy Dwight Spooner. This would now be the department's standard operating procedure for new sheriffs and deputies. Billy hired an administrative assistant to handle paperwork and filing using county budget enhancements recently granted and endorsed with enthusiasm. Proper paperwork and filing was, after all, part of law enforcement.

In addition to training development, Dwight helped Billy create their own small-scale criminology lab in the fish tank—the glassed-in office—not too far from his desk in the Lyon County Law Enforcement Center. They set up a table for a permanent case "sheet"—they called it their *case board*—hoping to never use it for anything other than solving a complex bicycle theft ring, or the like. The county purchased a microscope—with infrared capabilities—and innovative finger printing comparison equipment. Plus, they acquired a few other pieces of equipment recommended by Doc Gustavsen for his use when he was in residence. Doc Gus agreed to become the de facto Lyon County Medical Examiner on a part-time basis, as needed. The County Board of Commissioners provided whatever funding Billy felt they needed. Even got indoor plumbing to both of their cells. Billy ran unopposed in the next election, and won.

৩৯৫

WALT RECOVERED FROM THE WOUND TO HIS ABDOMEN AND the bullet that creased his left temple. His head wound caused his unconsciousness at what came to be known in county folklore as the *Battle at Rustywire*. But he was pissed that he missed most of the action.

Chief introduced Walt to the Lakota Sioux tribal elders in Fort Tate, North Dakota. Since he was a minor celebrity on the Dakotas casino circuit, they hired him as floor manager for their casino, a lucrative new venture for the tribe—and they paid well. After all, nobody spotted the grift like a grifter. But Walt explained this was only temporary. He would need to get back to his family in George to help raise his godchild.

Jake and Sophie missed Walt and looked forward to the day when he would return. But Sophie Hardt and Edie Rustywire (though she hadn't actually married Chief), now neighbors, filled lonely hours on their farms together, the closest of friends, like before. Their relationship and their dependency on each other deepened further with time.

⚜

MEMORIAL SERVICES FOR OWEN BUNN AND SEPPEL TOLLEY, who took their selfless courage to their graves, were well-attended by profoundly grateful folks from across the county. Statuary of the pair of local heroes held a place of honor in the new George Town Square after it was completed.

⚜

DEPUTY DWIGHT SPOONER ACCOMPANIED SHERIFF BILLY Kershaw to visit Deputy Roddy Braddock's widow. She had mellowed from her initial anger with the sheriff over her young husband's death. Billy explained that they had discovered who murdered her husband, and that they had killed the cowards in two different police actions with the help of a federal agency.

Billy described how Roddy's death surfaced what could have otherwise been a disaster on a national scale. He was a hero. Told her a bronze memorial plaque would soon hold a place of honor in City Hall, and she would be present for the dedication ceremony. Billy apologized to Sara Braddock that he should have ensured Roddy was better trained for his job. He got a lump in his throat and asked Dwight to describe what they were doing about that.

Dwight told Sara that this type of training was the exception, not the rule, in rural departments, and that he was proud to serve with a sheriff like Billy. Sara realized how difficult this must be for Billy and hugged him. Both cried.

Dwight came close to tears, too, even though he had never met Roddy.

They chose not to share with the murdered deputy's young wife that they discovered what remained of Roddy's uniform. They had found a charred boot and equipment belt in the burned-out hulk of his police cruiser in the ditch of a field road fifty miles away on the far side of Osceola County. Nobody ever learned the complete story. They could only speculate. They decided that was one mystery best left unsolved, or at least, one story left untold.

৩৫৩

THE FBI HAD WORKED THEIR RADIO MAGIC AND TRACKED down Klein's collaborator in Newark. As a paraplegic, one Hans Graber was unable to flee. How ironic that one paraplegic patriot of German heritage was responsible for the demise of a paraplegic traitor who shared the same heritage, but held very different political views. But that story was suppressed. After all, no normal citizen wanted to know too much of the all-too-frequent apocalyptic brinkmanship played on national and international stages. And an alliance between the inventor of this new fuel and government scientists at Princeton benefitted all concerns. With the aid of a few very official oaths of secrecy, they kept the entire affair on the QT.

When they discovered the traitor's location in New Jersey, Agent Cobb and his team uncovered an incredible stash of cash—billions of dollars. They learned through the use of enhanced interrogation techniques with Herr Graber that the money was counterfeit, otherwise indistinguishable from government-minted bills. A near-microscopic *hakenkreuz*, or hooked cross (swastika) could only be detected under a microscope equipped with a beam of infrared light on the

353

president's lapel in each bill. But nobody outside of the US Government would ever learn of this near-miss either.

Agent Milford Langford Eubanks gained a new appreciation for the crime-fighting capabilities of farmers and small-town folk. Remarkable. But that paled to his newfound respect for their obvious affection—even to offering their lives—for their community and for each other. These folks tolerated, even respected, their differences. Lang reflected that, *Catastrophe has a way of crystallizing apathy and confusion. Of greater importance, it provides perspective, does it not?*

True to Lang's word, he erased Walt Weller's tax bill. For invaluable services rendered to the agency, and to the nation, Lang arranged a consulting fee that covered Walt's federal tax bill, plus, what he owed to the state of Illinois, plus all late fees. Walt was a law-abiding citizen once more, even though more than half of his stash of cash buried below the floor planks of Jake's barn were too charred to save when the ashes cooled. Fickle fate. Sophie might say, "The Lord giveth, and the Lord taketh away."

LANG SMILED TO HIMSELF. HE RECEIVED A PERSONAL commendation from President Roosevelt. FDR understood the implications of their success in preventing the national distribution of this seductive Black Gold toxin during a time when the nation was perhaps at its most vulnerable. What was left unspoken was the supporting classified evidence of the traitorous machinations of one Leuther Kleinschmidt (Lester Klein), a.k.a. Mr. Shade. The thwarted theft of a revolutionary aviation fuel process could have played a damaging role to America and its allies in yet another war. And such a war was bound to break out in Europe within a few years, no doubt with American involvement once more. Additionally, the president lauded their discovery of a massive foreign counterfeit ring so sophisticated that it could have further devastated the US economy to the point of no return.

⊙⚜⊙

A LARGE GRINGO OPENED A NEW CANTINA IN THE HISTORIC *City of the Sun*, Hermosillo, the state capital. Roy Davidson's establishment grew to be the largest business concern run by an American in the entire state of Sonora—in Northwestern Mexico. He became a well-known local fixture, recognized by his distinctive olive-drab hat with four dents in the crown— gringo state-trooper-style. They also said he distilled some of the finest liquor around. He branded it *oro negro*.

⊙⚜⊙

AGENT EUBANKS DECIDED IT WAS TIME FOR A VACATION. Maybe a few days in Northwestern Mexico would do the trick before the next case pressed his schedule. Of course, he now traveled nowhere without his trusty pearl-handled forty-five—confiscated from the recent Roy Dillworth raid in Iowa, and reconditioned from getting partially baked by a Chief-bomb. Its previous owner had no further use for it. Lang gained tacit approval from the Mexican Federales to carry this marvelous acquisition. He had heard tales of a new cantina in the charming old city of Hermosillo. Yes, some sun would do him a world of good. And maybe he'd look up the gringo who ran that cantina—Roy Something-or-other.

⊙⚜⊙

LIFE IN NORTHWEST IOWA SETTLED INTO A COMFORTABLE rhythm once more, still scarred by the occasional black storm, drought conditions, and dubious strangers passing through. But farmers dedicated to their craft, and those dedicated to supporting farmers, realized such trials, while testing their mettle—which was stronger than ever—would not last forever. What mattered most was that people could overcome their differences, battle their enemies, inside and out, and depend on each other for help. That they could come to terms with what really was most important in this short life on this tiny planet—their internal light illuminating humanity's dark corners, together, through perseverance, and loyalty, and faith.

The End

Turn the page to explore the complete cast of characters, their relationships, a glossary of terms, and maps of key locations.

What's next?

Look for **the next Lyon County Adventure** in the Fall of 2022: The circus comes to town!

It's 1934. While investigating the murder of a gypsy circus "freak" in Northwest Iowa, Sheriff Billy Rhett Kershaw and his deputy, Dwight Spooner, juggle slippery politics and tangled biases of their prejudiced constituents. *But when bizarre forces trip up their investigation almost immediately, jeopardizing more lives in the process, they must step up their game. Holmes and Watson are imperfectly reincarnated as Billy and Dwight in the Midwestern Dust Bowl during America's Great Depression. Neither are above considering clues beyond scientific comprehension. Nor are they beyond leveraging the insights of an intuitive but reluctant amateur sleuth—Sophie Hardt—who comes to their aid.*

APPENDIX A - CAST

꧁꧂

Cast of Major Characters (in alphabetical order):

- **Sophie Bairns:** New wife of Jake Hardt
- **Henry Bairns:** Sophie's father; proprietor of Bairns Motors, George, Iowa; of German immigrant descent
- **Hilda (Hildie) Bairns:** Wife of Henry Bairns; Sophie's mother & friend; of German immigrant descent
- **Dwight Spooner:** ex-Minneapolis homicide detective & friend of Sheriff Billy Rhett Kershaw; later Billy's deputy
- **Rodney (Roddy) Braddock:** Sheriff Kershaw's murdered deputy
- **Owen Bunn:** mechanic at Bairns Motors, Great War vet; soft on Sophie; of German immigrant descent

- **Reese Cobb:** FBI Executive Special Agent in Charge (ESAIC), Newark, NJ
- **Roy Dillworth:** President Worthington City Ford; local liquor producer; Malone collaborator
- **Milford Langford (Lang) Eubanks:** Senior Agent for Alcohol, Tobacco & Firearms (ATF); a "G-Man" (Government Man)
- **Edith Everniss Winkels:** Sophie's only real friend
- **Hans Graber:** A Newark, New Jersey businessman (warehouse/distribution); code-name *Mr. Tree*; German immigrant
- **Sheriff Duane Graves:** Osceola County sheriff; Malone collaborator
- **Jacob (Jake) Hardt:** primary protagonist; farmer; inventor
- **Charles-Royce Hugo:** ATF informant, Lakehurst, New Jersey
- **Silas Hummel:** Jake is indebted to Silas who is a friend to, and customer of Sophie's father, Henry Bairns; of German immigrant descent
- **Sheriff Billy Rhett Kershaw:** Lyon County, Rapid City; soft on Sophie
- **Lester Klein (a.k.a. Leuther Kleinschmidt):** Code name *Mr. Shade;* George Grain Elevator Owner/Operator; German immigrant; Second Reich operative
- **Aghaistín (Sticks) Leary:** Finn Malone's senior lieutenant and gunsel; Irish immigrant
- **Jimmy Lenert :** Loyal but youthful Lyon County deputy
- **Finn Malone:** Henry Bairns' "banker" and Chicago gangster; Irish immigrant

- **Zachary (Zach) Mutter:** George City speakeasy owner/operator
- **Dan (Chief) Rustywire:** Jake's friend; chemist; inventor; pilot; half-breed (Native American and Irish)
- **Annie Cavendish Rustywire**: Chief's Irish mother
- **Bear Rustywire:** Chief's Indian father
- **Seppel (Sep) Tolley:** mechanic at Bairns Motors, Great War vet, soft on Sophie; of German immigrant descent
- **Jacko Ulster:** one of Malone's Chicago crime bosses and friend; Irish immigrant
- **Ritchy Winkels:** Edie Everniss' abusive husband; minor liquor distributor
- **Walter (Walt) Weller:** Jake Hardt's cousin; erstwhile drunk; expert gambler
- **Allan (Kookie) Westerhall:** Chief Dan Rustywire's college roommate and fellow alcohol chemist ("cooker"). Works for Finn Malone as his "Minnesota cooker."

APPENDIX B - RELATIONSHIPS

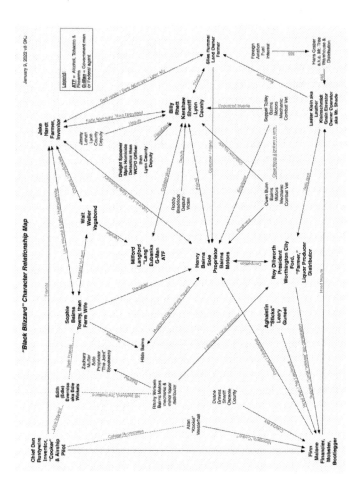

"Black Blizzard" Character Relationship Map

APPENDIX C - GLOSSARY

Glossary of Terms:

- **a.k.a. :** *also known as*, an abbreviation for an alias or an acronym.
- **ATF:** Alcohol, Tobacco & Firearms is an agency within the US Department of Justice in 1933.
- **Black Gold:** an illegal strong drink that is both addictive and toxic - physiologically and psychopathically.
- **Cooker:** An expert distiller of strong spirits.
- **German Empire:** The German Empire or the Imperial State of Germany, also referred to as Imperial Germany, the Second Reich, the Kaiserreich, as well as simply Germany, was the period of the German Reich from the unification of Germany in 1871 until the November Revolution in 1918, when the German Reich

changed its form of government from a monarchy to a republic.

- **G-Man:** Slang term for "Government Man," usually referring to a federal agent who either works for ATF, FBI or IRS.
- **Great War:** World War I
- **Gunsel:** A hoodlum or other criminal, especially one who carries a gun; a hired shooter.
- **Hobo:** The historical term for a homeless person; one who wanders from place to place without a permanent home or a means of livelihood.
- **Hooch:** Slang term for alcohol (a.k.a. booze, moonshine, etc.)
- **Second Reich:** The predecessor to the Nazi Third Reich. Also see German Empire.
- **Weimar Republic:** The democratic republic established in Germany after the people's revolution in November 1918 and the fall of Kaiser Wilhelm II at the end of the Great War.
- **Whoopee Party:** Slang term for a social gathering where strong drink is served.

APPENDIX D - MAPS

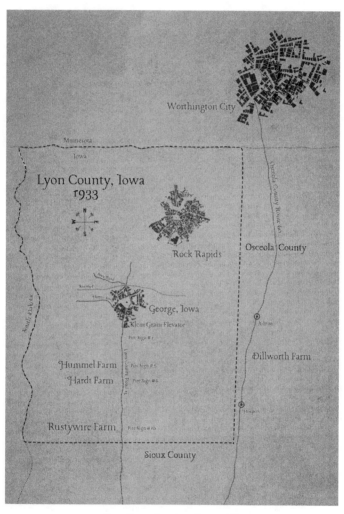

Lyon County, Iowa 1933 (not to scale)

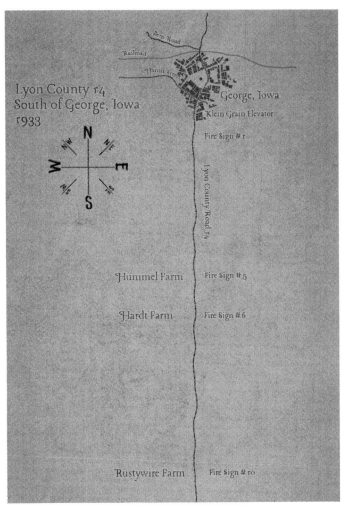

Lyon County Road 14 South of George, Iowa

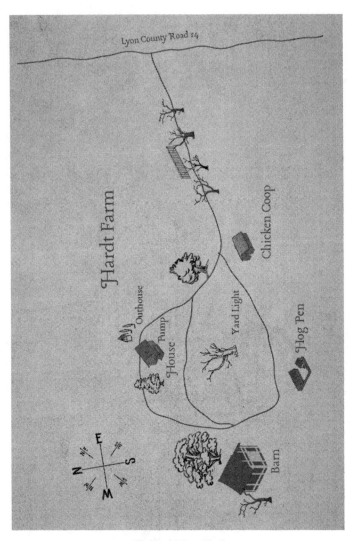

The Hardt "Home Place"

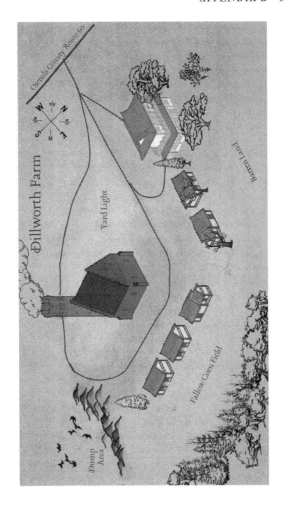

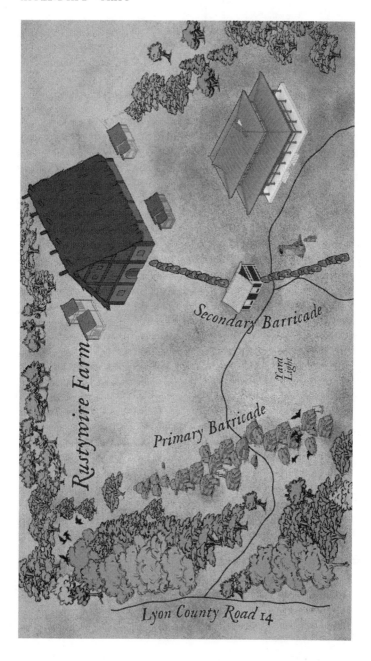

Secondary Barricade

Yard Light

Primary Barricade

Rustywire Farm

Lyon County Road 14

AUTHOR'S NOTE

The idea for this book started as an homage to my parents who always provided for their children during an unimaginably difficult time for them and for so many others.

As I researched 1930s rural America, I witnessed my original story idea transform into a compelling metaphor representing the struggles of contemporary America. Back then, they too suffered from crippling prejudice against immigrants, a pandemic—two, in fact—racial injustice, nationalism, social and financial inequality and political anxiety, all through no fault of their own. Just like today.

They envisioned a community—a nation—isolated and divided by all these factors, coming together in a time of adversity, to battle a common foe, much like we saw America briefly come together after September 11, 2001 and during COVID-19.

I needed to write this story for deep-rooted emotional reasons I cannot articulate. That doesn't matter now that it's finished. I sincerely hope you enjoyed reading "Black Blizzard" as much as I loved writing it.

facebook.com/genejurrens
twitter.com/gjurrens1
instagram.com/gjurrens

ALSO BY GK JURRENS

Other books by GK Jurrens:

Fiction:

Dangerous Dreams - Dream Runners Book 1

Fractured Dreams - Dream Runners Book 2

Underground - Mayhem Book 1

Mean Streets - Mayhem Book 2

Post Earth - Mayhem Book 3

A Glimpse: Companion Guide to the Mayhem Trilogy

Murder in Purgatory - A Lyon County Mystery

Non-fiction:

Moving a Boat and Her Crew

Restoring a Boat and Her Crew

Why Write? Why Publish? Passion? Profit? Both?

BEFORE YOU GO

Please write and post a brief review of the book you just read!
Whether you enjoyed this labor of love or not, I would be in your debt if you'd post a brief (or lengthy) review where you bought this book, or just email your reaction to this story at gjurrens@yahoo.com

Remember, other readers and I need to know what you *really* think about this or any of my books.

And consider following me on social media at:
www.facebook.com/genejurrens
https://www.linkedin.com/in/gkjurrens
www.twitter.com/gjurrens1
www.instagram.com/gjurrens

Also, feel free to browse or subscribe to GKJurrens.com for announcements and giveaways.

ABOUT THE AUTHOR

GK Jurrens writes with undiluted passion. He also teaches writing and publishing on the road. More often than not, GK and his wife live and travel in a motorhome when they're not spending time at their condo in Southwest Florida. They wander their beloved North America as a source of endless inspiration.

After studying Liberal Arts and Electronics Engineering Technology, GK earned a Bachelor of Science degree in Business and a Master of Science degree in Management of Technology from the University of Minnesota, USA. He is the proud father of two adult children and the equally proud grandfather of three almost-adult grandchildren.

Six years of government service and a successful three-decade career in global high-technology preceded more than a few years of sailing America's waterways, the Florida Keys, and the Eastern Caribbean from the British Virgin Islands to Granada, near the coasts of Venezuela and Trinidad, with a brief foray sailing around the Greek Cyclades Islands in the Aegean Sea.

GK now pursues his life-long penchant for the creative arts: prose and poetry, painting (watercolor), traveling (North America), playing guitar (acoustic-electric) and playing his growing collection of Native American flutes, some of which he crafted while living in the Arizona desert.

He enjoys quiet evenings reading and exploring movies,

when not writing or sitting by a campfire alongside his copilot and soulmate of over half a century—Admiral Kay.

If you'd care to offer the author feedback, for which he'd be grateful, consider emailing **gjurrens@yahoo.com** or visit **GKJurrens.com**.

Made in the USA
Middletown, DE
04 February 2025

70115421R00236